STACY M. JONES

Boston Underground

First edition

ISBN: 978-0-578-88379-3

This book was professionally typeset on Reedsy.
Find out more at reedsy.com

For J.S. - Boston always reminds me of you

Acknowledgement

Special thanks to my family and friends who are always a source of support and encouragement. Thank you to my early readers whose feedback was invaluable. Sharon Aponte, a wonderfully-skilled graphic designer, thank you for bringing my stories to life with amazing covers. Thank you to Dj Hendrickson for your insightful editing and Liza Wood for proofreading and revisions.

Thank you to the two former CIA officers who shared their knowledge with me and answered my endless questions. Their insight was more than I could have ever expected. I learned so much for the story and for sleuthing around.

Thanks to my readers who have been with me since the first in the series and new readers just finding my books – I hope you enjoy reading these stories as much as I enjoy writing them.

Chapter 1

The clock flicked to 3:18 a.m. as I opened my eyes and angled my head to look at the clock on the bedside table. What sounded like ice crystals hit the window directly next to the side of the bed. The repetitive noise had roused me from my dreamless sleep.

Det. Luke Morgan, my husband, slept on his back with his head turned away from me and had one protective hand in the groove at the top of my thigh. We were snuggled under warm soft blankets. The fire he had started in our hotel room fireplace after our wedding the night before had gone out. The Lake Placid air held a chill even I wasn't used to.

Although it had been unseasonably warm for the wedding, the weather had been predicted to turn colder. Snow hadn't been expected, which made the sound against the window even stranger. I gently moved Luke's hand, peeled back the blankets, and rolled out of bed, planting my feet on the cold floor. I reached for my robe tossed across the bottom of the bed and wrapped it around me before stepping toward the window.

The silk curtain slipped through my fingers as I drew it back and peeked through the blinds. The ground remained green and free of any white powder. I didn't have a chance to look around because I instinctually jumped back as the window took another direct hit. It wasn't ice.

I moved back to the window and parted the blinds with my fingers. Below the window stood a silhouette of a person looking up at our room. They waved to me and I waved in acknowledgment. When they stepped closer into the light cast from the hotel, I saw my sister's hot pink hoodie pulled over her head and small pebbles in her gloved hand. I had no idea what Liv was doing out there this time of night. The last time I saw her, she had been drunk and chatting with a guy at the hotel bar.

I worried she might be in trouble. I held up my finger to indicate that I'd be down in a minute. I stepped back from the window and fished around for clothing in the dark so I wouldn't wake Luke. He had a few beers at our wedding reception and that always knocked him out. He needed the sleep, and there was no way I was going to wake him to deal with my sister's antics. No one needed to start a marriage that way.

I found jeans, a thin long-sleeved shirt, a heavy sweater, socks, and boots. I didn't grab my coat. The sweater should keep me warm enough while I dragged Liv back inside and tucked her into bed. I found the room keycard on the desk and left the room, easing the door closed behind me. We were on the third floor and I took the elevator to the first. I assumed there'd be someone at the front desk, but as I passed by, there wasn't a soul in sight.

I walked toward the automatic doors and they slid open as soon as I got close. I stood outside for a moment to orient myself in order to decide which direction I needed to go to find my sister. I made a right and walked around to the side of the building. Down a small hill and standing in the shadow of the building, Liv stood with her head tilted up to my room.

"Liv," I said, more hushed whisper than full voice. No one sleeping in the hotel needed to hear my big mouth in the dead of night. She didn't turn to look at me, so I assumed I wasn't loud enough. As I approached, I called her name again. When she still didn't turn to acknowledge me, I groaned. "Liv, how drunk are you? You're going to freeze to death."

I realized too late it wasn't Liv. The person didn't have Liv's long blonde hair or ample chest. I called her name one more time in the hopes I was seeing things, but a crack on the back of my skull silenced me.

The ground came rushing toward my face faster than I could reach out to brace myself. The person who I thought was Liv finally turned, and under the hot pink hoodie appeared a man with a sick twisted grin spread across his face.

As my head smashed into the earth and before the lights went out completely, he let out a menacing laugh. "This will make your father come running."

Chapter 2

Luke opened his eyes and yawned as he ran a hand down his stubbled face. "I don't think I've slept like that in a long time. Are you awake?" When Riley didn't respond, he rolled to his side to pull her into his arms but was met with an empty bed. Assuming she might be in the bathroom, Luke rolled over onto his back and closed his eyes again.

He wasn't sure how much time passed, but he opened his eyes again and looked at the clock. 7:47 a.m. "Riley," he called out fighting his groggy voice. When she didn't respond, Luke sat straight up in bed. He blinked away his sleep and rubbed his eyes. "Riley, are you here?"

The room remained dark except for a little light peeking through the blinds. Luke tossed back the covers and got up. He clicked on the bedside lamp. Riley's phone was plugged into her charger and sat on the table on her side of the bed. Luke walked into the sitting room attached to the bedroom in their suite. Her purse rested on one of the chairs, her suitcase appeared slightly tossed, like she had been searching for clothes, and the room key was gone from the desk.

Luke walked back to the bed and reached for his phone on the nightstand. He sent off a quick text to Cooper Deagnan, his best friend since college and Riley's investigative partner.

Is Riley with you? If she is, tell her I'm going to shower and I'll be right down for breakfast.

Luke assumed Riley had gotten an early start and let him sleep in. He grabbed some clothes and headed for the bathroom. As he turned on the water, he noticed that the shower stall wasn't wet. Riley hadn't showered before she went downstairs, which wasn't like her at all. He stepped into the shower and let the hot water run over his head and down his back. He remembered her phone sitting on the nightstand and a chill chased the water down his spine. She never left her phone. Luke exhaled and chuckled, chastising himself for being a detective and making more out of something than it was.

Riley probably woke up excited and went to have an early breakfast or maybe even a walk with her mother and sister. "Not everything is a crime," Luke said to himself as he finished his shower.

Twenty minutes later, dressed and ready for the day, Luke still hadn't heard back from Cooper. He left the room in search of Riley and the rest of their family and friends. As he reached the lobby and headed for the dining room where breakfast was served, he ran into Cooper holding an empty white plate and heading for the buffet.

"I saw your text. I haven't seen Riley yet this morning. She wasn't in your room?" he asked.

"No," Luke said, looking past Cooper into the dining room. Luke's parents and Riley's mom with her boyfriend Jack sat at a table eating breakfast. "I figured she came down here already or was with her mom or Liv."

"Liv hasn't come down yet. Maybe Riley is in her room." Cooper stepped closer to Luke. "Liv was wasted last night. I tried to stop her from going off with some guy she met, but she wasn't listening to me. She's a grown woman. I figured it wasn't my place to stop her from having fun."

Luke nodded and made his way into the dining room. His parents, Lucia and Spencer, stood to greet him. "I figured you'd sleep in," Lucia said as she wrapped her arms around him.

He hugged his mother and when she let go, Luke stepped back. "I'm looking for Riley. Have any of you seen her this morning?"

"She wasn't in your room when you woke up?" Karen, Riley's mother, asked.

"No. I figured she'd be down here. I can't even call her because she left her phone plugged into the charger."

Karen laughed. "She can't be far. She never goes anywhere without her phone."

"I know. That's what I figured, but the shower was dry, too. Maybe I'm worried for nothing, but Riley rarely leaves the house without taking a shower."

Karen smiled up at him. "It's that hair. She's like a wild woman if she doesn't shower in the morning." She took a sip of her coffee, seeming unconcerned. "Check Liv's room. Maybe Riley went to check on her. When those girls get talking, they lose all sense of time."

"What room is she in?"

Karen took the napkin off her lap and stood. "Come on, I'll go with you. I have one of Liv's keycards. She asked me to hold on to it last night in case she lost hers."

Luke appreciated that. He still wasn't accustomed to Liv's sense of humor. Right before the wedding, when they were at Karen's house, where Riley grew up in Troy, New York, Liv had teased him about them getting together when Riley was done with him. Liv laughed while he stood in the hallway dumbfounded. Needless to say, while he liked Liv, he wasn't always comfortable around her.

"Your parents are lovely," Karen said, drawing Luke's attention as they made their way to the elevator. "It's too bad we don't live closer."

Luke nodded in agreement. Anxiety had spread through his gut and made his pulse race, making it hard for him to hold a conversation. He couldn't shake the feeling that something was wrong.

Karen reached for Luke's hand. "It's going to be okay. I'm telling you Riley probably went to Liv's room and they are talking or they fell back to sleep."

Luke wanted to be reassured, but his gut instinct as a homicide detective told him otherwise. He knew Riley's habits far too well. They reached the fourth floor and walked the length of the hallway to Liv's room. Karen knocked once, calling out both girls' names. They were met with silence.

Karen, who stood about five-four, raised her blue eyes to him. "Now, I'm worried."

Luke knocked on the door again and called Riley's name. When no one responded, he said, "Let's use the key and check the room."

Karen pulled the key from her pocket and slid it into the slot. The lock lit green and the door unlocked. She reached down and turned the handle and pushed open the door. As they stepped into the room, Luke wasn't sure where to look first. There were clothes thrown on the floor, a suitcase tossed beside them, and shoes scattered haphazardly. The bed looked like it hadn't been slept in.

On edge, Luke told Karen to wait at the door and he stepped farther into the room. He walked around the clothes and called over his shoulder. "Is Liv always this messy?"

"Yes, unfortunately," Karen said, tsking.

Luke checked the bathroom next. Makeup littered the sink countertop and the hair dryer sat precariously on the edge of the sink still plugged in. Much to Luke's dismay, there was no sign of Riley or Liv. He walked back to the door, but couldn't meet Karen's worried look.

"They aren't here and it doesn't look like anyone slept here last night. I don't see Liv's phone or purse either."

Karen swallowed hard. "Let me try to call her." Karen pulled her phone from her pocket and called Liv, but the call went straight to voicemail. Karen said that wasn't unusual because Liv often forgets to charge her phone. "What do we do?"

Luke ran a hand over his bald head. As soon as the police were called, they'd suspect him. It didn't matter that he was a detective. They'd suspect him, and he couldn't blame them. If he were called to a similar case, he'd first suspect the spouse. The only thing he needed right now before the cops arrived was information and to gather his team.

Luke stepped out of the room and closed the door. "We need to call the police. But, Karen, you have to know as soon as they arrive, they are going to suspect that I did something to Riley. I would never hurt her, you know that. Our entire relationship is going to be under the microscope. It will impede me from doing my job and finding them."

Karen reached her hand out to Luke. "I know you'd never hurt her. What do you need before we call the police?"

"I want to get Captain Meadows and Det. Tyler and look at the surveillance footage first."

"That's what we'll do. You find them and, in the meantime, I'll go downstairs and tell Jack and Cooper to speak to the hotel staff and get the surveillance video." Karen headed down the hall but turned back to him. "Luke, if anyone is going to find my daughters, it's you."

Luke breathed a sigh of relief knowing Karen was on his side. He had no idea what he would have done if she didn't trust him. He headed farther down the hall to find Captain Meadows and Det. Tyler. He had worked with them at the Little Rock Police Department for nearly all his law enforcement career. Luke had been promoted to the head of the detective's bureau a few years ago. He was the first African-American man to head up the department. Det. Bill Tyler, who always just went by Tyler, had been his partner and one of his most trusted friends for more years than he remembered.

Luke knocked on Tyler's door and within seconds, it opened. Tyler stood on the other side dressed and looking a bit embarrassed. "I know I'm late for breakfast. We slept in," he said with a knowing wink.

"It's not that," Luke reassured. "Riley wasn't in bed when I woke up this morning, and now, we can't find her or her sister, Liv."

Concern came over Tyler's face. "Did you try to call Riley?"

"Her phone was still plugged into her charger and her purse was in the room." Luke looked down at the ground and shook his head, trying to hold back tears. The last thing he wanted to do was cry in front of his partner.

Tyler reached out his hand and gripped Luke's shoulder. "We'll find her, Luke. We are all here."

"I know," Luke swallowed. "But we always find dead bodies. We rarely bring victims back alive."

"No, no, don't think that way. Come on, you know Riley, she is a fighter." Tyler stuck his head back into the room and explained to his wife what was happening. He told her to go on to breakfast without him. "Let's get Captain Meadows and ask for the surveillance footage."

"Cooper's already on it."

"Good," Tyler stepped into the hall. "We are already ahead of the game."

"We need to call the local police," Luke said with a look.

"Not yet," Tyler responded. "We both know what's going to happen if we do, and I'm going to take the fall on the delay in calling them."

"I can't have you do that."

"You can and you will." Tyler and Luke set off to find Captain Meadows and then join the rest downstairs.

Chapter 3

After Karen arrived back at the breakfast table frantic and wringing her hands, she explained to everyone what was happening. She asked Cooper and Jack to deal with hotel security. The two of them headed to the front desk to ask for surveillance footage.

Jack, who was a retired homicide detective from the Troy Police Department, had worked with Riley on two cases. Cooper trusted him completely. He let Jack take the lead at the front desk.

Jack explained the situation to the young woman behind the desk. She remembered Riley from the wedding the evening before. "We aren't sure what happened to Riley and her sister, but we are hoping to look at the surveillance footage."

Cooper added, "Last night, I saw Riley's sister, Liv, talking to a man at the hotel bar. I tried to get her to come upstairs with me, but she insisted she was fine. If you could pull surveillance footage of that, too, it would be helpful. That happened right around midnight."

The young woman expressed her concern for them and picked up the phone to call the hotel's security office. She spoke to someone on the other end and explained the situation. When she hung up, she said, "Let me put all of you in one of our unused conference spaces and security will meet with you."

"Are they bringing the surveillance videos?" Jack asked.

"As far as I know," the young woman said and motioned for them to follow her. She walked through the main lobby and took a corridor to the right. Cooper and Jack followed until they reached the room. She unlocked the door for them. "If you need anything else, please let me know."

Jack and Cooper walked into the room, which had a small conference table and a phone but not much else. "Let me go get everyone else," Jack said, turning and leaving the room.

Cooper couldn't sit. All he wanted to do was get out there and search for Riley. He cursed himself for not stopping Liv the night before. He should have insisted she go upstairs with him and his girlfriend, Adele. Riley and Luke's wedding had been small. It was just family and close friends. Cooper and Adele had been the last of the wedding guests in the bar. He shouldn't have left Liv there.

Cooper continued to berate himself until everyone else joined him in the room. Jack and Karen took a seat at the table across from Luke's parents. Adele entered and wrapped her arms around his middle and kissed him on the cheek.

"Are you feeling as much guilt as I do for leaving Liv at the bar with that guy?" she asked, her voice quiet so only Cooper could hear her.

"More than you know." They took a seat at the table and Cooper wondered what was taking Luke so long. He reached for his phone to call him but didn't even get the chance because hotel security walked into the room.

The man stood about six-one, an inch taller than both Luke and Cooper, and looked like he worked out daily. He was young with dark hair and a pleasant enough face. Cooper wondered how long he had been on the job. "I'm Owen with hotel security. I've put a call into the Lake Placid Police. They should be arriving shortly."

Jack stood and walked over to shake the man's hand. He told Owen that he was a retired homicide detective with more than thirty

11

years of experience and was now a licensed private investigator. "We don't even know what we are looking at. We were hoping to see the surveillance video for more information."

Owen shook his head. "I appreciate your experience, but I can't share that with you."

"Why not?" Cooper asked. "I'm a licensed private investigator in Arkansas and one of the missing women is my partner. She is a licensed private investigator here in New York and Arkansas. We routinely have hotels share surveillance footage with us. I don't understand the problem."

Owen shoved his hands in his pockets and rocked on his feet. "That's not the way we work up here. When the detective gets here, if he wants to share it with you, that's fine by me."

The door to the room opened and Luke entered with Captain Meadows and Det. Tyler. Owen introduced himself. Luke, in turn, flashed his badge along with Captain Meadows and Det. Tyler.

"Where is the surveillance footage?" Luke asked.

"Det. Morgan, I was just explaining that we are waiting for the Lake Placid Police to arrive. I can't share the surveillance footage with you."

Luke shook his head in disbelief. "That's the most ridiculous thing I've ever heard. My wife and her sister have been gone for who knows how long. We can't sit around here and do nothing. You have decades of law enforcement experience in this room. Let us get to work doing what we do best."

Owen clicked his tongue. "I'm afraid I can't do that."

Luke clenched his fists and Cooper was sure he was going to punch the man. Cooper got up from his seat and walked over to Luke to calm him down. "The detective should be here soon. Let's just strategize while we wait."

Luke let out a breath. "All right, okay."

"Have you checked outside? Maybe they drove off somewhere,"

Owen suggested.

"That's not possible," Karen said from the end of the table. She explained Riley and Liv were her daughters. "Liv didn't have her car with her. She drove with me and Riley rode with Luke."

Luke had his keys in his pocket and Riley didn't have a key to his SUV with her, so he was sure they didn't leave on their own. "How long have you been doing your job?" Luke asked.

"About a year," Owen said. "Nothing like this has ever happened here before."

That's what Cooper thought. "Time is critical when someone goes missing. Keeping us waiting in this room is taking up time we don't have."

"It's what the local cops asked me to do, so I'm doing it." Owen stood ramrod straight in front of the door.

Cooper was sure Luke was going to lose his cool at any moment. Even Captain Meadows tried to talk some sense into the young security officer, but he wasn't having any of it. Cooper felt helpless at that moment to do anything productive. He looked to Adele who was a criminal defense attorney, but she didn't have anything to offer either.

Cooper walked to the far end of the room and pulled out his phone. He looked up the number for the Lake Placid Police Department and called them. With his back turned to the room, hoping they couldn't hear him, he explained the situation to the woman who answered the phone and stressed the need to get a detective there immediately, especially since they couldn't do any of the investigative work that they were all trained to do. The woman put Cooper on hold and when she came back on the line, she assured him that Det. Grant Perry was on his way.

Cooper turned back to the group who were all staring at him. He shrugged. "I figured if we are going to be trapped here doing nothing, I might as well make sure they're on their way. Det. Grant Perry should be here any minute."

Captain Meadows thanked Cooper. "Before the detective gets here, does anyone have photos of Riley and Liv other than the wedding? I'm sure those are good photos, but let's go with an everyday photo without all the makeup and fancy dress."

Cooper scrolled through his photos and so did Karen and Luke. They had a few photos to choose from and they picked the best and most representative of Riley and Liv. As they finished choosing the photos, someone knocked on the door and opened it.

The man looked around the room at all of them and introduced himself. "I'm Det. Grant Perry, is there a Det. Luke Morgan here?"

Luke stepped forward and shook the man's hand. He had to look up to meet Det. Perry's eyes. The man stood about six-four and had a thick, hearty lumberjack build.

"My wife, Riley, and her sister, Liv, are missing." Before Det. Perry could say anything else, Luke introduced everyone in the room. Cooper wasn't surprised that Luke made sure to include their law enforcement experience.

Det. Perry whistled. "I'm not sure why I'm here. You all have enough experience to handle this. Have you seen the hotel's surveillance video?"

"No," Cooper said with disgust in his voice. "We were told we weren't allowed."

Det. Perry stepped toward the door and waved for Luke to follow him. "Det. Morgan, since you can identify both of the women, let's take a walk and you can fill me in. We can look at the surveillance video together."

Chapter 4

L uke followed Det. Perry out into the hall with a growing sense of anxiety rushing over him. The detective separated him from the others for questioning no matter what he said about looking at surveillance footage. Det. Perry confirmed Luke's suspicion when he asked Owen to go ahead and queue up the video for them while they talked.

Det. Perry slowed his pace and let Owen go ahead. "Tell me what happened this morning, Det. Morgan."

Luke took a breath and went through the story one more time, leaving nothing out. When he was done, Luke said, "I know you have to ask me these questions. I'd be doing the same, but let's not waste too much time. My wife and sister-in-law are out there in the cold and my only focus is finding them. Interrogate me. Give me a lie detector test. Do whatever you need to, but do it fast. We both know time is of the essence."

Det. Perry didn't respond to Luke's request. "Have you and Riley argued recently? Is there any reason she would have left on her own?"

"We haven't been arguing at all," Luke stressed, trying to rein in his temper. "We just got married last night. If Riley left on her own, it was because her sister needed something. Riley is extremely responsible and would never take off like this."

"Riley has no history of taking off without anyone knowing where she is?"

"Absolutely not," Luke said, stressing his point. He said the words but did have a moment's hesitation. At the start of their relationship, Riley left him. Everything was fine and then she went back to New York without telling him or taking his calls. She had always been a little gun shy about commitment, but Luke was sure she wouldn't have left her phone and purse behind. Even if she were suddenly freaked out about getting married, she wouldn't scare her mother like this.

"You said you took a shower before you went looking for Riley. Is that correct?" Det. Perry asked and Luke confirmed. The detective looked at him wide-eyed. "It seems to me if you knew your wife was missing, a shower wouldn't have mattered."

Luke stopped walking. "I didn't wake up, see that Riley was gone, and assume she was missing. Her mother and sister and our friends are here at the hotel. I figured she went down to breakfast before me." Luke dug out his phone from his pants pocket. "You can see I texted Cooper to ask if Riley was down there. I wasn't concerned until I went downstairs and saw that Riley wasn't with everyone else. Then her mother and I checked Liv's room."

Det. Perry nodded his head in understanding, but Luke wasn't so sure. "Why didn't you call us right away? It was the hotel who called the police."

"Are you serious?" Luke asked with annoyance in his voice. "The first thing I did was go get my partner, Det. Tyler, and Captain Meadows and asked Cooper to ask for the surveillance video. I immediately went into doing what I'd do as a detective. Besides, most jurisdictions still stick to that old missing for twenty-four hours rule. Riley and I went to sleep around one-thirty or two this morning. I wasn't looking at the clock though. It had only been less than six hours. I was going to call after we looked at the surveillance video to see what we were dealing with."

"Are you sure you didn't call the police right away because you knew we'd suspect you?"

Luke put his hands on his hips and glared at the man. "Sure, that was a thought but only because it would slow down the process of searching for Riley. Like what's happening right now. Not because I did anything wrong. If we watch the surveillance video, you'll see I didn't leave the room all night."

"What were you doing all night?"

Luke smirked. "You want all the details about what I did with my new wife after our wedding reception?"

Det. Perry looked away as red crept up his face. "Yes, I think given the situation it's warranted."

"Okay fine," Luke said, growing angrier by the second. "We enjoyed our wedding reception. Riley doesn't drink often, but she had a glass of champagne at our toast. She drank water the rest of the night. I had a few beers. We danced, laughed, and spent time with our families and friends. We left around eleven and headed up to our room. We showered together and started to fool around, but Riley joked we were going to slip and fall in the shower. We got out, dried off enough, and made love, twice. Then we fell asleep. I slept like a rock. I was exhausted and beer always sends me into a deep sleep. I woke up just before eight to find Riley wasn't in our room. Is that enough detail or do you want the down and dirty version?"

Det. Perry waved him off. "That's fine for now. Let's go look at the surveillance video."

"Finally," Luke sighed. They walked the rest of the way in silence. Luke tried to dull his simmering rage. He had to remain calm if he was going to get anywhere and not come across like a lunatic.

They met with Owen in the security office. He had the first clip of the video all set up. Luke looked at the screen and saw several people standing at the bar. The time stamp said 11:55 p.m.

"I queued it up to start right before your friend said he saw Liv at the bar." Owen clicked play and the screen jumped to life.

Cooper was right on the money regarding the time. About two minutes later, the video showed Cooper and Adele walking up to Liv, who stood at the bar chatting with a man with dark hair. He wore jeans and a button-down shirt. From the current vantage point, the man's back was turned to the camera. Luke couldn't see his face.

Liv swayed as she talked to Cooper. Luke understood why Cooper wanted her to leave with them and go to her room. Liv was clearly intoxicated. She barely stood on her own. Cooper took a drink out of Liv's hand and set it down on the bar. He turned her around so she faced him and then both Cooper and Adele said something to her. Liv waved them off and laughed while Cooper and Adele shared a worried look. Cooper tried again, but it was obvious Liv wasn't going anywhere. The video continued for another fifteen minutes after Cooper and Adele walked away. Liv and the man kept talking and then they left the bar and headed for the elevators.

"She is probably going up to her room," Luke said and gave Owen the room number. They waited while Owen scanned through the video of the hallway and got the right time as the two walked off the elevator in the direction of Liv's room. The man looked to be in his late thirties or early forties. There wasn't anything distinctive about him. The video showed them going into Liv's room and the door closed behind them.

Owen looked back at them. "Should I skip to Riley's room now?"

Luke responded before Det. Perry. "No, she left that room at some point. Scan through the video on three times the speed."

Owen didn't like that answer, but he turned back and did as Luke asked. They didn't have to wait long because not even thirty minutes later, Liv left the room in a change of clothes. She had ditched the dress she had worn to the wedding and now had on jeans, a long sleeve shirt, and boots. She carried a pink hoodie.

Owen changed the video and scanned the bar area, but they weren't there. He caught them on video walking out of the hotel together. Det. Perry asked. "Do you have video of the front of the hotel?"

"Right outside the door. We had video surveillance in the parking lot, but the cameras haven't been working."

Det. Perry cursed loudly. "Let's go to Luke and Riley's room now."

Owen scanned through the video starting at eleven at night. Luke's heart thumped as he saw himself and Riley in her wedding dress exit the elevator. They had stopped to kiss each other in front of the door to their room. Luke hated that a display of affection like that was now being viewed by security and Det. Perry, but he hoped it showed they were happy.

Owen hit fast forward after Luke and Riley entered the room and the door closed. More than two hours of video flashed by on fast forward.

"Stop, right there!" Luke called out when Riley appeared leaving the room at 3:24 a.m. She was dressed in a sweater, jeans, and boots. She had her long auburn hair thrown up in a messy bun at the top of her head. It looked to Luke like she had just woken up.

Owen stopped the video as Riley walked down the hall and took the elevator to the lobby. Another video caught her walking right out the front door. Det. Perry asked him to find the video of the front of the lobby as Riley walked out. A few minutes later, they watched as Riley left the hotel, stood still for a moment, and then walked around the side of the building.

Det. Perry turned to Luke. "Have you looked outside for them?"

Luke shook his head not sure whether to feel vindicated that he hadn't done anything to Riley or stupid for not having checked outside. He wanted to rush outside and check.

"Go back to Luke's room and play the video through until morning,"

Det. Perry directed, preventing Luke from leaving.

Owen switched the video again and he played it on fast forward. Riley never came back to the room and Luke didn't leave until 8:21 a.m.

Det. Perry pointed to the screen. "Make me two copies of those videos and loop them together in sequence. Find me video of the man who left with Liv where we can see his face." He turned to Luke. "Let's go look outside."

A few minutes later, Det. Perry and Luke stood in the spot outside the door where Riley had stood. They turned right and went to the side of the building in the same direction as Riley had on the video. Luke held his breath. He almost expected to see her out there, but there was no one. They walked halfway down the length of the building when Det. Perry stopped.

He pointed to the ground. "Look at all these pebbles. There is a whole pile right here in one spot." He walked up closer to the building and saw several more. "There is a pebble garden in the front of the hotel but not out here."

Luke wasn't sure what the detective was driving at until he looked up and started counting rooms from the front of the building. "I can't be sure, but it looks like it's right under our window."

Det. Perry blew out a cold breath. "Any chance Liv came back and tried to get Riley's attention? Maybe she came out here looking for her."

"That's possible," Luke said, looking around. "That still doesn't answer where they are now."

Chapter 5

The motion and feel of grated metal under my back woke me with a start. My eyes flew open, but I couldn't focus on anything. My vision was blurred and I couldn't make sense of where I was. The feeling disoriented me. I searched for my last memory but came up blank. I tried to move my hands but they were cuffed. The feel of plastic dug into my skin. At least, my hands were cuffed in front of me and not behind my back. I awkwardly reached for my face and rubbed my eyes.

"Riley," someone said above me with a hoarse and hushed voice. "I'm so scared, Riley. What's happening?"

I turned my head to the left where the sound came from. There were boots and jeans and when I scanned up, I realized it was my sister. I tried to sit up but dizziness forced me to lie back down. "Liv, where are we?"

Liv's soft cries filled the space between us. "In a cargo van. You've been unconscious for a long time. I thought you were dead."

"Are you okay?"

"No, but I'm not hurt or anything if that's what you mean."

"How did we get here?" I couldn't remember anything after going to bed last night.

"I don't know how you got here, but I left the hotel bar with a guy last night. We left in his car, and as soon as we got away from the hotel, he pulled over to the side of the road and handed me off to another guy. He cuffed me and threw me in the back of this van. I screamed and tried to get away, but he smacked me and told me if I kept it up, he'd kill me." Liv sobbed uncontrollably.

"Calm down, Liv. We have to stay calm." I tried to swallow but my mouth was so dry my tongue felt like thick cotton. "Do we have any water in here?"

"No, there's nothing back here except us." Liv stared down into my face. Her makeup streaked under her eyes, which were swollen and red like she had been crying all night, which she probably had been. "We have to get out of here."

I tried again to sit up. This time, I inched myself back against the bench that ran down both sides of the van. I had been on my back between them. I breathed a sigh of relief to be in a sitting position and looking at my sister directly.

I focused on my sister's face as a memory came flooding back. "I thought you were throwing pebbles at my window last night. You had on your pink hoodie."

"The guy I left the bar with took that from me when he passed me off to the other guy." Liv started crying again and then calmed herself down almost immediately. "I don't know any of their names. I don't know how many are in here with us, but we haven't stopped driving for hours."

I scanned the space. There were no windows on the sides of the van or in the back doors. I had no way of assessing where we might be. We were completely blocked off from the view of the driver's area, so I had no idea who was up there. Lake Placid isn't far from the Canadian border, but I had a distinct feeling that wasn't the direction we were headed.

"Do you know if we stopped at any tolls or went through the border crossing at the Canadian border?"

"No, nothing like that. We were on one road for a short period and then it felt like we got off an exit and then went onto a different road."

"Have they stopped and let you use the bathroom?"

Liv shook her head. "When they threw you into the van, one of them walked me into the woods and let me go. He said if I ran or screamed for help, he'd kill me."

I remembered the man said something about Sully before I blacked out. "Liv, when we were in Lake Placid, did you see Sully at all?"

Patrick Sullivan was our father but hadn't been in our lives for most of it. He popped in and out. As the story goes, he was heavily involved with the Irish mob and the head of a crime syndicate in Europe someplace and our mother had banished him from having anything to do with us. She told us more than once he wasn't even allowed in the United States. His family's homestead was in southern Ireland, but she didn't even know how frequently he was there.

I was sure I had seen him at the wedding the night before. It was only a glimpse of a man who looked like him and I could be mistaken.

Liv shook her head. "Why would he be here?"

"I thought I saw him. You know he called Luke when he was driving up to New York with Cooper and Adele. I haven't spoken to him in years, but Mom said he keeps tabs on us. He knew about the wedding. I'm sure he even probably knew where I was having it."

"That's crazy, Riley. Besides, what does he have to do with any of this? We've probably been kidnapped into a human trafficking ring or something."

"Unlikely."

"You see it all the time on Facebook. All those stories and warnings." Liv sniffled back tears.

I looked at my sister. "Liv, most of those stories on Facebook aren't true. Besides, human trafficking isn't as common as people think it is here in the United States. Don't get me wrong, it happens, but there aren't men trolling around Walmart looking for victims. This isn't human trafficking."

"What if it is?" she cried.

"They aren't going to get us out of the country alive," I assured her. "I'm going to scream, kick, fight and do whatever I can. If they kill me, they kill me. It's better than wherever I'd end up. You're going to get it together and do the same." I paused because Liv's face had turned to absolute terror and I realized I had gone too far. "Trust me, Liv, that isn't what this is. I'm sure it has something to do with Sully."

"How do you know that?"

"Because right before I lost consciousness, the guy said something about Sully. I can't recall what it was exactly, but it was along the lines that this will make him come running. Like they are trying to get his attention."

"Are you sure?" Liv looked at me, skepticism written all over her face.

"I'm positive."

"Riley, I don't think our father kidnapped us."

"No, Liv, that's not what I'm saying. I think someone who is after Sully took us or maybe they have him, too. I think no matter how it went down, they followed him to the wedding." I raised my eyebrows as a reckoning took hold. "This is what Mom has been worried about all along. That we'd be collateral damage."

"You are not making this any better." Liv started to cry again.

"Stop! I need you to get it together. This is scary, but if they wanted to kill us, they would have done it already."

I knew I was being too hard on Liv, but I didn't have time or the energy to take care of her while I was trying to get us out of the situation. I believed what I told her. What I didn't tell Liv was that I had also wondered if they were keeping us alive to torture information out of us. Not that Liv knew anything, but I did. There were secrets I had vowed to take to my grave.

"Aren't you scared?" she asked me, trying her best to stop crying.

"Of course, I'm scared, but we can't lose our heads right now. That's the worst thing we could do. We have to have a plan."

"Do you have a plan?"

"Not yet."

I got myself to my knees and then planted my feet on the floor and stood. It was no easy feat. The dizziness still came in waves and the van rocked us back and forth. I inched my way to the front of the van and pressed my ear against the metal to see if I could hear anything. A radio was on, but no one was speaking. I had hoped I'd hear a conversation, anything to indicate who they were or where we were headed. I waited there a while longer with my ear pressed to the wall even as the van bumped and jostled me. I planted my feet firmly and tried my best not to move. I gave up after a while and sat down on the bench across from my sister.

"It might be one person up there. I don't hear talking or anything other than the radio."

Liv didn't say anything. She stared off into space. I worried that she didn't have the strength to deal with whatever came next.

"Liv," I said gently, "I'm sure Luke and everyone else is up by now. They are going to know we are missing. My purse and my phone are in the room. Luke knows I don't go anywhere without my phone. I'm sure they have already started searching for us. They probably called the police and watched surveillance video from the hotel. They will see the guy you left with."

"Even if that's true, all they are going to see is both of us leaving on our own. Luke is going to think you bailed on him."

"Never. He would never think that."

"You did before," she said sarcastically, reminding me of a shameful time in my life.

I took a breath. "That's different, Liv. We got married last night. Luke knows I'm not going to run away." I wasn't sure I believed my own words. Cooper would talk sense into him. "They are searching for us. I'm sure of it."

Liv shrugged. "Let's hope they find us before it's too late."

Chapter 6

L uke walked back to the conference room with Det. Perry, unsure about what he had seen. He had no idea how to identify the man that Liv had left with and no idea where either of them had gone. The only thing they could do right now was search the property and Lake Placid with Riley's and Liv's photos to see if anyone saw them last night or this morning.

"Det. Perry, there's one thing I haven't done and it would be great if you could come with me."

"What's that?" Det. Perry asked, walking in step with Luke.

"I left Riley's phone on the charger and never looked at it this morning. It occurred to me after we saw the surveillance video that if Liv was in trouble, she might have texted or called Riley first before she came to the window – if that's even what those pebbles were for. We have no way to confirm that."

"Let's go look," Det. Perry said, his voice constrained.

Luke stopped walking and looked at the man. "Is there something wrong?"

The detective stood with his hands on his hips. "I know you think your wife is missing and something has happened to her, but I don't have any evidence of that. Your wife and her sister are both in their late thirties and have every right to leave a hotel, even in the middle of the night. I don't see any evidence of foul play or a crime. This isn't a police matter."

Luke's mouth dropped open. "You're not going to do anything?"

"There's nothing for me to do." Det. Perry shrugged. "We have a small police department and not a lot of manpower. I don't have the staffing capacity to help track down two women who left a hotel on their own volition." Luke was about to speak but Det. Perry asked him to stop. "Listen, Luke, I don't believe you did anything to your wife and her sister. You were in the room the whole night, but it doesn't look like anyone did anything to her. Your sister-in-law left with a guy she was involved with and hasn't returned yet. She will probably sleep in and be back later today. She might know where Riley took off to. Your wife sounds like an intelligent woman, I'm sure if she didn't want to be here anymore for whatever reason, she could leave even without having a car here."

Luke let out an incredulous laugh and counted the evidence on his fingers. "You're telling me she left with no money, no phone, no coat in frigid temperatures, and no ride up here in the middle of nowhere? That makes less sense than you suspecting me of wrongdoing."

Det. Perry didn't say anything. "I'll go with you to look at the phone, but if there isn't evidence of anything, I can't be of help."

Luke wanted a witness when he went through Riley's phone in case later someone accused him of deleting anything. He knew how the game was played. They walked to the room and Luke unlocked the door. He waved Det. Perry past the small sitting room and into the adjoining bedroom.

Luke walked around the unmade bed and grabbed Riley's phone. It occurred to him as he did that Det. Perry hadn't even searched their room. It was the first time he had entered it. That's not a mistake Luke would have made had this been his case.

Luke carried the phone over to Det. Perry and Luke typed in Riley's password. He scrolled through the text message log and call log but found nothing new. Liv hadn't called or texted Riley the night before at all.

Det. Perry lowered his eyes to Luke. "I'm going, but if you find out anything else, call me. I'll make sure Owen brings you a copy of the video surveillance. I'll keep one with me for now in case..." He paused and gestured awkwardly with his hand. "Well, in case it's needed later."

Det. Perry left the room and Luke followed and said goodbye to him in the hallway. He assured Det. Perry that he'd explain to the others why local law enforcement wouldn't be involved at this time. There was no point trying to convince the detective that something had happened and that he was sure Riley and Liv were in danger. He couldn't blame Det. Perry. He might do the same in his shoes. Luke felt lucky that he had his work colleagues and Cooper and Jack with him.

As Luke walked down the hall toward the elevator, he decided to call Det. Miles Ward with the Troy Police Department. He had been assigned to a missing person and homicide case that Riley had helped Jack with right before their wedding. Luke and Cooper had assisted, too. Luke suspected Miles had a crush on Riley and she had admitted to flirting with him. Luke hated to call him but someone should check Karen's house to see if Riley or Liv had returned home.

Luke stepped away from the elevators and went through Riley's contacts until he found the number. Luke debated for only a moment before placing the call.

Miles answered almost immediately. "Tell me you're still single and I'll run away with you right now."

Luke cleared his throat as anger bubbled up. "Excuse me?" he said and was met with dead silence. "Miles, this is Luke. Riley and her sister, Liv, are missing. We got married last night and I woke up to find Riley and her sister gone this morning. The hotel surveillance video shows Liv leaving the hotel with an unknown man. In the middle of the night, Riley also left the hotel alone. She walked outside and turned right like she was walking to the side of the building. She left her phone and purse in the room and wasn't even wearing a coat."

"What do you need, Luke? Anything you need I'm on it," Miles said and then awkwardly apologized for the way he answered the phone. "I knew you got married yesterday so I was surprised Riley was calling. I was teasing her. That's all, I swear."

"It's fine," Luke said stiffly. "I need you to check Riley's mother's house to see if either of the girls are there. Riley mentioned to me before that her mother keeps a key on the far side of the porch under the rug near the chairs. If the key is still there, check the house."

"Where's the dog?" Miles asked.

"At the neighbor's house. Ask around with the neighbors if anyone has seen anything suspicious at the house or if they have seen Riley or Liv in the past few hours." Luke gave Miles his phone number to call instead of Riley's.

"I'm on it." Miles hesitated before he hung up. "You'll find her. Riley wouldn't have run away. I know I don't know Riley anywhere as well as you do, but she was genuinely excited about getting married. She wouldn't have taken off like that. I'll help you in any way I can. Whatever you need, don't hesitate to ask."

Luke thanked him before hanging up. He didn't know why hearing those words from Miles made him feel better. Everyone had said it to him, but the lack of support from Det. Perry made him doubt Riley for a moment. He wouldn't do that again.

Luke went downstairs to the conference room and found everyone just as he had left them. Cooper paced the room and Karen's eyes had become puffy and red.

"What did Det. Perry say?" Cooper asked, rushing to Luke.

"He can't help us."

"What?" Karen yelled. "My daughters are missing and local police are doing nothing?"

Luke held up his hand for them to wait. He explained what he had seen on video and told them he had called Det. Miles Ward to check the house. "I hope you don't mind, Karen. I told him where the spare key is hidden on the porch. I figured he should search inside the house and talk to the neighbors, too."

"That's a good idea," Jack said, putting his arm around Karen and reassuring her it would all be okay.

"What do we do now, Luke?" Karen asked.

"We need to search the area first. Get out and talk to people and see if anyone has seen Riley and Liv. I'll text you all photos so you have them to show people." They didn't even have many leads to go on. The only one they had was the guy Liv left with, but even at that, they had no information.

"Should we get the media involved?" Captain Meadows asked.

Luke had thought of that, but he had no idea what they were dealing with. He didn't know if doing that would put them in more danger. "Let's wait until we know more. I want to put the photo of the guy Liv left with into our database and see if anything comes back."

Captain Meadows stood. "I'll go get my laptop."

Everyone cleared out of the room to get ready for the search. They planned to meet back in the conference room in twenty minutes to decide who was going to search where. The only people left with Luke were his parents. His mother got up and wrapped her arms around him and his father patted his back.

"It's going to be okay," his father, Spencer, reassured.

"I'm sorry your vacation is ruined." His parents had planned a few days after the wedding as a mini-vacation to explore Lake Placid and the surrounding areas. They didn't get out of Little Rock much and deserved the break. "If you want to go, we can keep you updated."

Luke's mother, Lucia, looked up at him. "We aren't going anywhere.

Text your father the photos of the girls and we will search. There's nowhere we'd rather be than with you."

Luke nodded and held back tears he knew would come as soon as he was alone. Riley teased him that he was the more emotional of the two of them. It was true. He couldn't deny it.

As Luke walked out of the conference room and into the lobby, he stopped at the front desk and asked the woman to hold the conference room for them. She assured Luke they could have it as long as they needed. He asked that Owen leave the security footage with her and that he'd pick it up later. Then he went upstairs to get ready to search for his missing wife – something no new husband should ever have to do.

Chapter 7

I sat on the bench across from Liv in the van for probably an hour. The driver left the highway and hit stop and go traffic. Without being able to see outside, I couldn't confirm where we were, but it was clear we were no longer cruising at a high rate of speed the way we had been. The jarring starts and stops indicated we were on city roads.

I attempted some math to determine where we might have been given the amount of time that I thought we had been traveling, relying on the time Liv said we left. Given how small New England was, we could be in one of a few states or even as far as New York City. I estimated we had been gone about four to five hours.

A few minutes later, the van came to a stop with the brakes screeching under us. The engine cut off and the front door opened and slammed shut. Another car approached from behind us and a man's voice drifted inside of the van. I couldn't make out what he was saying though.

Liv looked at me. "What are we going to do?"

"I don't know yet. I can't see where we are and I can't fight with handcuffs on my hands." I looked to the back door as someone unlocked it. "Don't say anything. Let me do all the talking. Look around if you can and see if anything looks familiar."

Liv shook her head. She had never seemed more scared to me than she did at that moment. "We're going to be okay," I promised even though I had no way of knowing I could keep that promise.

Both of the van doors swung open and two men stood staring up at us. "Good to see you're alive," the taller one said as he raised the hem of his shirt and flashed a gun in his waistband. He had dark hair, blue eyes, and a freckle under his right eye. He had a clean-cut appearance, and if I saw him in a store or walking on the street, I would have found him attractive. I scanned his face taking in everything I could.

The other man was short and had a protruding belly under a snug shirt. He reached down twice to tug up his pants. There wasn't a thing attractive about him. He seemed less confident than the other and I assumed he wasn't in charge.

"Who are you?" I asked, walking toward him slightly hunched over so my head didn't hit the ceiling of the van. I could see that we were parked on a narrow street with tightly packed row houses on each side. When I got to the back of the van and could more clearly see outside, I spotted a car parked across the street and noted the Massachusetts license plate.

"You'll find out soon enough." The man who had flashed the gun motioned for me to get down, which seemed impossible because I couldn't hold on to anything to get down to the pavement. When I didn't move fast enough, the shorter one reached up, grabbed my arm, and yanked me to the ground, causing me to land on my knees. I couldn't believe this happened in broad daylight, but there didn't seem to be anyone around.

He gripped my arm again, hard enough to leave bruises, and got me to my feet. Defiance raged in me, but I worried about keeping Liv safe.

"Can you at least tell me what to call you?"

The one that had my arm shook his head at me, but the other with the gun said, "Call me Holden. That's Collins."

34

Collins pulled Liv out of the van in the same rough way he had brought me to the pavement and then they pushed us onto the sidewalk toward a rundown two-story house with dirty blue siding. The front screen door hung loosely from its top hinge. I shifted my eyes up the road as we walked up the driveway and to my left, there were street signs at the small intersection. We were at the corner of East 3rd Street and P. Street. Right before Collins gripped my arm and forced me to walk faster, I noticed the block dead-ended at what looked like a park and then water. I wasn't sure if that was a river, harbor, or the ocean. Nothing seemed familiar to me.

They guided us around to the back of the house and Collins pulled keys out of his drooping pants to unlock the back door. I thought about screaming or running or doing something to draw attention to us, but there wasn't a soul in sight. I could outrun the big one but not Holden, who seemed fit and agile and not someone I'd beat in any race.

Collins held the door open and shoved me through. He shoved Liv in after me so hard that she hit my back and nearly knocked me to the floor. We entered a kitchen that was as outdated and rundown as the front of the house. Collins grabbed a door off the right and nudged me down concrete steps before I could see the rest of the house. The basement had no lights so as hard as I tried it was impossible to keep my balance going down the steps. I pitched forward, but Collins grabbed the back of my shirt and righted me before I nosedived to the bottom.

He held onto me until we reached the floor and he flicked the lights on. It was a little like stepping back in time. The orange shag rug, dark end tables and coffee table, and autumnal-colored picture-patterned sofa brought me right back to photos I'd seen of my grandmother's living room in the 1970s. I leaned forward and squinted at the couch. It had a picture of a farmhouse on the back cushions.

Holden walked Liv over to the couch and dropped her down. He wasn't as rough as Collins, at least. "You girls can make yourselves at home here. There's a bathroom off that narrow hall." He pointed to a darkened space I couldn't see. "Don't try anything stupid. I have no problem killing you ahead of time."

"You're going to kill us?" Liv asked.

Holden nodded. "I have to. That's how it works."

I turned back to him and caught the look on his face. It seemed pained and uncertain. "That's how what works?"

"Revenge," he said locking his eyes with mine.

"Revenge for what?"

He shook his head. "Not for you to know right now."

Liv sniffled back tears and looked up at me. "I don't want to die."

"We aren't going to die."

Holden took quick steps toward me and cupped his hand under my chin, lifting my face to him. "You are going to die. You better make your peace with it right now."

I did everything I could to not show fear, but it coursed through me and a wave of nausea took hold. "Does this have something to do with our father?"

Holden stepped back and smiled a satisfied grin. "They told me you were the smart one. Not only am I going to kill you, but I'm going to lure him here and make him watch me kill the two of you. Then I'm going to kill him."

"You said before this was about revenge. What did Sully do to you?"

"She is baiting you," Collins said from across the room. "You already told her too much."

Holden turned to him, his face turning red. "I make the decisions. I know exactly what she's doing and it's not going to work."

"I'm not trying to do anything but get to the truth. If you're going to kill my sister and me, I'd like to know why we are going to die." Holden still didn't say anything. "I hope you understand that my father may not look for us. We haven't been in his life. He might not even care that you have us."

"She's right," Liv said, her voice hoarse. "Our father hasn't been in our lives at all. He's a criminal and we have nothing to do with him."

Holden stared at me as if searching my face for the truth. "When was the last time you saw him?"

"It's been years. He doesn't even live in the United States," I explained.

"It's been years. You expect me to believe that?"

"It's the truth," I said more defiantly than before.

Holden shook his head. "He was at your wedding. We followed him there and he led us right to you."

I let my mouth open in fake shock and shook my head. "That can't be. He would have said something to us. Liv, did you see him?"

"No," she said softly. "The place wasn't that big. If he was there, we would have known."

"You didn't know?" Holden asked, his eyes shifting between us.

"If my father didn't tell me he was there or join us, how would I know? I was focused on getting married."

Holden stepped back and breathed out. For a moment, I thought he might admit his plan was stupid or not going the way he thought, but he laughed. "Patrick Sullivan will know I have you. It will be all over the news soon enough. With two girls like you, one missing right after she got married, the news will be international before we know it. He is sure to see it and will know the message we are sending."

His laugh faltered as he said the words and it gave me a bit of hope. "Have you ever kidnapped anyone before?"

"What's your point?" Holden snapped back, not denying it.

A laugh escaped and I bit my lip to hold it back. I shook my head looking at him as I plopped down in an ugly burnt-orange chair with a tear on the arm. "Some guy, I assume you're working with, walked out of the hotel with Liv, and then I walked out of the hotel on my own. All the cops are going to see is both of us leaving the hotel of our own free will. Law enforcement isn't even going to take this case. It's not going to hit the news because my husband, a homicide detective, hates the media. All you did was make sure that several cops, my dogged investigative partner, and my mother, who will rip you from limb to limb if you hurt one hair on our heads, will be hunting you down probably as we speak."

"We took a cop's wife?" Collins asked, not even bothering to hide his shock.

"Go upstairs and wait for me," Holden snapped and Collins walked up the stairs without saying another word.

"I don't understand," I said, still watching him. "How will my father know the message you're sending if he doesn't even know we are missing? I think your plan has some holes in it."

Holden turned back to me. "Trust me, once he sees the surveillance from the hotel, he'll know. He'll come for you."

I had my doubts. I held out my cuffed hands. "In the meantime, because it seems like we are going to be here a while, can you uncuff us?" I looked around the room. "There are no windows that I can see and nothing to make a weapon out of. We will stay quiet down here while this plays out."

Holden didn't respond to me, but my confidence seemed to light a spark in Liv. She raised her eyes to him. "As long as we are requesting things, can we get something to eat? I haven't eaten since the reception last night and I'm starving. A Starbucks café mocha would be great, too."

It was hard to hold back my grin. Holden didn't seem amused and turned and walked back to the stairs muttering to himself. We had shaken him, that much was obvious.

38

Chapter 8

L uke returned to the hotel frustrated and tired after spending the last three hours searching in Lake Placid for Riley and Liv. They had paired off to search. Karen and Jack, Adele and Cooper, his parents, and Det. Tyler and Luke. Captain Meadows remained at the hotel in case there was any word. He had planned to use law enforcement databases to see if they could get any information on the man that left the hotel with Liv.

Luke spotted Emma and Joe, Riley's best friends and their neighbors in Little Rock. Emma rushed up to Luke as soon as she saw him and threw her arms around him. "We were late to breakfast and saw Captain Meadows who told us what happened. Have you found them?"

Luke returned the hug and shook Joe's hand. "No, no one has seen them. I'm not sure what we are going to do. The local cops here think Riley and Liv took off, but we know that isn't true. I'm going to see if Captain Meadows found anything about the guy who was seen with Liv."

"We'll go with you," Joe said.

Luke walked with them in the direction of the conference room. "I was out searching with Det. Tyler and he came back early to meet his wife. Have you seen anyone else?"

"Karen and Jack are back up in their room, but I haven't seen anyone else." Emma put her hand on Luke's arm before he could open the door. "I think there's something you should know. At the reception last night, Riley told me she thought she saw her father right after the wedding ceremony. It freaked her out. She told me he called you the other day."

Luke confirmed the call and furrowed his brow. "Riley saw her father here? She didn't mention anything to me."

"She didn't want to upset you. Riley told me she was going to tell you later. She wasn't hiding it from you. She wasn't one hundred percent sure it was him and didn't want to make an issue of something that might not be an issue. Riley only saw him for a few seconds off in the distance right after the ceremony."

"I understand," Luke said, even though he wasn't sure that he did. Riley potentially seeing her father at the wedding was a big deal. Luke shook off the annoyance and opened the door to the conference room.

Captain Meadows sat at the table behind a laptop and a stack of printed out pages. He looked up as they came in. "I found some information, Luke, but it doesn't make a lot of sense to me."

Luke sat down next to him and Emma and Joe took seats across from them. Captain Meadows moved the stack of papers over to Luke. "The guy Liv left with has ties to the Irish mob out of South Boston. He has a rap sheet a mile long, everything from petty theft to assault. I called a Boston detective I know and this guy has been on their radar for a long time. He's not high up in the ranks of the Irish mob. He's an underling. What would a guy like this be doing up here?"

Emma's hand flew to her mouth. "Riley's father."

Luke wasn't sure what she meant. "You think Riley's father has something to do with this guy?"

"Riley always said her father was involved in the Irish mob, right?" Emma said, tears forming in her eyes.

"Riley's father is in Ireland," Luke explained. "I don't know of any connection he has to Boston."

Captain Meadows had been completely out of the loop so Luke explained about Riley's father, his criminal ties, and that Riley told Emma she thought she had seen him at the wedding.

"Would he kidnap his daughters?" Captain Meadows asked.

Luke shrugged and looked across the table at Emma. "What do you think? Is that something he would do?"

"I have no idea. Riley hasn't told me enough about him for me to even venture a guess. At least, if they are with him, Riley and Liv are probably safe."

"Probably?" Captain Meadows asked with raised eyebrows. He asked for Riley's father's name, an approximate age, nationality, and other identifying information.

Luke gave him the details he knew. "Are you going to search for him? I've never searched although I wanted to. I didn't want to invade Riley's privacy like that."

Captain Meadows didn't respond. Instead, he typed information into the database and waited. He shook his head twice and typed in more information. Luke looked over at the screen and didn't understand what he was seeing. Patrick Sullivan's name was there along with a photo, but the information wasn't accessible. It was all marked confidential.

Captain Meadows turned to Emma. "Can you and Joe go up and get Karen and Jack for me, please?"

Neither said a word but both got up and left the conference room. When they were gone and the door closed behind them, Captain Meadows turned his screen to Luke. He pointed to a number in the corner of one of the reports. "As you know that number means we can't touch him. He's connected to the government."

"Is he an informant?"

"No." Captain Meadows shook his head. "It means Patrick Sullivan isn't who he says he is. He's working for the government or possibly another government."

"FBI?" Luke asked, his stomach dropping.

"No. These files can only be accessed by the highest-level security clearances. If I have the right guy, Patrick Sullivan isn't a criminal at all." Captain Meadows locked eyes with Luke. "I can't access the information though. It goes much higher than both of our pay grades."

Luke's mind spun with the information. He wondered if Riley had been lying to him this whole time or maybe she hadn't even known her father's real identity. None of it made any sense to Luke.

"Did you find anything in your search?" Captain Meadows asked.

"No, nothing. Not one person has seen either of them." Luke rubbed his bald head. "I think we might need to go to the media even though I hate even the idea of it. We are running out of options."

As they waited for Karen, Luke called Miles to see if he found anything in Troy.

"I was just about to call you, Luke," Miles said as he answered. "I don't have any news for you. No one had been at the house and none of the neighbors I spoke to had any information. Have you found anything yet?"

"Not anything that makes sense," Luke said, which wasn't a lie.

"I called some of my contacts up there. I have a team on standby with some dogs to trace their scent if you want their help. You mentioned you saw Riley go to the side of the building. Maybe you can trace her scent from there."

Luke had thought of that earlier but didn't know who to call given local law enforcement wasn't interested in getting involved. At that moment, he was beyond grateful to Miles and told him so. He added, "I'm here anytime they want to show up. I don't have a plan of action yet. We might take it to the media, but if we can trace their scent, I'd rather start there. It would be more than we know now."

Miles told Luke he'd call the team with the dogs right away and text him the information. "Let me know of anything else you need. I'm here on standby for you," he said before hanging up.

As Luke ended the call, Karen shoved open both doors. "You think this has something to do with my ex-husband?"

Luke waved her over to the table. "We don't know, but I need you to tell me everything you know about him."

Karen shook her head. "I can't do that."

"What if he took them?" Luke insisted. "Captain Meadows found the guy who was last seen with Liv. He's connected to the Irish mob, which connects to Riley's father."

"What's his name?" Karen asked, folding her arms across her chest.

Luke leaned over and glanced at the screen Captain Meadows pulled up for him. "Noah Byrne."

Karen nodded and walked out of the room without saying another word. Luke wasn't having any of it. He got up so fast his chair tipped over backward and hit the wall behind him.

He followed Karen out into the hallway. "You need to tell me what's going on right now."

Karen turned to him. "If I could tell you, I would. I promise you that, Luke." She kept walking at a pace faster than Luke had ever seen her move.

"Where are you going?"

"I need a phone, one of those disposable ones. Right now!"

This wasn't making any sense to Luke, but if it meant it would help find Riley, he'd do whatever it took. "Come on," Luke said, guiding her by the arm. "There's a store right down the road where I saw some."

Karen seemed hesitant to go with him, but finally gave in and followed Luke out of the hotel.

Thirty minutes later, after they had gone to a store and then enabled the phone, they sat in Luke's SUV. Karen sent a text to a number Luke didn't recognize. He peered over at her as she typed. The message didn't seem like anything important, but Luke assumed it carried more weight than the actual words. It was a simple question.

Can you send me the recipe for your mother's lasagna?

Chapter 9

"I don't want to die, Riley," Liv cried as the door slammed shut at the top of the stairs.

Holden didn't unlock our handcuffs before he left, but I hoped he was getting us food. I needed something to keep my strength up until I could find a way out of here.

I needed to refocus my sister's attention on something helpful. "Tell me what you saw outside. I need to figure out where we are." I got up from the chair and looked around the basement. The small room we were in didn't have any windows. I flicked on a hall light and walked to the bathroom. There wasn't a window in there either, just an endless sea of pink. The pink sink and tiled walls probably hadn't been updated in fifty years or more.

I walked out of the bathroom and went farther down a short hallway that grew darker the farther I went. I ran my hands along the wall for another light switch. When I found it within a few feet, I turned on another light. The hallway led into another area of the basement. The carpeting in the main room gave way to concrete floors in what appeared to be an unfinished area. A hot water tank and furnace sat off to my right and a washer and dryer off to the left. I wasn't sure whose house this was but someone lived here. A pile of folded laundry sat on top of the dryer. By the look of them, the clothes belonged to an older woman. I didn't know anyone other than grandmas who wore polyester pants.

There were two small windows above the washer and dryer but they weren't big enough for a person to fit through. From the cobwebs and inches of dirt that covered them, they probably hadn't been opened in a long time. I didn't even think I could get up there to open one and call for help.

Frustrated, I went back to Liv who sat on the couch with her eyes closed. "You never answered me," I said drawing her attention. "What did you see outside?"

Liv turned her head slightly to look at me. "I think we are in the Boston area. I saw the Massachusetts license plates and a friend of mine lived in a neighborhood like this a few years ago. It reminds me of that."

I had thought the same, but nearly every neighborhood outside of Boston looked like the one we were in. There were more small towns and cities in the surrounding area than I could count. I didn't know if we were north of Boston or south. We were near water and I had the street names. That's all I knew, but it wasn't like I had my phone or a laptop and could look it up.

I slumped back down on the chair. "Does this guy seem familiar to you at all?"

"No."

"Tell me about the guy last night? Did you hook up with him?"

Liv raised her eyebrows. "Is this really the time to give me a lecture about casual sex?"

"I don't care about that. I'm trying to figure out who these people are and any information will help. Did he say where he was from or what he was doing in Lake Placid? Did he say anything strange to you?"

Liv reached her cuffed hands up to her head and rubbed across her forehead. "I wasn't kidding before. I could use some food and coffee."

She paused and closed her eyes. "His name was Noah, but now, I don't know if that was real or fake. He told me he worked in a bank in Albany. Because he mentioned Albany, I told him I was from Troy."

"Anything else? Any strange conversation? Anything about Sully?"

"No nothing about him..." Liv trailed off. "There was one thing. When he came up to me at the bar, I told him my name was Liv and he said he knew. I asked him what he meant and he brushed it off that he had heard all of us talking, which seemed to make sense at the time. I'm assuming he probably knew everything about me."

"That's what I assume, too."

"Right," Liv said sarcastically. "I know what you're going to say. If I hadn't been so gullible and slutty none of this would have happened."

I shook my head. "Liv, I wasn't going to say that and I haven't thought that once. This was coordinated and planned. If they hadn't grabbed us there, it would have been someplace else. I'm not focused on why or how it happened; I'm focused on getting us out of here."

"What can I do to help?"

"Be observant and keep your head down as much as possible. Right now, letting them underestimate us is the best thing we can do." I looked over at my sister and didn't want to say the next part but had to. "When the time comes and I tell you to fight, do it as if your life depends on it because it does."

Liv didn't say anything but she half-smiled at me in understanding. She reached for the television remote control that sat on the coffee table. "Were you being serious about Luke not going to the media? I wasn't sure if you were saying that for their benefit or if it's true."

It occurred to me that they might have some audio wired in the basement to be able to listen to our conversations. I scanned around the room looking for wires or anything odd but didn't see anything. If they were listening in, I couldn't do much about it.

"I was serious. Luke is going to look at this like a typical missing person's case. He's going to run down every lead and uncover as much evidence as he can about what happened before getting the media involved. He will only do it as a last resort or if he thinks it advantageous to finding us. After all this time, I know how his mind works. He's as stubborn as I am."

"I don't know how they are going to find us." Liv turned on the television and flipped around to a national news station. We watched for a few minutes and, as expected, there was nothing about us.

"Liv, don't get discouraged. Think about who was at my wedding. You have Luke, Cooper, Jack, Det. Tyler and Captain Meadows. Plus, you know Mom is like a bloodhound. They will find us." I believed that. If I had to go missing, there wasn't a better team I wanted searching for me.

A few minutes later, the door at the top of the stairs creaked open and Holden came down carrying a food bag from a local fast-food place and coffee from Starbucks. He wouldn't look either of us in the eyes. He dropped the bag and the coffee cups on the table and then walked over to each of us and unlocked our cuffs. Both Liv and I moved our hands around happy to have freedom of movement for the first time in hours.

When Holden was done, he reached for a cup on the table and handed it to me. "Your sister was specific, but I didn't know what you wanted. I got you regular coffee with cream and sugar."

I took the cup and thanked him. This wasn't the gesture of a killer. If I wasn't so in need of caffeine I might have stopped to wonder if he drugged or poisoned anything. If I had to go out, poisoned coffee wouldn't be the worst way to go.

I took a sip and caught his eye. "I appreciate you feeding us. As you can imagine, it's been a rough night." Holden didn't say anything but turned toward the stairs. I called to his back. "Do you think I can talk to you for a moment?"

He turned and waited for me to speak, but I wanted to get him alone. I stood and motioned with my head to walk down the hall with me. I hid my surprise when he followed. I flicked on the hallway light and walked to where the washer and dryer were.

"I hope you're not planning to do something stupid like attacking me. I can overpower you and put you right back in the cuffs," Holden said, eyeing me.

"I just want to talk out of earshot of my sister." I paused still not exactly sure what I was going to say. "I know you think taking us is some revenge on our father for something he did to you, but he's done a lot to us, too. I'm closer to my father than Liv is. She is closer to my mother. Let her go and keep me. You can kill me if it comes to that, but let her go."

"That's admirable, but it's not going to happen. Even if I wanted to, she knows too much now."

"What does she know?" I asked, stressing the point. "We have no idea where we are. Blindfold her, cuff her, and drive her far away and dump her someplace. Liv can figure it out from there." I didn't know if that was technically true. My sister had a horrible sense of direction and wasn't very good on her own, but anything was better than here.

When Holden didn't say anything, I pressed on. "It's obvious my father hurt you somehow, but he's been hurting my family for years. There is no point killing my sister to hurt my mother because that's all you'd accomplish."

Holden stepped closer to me and I backed up. "What would you do if someone killed your sister?"

"I don't know," I said honestly, not even able to imagine it. "I'd want justice. I'd probably make them pay."

Holden's mouth set in a firm line. "Now you know how I feel. Your father killed my brother."

"Are you sure? Do you have proof?" I didn't doubt the possibility of that, but I wanted to make sure he was operating on facts.

"I have all the proof I need."

"So, no?" I looked Holden right in the eyes and I could tell there was uncertainty. "Before you go down this road, don't you at least want to make sure that he did it? If not, the real killer will go free and you'd have killed us for nothing. How is that justice for your brother?"

Holden watched me but didn't say anything. There was something about his eyes that gave him away. He wasn't sure and he had no idea what he was doing. "Let Liv go and I'll help you solve your brother's murder. If my father did it, you can kill me. I won't even try to fight you."

Holden blinked twice. "You're wagering a lot on your investigative ability and your father's innocence."

I shrugged. "You're going to kill me anyway. What have I got to lose?"

Chapter 10

"Cooper, you have to stop blaming yourself," Adele said, sitting on the side of the bed watching as he beat himself up over the events of last night. "What can you do to help?"

"I feel too paralyzed to do anything." Cooper sat down and dropped his head in his hands. "We searched the entire area of Lake Placid, but no one has seen or heard anything about Riley and Liv."

Adele moved up on the bed to put her back against the headboard and got comfortable. "Luke is emotional, which means he isn't thinking straight so that's what you need to do. Let's talk it through like every other case you've had. What does your gut tell you?"

Cooper didn't say anything for a moment and then turned to look at Adele. "They aren't here anymore. My bet is someone took Liv and then lured Riley away. If someone had Liv and Riley knew, she'd do anything to protect her sister even if it was foolish and stupid."

"That's her weakness then and it's got to be someone who knows how to exploit that."

"If that's true, then it's someone Riley knows or someone who did a lot of research on her."

"Which means planning," Adele added.

"Right," Cooper said, letting that sit for a moment. Adele had a way of talking him through cases. It was the defense attorney in her. That's why they made the perfect pair. "It means it's not a typical kidnapping.

They didn't take Liv and Riley for the usual reasons – sexual assault and murder."

"They could do that here, and there's no sign of them anywhere." Adele watched him. "So, what's the next step?"

Cooper mulled over the limited options they had. He was interrupted by a knock on the door. He got up to answer it and found Luke standing there. "You find out anything?"

"We need to talk," Luke said, stepping into the room. "I have something to ask you."

"Ask away," Cooper said.

"Captain Meadows and Det. Tyler are going to need to go back to Little Rock. They rescheduled their flight for a later one, but we have cases pending in Little Rock. Are you free to stay and help me search for Riley and Liv?"

"You couldn't make me leave." Cooper looked at Adele.

"I have all week," she said. "I have a case in court next week, but I can wait it out until the weekend and figure it out from there."

Relief washed over Luke's face. "I don't know what I'd do without you both."

Cooper sat down in the chair. "Did you find out anything about the guy Liv left with?"

"Noah Byrne. He's connected to the Irish mob in Boston."

"Adele and I were talking about the kidnapping. There had to have been a good deal of planning and research ahead of time. Is there a connection between this guy and Riley or Liv?"

"Possibly," Luke said and sat down. He met Adele's stare and then turned to Cooper. "This can't leave this room. We can't tell Emma and Joe or even my parents. I believe it might have something to do with their father. I went to ask Karen about it and she won't tell me anything. I went out with her and she bought a burner phone and texted someone a very strange message, almost like talking in code.

She's downstairs with Captain Meadows and Det. Tyler right now waiting for a response."

"What do you think is going on?" Adele asked, moving to the edge of the bed.

"If I had to guess, I'd say that Karen and Sully have a way to communicate with each other that no one else will understand." Luke dropped his voice lower. "When Captain Meadows looked him up in the database to see his priors, he came back with confidential files that need top-level security clearances to open."

"He's law enforcement?" Cooper asked, trying to remember everything Riley had ever said about her father.

"I don't think so. That wouldn't require that kind of top-level security clearances."

"He's a spy," Adele said, a broad smile appearing on her face.

Cooper turned to face her. "Like CIA?"

"We don't know." Luke sat back and clasped his hands in front of him. "Whatever information we get about Riley's father, we will need to keep it close to the vest. I know Emma and Joe don't want to go back to Little Rock, but I think we need to convince them to do that. I need my parents to go on their vacation or back to Little Rock. I need them safely away from this. I can handle my parents, but can you talk to Emma and Joe? Then we need to meet back downstairs, and hopefully, Karen hears back soon."

"I can handle Emma and Joe," Cooper assured. "Their kids are with her parents so I'm sure they want to get home. I'll promise to keep them updated."

The three of them made a plan and then Luke left. As Cooper shut the door, he turned to Adele. "What do you think?"

Adele stood from the bed and grabbed her cardigan and pulled it on. "I think it makes sense. Think about the call you got from Sully while we were driving up to New York. He told Luke to keep a watch on

Riley. He even alluded to the fact that people might want to do him harm. His daughters could be an extension of that."

"You don't think he took them?"

"I don't know anything about him, but I've never heard Karen say anything that would hint at that. It doesn't seem like there was violence in their relationship, and I don't think a father would kidnap his daughter right after her wedding."

Cooper considered what Adele said and wasn't sure if that made him feel better or worse. At least if Sully had them, they might be safe. The alternative was too much to think about. "Let's go talk to Emma and Joe."

"Can you do that alone?" Adele asked, checking her phone. "I need to make a few calls on an upcoming case."

"When you're done, check down in the conference room for us."

Cooper walked down the hall to Emma and Joe and knocked on the door.

Emma answered, wringing her hands. "Do you know something?"

"No. Nothing yet. I want to talk to you both if you have time."

Emma stepped out of the way and let Cooper in. "I needed to speak to you or Luke as well."

Cooper walked into the room and took a seat at the table with Joe. Emma had a look of uncertainty as she spoke.

"Let me go first if it's okay." When Cooper didn't argue she continued. "Joe and I need to go back to Little Rock. We have two kids and Joe needs to get back to work. I have work pending, too. I know that probably seems horrible of me and we'd stay if we could. I don't know how long that will be or how we could help. Please don't hate me. I love Riley so much, but I don't feel like there's much I can do and my kids need me."

Relieved, Cooper said, "Emma, don't worry. I was coming here to talk to you both about going back to Little Rock. There isn't anything

54

for you to do here, and we need eyes and ears in Little Rock. Luke was going to send you back with the house key so you can check the house for us. I don't think Riley went back there, but we need someone to confirm that. Det. Tyler and Captain Meadows are heading back, too. Luke is talking to his parents right now about doing the same."

Emma sat down on the edge of the bed. "I feel so much better. I felt awful about leaving."

"No need. We all know how much you both love Riley. I'll call and keep you updated when I know more." Cooper shook Joe's hand and then hugged Emma before he left.

Cooper headed to the elevator happy that went better than he had planned. He didn't even have to bring up Sully. No one liked feeling cut out of the loop. Cooper entered the elevator at the same time as another man. As the elevator doors closed, he turned to Cooper.

"Is there something happening at the hotel with two women missing? I heard some other guests talking."

Cooper introduced himself. "Two of my friends went missing last night. We have been asking around if anyone has seen them."

"I have some information, but I'm not sure if it's relevant."

The elevator reached the ground floor and the doors slid open. "Let's find someplace quiet and you can tell me," Cooper said, looking in the lobby away from everyone else. He turned the corner and found two chairs not far from the fireplace.

As they sat down, Cooper asked, "What did you see?"

The man told Cooper his name was Peter and explained he and his wife were visiting Lake Placid for a few days. "Last night, I woke up because something kept hitting our window. I looked out and there was a person down there throwing something at the window next to ours. They must have missed a few times and hit ours instead. It was too dark to make out who was down there. I stepped away from the window to throw on my pants and grab a jacket. I was going down to yell at them to stop. When I got outside, no one was out there. As I walked back up the small hill toward the hotel, I saw a car taking off out of the parking lot. Two men were driving. I didn't see anyone else, but I caught the make and model of the car." He pulled a slip of paper from his pocket and handed it to Cooper. "As I said, I have no idea if this is connected, but I thought it strange that they took off out of the parking lot right after I saw someone throwing something at the window."

"What room are you staying in?"

Peter told him the number. It was the room next to Luke and Riley. "Do you think I saw something that can help? I wasn't sure who to reach out to. When I went down to the lobby last night, there wasn't anyone at the desk and I didn't want to stand around all night waiting."

"Understandable. Is there anything else you can tell me?"

"I watched as they left the parking lot and they went to the right." Peter gave Cooper a basic description of the two men but it wasn't detailed enough for them to do anything with. It had been so dark; Peter was lucky he saw anything.

"I hope you find your friends," Peter said, standing. He gave Cooper his cellphone number in case he had more questions.

Chapter 11

It hadn't been the easiest conversation, but in the end, Spencer helped Luke convince Lucia that they would be better off at home in Little Rock. Luke encouraged them to take a few days and continue with their trip, but he wasn't sure they would do that.

Luke's parents felt like they were abandoning him in his time of need. He had tried his best to convince them otherwise. After much discussion and reassurance, they finally gave in and agreed to go only if Luke promised to keep them informed of what was happening.

When Luke made it back down to the lobby, he stopped at the front desk and was pleased a copy of the video surveillance was ready for him on a flash drive. As Luke headed back to the conference room, he received a call that the dogs were there with their handlers. He reversed direction and went back up to his room to grab something of Riley's so the dogs would have her scent. From a pile of clothes Riley had said was laundry, Luke grabbed one of the shirts that she had worn on the drive up to Lake Placid.

A few minutes later, Luke met the dog handlers at the front of the hotel and handed over Riley's shirt. The handlers took it from there. Luke stood back a safe distance and let the dogs go to work. They immediately picked up Riley's scent from the hotel doors and followed the same path Luke had taken with the Lake Placid detective earlier that day. They picked up on one particular spot near the small pile of stones and then they took off back up the hill toward the parking lot.

Luke wasn't sure if it meant anything because Riley had been in the parking lot a few times getting things from their car, except the dogs didn't follow a path to Luke's SUV. They went to another section of the parking lot and stopped near an open space. They sniffed around the area and indicated Riley had been there, too. Luke looked around and didn't see any familiar cars. Everyone that had been with them had parked near Luke's SUV. Luke didn't think Riley had even walked to that area of the parking lot. Of course, he could be wrong, but he didn't think so.

"What does this mean?" Luke asked one of the handlers.

"I'd say it's fairly certain she got into a vehicle. Now whether that was on her own or not, the dogs won't be able to tell." The handler asked if Riley had been to that area before and Luke said no. "Whatever happened, she was on the side of that hotel and then in this area of the parking lot. That's all I'm able to tell you."

Luke thanked them for their time and headed back into the hotel and ran right into Cooper. He thrust a slip of paper at Luke and explained about the witness who had come forward. Luke absorbed the information and tried to temper his excitement. He turned in the direction of the conference room with Cooper right behind him.

Luke walked into the middle of a discussion between Captain Meadows, Karen, and Jack. They stopped talking when he entered and turned their eyes to Luke.

"What's going on?" he asked looking at the three of them. He tossed Riley's shirt on the back of a chair.

Karen stepped toward him. "I received a message from the one I sent earlier. We need to leave the hotel and meet someone. You are going to have to trust me because I can't tell you anything right now."

Captain Meadows caught Luke's eye. "You need to trust them, Luke. Listen to Karen with an open mind and don't jump to conclusions."

That sounded more ominous than Luke liked, but he agreed. "If it gets us closer to finding Riley and Liv, I'm in." Luke turned back to Cooper. "I want Cooper involved. I'm not doing anything without him."

Karen nodded. "Cooper and Adele can both come with us, but we need to go quickly. I'll meet you in the parking lot when you're ready." Karen and Jack both left the room.

"What's going on?" Cooper asked Captain Meadows.

"It's not my place to explain, but there has been a significant development. All I'll say is that Riley's father is here in Lake Placid and he wants to speak with all of you. Karen doesn't know more than that, but she wants to fill you in on his background." Captain Meadows went to the table and shut down his laptop and gathered his things. As he headed back toward the door, he said, "Take as much time as you need here, Luke. Your job will be waiting for you when you get back. If there is anything that we can do for you, call us."

"Tell Tyler I'll call him when I can." Luke and Cooper walked out of the conference room with Captain Meadows and said goodbye in the hallway. Cooper texted Adele and told her they needed to leave as soon as possible and to meet him in the lobby. She responded almost immediately that she'd be right down.

They waited for Adele and then headed out of the hotel. They climbed in the back of Karen's SUV, with Adele in the middle, and closed their doors.

"Can you tell us what's going on now?" Luke asked, wishing his voice didn't have a tinge of impatience. He wasn't frustrated with her, just the situation.

"Not yet, Luke. We need to be someplace secure." Karen turned around to face him as Jack drove. "I promise you, give me about fifteen minutes and it will all become clear."

Jack drove them out of Lake Placid village and into the Adirondack mountains. They drove several miles before Jack turned off the main road and climbed a steep hill. If it had recently snowed, Luke had no idea how they would have reached their destination. Luckily, the roads were clear. Jack turned twice taking a left and a right, bringing them into more dense woods until finally, a small cabin came into view.

A man, about six-four with thick defined muscle and dark wavy hair, stood on the porch. Luke had no idea what to expect, but as soon as he was close enough to see the man's face, he knew without question, it was Riley's father. They shared the same eyes, nose, and cheekbones. It was obvious which parent Riley looked like.

Jack parked and they all exited the vehicle, walking slowly up to the porch.

"Welcome, all," Sully said with his thick Irish accent. "Come on in." He opened the door and stood out of the way. Luke sized him up as he passed and didn't like the feeling that if Sully were so inclined, he could probably snap Luke and Cooper in two without breaking a sweat.

They all took a seat in the living room and waited for Sully to join them. He had lit a fire and the space was comfortable and warm, a direct contrast to how Luke felt. Karen introduced each of them and explained how Cooper and Adele were connected to Riley. Sully seemed to already know.

Sully stood in the center, glancing at each of them. "I brought you here because I know it's secure. You'll have to excuse all the cloak and dagger, but this is the norm in my line of work."

"What is your line of work?" Luke asked, inching forward on his seat. "Riley told us all that you were a criminal, part of the Irish mob. None of this makes sense to me. Why are you here?"

"I can understand your confusion," Sully said, dropping his voice. "Riley told you what she has been instructed to say since she found out the truth about me."

Luke, Cooper, and Adele shared a look among themselves, still not understanding. "What does this mean exactly?" Cooper asked.

Sully glanced down at Karen and allowed her to explain. "Sully is a CIA officer. He has been a part of the CIA's National Clandestine Service since our twenties. He had already gained citizenship in the United States, planning to make his life here but was recruited right out of grad school."

Even though Luke had been warned and had suspected something like this was coming, it still came as a shock to his system to hear the words and have confirmation. It also meant Riley had been lying to him this whole time. "You knew, Jack?"

Jack nodded. "Only for a few months. I stumbled onto some documents while helping Karen clean the attic. She didn't have much choice but to tell me."

"Riley has been lying to me this whole time?" Luke said, not able to shake the feeling of being betrayed.

Sully walked over to him but stopped when Luke raised his head. He was sure the expression on his face gave Sully pause. Luke wasn't happy, to say the least.

Sully explained, "Riley asked her mother if she could tell you and was told no. This wasn't a lie she wanted to keep from you. She was given no choice. If it makes you feel any better, Liv doesn't know the truth either."

Chapter 12

After Holden left me standing in the back area of the basement and went upstairs without giving me an answer, I joined Liv and drank my coffee and ate the breakfast that had been bought for us. Liv asked me twice what we had talked about. All I would tell her is that I was hoping to have her released. She argued that she wouldn't leave me behind.

I told her that she would go if I had to force her out. I whispered directly in her ear that she'd have to remember every detail she could and get us help. That would be her mission if released. If we had any chance of pulling this off, she'd have to pretend to Holden that she'd never do anything like that and she didn't know anything about where we were being held. I had no idea if she could pull that off or not, but our lives might very well depend on it. At least, Holden hadn't said no to my offer to help him if he let Liv go. We still had a shot.

After she finished eating, Liv fell asleep on the couch for a couple of hours while I flipped through channels looking for any information I could find on the news. It occurred to me that Holden must not care or he forgot that we could watch a local news station, which would give us a general idea of where we were.

A few things weren't adding up about Holden. He wanted us to believe he was capable of killing us for revenge, but his actions said otherwise. Killers don't buy hostages breakfast. They don't unlock handcuffs and leave hostages free to roam around a basement. They certainly don't provide a television if they want to keep a location secret.

All I could get on the local news station was that we were in the Boston area, but that still didn't tell me much. There were too many towns to narrow down specifically, but at least, what we had guessed before was correct. I shut off the television and rested my head back on the chair. I closed my eyes for what felt like a few minutes, but I woke rested sometime later with Holden standing over me nudging my arm.

I raised my eyes to him. "How long was I asleep?"

"A couple of hours." He stood back and waved to the back area of the basement. Liv was still asleep.

"You didn't drug us, did you?" I asked as I joined him.

Holden furrowed his brow. "Why would I do that?"

"You know, killer and all that." For some reason, I had forgotten how to stand. I didn't quite know what to do with my arms as I stood there with the man who kidnapped me. It wasn't a friendly chat, but here we were locked in conversation like we were buddies. I shoved my hands in my pockets, unsure of what to do with them.

Holden noticed my fidgeting but didn't address it. "What does your sister know about your father?"

"Almost nothing," I said honestly. "My mother didn't tell her much about my father growing up. What was there to tell? He was a criminal and out of our lives. Neither of us asked too many questions. It never seemed like a good topic of conversation in our family. Besides, as I said, my sister is much closer to my mother."

"What about you? How much do you know?"

"Not much more than Liv," I lied with ease, used to it now. "I saw my father some when I was younger but have few memories of him. As an adult, it hasn't been much at all. He could be remarried, have other children, or live in France for all I know." I locked eyes with him. "No offense, but you didn't do enough homework."

Holden narrowed his eyes. "I did enough research that I got you here easily enough."

I reached up and rubbed the sore spot on the back of my head where I had been struck. "Fair enough. Who hit me?"

"A friend of the guy who lured Liv out of the bar."

"Were you in Lake Placid at all?"

"No. I was here preparing for your arrival."

A deep belly laugh escaped and I bit my lip. "You stole some old lady's house. What's to prepare?" Then it dawned on me. I hadn't seen the homeowner and hoped she wasn't dead in a closet upstairs. I hated to even ask the question. "You didn't kill the homeowner, did you?"

Holden's face registered a horror I hadn't been expecting. "Of course not. What do you take me for?"

I gestured with my hand. "Well, you kidnapped me and my sister and told us you were going to kill us. It's easy to make the leap."

All Holden offered was a half sheepish shrug I didn't quite understand. "I think you're right that I miscalculated what would happen if I kidnapped you."

I couldn't believe he was admitting that. "What do you mean?"

"I figured it would have made the news by now and your father would have found out."

I hated to tell him, but I wasn't Bill Gate's daughter or royalty. No one would care if I was gone except the people closest to me who hated to involve the media.

"I'm sure my husband is searching for me." I paused because that was the first time that I said *husband* aloud. I wanted to smile, but given the circumstances, it wasn't appropriate. "As I was saying, I'm sure people are looking for us, and it might hit the news eventually. I can assure you though it's not going to hit the international news so my father is probably not going to hear it."

"My understanding was that he'd be in Lake Placid at your wedding."

I shook my head. "I don't know who you're getting your information from, but even if my father was there yesterday, he would have left right after. He doesn't hang around in the United States too often. If you were an international criminal wanted by every law enforcement agency, would you?"

Holden didn't respond, so I pushed harder. "Who is giving you information about Patrick Sullivan? Who told you he killed your brother?"

"Some of my brother's associates," Holden admitted. "They said they were sure that Patrick Sullivan killed him in a deal gone bad. It makes sense given who my brother was."

If we were going to stand here and have this awkward conversation like old pals, I was at least going to sit. I walked over to the washer, closed the lid, and hopped up on it.

"Holden, I have to tell you, I don't think you're getting information from reliable people. If your brother was a criminal, then your brother's criminal friends are the least likely source of information."

Holden leaned against the dryer and bit the inside of his cheek, making a popping sound when he let it go. He watched me and didn't say anything.

I pointed to the ceiling. "Is Collins up there one of your brother's associates?"

"He was back in the neighborhood growing up. Not as much recently."

"Listen, Holden," I said more dramatically than I meant. "I don't want to insult your ego, but I've been an investigator for a long time. I was an investigative journalist and now a private investigator. You don't strike me as a criminal, not a kidnapper, and not as someone who would kill two women – even for revenge." The way Holden looked away told me I wasn't wrong.

I pressed harder. "Were you going to kill us or have someone else do it?"

"Someone else," Holden said quietly with a tinge of embarrassment and failure in his voice.

"Holden, there is nothing wrong with you that you can't kill us yourself. Quite the opposite." I had no idea what to say to him. My instinct told me to keep him talking. It's not like I had been in this situation before, but I saw an opening so I was taking it. "How did this plan come together?"

"My brother, Eddie, was murdered about two years ago. Some of the guys in his old crew came to me and said we had to get revenge for his death. Eddie had been living in Europe and was killed in Boston one weekend he came back to visit. His old crew members pointed to Patrick Sullivan. They said he had tried to kill Eddie before and finally succeeded."

Holden exhaled. "They got me involved and assumed I'd want the same revenge as them. Initially, I said no, but they said I was spitting on my brother's memory and that I was a coward. I had the money to pull this off."

"But not the brains," I said to myself.

"What?" Holden asked.

"Nothing. It's obvious your heart isn't in this and it's not what you want to be doing."

"It's too late now," Holden argued. "The plan is in motion. I can't back out now. If I do, my life might be in danger. Eddie's associates want blood. I don't know if they care at this point if it's mine or yours."

I shook my head. "As long as we are still breathing, it's not too late." A plan formulated in my mind, but I wasn't sure it could work. I needed to get Liv to safety and then find out who killed Holden's brother.

I reached my hand out to Holden and put it on his shoulder. He didn't flinch or move it. I looked him directly in the eyes. "You said something a few minutes ago that reinforced that it wasn't my father who killed your brother. If there is one thing I know, he doesn't try to kill people. If Sully wants you dead, you're dead. There's no try about it. One shot, one kill, the first time."

Holden let out a string of curses. I think he was finally starting to see how much over his head he had gotten himself. He raised his eyes to mine. "What do you suggest?"

"I think I might have a workable plan."

Chapter 13

L uke stood, a wave of disgust and anger washing over him. "What do you mean Liv doesn't know you work for the CIA? How can you not tell your daughter?"

"Luke, calm down," Karen said from across the room. "You know Liv. Does she seem like someone who could keep a secret? We didn't tell Riley until after she graduated college when she was an adult fully capable of processing the information and all its implications for our family. We planned to do the same with Liv, but she is a different person as you know. She drinks too much. She isn't the most responsible. I know Riley likes to tell people that Liv is my favorite. That's not true. Liv needs more support than Riley. She always has."

Luke still didn't understand and he exhaled but said nothing.

Karen continued. "When the time came, Sully and I decided it wasn't safe to tell Liv. I can't tell you the number of times Liv has been drunk with friends or at a bar and she told people her father was an international criminal. Luckily for us, people rarely believe that tale and tend to let it go at that. Can you imagine what would happen if she knew the truth? All of our lives would be at risk."

Sully looked directly at Luke. "The bottom line is Riley could stand up to interrogation. She'd be able to handle herself where Liv would crack."

"Interrogation?" Luke said, knowing exactly what Sully meant. "You mean torture."

Sully turned his head away. "Riley would take our family secret to the grave."

Luke lunged at him, reaching his hands out to Sully's throat, but he never got the chance to make contact. For as skilled and powerful as Luke was, Sully was better. He was too big and far too strong to be taken down by Luke. Sully countered and had Luke in a headlock before he even realized what was happening.

Cooper jumped up but must have thought better of it because all he did was look down at Luke with pity in his eyes and admiration for Sully. At that moment, Luke wanted to punch him in the face. He struggled free of Sully when the grip around his neck loosened. He pointed his finger at the man and raised his voice. "Don't ever touch me again!" Luke pulled away and straightened out his shirt that had ridden up his midsection.

Jack stood. "Let's take a break. Luke, let's go for a walk."

"I don't think that's a good idea," Sully said, moving in his path.

Jack stood his ground. "With all due respect, I don't care what you think right now. Luke's wife is missing and the last thing he needs to hear is that she lied to him and would hold up well under torture." Jack stepped toward him. "If you don't move, you're going to have to take on both Luke and me and that isn't going to end well for you."

Sully stood defiant until Karen told him to knock it off and get out of the way.

Jack moved toward the door and waved at Luke who followed him out. Jack waited until they were several hundred feet away from the house on a dirt path before he spoke. "I don't know if I felt the same as you when I found out so I won't pretend I did. But it was a shock and wasn't something I was sure I could take on. I worried for Karen and the girls but also worried about Sully's influence in their lives. I felt betrayed and it's hard to keep it secret, especially from you. I nearly told you at Karen's house. Do you remember?"

Luke started to say no but then recalled a conversation from a previous visit. "It was when you told me that investigation was in Riley's blood. You said her grandfather. Was that a lie?"

"It wasn't the whole truth like you deserved. Sully's father was a detective in Ireland and Sully followed in his footsteps and so did Riley. They may work different kinds of investigations, but it's all the same." Jack stopped walking and turned to Luke. "Get it all out now because when we go back in that house, you have to keep it together. Sully isn't the enemy. I don't like him and I'd like nothing more than to knock him on his backside, but he might be the key to helping us find Riley and Liv. That's all that matters to me right now."

Luke knew Jack was right. "I don't want to feel betrayed by Riley but I do."

"It's normal," Jack reassured. "Riley fought with her mother to tell you, but part of the issue was finding a secure enough place to do that. She's a spy's kid, Luke. She's been playing the game since she was twenty-two. Old habits are hard to break."

Luke didn't say anything so Jack asked, "If Riley had told you when you first met or before the wedding, would it have changed anything? Would you have broken up with her or not married her?"

"No, of course not. I love Riley and there isn't anything I wouldn't do for her."

"I figured as much. Then it shouldn't matter now. What you can do for Riley right now is put your feelings about this on the backburner and go forward like every great detective does when something hits really close to home."

They walked for a good while longer and then turned around and headed back toward the house. Luke had a chance to think things through and calm himself down. He appreciated Jack having the sense to get him out of the house. Luke had to force himself to remove his emotions from the equation and start thinking rationally about how to find Riley.

Before they reached the door, Jack slapped Luke on the back. "I'm on your side. Anything you need, I'm there even if it's keeping Sully away from you."

"I appreciate that." Luke rubbed his forehead, hoping to dull the headache coming on. "As you said, this isn't about me. I need to put my issues aside and focus on the mission at hand, but heaven help me if he did anything to put Riley and Liv in danger. You might as well lock me up right now."

"You and me both." Jack pulled open the door and let Luke walk in first.

Luke stood a few steps from Sully, who still stood in the center of the living room, commanding everyone's attention. His personality seemed larger than life. Luke hoped for his sake, the man's ego wasn't the same. Luke moved toward him and extended his hand. Sully gripped it in his meaty paw. He hated that Sully's hand enveloped his own. There was nothing small about Luke, but next to Sully, he felt pint-sized.

"Let's get busy finding Riley and Liv." Luke pulled a removable drive from his pocket that contained the hotel surveillance video. "You need to watch this to see if you know the man leaving with Liv."

"We have other things to discuss first," Sully said.

"No, we don't, unless it directly relates to who took Riley and Liv," Luke insisted. "We're here for one reason and that's to find them. You're either on board with that or it's time for us to go and find them without your help." Luke stood his ground. Sully may be bigger, meaner, and more skilled, but Luke didn't take his orders from him and never would.

"Time is wasting, Sully," Jack reiterated.

"Fine," Sully said, closing his fingers around the drive and walking out of the room. A few minutes later he returned carrying a laptop. He set it down on the coffee table and took a seat on the couch. He hit play and watched it. Luke knew within moments that Sully knew the guy. He could tell by the way his face constricted and his body pulled back.

"Who is he?" Luke asked. Before Sully could say anything, he added, "I know that you know him from your reaction. You may be CIA but I've been a homicide detective for a long time. I read people almost as well as your daughter."

Sully raised his eyes to Luke. "That's Noah Byrne."

"I'm aware of that already. We haven't been sitting around on our hands all day." Luke pointed at him. "What I want to know right now is his connection to you."

"He is an associate of someone who was involved in one of my operations."

"Explain more," Luke demanded.

Sully shook his head. "It's above your pay grade."

It took everything Luke had not to leap across the room and attempt to beat it out of him. He breathed until he grew calm and said slowly, "If you cannot tell us anything, then why are we wasting our time here? Your daughters are missing. I need to know right now if you've had something to do with that."

Sully looked around the room at Karen and then at Jack and finally landed back on Luke. "You think I've done something to the girls?"

Karen stood and walked to him. "Sully, no one thinks you've hurt the girls, but we are desperately trying to find them. What Luke is trying to say is that there is a chance one of your operations might have put them at risk. You're here after all and that could have led someone directly to them."

"That's not possible."

Luke moved swiftly to the laptop and jabbed at the photo of Noah with his finger. "You know this man. It's not a coincidence he's here and talking to Liv. He is the only lead we have to go on and you know him, so you need to stop playing games and start talking."

Sully exhaled and shifted his eyes around the room in much the same way Riley did when she debated what she was going to do. Luke knew the look all too well. After a beat, Sully explained, "I'm not sure where to start."

No one responded but all sat on the edges of their seats waiting for information. Sully started, "There is a rumor circulating that I killed a man by the name of Eddie Stone. He was an international criminal from Boston."

"Did you?" Luke asked, running a hand down his stubbled face. He had shaved for the wedding and his face felt as rough as the rest of him.

"No, but for a reason I can't figure out, it's been blamed on me." Sully averted his eyes. "I guess there is a chance his associates could be out for revenge. An eye for an eye so to speak."

Chapter 14

"Now we are getting someplace," Luke said not feeling the least bit relieved. "Go on with the rest of it."

"None of this information can leave this room. I can lose my security clearances and be fired for even telling you this." Everyone readily agreed so he went on. "Eddie Stone grew up in an upscale part of Boston. He came from considerable wealth and went to the best schools, but he was always causing trouble. He'd go to South Boston and hang out with dropouts and gang members. He got hooked up into the Irish mob, even though he didn't even live in the neighborhood. He ran drugs and gambling and all sorts of petty crimes. The old bosses took Eddie under their wing. They probably liked the wealth he had and figured they could exploit that. That's not what happened though."

Sully sat back and folded his hands. "When Eddie's parents found out he wasn't in school and where he was spending his time, his father sent him away to a boarding school to remove the bad influences from his life and straighten him out. The problem was Eddie was his own bad influence. He made connections at boarding school that would later fuel his criminal empire. Eddie ended up being kicked out of boarding school. At that point, he dropped out of high school completely. His father kicked him out of the house and cut him off financially. Where do you think he went?"

"Back to South Boston and his old crew," Adele said.

"Exactly," Sully said, nodding his head. "Eddie wasn't satisfied with being a small-time guy. He didn't want to rule a neighborhood. He wanted to rule the world and that's what he set out to do. Through his prep school connections, he had doors opened for him in the world of finance and business and international commerce." Sully paused for a moment. "The thing you have to know about Eddie is he was extremely intelligent, even with dropping out of high school. He could have been a straight-A student. He could have gone on to the best university. His father would have paid for it all. It wasn't the path Eddie wanted. But he used his natural charisma, good looks, and intelligence in criminal ways. Eddie never forgot his old crew back home where he got his start, that's why they are so loyal and that meant something to Eddie. His parents passed away a few years ago, both of them from cancer. His father passed first and then a year later his mother. They left Eddie and his brother a fortune, not that Eddie needed it by then. His brother is the only family left."

Luke had so many questions he wasn't sure where to start.

Jack helped him out. "Tell us how you first came in contact with Eddie."

"Illegal arms trade. Eddie didn't care who he worked with. Russians, Chinese, Saudis, Iranians, the Brits...he didn't care. He also didn't care who he double-crossed." Sully waved his hand. "I can't get too much into my mission, but suffice it to say, our paths crossed a few times."

Luke asked, "You said he was from Boston. Was he killed there?"

Sully nodded. "That's the odd part. Eddie wasn't killed overseas where he had based his operation in London. He wasn't killed during a deal in some foreign country he wasn't supposed to be in. Eddie came home for Christmas break and was murdered right in Boston. They laid in wait until he came out of a restaurant and gunned him down on the street. If there were witnesses, no one talked. Everyone in that city knows who Eddie Stone was and the power he held. They also know how much money he funneled back home and into local charities."

Sully stood from the couch and stretched his long legs. "His hometown crew isn't going to let go of the fact that Eddie was murdered right there in Boston. It was adding insult to injury."

"I assume the case was never solved?" Luke asked.

"They never even had a real viable suspect."

"I still don't understand how Eddie's crew would know about you," Jack said catching Luke's eyes. Luke felt it too, like there was a part of the story missing. "My understanding is you use an alias at work."

"That's true and the part of the puzzle that's missing for me. How he came to know about Patrick Sullivan, I don't know."

Luke hadn't known Sully had used an alias. He didn't ask because he assumed that was above his pay grade, too. "Tell us about your relationship with Eddie."

"I can't go into that," Sully said, stonewalling again. "All I can say is that by all appearances Eddie and I had a contentious relationship. Eddie never knew my real identity though. How his associates are pointing the finger at me, I can't say. But that's the word on the street."

"I assume you use an alias on most operations?" Jack asked.

"Always," Sully confirmed. "No one other than family knows me by Patrick Sullivan."

Jack pressed. "How would they have connected Riley and Liv to you?"

Sully shook his head. "I don't know. At some point, Eddie must have gotten ahold of my real name, but I don't believe he would have passed that on to anyone. I don't believe Eddie would have told anyone about his association with me."

"Why is that?" Jack asked, confusion in his voice.

Sully remained silent and Jack didn't insist further. It was obvious there were things Sully wouldn't tell them. The story didn't make much sense to Luke, but fighting Sully for information wasn't going to work.

Luke looked to Cooper, and, having worked together for so long, they could read each other's thoughts. "Tell us about Eddie Stone's brother," Luke demanded, turning back to Sully.

"Holden Stone is a tech genius in California. He is the exact opposite of his brother. He licensed some satellite tracking software a few years ago and sold it to the military. He is worth millions – possibly billions. I highly doubt he is going to risk his reputation for his criminal brother. The intel I have is they rarely spoke, but they are the only real family each other had."

Jack suggested the obvious. "A tech genius could do enough research and connect the dots on Sully's connection to Riley and Liv."

"How?" Sully asked. "As I said, Eddie never knew me as Patrick Sullivan. I never met any of his associates in Boston. Our interactions were in the United Kingdom predominantly."

. Luke turned to Jack. "What's your gut on this?"

"It's not a coincidence that Noah Byrne was seen on video talking to Liv and has a connection to Sully. That's the only lead we have right now that makes any sense, so we run it down."

Luke would take hardheaded old-school homicide detective over CIA spook any day of the week. "I agree. Sully, where can we find Eddie's crew members?"

Sully looked to Jack and then to Luke. "I need to handle this on my own. You should go back home."

Luke cursed. "That's not happening. I'm going to find Riley and Liv with or without your help."

"You don't know what you're getting into."

"Then tell us!"

Sully stood stone-faced. "I'll tell you this much. Most of Eddie's associates are in jail. Some are in Boston in the old neighborhood but I don't think they'd take the girls there. As I said, his brother is in California. They also have connections in New York City. All that aside, I need to handle this on my own."

Luke looked around Sully's living room, the anger rising in him. "I can't work like this. I need to go back to the hotel."

"What about going back to Troy?" Jack asked. Luke started to argue but he pressed on. "Listen, I can get you a secure server at the Troy Police Station. It's closer to Boston and a major airport if you need to go to California. There's nothing up here."

When Luke thought about it, it wasn't a bad idea. "What are you going to do?" he asked Sully.

Sully shifted his eyes over to Karen as if asking a question. When she didn't say anything, he said, "If I can't stop you from going on your own then I'll be going with you. Instead of the Troy Police Department, I have secure lines and a safe room in the basement at the house."

Luke remembered the time he had been at Karen's house while working to solve his sister's murder and Karen pulled out a cache of weapons from the wall safe. He had thought it odd then but didn't question it. Now, he finds out there is a safe room in the basement. Luke wasn't sure he wanted to know more.

"Fine," Luke said frustrated. "Let's get going. We don't have any more time to waste."

As they gathered their things and headed for the door, leaving Sully alone, something occurred to Luke that no one had asked. Luke turned to him. "Why are you here in Lake Placid?"

For the first time, Sully's face softened. "I wanted to see my daughter get married and meet my new son-in-law. I had heard great things about you. It appears to all be true."

Luke barely broke a smile and didn't believe half of what Sully said.

CHAPTER 14

As far as Luke was concerned, he wasn't someone to be trusted.

Chapter 15

Holden disappeared again after we spoke, and I was left waiting in the basement for hours. By late afternoon, my stomach growled again. Liv had dozed for most of the day. She got up at one point and went in search of a cup so she could drink water from the bathroom faucet. In the end, Liv hadn't found anything she could use, so she rinsed her coffee cup until it was clean and drank from that. She was probably dehydrated from all the alcohol the night before.

My head had started to throb more from stress than anything else. I had no moves left if Holden didn't accept my offer and roll out the plan that I had detailed for him. I had made suggestions, he countered, and we finally agreed on a workable idea. There was a diabolical side to my personality that proved useful for crime-fighting. Luke had told me more than once to make sure I used that side for good instead of evil. Sometimes you had to shimmy the line to get things done. Right now, it was my only play.

I closed my eyes to see if I could get some sleep, but moments later, the familiar creak of the upstairs door indicated someone was on their way down. When I opened my eyes, I was surprised to see two sets of legs approaching. Holden with Collins shuffling behind him.

"Get up, both of you," Holden barked. "We have a change of plans."

"You're not going to kill us for revenge?" I asked somewhat

sarcastically.

"You, I'm still killing," Holden said, pointing at me, "but your sister I'm letting go."

Liv jumped up. "I'm not going anywhere without Riley."

I turned my head and saw the look of fear on her face. She didn't believe that she was going to be let go. "Liv, if you have a chance to go back to Mom, you have to take it. I'll be okay. No one is going to kill me." I refocused my attention on Holden. "Why are you doing this? What's to stop Liv from going to the cops and ratting you out?"

Holden looked at Liv with a stern cold look on his face. "If your sister goes to the police, we will find her and kill her. Then we will kill you. It's that simple."

I shook my head. "I still don't understand."

"You were right that your disappearance wouldn't make the news," Holden admitted. "I miscalculated the attention your kidnapping would get. You two aren't important enough to rate a news story. Your sister will be sent back with a message she is to give to your mother who will give it to your father. He'll know what it means."

"My husband is a detective. How do you plan to keep it away from him?"

"Your father will do that for me. A criminal isn't going to get the cops involved. No, he'll come to find you alone. When that happens, I'm going to kill you and then kill him."

Liv didn't want to go. I could tell by the look on her face. "Are you okay, Liv?"

"No, Riley. I'm not going anywhere without you."

I planted my hands on the arms of the chair and pushed myself up to a standing position. "How are we doing this?" I asked, ignoring my sister's pleas. She could hate me now, but all I cared about was getting her to safety.

"Collins is going to blindfold your sister and dump her far away from here. She can make it back to your mother's and then give her the message."

"How will I know she made it unharmed?"

Holden turned to Collins and stressed, "She will make it to the drop we discussed without one hair on her head touched, understand? This only works if she makes it back to her mother. You are not to implicate yourself in any way that leaves evidence behind."

Collins didn't look happy, but he gave a nod of understanding.

Holden turned back to me. "She will be given an untraceable phone number to make a call once she's back at your mother's house to let us know the message has been delivered. She can tell them not to bother trying to trace it either because it's untraceable. Your mother's only focus should be getting a message to your father."

"My parents haven't spoken in years," Liv cried. "What if she can't reach him?"

Holden locked eyes with Liv. "Then your sister will die. If you don't let me know that the message has been delivered within twenty-four hours, I will kill your sister and then I'll come for you and your mother."

Liv screeched and big fat tears rolled down her face. I didn't like that Collins was taking my sister anywhere alone, but at least it wasn't Noah, who had knocked me unconscious. "Liv, you need to calm down. You can do this. I'm sure Mom will know how to reach Sully. You'll figure it out."

"Remember no cops," Holden stressed.

"Can I have a minute alone with Liv before you take her? I can get her to calm down," I said and Holden hesitated. "Do you think Collins is going to want to deal with a hysterical woman?"

"I don't," Collins said from behind Holden.

Holden relented, looking at me with suspicion in his eyes and not happy about my request. As they turned and headed up the stairs, I rushed to Liv and pulled her by the arm to the back of the basement. I couldn't tell if she was in shock or terrified, but she didn't look at me or say a word. Earlier, while speaking to Holden, I noticed a Sharpie sitting on a shelf. I grabbed it now hoping it worked.

I lifted the sleeve of my sister's shirt and pressed the tip to her arm. A black dot appeared and I wrote Cooper's cellphone number on her arm. "When you are dropped off, go to the nearest phone and call Cooper. Do not call the police or the media, Liv. Never call the cops or the media, do you understand? Do not let anyone else call the police or the media. Understand? My life depends on it."

Liv bobbed up and down while her eyes remained vacant and terrified.

"Cooper will know what to do," I reassured her, pulling down her sleeve. "He will be calm enough to get the information to Mom and go from there. Luke will be too emotional right now. I need saner heads to keep me safe. If Cooper knows first, he can tell Luke and keep him calm. It will give Cooper time to come up with a plan."

Liv turned her eyes toward me. "What if Sully doesn't come?"

"Don't worry about that right now." I wiped my sister's face with my hand. "You have to pull yourself together. Do not tell Cooper anything over the phone. Tell him where you are. When he picks you up, tell him everything. Got it?" I didn't wait for an answer, I dragged Liv by the arm back to the main part of the basement and was grateful Holden and Collins hadn't returned.

As the door creaked open again, I threw my arms around Liv in an embrace that she didn't quite return. This was all too much for her. I kissed her on the cheek and told her how brave she was and assured her that she'd be okay. She told me she loved me and hoped this wasn't the last time we'd see each other. I assured her it wasn't.

A moment later, Collins dragged her up the stairs away from me. Liv looked back once and the sad look on her face nearly tore me apart. I sat back down on the chair and waited for Holden to return down the steps. All that mattered right now was that he trusted me completely.

It took longer than I liked for him to return. I wondered what he was doing, and it was hard to resist going upstairs to check. I wondered if this was a test to see if I'd try to run from him, but a deal was a deal. Holden would let Liv go and I'd help him find out who killed his brother. I hoped it wasn't Sully. Otherwise, my life would still be in danger.

"Riley," Holden called my name from the top of the stairs. "Come up!"

I stood and took a breath. Pulling this off would take every ounce of acting skill I had to not only make sure I lived but to keep Sully alive as well.

I got to the top of the stairs and nudged the door open. Holden stood at the back door ready to go. The sky had already turned dark and there wasn't much light in the kitchen. Holden had a backpack slung over his shoulder and he held the door open. He waved keys that jingled around in front of his fingers. "Let's go. We don't have much time. Collins was a hard sell on letting Liv go and took a lot of convincing. He's not the brightest guy, but he was suspicious. We've only got a few hours before Collins tells some of the other guys what's going down."

"He won't tell Noah or anyone right now?"

"I hope not. I pretended to call Noah and run it by him. It's what convinced Collins to go along."

"That was smart thinking." As much as Holden had to trust me for this to work, I had to trust him, too. I followed him out of the back door into the night.

Chapter 16

Cooper bounded up the stairs to the spare bedroom he always used when he was at Karen's house. They had made it back to Troy in record time and then Karen had made dinner for them all as they sat around the kitchen table discussing the next steps.

Cooper had no idea how Karen was holding it together let alone cooking. Adele had offered to help as had all of them. Jack had his phone in hand ready to order something but Karen insisted. She said it made her feel useful.

The tension was high with the addition of Sully in the house. He didn't seem to know what to do with himself even though this had been his home for a time. Cooper had asked him the last time he had been inside, and he couldn't recall.

Jack and Luke did nothing to make Sully feel welcome. Luke had snapped at every suggestion Sully made and Jack had sided with Luke. Cooper didn't think that would serve anyone, but nobody had asked his opinion. He kept quiet for the most part and tried to stay out of it. That's why, when he got the chance to retreat to the bedroom under the guise of getting laundry together, he took it.

He couldn't handle the sniping at one another any longer. It was stressful enough worrying about Riley and Liv. Cooper stood at the side of the bed unpacking his suitcase, separating clean clothes from dirty. Adele had a pile of clothes on the other side of the room ready to go. As he launched an undershirt across the room into the pile of dirty clothes, his cellphone rang.

Cooper pulled it from his pocket but didn't recognize the number or the area code. "Hello," he said expecting a client to ask about investigation rates. What he heard on the other end made him nearly drop his phone.

Liv's voice was rushed and quiet. "Cooper, it's me, Liv. Don't tell anyone I'm calling, just listen."

"Are you okay?"

"I need you to come to get me. Don't tell anyone yet. I need to tell you a few things before we tell everyone else." Liv spoke to someone else and then came back on the line. "I need your help, Cooper. Riley needs your help. Her life depends on it."

Cooper gripped the phone so tight his knuckles turned white. "Where are you?"

"I'm in Bennington, Vermont. Are you still in Lake Placid?"

"No. I'm at your mom's house."

"Good," she said relieved. "Bennington is about thirty miles from Troy, but it will take you about an hour. It's all backroads and not well lit at night." Liv paused and then stressed, "Cooper, make sure you come alone."

Liv gave him the address where he could find her and a phone number if he had trouble. She said she was in the home of a couple who had let her use their phone. Liv assured Cooper she was fine but that he needed to hurry.

Cooper ended the call and grabbed his wallet by the bedside table. He slowed his pace as he walked down the stairs, trying to calm himself as he went. Cooper had one major problem to address before he could go anywhere. He didn't have a car. He had driven up to New York with Luke in his SUV. He had no idea how he'd pick up Liv without the wheels to do it or without telling anyone. It's not like he could

Uber there.

Cooper walked through the hall and into the kitchen in the back of the house. "Adele, can I talk to you for a second?" he smiled sheepishly and shrugged. "I have a laundry question."

Adele finished drying the dish in her hand and set the dishtowel down on the counter. She followed Cooper back into the hall near the stairs. "What's going on? You do our laundry all the time."

Cooper dropped his voice to a whisper. "I need you to not freak out or say anything at all. Promise?" Adele nodded and he continued. "Liv just called me and she needs me to pick her up in Bennington, Vermont. She didn't tell me anything just that I need to hurry because Riley's life depended on it. I don't have a car."

Adele pinched the bridge of her nose. "It sounds like a trap, Cooper. How did she get there?"

"She didn't say," Cooper said, realizing he hadn't considered that someone could be holding Liv and luring him there alone. He wasn't even armed. All in all, he seemed the worst person for the job. He needed help.

He snapped his fingers as the idea sparked. "I need you to stay here and distract Karen, Luke and Sully. Right now, I need you to tell Jack to meet me outside as discretely as possible with the keys to his car. I don't know what's happening, but there is no reason to get anyone excited or have Luke or Sully go off half-cocked. Make some excuse if anyone is looking for me."

Adele kissed him goodbye and walked back into the kitchen as Cooper quietly slipped out the front door. He walked to Jack's car and waited in the dark. It was cold enough that Cooper could see his breath. He shoved his hands in his pockets and waited, hoping it was Jack who met him and not Luke or Sully.

Just when Cooper had nearly run out of patience and was about to walk back into the house, Jack appeared at the front door, craning his neck around looking for Cooper. He waved and Jack slowly jogged over to him.

Jack handed Cooper his keys. "Adele said you needed my car and to be stealthy about it. What's going on?"

Cooper glanced around to make sure no one had followed Jack out. He explained about the call from Liv and that he was going to pick her up. "I don't know if it's a trap or if she escaped or what's going on, but she didn't want me to tell anyone. She said she'd explain when I picked her up, but I don't have a car."

"You've got mine. Take it and take this, too." Jack pulled the Glock from his hip holster and handed it to Cooper. "Don't worry about being licensed in New York and Vermont. We'll worry about that later. All I care about is you getting Liv back to us safely." Jack walked off but then turned around. "Be careful of the deer. Lots of them out there on those roads this time of year."

Cooper thanked Jack and then unlocked the man's car and slipped into the driver's seat. He placed the gun in the console between the seats and plugged directions into his phone. Liv had been right about the distance. She was only about thirty miles away, but it was all backroads. Cooper took off up Pawling Avenue, trying to maintain his speed.

The farther he went, the more surprised Cooper grew at how much rural land covered upstate New York. He had no idea and imagined the drive would have been beautiful in daylight. In the dark, all he could focus on was the road and making sure not to smack right into a deer as Jack had warned. He saw several that caused his back to tense and his eyes to remain laser-focused.

Cooper passed a sign for Vermont and then later saw a sign for Bennington. He continued to follow the directions until he took a right and the address Liv had given him came into view. Liv told him she was at an old white farmhouse with several acres of land attached.

Cooper pulled the car over and assessed the area. He put the address in the search engine and pulled back information on a couple who owned it. Nothing nefarious jumped out at him.

A moment later, a porch light turned on and two women appeared under the glow. One of them looked like Liv. Cooper grabbed Jack's gun and slipped it in the waistband of his pants for lack of a better place to put it. The metal felt cool against his skin and he wondered how people walked around like this. He walked a few feet and thought better of it and took the gun out and carried it at his side in his right hand. He made his way slowly up the driveway and called Liv's name.

Both of the women turned in his direction and Liv set off in a sprint towards him. Cooper braced himself as she barreled into him, looping her arms around his neck and burying her face into his chest. He awkwardly looped his arms around her back and comforted her, assuring her that she was okay. He shifted his eyes left and right, on high alert, making sure he hadn't walked into an ambush.

"Are you alone?" he asked as Liv pulled back.

"Yes, the kidnapper dropped me off and I walked here. This was the first house I saw with lights on. They were nice enough to let me use their phone. I didn't tell them what was happening. I said I had a fight with my boyfriend and he took off without me. I told them I needed to call a friend." Liv turned and waved to the woman standing on the porch. She waved back and then went inside.

Liv appeared okay to him other than smudged makeup and hair all askew. "Did they hurt you?"

"No," Liv said, shaking her head. "We need to get back home."

Together they walked to the car and got inside. Cooper explained about having to tell Jack to borrow his car. Liv seemed okay with that. She rested her head back and closed her eyes. Cooper waited for a breakdown that never came.

As he navigated the country roads back to New York, Liv finally opened her eyes and explained how she had been taken and then how they lured Riley. She told Cooper about the van and gave him a detailed description of both men.

"I believe we were being held in Boston near the water. I'm not sure if it's a lake or the ocean. We weren't close enough to see. Riley said to remember the cross-streets East 3rd Street and P. Street. She saw the street signs as they brought us into the house."

Cooper asked several questions and decided the kidnappers weren't professionals given they held Riley and Liv in a basement with television access and someone had brought them coffee and breakfast. Liv spoke until she got to the part about Riley and then she choked up.

"Cooper, she has no idea I know what she did. She thought I was asleep but I wasn't. I watched as Riley took Holden into the back of the basement and then I crept behind a bookshelf and listened. She promised to help him find who killed his brother in exchange for letting me go. She laid out the entire plan for him."

Cooper wasn't surprised. Riley would do anything to keep Liv safe, but she was out there alone now with someone she couldn't trust, unarmed, and with no help.

"This guy thinks Sully killed his brother. My father is a criminal. What happens to Riley when they find out it was Sully who killed him?"

Cooper expelled a breath. He had forgotten that Liv had no idea about Sully's real occupation and the question still lingered if Sully did kill the guy. No matter how much Sully had protested that he wasn't responsible, the fact that he was a trained liar didn't escape Cooper's attention. No matter what happened, he'd have his eye on Sully going forward.

Chapter 17

Luke tossed and turned in the bed in Riley's room. He kicked the covers off only to pull them back around him a few minutes later. He couldn't find a comfortable spot and he went from hot to cold, never settling on the right temperature. Worst of all his mind raced thinking of the things that could be happening to Riley while he slept. He knew he needed rest, but it didn't seem fair when Riley was in danger.

Everywhere Luke looked reminded him of Riley. This had been her bedroom since childhood. Even after she left for college and found her own place to live, Karen had left the room for her. It had been painted and updated, but most things remained the same. It gave Luke some comfort to be surrounded by so many things that reminded him of her, but it also tore out his heart to know she was out there and he couldn't protect her.

Riley had taken months to plan the perfect wedding, and they had a blissful perfect day. He had gone to bed so happy and peaceful that he thought the feeling would have at least lasted longer than a night. He couldn't lose her. No, he *wouldn't* lose her.

Luke tried to quiet his mind and willed himself to sleep, and he was almost there when someone, he assumed Karen, shrieked outside of Luke's door. He threw off his covers and raced barefoot to make sure she was okay. He yanked open the bedroom door but there was no one in the hall. The noise came from the floor below.

Luke ran down the stairs and made it about halfway when he heard Liv's voice. His chest expanded thinking Riley was safe. He ran down the rest of the steps and then pulled up short when he didn't see her among them in the living room.

Liv stood with Jack and Sully on either side and Karen had her arms wrapped around her. Cooper and Adele stood off to the side watching the scene. Riley wasn't anywhere in sight. Luke didn't understand what was unfolding in front of him.

"Is Riley with you?" he asked, stepping forward. The reality that she wasn't came over him slowly, like sinking under the water with nothing to pull him up.

Liv let go of Karen. She rushed toward Luke and wrapped her arms around him. "I'm sorry. Riley is still with him, but she's going to be okay. I know she is."

Luke shook her off and stepped out of her embrace. "What's going on? How did you escape?" He had so many questions he wasn't sure where to start. Not that Luke wasn't happy Liv had made it home, but he realized the moment he saw Liv's face that he blamed her for Riley's disappearance. It wasn't charitable of him. It wasn't even rational, but deep-down Luke believed that if Riley hadn't been trying to protect her sister none of this would have happened.

Liv's face fell as she stepped away from him. She looked like she wasn't sure what to say. "I'm sorry, Luke. I really am. I know where to find her though."

"How did you get here?" he asked, still not understanding how all of this played out. His anger grew because he felt like they were keeping things from him. "How long have you been back?"

Karen stepped toward him and placed her hand on his arm. "Cooper and Liv got back only a few minutes ago. Jack was about to wake you."

Luke turned his head to Cooper. This was the second time today he felt like Cooper had betrayed him – the first with Sully and now this. "What do you mean you got back with Liv? What is happening here?" he yelled, not caring that his voice was raised.

Cooper stammered, surprised by Luke's anger. "Luke, calm down. Sit and I'll tell you what happened."

"You left Riley there?" Luke accused, shaking his head. The floor below him seemed to rock and pitch him forward while the room closed in around him. He swayed and the room spun. Before he knew what was happening Jack and Cooper had both of his arms and led him to the couch. Luke found it hard to catch his breath and his chest constricted in pain. He moved his hand over his heart, which felt like it was breaking into a million pieces.

"Just breathe," Jack said, guiding Luke back to the couch. "Karen, give Luke and me a few minutes and take everyone in the kitchen. I'm sure you and Sully have a lot to tell Liv."

Cooper and Adele excused themselves to go upstairs while Karen, Sully, and Liv went into the kitchen. Luke laid his head back on the couch and focused on his breathing. In time, the dizziness subsided and his breathing returned to normal. He turned his head to Jack who sat there with him unmoving and not pressuring him to speak. "What happened?"

"A little overwhelmed or maybe some anxiety. Has that ever happened before?"

Even though he was embarrassed by what had happened to him, Luke appreciated Jack's calm and steady demeanor. "Never. I thought I was having a heart attack."

"That's what a panic attack can feel like. This has been a lot for anyone, Luke, and you're trying to be detective and husband. It's too much for anyone."

Luke sat forward and looked at Jack. "What happened with Cooper and Liv?"

Jack explained about the call Liv had made to Cooper and that he didn't want to upset everyone until he knew what he was dealing with. "He meant no harm, Luke. Don't look at it as a betrayal. Cooper was trying to help. If anything, he was willing to take on a lot of risk to protect the rest of us. He had no idea what he was walking into."

Luke couldn't hear a defense of anyone right now. He wanted facts and only facts. "Did Liv say anything about Riley or where she is?"

Jack nodded his head. "You came down about three minutes after they got here. I don't have much information yet. Let's give Karen and Sully a chance to explain things to Liv and then we can speak with her."

Luke wanted to race to the kitchen and interrogate Liv like a suspect, but he wasn't even sure he could stand up without falling. He waited there on the couch until Jack got up and went to the kitchen a few minutes later to see if Liv could talk.

Jack came back into the living room a few minutes later with a glass of water for Luke. Liv followed behind him, her face looking more shell-shocked than she had when Luke first saw her.

"It's a shock, right?" Luke said.

"I'm not sure whether to be angry that they lied to me all these years or comforted that I didn't have to carry that around with me." Liv sat down on a chair at the end of the couch.

"I know the feeling." Luke asked Liv a few questions about how she was taken and what she knew about Riley's disappearance.

"It was planned. That's all I can say. I feel horrible like it's all my fault, but Riley assured me that no matter how it played out, they were going to take us."

"Why let you go then?"

Liv leaned back and crossed her legs. "Because you wouldn't go to the media. Riley said that given how we were taken the local police wouldn't get involved. She knew you'd do everything you could to delay going to the media. Riley convinced them if the goal was to lure Sully, he would have no way of knowing they had us if the story didn't hit the national or international press."

Luke went to say something but Liv stopped him. "They weren't professional kidnappers. Riley kept saying they had no idea what they were doing. Holden, the main guy, at first tried to come off mean and hard. He flashed a gun at us and threatened us, but I asked for breakfast and he went and got it for us. He said he wanted to kill us in front of Sully for revenge. Riley figured out quickly that he wouldn't kill anyone. That's not to say another of them wouldn't do it, but I don't think Holden would and that's who Riley is with now."

"What do you mean she's with him? Where is everyone else?" Luke pressed, not understanding.

"There were four of them. Noah and his friend kidnapped Riley and me and then Holden and Collins held us in Boston. Holden said Sully killed his brother."

Luke leaned forward. "Do you know where Riley is now?"

Liv explained how she had hidden and listened as Riley had negotiated her freedom in exchange for helping Holden figure out who killed his brother. "Riley came up with the whole story about needing to let me go so Sully knew we were taken. She told him the plan and he went with it. That's why I think she's going to be okay. I think Riley knows what she's doing. Holden told her they only had a short time or the rest of the guys would figure out what was going on and kill them both."

Jack clasped his hands in front of him. "Liv, this is important. Is there anything you can tell me about where they kept you? Anything at all will help."

It wasn't Liv who answered but rather Cooper from the bottom of the stairs. Luke hadn't heard him come back down. "On the car ride here, Liv mentioned Riley had seen two cross-streets - East 3rd Street and P. Street. While you were all talking, I did a search and it's in South Boston near Boston Harbor. Liv, you said you saw water. That must be the place."

"Thank you," Luke said, not even glancing over at him. "Liv, would you recognize the house if you saw it again?"

"Definitely, but I'm not going back there," Liv said.

Jack understood and explained there were other ways she could help them. He asked her to describe the house so she did in detail.

Liv described the outside of the home and the interior including every detail she could remember. "I don't think they will still be there. Holden told Collins to get rid of the van and lay low and not to come back to the house. I assume he told him that to give him and Riley a head start."

Luke assumed as much, but that's where they would start their search. "Can you remember anything else about them?"

Liv sat back and closed her eyes as if recalling a memory. "Collins was portly and sloppy. He shuffled when he walked and kept pulling his pants up. Holden looked like a rich guy you'd see at a pub dressed well and composed. He was well-spoken and had expensive shoes on."

Luke furrowed his brow. "How do you know they were expensive?"

"I'm into fashion, I know these things." Liv rattled off the designer labels of Holden's clothes. It meant nothing to Luke. He hadn't even heard of half of them.

"The point is he has the money to pull off whatever they think they are doing," Liv stressed.

Cooper walked over to Liv and handed her his phone. "Look at that photo. Does that look like anyone?"

Liv only glanced down at it for a moment before her head snapped back up. "That's Holden."

"Are you sure?" Luke asked.

"There's no doubt in my mind. Same guy. Different haircut and he has the start of a beard now, but it's the same guy."

Jack groaned. "I'm not sure whether to be more worried or less. Riley is with her kidnapper who is a tech guy with no investigative experience hunting down the killer of an international crime boss."

"Even if she's safe from Holden, Riley is in way over her head," Cooper said.

Luke agreed. "We need to get to Boston."

Jack turned to him. "We all need to get some rest, but we'll leave first thing in the morning. Should we call the Boston police?"

"No, don't do that. Riley said no cops," Liv said. "I think we have to trust her right now."

Chapter 18

After we left the house that Liv and I were held in, Holden drove us to get something to eat, and then we went right to Boston's Back Bay neighborhood. He parked in a nearby garage and we walked a few blocks along cobblestone streets to a narrow three-story brick house that had black shutters and handrails that lined the two steps to the door.

It was only after he pulled out a key and unlocked the door, Holden finally explained this was a house he had bought when his parents passed away. Holden said he didn't use the place often but had recently stocked it with food and other provisions in case he needed to crash there. He assured me that the house wasn't in his name and no one even knew he had it so we should be safe.

He directed me to the back of the house and we sat at a square kitchen table near a window. When I asked him questions about his life, he shut me down fast. Not that I could blame him, but he already knew so much about me I figured fair was fair. Plus, he was more relaxed when I kept him talking.

I wanted to call home to assure Luke and my mom that I was okay, but I hadn't seen a home phone, didn't have my cellphone, and figured Holden would say no. I did the only thing I could and sat there with Holden until Liv texted the phone number he had given her and let him know that she had delivered the message to Sully. At least, I knew she was safe.

Close to midnight, he directed me to a bedroom on the second floor, handed me a pair of pajamas, which I assumed were his, and told me to sleep well. He left me standing in the middle of the room and shut the door and locked it behind him from the outside. Not that I planned to escape, but I didn't like being locked in.

The bedroom at least had an attached bathroom. I flipped on the light and rummaged around in the bathroom cabinet until I found supplies to take a shower and brush my teeth. I had been up for close to twenty-four hours and didn't think I would last much longer.

I pulled back the blue and gray checkered comforter and climbed into bed. The sheets felt good against my skin and the room was warm and cozy. I felt safe enough given the circumstances.

Before I allowed myself to drift off to sleep, I considered whether I'd try to escape from Holden. He had held up his end of the deal and released Liv but he was still holding me hostage. If I did escape, there's no reason he wouldn't come for us again. If not him, then his brother's associates would kill us for sure. I wrestled with the decision until sleep pulled me under.

I slept so soundly that I didn't hear Holden unlock the door and enter the bedroom in the morning. He stood in the doorway calling my name. "I let you sleep as long as I could, but we need to get moving if we are going to solve my brother's murder," he said, his tone soft but insistent.

I opened my eyes, stretched my arms, and pushed myself up against the headboard. The fact that Holden hadn't killed me in the wee hours of the night and seemed ready to find the killer gave me hope that maybe he was starting to trust me. "Do you have any clothes I can borrow?"

Holden pointed to the six-drawer dresser on the wall opposite the bed. "You should be able to find a few things in the dresser and closet.

That's why I put you in this room. It had everything including the attached bathroom."

"I appreciate that," I said and meant it. "Let me get ready and I'll meet you downstairs. We can make a plan for the day." Holden agreed and turned to leave, but I called him back. "There are things you might not want to tell me about your brother that I'm going to need to know. If we have any chance of catching his killer, I need to know everything. It's the only way it can work."

Holden seemed on the verge of saying something but didn't. He turned and left without saying another word. I worried that he would lie to me and then the whole investigation would be pointless. I couldn't find who killed his brother if he held back information. Unless that was his goal – he wanted the killer to be Sully and he was toying with me until he killed me. I had to keep that in the forefront of my mind. I shouldn't trust him too much.

In the dresser, I found women's clothing including underwear, pants, and shirts that still had tags on them. They'd fit well enough. In the closet, there was a men's cardigan sweater that would keep me warm.

When I got to the bottom of the stairs, Holden sat in a chair in the living room waiting for me. "There's breakfast out there if you're hungry and I just made coffee."

I thanked him and made my way into the kitchen and poured myself a cup of coffee and grabbed a banana from a basket on the counter.

Leaning against the center island, Holden asked, "What do you need to know about my brother?"

I wasn't sure where I wanted to start but figured getting his list of suspects would be a good bet. I took a sip from my cup and turned to him. "If Sully didn't kill your brother, who else would you suspect?"

Holden mulled it over. "I don't know," he said sounding unsure. "I've always been told it was Patrick Sullivan, Sully as you call him, and I never questioned it. My brother wasn't a good guy. He had many

100

international criminal connections. For as many people loved him here in Boston, he made enemies, too."

Holden and I sat down at the table where we had sat the night before. "Start with local connections and then we can work our way out." I stopped and debated in my head for a moment if that was the best approach while he watched me.

I urged him on. "Yes, let's do it that way. I'm sure an international killer could have followed him to Boston, but there are easier and more lenient countries to get away with murder. Why risk exposure if you're an international criminal, unless they were specifically sending a message that they could get him on his home turf."

He thought for a moment. "The Irish mob runs pretty deep in South Boston. The FBI took down a few people like Whitey Bulger, but it's still active. Eddie was charismatic enough that he garnered respect with some but others couldn't take him. Whether it was jealousy or what I don't know. The two main Irish mob families in South Boston are run by Danny Devaney and Frank Coonan. They ran gangs out of South Boston and Eddie brought them some competition in gambling and drug sales."

"How did he end up in London?"

"Eddie wasn't satisfied being small time. He got into insider trading, money laundering, and big black market deals including art theft, arms dealing, and international drug rings. There's a chance Danny or Frank had enough of Eddie."

"Why wait until Eddie is long gone to London?" I asked, not sure this theory made sense.

"I don't know. Eddie still had associates here. Maybe they just didn't like that he was making more money than them. Who knows? I don't think those kinds of people think logically."

"Any street cred gained by taking out Eddie?"

"If there was, no one heard about it. No one ever took credit, and with something like that, I'd assume they want credit."

"Fair enough." I unpeeled and ate the banana, thinking about what information we'd need. "What about police reports? Autopsy reports? Do you have anything like that?"

"No. I wasn't living in Boston and hadn't spoken to my brother in a few years." Holden looked away and exhaled. "I'm ashamed to say it but I assumed it was only a matter of time until someone killed him. That's how that life goes. When I got the news of Eddie's death, I didn't care about who did it."

That didn't make any sense to me. He had told me before he had been plotting my kidnapping for a year and wanted revenge. I told him as much. "If you're not passionate about all this why put your life on the line and risk prison for a long time if it didn't matter to you?"

"Eddie mattered to me. It wasn't that. It was a sad ending for what I considered a sad life." He shrugged. "It's like when you know someone is sick for a long time, you know the inevitable is death, but you can still hate the way they went out. When Eddie's guys came to me and told me they knew who killed him, they convinced me, as Eddie's only surviving family, I had an obligation to get retribution." Holden sat back and took a long sip of coffee, locking eyes with me over the rim. "I'm fulfilling that obligation now."

Chapter 19

While I knew guilt could do strange things to a person, I thought Holden's method of seeking justice for his brother was misplaced. I fought the urge to feel bad for him because I wondered if I was at risk of Stockholm Syndrome – emotionally bonding with my captor. I was afraid that it might already be too late. I couldn't summon up fear of Holden.

"Is a banana enough for breakfast or would you like something else?" Holden asked as he stood and carried his coffee cup to the sink.

"I'm fine, thanks," I said like I wasn't his hostage. He kept doing things to garner more of my trust and that frustrated me to no end. I stood from the table. "We need to make a plan and the first thing we need is access to information about the murder."

"How do we get that?" Holden asked, leaning against the counter.

"We have to go to the police."

"If I take you to the police, you're going to tell them I kidnapped you, and then where will that leave us?" He eyed me seeming to call my bluff.

"I can't investigate in a vacuum. I have to have access to information. Who was the detective you dealt with after Eddie was murdered? He's the best place to start. Call him and tell him it's bothering you that there's been no justice for your brother and you want to look into a few things. You need the police reports and autopsy records."

"You think that will work?"

I walked over to him. "We don't have a choice, Holden. It's what we need." I locked eyes with him. "Would it help if I promised not to escape or tell them you kidnapped me?"

Holden lowered his eyes to the floor and said softly, "I wish I hadn't kidnapped you. I didn't think things through. Eddie's guys had been so adamant that they needed my help to seek retribution that I wasn't thinking straight. They suggested that if I didn't help that maybe I had something to do with my brother's murder since Eddie and I weren't speaking at the time."

The hardest part for me was figuring out if Holden was telling me the truth when he said things like that. I had to keep a hardnosed approach. "What's done is done and we can worry about that later. Who was the detective on the case?"

Holden straightened his posture. "Det. Stephen Nixon. He tried to call me a few times after the murder, but after I took care of the funeral arrangements, I went back home and tried to forget about it."

"Do you have other family?" I asked, hoping he'd at least answer that.

"None that I'm in contact with. My parents had distant relatives we saw on holidays and from time to time but no one close." Holden turned and started to wash the dishes in the sink. He angled his head to look at me. "No wife or kids if that's what you're wondering. I had a girlfriend but we broke up. That's whose clothes are upstairs. My life is mainly focused on work."

"You need to call Det. Nixon and tell him what I said. We can go by and pick up any documents they may have." Holden's face registered a moment of worry so I reassured him again. "I promise not to escape or alert the cops in any way. I never break a promise."

When he still didn't look convinced, I leaned against the counter and looked up at him with the most sheepish compliant face I could muster. "Last night I thought about escaping, but then I thought it through. If I do, nothing is stopping you or Eddie's guys from coming to get me or Liv again. If they are convinced Sully killed Eddie, they are going to come for us. I might survive it but Liv won't. I will not put my family in danger."

I extended my hand to him. "For better or worse, we are in this together. If all goes well, you won't hurt me and I won't have to kill you when this is all over."

For some reason that got Holden to laugh and when he did, his whole face lit up. His grumpy scary scowl was gone and he looked like an average guy who I might otherwise have been friends with. He dried his wet hand on his pants and extended it to me. "You have a deal," he said, still smiling. "Have you ever actually killed anyone?"

I nodded. "Once and funny enough, he had taken me hostage, too. Let's just say I'm one and one in the game."

A look of shock spread over Holden's face. "I guess I got more than I bargained for with you."

"That's a common refrain from people who don't know me too well."

"Since you've killed someone and I haven't, I'm going to watch my step with you."

"You should. Now, let's get down to business." I walked to the counter where he had left his phone and grabbed it. Holden jerked forward like he was afraid I might call someone, but all I did was hand him the phone. "You need to call that detective. Once that goes off without a hitch, I want to call home and let them know I'm okay. I can use the phone you had Liv call, but unless you want that traced, you're going to need to ditch it after I do that."

While I wanted Luke and Cooper's help, the last thing I wanted was the cops showing up. I couldn't see any way that would help. They hadn't had any luck finding Eddie's killer.

Holden stood back appraising me. "Why do I have a feeling you'd be better at kidnapping someone than me?"

"Because I would." I left him standing there with his mouth slightly open holding the phone in his hand. I walked down the hall toward the stairs feeling confidence I hadn't felt before. Before I climbed the stairs, I yelled, "Holden, you really should rethink your life of crime – you're truly terrible at it. I knew from the moment I stepped out of the van, I was in South Boston and you had no idea what you were doing."

Holden choked back a laugh, but he did as I asked because a moment later, I heard him ask for Det. Nixon. Now, we'd at least have a starting point.

An hour later, we sat in the back corner of a coffee shop not far from Holden's house waiting for Det. Nixon to arrive. He had been both curious and pleased to hear from Holden about Eddie's murder.

I had meant what I told Holden earlier. I wouldn't attempt an escape. I was in full investigator mode ready to get down to business. We sat chatting in the back of the shop until the detective arrived. He stood about five-foot-ten, taller than me but not quite to Holden's height. He had a wave of blond hair and an easy smile. Holden waved when he saw him and Det. Nixon strode toward us with files under his arm.

Det. Nixon reached out and shook Holden's hand. "I'm surprised to hear from you. I didn't know you had come back to the city."

"I'm here for a few weeks and hoping to make some progress on Eddie's murder." Holden nudged out the chair next to him for the detective to sit and introduced me as a friend who also happened to be a private investigator. We had made a plan for what he'd say before we arrived.

Det. Nixon sat down and kept the files close to him. He looked across the table at me. "If you've worked a few homicide cases, especially open and active ones, then you know we don't like sharing information with anyone. This case, though, we haven't had anything to go on. Every lead we had dried up days after the homicide. The people Eddie was involved with don't like to talk and no witnesses came forward."

He hitched his jaw toward me. "What makes you want to take this on?"

"I'm helping a friend that's all. I had some time in between cases and thought I'd take a crack at it. Sometimes fresh eyes can bring new leads," I lied and hoped it was convincing enough.

"That's true," Det. Nixon said. "Let me grab some coffee and we can get down to it." He shrugged off his jacket and hung it on the back of his chair. He went up to the counter and ordered a coffee in a to-go cup.

Det. Nixon pulled out his chair and sat down. He sipped his coffee and flipped open the first file. "I can't share any crime scene photos with you."

Holden confirmed he was fine not seeing them. Det. Nixon continued reading from a file, his voice flat and monotone. "I have no leads. We've shaken every branch we could find. We speculated that it might have been someone from an international criminal network given Eddie's connections, but a search turned up nothing. There were no reports of anyone on any watch list coming through the Boston airport around that time."

I interrupted, "You can't rule out someone coming in from another airport and driving here or someone not on any list."

"That's right," Det. Nixon agreed, "but there are too many variables at play. I absolutely can't rule out that someone came into the country and killed him. Big risk though when they could more easily do it someplace else."

"That's exactly what Riley said earlier," Holden said, seeming pleased we were in consensus.

"You've got a good investigator then," Det. Nixon said, glancing up

107

at me. "We questioned all the rival gangs and explored a few other options and there's nothing. Eddie was killed with two shots to his chest and one went astray and hit the door of the restaurant behind him. No one else was hurt. The murder was targeted like one of those old-style mafia hits."

"What kind of weapon was used?"

Det. Nixon rattled off the type of gun he believed based on the shell casings and witness testimony. The person shot from the passenger side of a large black SUV with tinted windows. No one saw the shooter or the driver in the dark or at least that was the story. There were no video cameras in the area that picked up anything either. Det. Nixon explained a few witnesses said the SUV had Massachusetts license plates but no one could confirm the numbers.

He tapped at the file. "As I said, not much to go on. We searched for the black SUV and checked rentals but nothing. No drugs came back in the toxicology report. Eddie had a few drinks with dinner but not anything that would have indicated he was under the influence."

"Who was he with that night?" I asked.

Det. Nixon looked through the file. "Melissa Patton. They had dinner and were on the way out of the restaurant when the shooting happened. She wasn't hurt."

"That's Eddie's old girlfriend," Holden explained to me. "Eddie wrote in his will that she should be taken care of so I've been helping her out financially. I never asked her any questions about that night though. As you know, Det. Nixon, I wouldn't even return your calls after your initial interview. I wanted nothing to do with this. I didn't know much about Eddie's life. I figured the less I knew the better."

"You're not your brother, Holden. You weren't a part of his life for good reason. You shouldn't take on any guilt. Eddie made his choices and you made yours. You came from a good family and Eddie went his own way." Det. Nixon shook his head. "If I were in your shoes, I might have washed my hands of this forever. I'm glad you're taking an interest now. While Eddie's murder still has an active status because it hasn't been solved, there are no resources spent on it. It's a cold case for us."

Chapter 20

They took two cars to Boston, which was a relief to Luke. He drove with Jack and gave Cooper and Sully his SUV. They planned to meet at the Boston hotel they had reserved. Karen, Liv, and Adele stayed at the house. Adele had to go back to Little Rock by the end of the week and had already scheduled a flight in case they weren't back in time. She figured Karen and Liv could use the support and Luke had been grateful for her reasoning.

Driving with Jack, Luke didn't have to deal with Sully. While he wasn't angry with Cooper – the bond between them had always been strong and had weathered difficult situations before – Luke hoped he could stay objective and not be enamored with Sully.

The drive would take about two and a half hours from start to finish on I-90 East. Luke remembered Riley telling him how much time she spent in Boston as a child from school trips to the New England Aquarium and Faneuil Hall Marketplace to Red Sox games. She had told Luke she went to Boston more than she went to New York City. The two cities were about the same distance from Troy. They had talked about going there together at some point. At least, Riley knew the area.

Luke searched the phone number for Holden Stone's business in California. The plan was to call and gather information. It would at least be a starting point. Luke and Jack debated if they should use a ruse, but they decided that it was probably better to play it straight. Luke punched the numbers into his cellphone as Jack drove. It rang a few times and a woman answered.

"I'm Det. Luke Morgan looking for information on Holden Stone," Luke said after she finished rattling off the name of the business and her name.

"I'm sorry, Holden Stone no longer works with the company."

"When did he leave the company?" Luke asked.

"About two months ago. Mr. Stone sold his share of the business to his partners. I can connect you with them if you'd like."

Luke didn't know if that would prove helpful. "Do you know how I can reach Mr. Stone?"

"I don't," she said and hesitated.

Luke took the opportunity to push harder. "I have an urgent matter to discuss with Mr. Stone. I must reach him. If you don't know, please connect me with one of the partners who might know more. Time is of the essence."

The woman sucked in an audible breath. "None of the partners can help you. All we know is that Mr. Stone went back to the east coast. He left in a hurry. He sold his share of the company, cashed in his stocks, cleared out his house, and left. We don't know any more than that. I don't even have a forwarding address for him and his cellphone that we had on file has been turned off. One of the partners tried to reach him a couple of weeks ago and had no luck."

"Any family or friends that you're aware of?"

"Mr. Stone's parents and brother are deceased. There is no other family that I'm aware of and none of his friends here have any idea where he is. We checked with his neighbors and they don't know anything. They said he sold the house fully furnished, took a few belongings, and left. If you find him, please tell him to get ahold of us."

"I appreciate the information," Luke said before hanging up. He turned to Jack. "He's been off the grid for about two months. Sounds like this is some sort of endgame for him, and he's not returning to his old life." Luke explained about selling his company and the stocks.

"He's flush with cash and has nothing to lose," Jack said solemnly.

"I bet he assumes he's going to get caught or killed in the process and got his affairs in order."

"Either way, it doesn't bode well for us or Riley." They had about thirty minutes left before they arrived. Jack changed lanes back to the slow lane and glanced over at Luke. "Do you think Riley knows what she's doing?"

"I have no idea. I know she'd say anything to save Liv and keep herself alive. For all I know, she's just buying herself time." Luke stared straight ahead. "Do you trust Sully? What if Riley finds out he did kill this guy's brother? Sully says he didn't, but I don't trust him."

"I think we have to put personal feelings aside," Jack cautioned. "I don't like the guy, but I keep reminding myself that he's one of us. He works for the government and we all have rules to follow."

"He's CIA, Jack. He doesn't play by the same rules we do."

"That may be true, but they can't kill Americans on American soil last I checked. Besides, if he was going to kill this guy, there are quieter ways to go about it."

Luke let that sink in. After contemplating for several moments, he still wasn't sure. "All I know is we only have the house they were held in to go on. We have no other leads."

"It won't be easy. Nothing ever is." Jack continued to drive the rest of the way, navigating with ease.

Luke assumed Jack had been to Boston enough times to know exactly where he was going because he drove without directions or needing to consult a map. They pulled into the parking garage of the hotel right after Cooper, who stood at the back of Luke's SUV. Sully was nowhere to be seen.

Luke opened the passenger side door and placed his feet on the pavement. "We need to talk," he said to Cooper who looked at him with eyebrows raised.

Cooper set his bag on the ground and motioned with his head to the other side of the garage. "Yes. We need to talk." The two of them walked off a distance from Jack and squared off facing each other. Cooper stood with his hands in his pockets and locked eyes with Luke. "I know you're angry with me because I failed some loyalty test, but all I'm focused on is finding Riley."

Luke hadn't been expecting Cooper to say what he did. It disarmed him and let out all the argument he had stored up for this moment. "You should have told me Liv called. Going alone wasn't smart."

"I did what I had to do. Liv asked that I come alone and so I went. I had no idea what I was walking into and you can be a hothead. I went for both of us." Cooper reached his hand out and put it on Luke's shoulder. "No matter what you think, I'm on your side. Yeah, Sully's CIA career is probably interesting and for a moment I was impressed. Not anymore."

"Why?" Luke asked eyeing him.

"It doesn't escape me that he lied to Riley and Liv their whole lives and his actions put them in danger. If not for him, you wouldn't have woken up the morning after your wedding to find your wife missing." Cooper shook his head, a look of disgust on his face. "I plan on keeping my eye on him. That's what I've been doing. I spent the car ride trying to get as much information out of him as I could."

Luke shifted his eyes to the left and right making sure Sully hadn't appeared. "Find out anything?"

"Not really," Cooper said with frustration. "He's a closed book. In that line of work you need to be, but Sully is too detached for my liking. Let me stay on him and you and Jack focus on Riley."

"You don't think that's his focus, too?"

"I don't know, Luke. If this were your kid missing because of your work wouldn't you be crazier right now? He told me at least five times during the trip that we should be letting him handle this alone. He told me we aren't needed. We should go home and wait. Did you see him last night? He barely even reacted when I brought Liv back."

Cooper ran a hand through his hair and exhaled. "Maybe he was nervous about having to tell Liv the truth or maybe Sully was worried about what she had learned about him while she was gone, but there's something not right in this situation."

Luke had noticed what Cooper was saying. He had cautioned himself that he might have a bias so he had let it go. Now that Cooper mentioned it to him, the feeling came rushing back. "You think Sully is lying about something?"

"Without question. How can we trust someone who has spent his life lying for a living?"

That was Luke's thought exactly. "I'm going to loop Jack in. He doesn't like or trust Sully either. If we find he's hampering our efforts, we are going to have to ditch him."

Luke waved to Jack that he'd be right there. He spent the next few minutes giving Cooper an update about what he had found out about Holden. "The bottom line is it sounds like this guy has put his affairs in order and isn't planning to live much longer. He is going to avenge his brother's death or is willing to die trying, and that doesn't bode well for Riley."

"Let's get to work then," Cooper said, giving Luke a good natured punch in the chest.

Chapter 21

As we walked out of the coffee shop and hit the sidewalk, I turned to Holden. "I didn't think Det. Nixon would have handed over the information to us so quickly. I figured it would be more of a fight."

Holden didn't meet my eyes. Instead, he stared off into the street at the traffic zipping by, and his voice sounded far off like he was lost in a memory. "Det. Nixon had been asking me to come back to Boston for more than a year now to discuss my brother's murder with him. I put him off. We had the initial interview after the murder in which he ruled me out as a suspect since I was out of state. I think he was probably grateful that I'm even interested in what happened to my brother. I believe he thought I might know more, but as he saw today, I don't."

"What did he think you knew?"

Holden focused back on me. "Det. Nixon had been working on a theory that Eddie may have been involved in some serious drug trafficking and it was a deal gone bad. He suspected that it was a rival gang. Not the Irish mob but the Italian Mafia or maybe a cartel. Det. Nixon had been trying to figure out if there was anything in Eddie's financial documents that would have given him a new suspect."

"Why didn't he subpoena those records?" I didn't understand why Det. Nixon would need Holden's help with that.

"I gave him access to everything I had here in Boston. Eddie had named me the executor of his will and left me all his money including property in several countries. He wanted to know what I found when I fully took care of Eddie's assets."

I looked up at him wide-eyed. "Did you find anything worth noting?"

"Not really. I have boxes of Eddie's things in the house tucked away in a bedroom. There wasn't much at Eddie's residences. It looked like he was rarely at those other properties, except for the house in London, where he had made his permanent residence. I found most of his papers there, including his will and financial documents. Other than the will and settling his accounts, I didn't go through the rest of the documents."

"I'm surprised that Det. Nixon didn't press for that information today in exchange for telling us what he did."

Holden sighed. "I think he's figured out he can't push me. He's probably worried if he did that I might shut down and retreat again. I assume he believes that since I'm looking into things now, I'll alert him if I find anything."

Financial documents were often the most telling and shed light on a person's habits, secrets, and scandals. "Did Eddie's financial records also include his criminal activities or was that separate?"

"It was all there. He had multiple accounts including offshore accounts. I closed everything that I found. What I didn't do was go line by line in his financial records. This money is mine now, and I'm not so sure I want to know where it all came from. I've considered donating it to good causes to help appease my guilt for my brother's actions. I've kept up the charities he donated to though."

I understood and looked up at Holden. "I'm not judging you. Those documents might reveal more than his financial affairs. They might give us clues to a suspect. We can worry about that later though. Let's go find Melissa Patton. Since she was with Eddie the night of the murder and had known him for a while, she must be someone he trusted."

"I doubt she will tell us anything," Holden said with skepticism in his voice.

"Leave that to me. I can be persuasive."

There was a hint of a smile on Holden's face. "I can see that. You persuaded me to start this investigation and I wouldn't have thought that was possible."

"Where does Melissa live?"

"She's in Somerville. We'll need to drive there."

About thirty minutes later, we stood outside of a small three-story row house with yellow siding and concrete steps that appeared in desperate need of repair. "Who does she live with?" I asked as we climbed the broken steps.

"I don't know," Holden said as he reached out and knocked on the screen door, which banged on its hinges. "My brother pays her rent." He glanced down at me. "Well, I pay her rent now. As I said, Eddie wanted me to make sure she was taken care of should anything happen to him."

That answered how Holden knew where she lived and drove there with such ease. I expected to see a woman who looked like every mob boss's wife portrayed in the movies – hair and makeup flawless, skinny, tall, and dressed to the nines. The woman who answered and launched herself into Holden's arms wasn't anything like I had imagined.

Melissa stood about five-foot-four, and like me, enjoyed her sweets too much. Everything about her was round from the shape of her face and blonde curls that came to a stop at her chin to her figure. She wore hardly any makeup and didn't need it. Her skin was flawless and her cheeks had a hint of red. She reminded me of a five-year-old who hadn't lost their baby fat.

After hugging Holden, she flicked her big round blue eyes toward me. "Sorry," she said, letting Holden go and pulling her shirt back down over her belly. "I didn't realize you had someone with you." She stuck a chubby hand out to me. "I'm Melissa."

I shook her hand in return. "I'm Riley, a friend of Holden's. Do you have a few minutes to speak to us?"

"Sure," she said and stepped out of the way. Melissa trusted Holden, and me by extension. "What's this about?" She guided us into a small living room and plopped down on the couch and drew up her legs to sit cross-legged.

Holden sat next to her and I planted myself in a chair that looked like it might be older than me. I expected the springs to give way under my weight. Instead, it enveloped me like a hug.

"We need to talk about Eddie," Holden said. "I don't want to upset you but you were with him the night he died. I came back here to Boston to figure out what happened to him."

Melissa set her mouth in a firm line. "I don't know what more I can say. I told the cops everything I know. I didn't see who killed Eddie that night."

"Can you tell me please?" I asked. "I know this is probably difficult but I'm a private investigator who is helping Holden. We need to hear it directly from you."

Melissa shrugged. "I guess so. Eddie was home for a few weeks for Christmas and he was killed on our way out of a restaurant one night." She smiled sadly recalling the memory. "We got all dressed up for the perfect night Eddie had planned. Dinner was amazing and we planned a walk after dinner. Before I knew what happened, he was dead on the pavement."

That wasn't all and I knew it. I hated to make any witness give me the down and dirty details of a loved one being murdered in front of them, but it was critical. "I need more details, Melissa. Did you walk out of the restaurant first? Were there other people around? Did you see Eddie get shot?"

Holden reached out and squeezed Melissa's hand. "It's important or we wouldn't be asking. I want to make sure the person who killed Eddie is brought to justice."

"Why do you care now?" she asked him.

"I cared all along," Holden admitted. "I never felt ready to deal with it. I'm sure you understand that."

Melissa didn't respond to Holden. She turned her head to me and explained, "Eddie held the door open for me and I walked out first. I noticed a large black SUV sitting at the curb, but I couldn't see in the windows because they were heavily tinted. I didn't think anything of it. I figured they were dropping off or picking up someone. I was in front of Eddie and had started to walk away from the restaurant down the sidewalk. I only made it a few feet when I heard the shots. Before I even understood what was happening Eddie was down on the ground and the black SUV took off. I didn't see them shoot. I ran back to Eddie, but he was dead before I got to him." Tears ran down Melissa's face. "I didn't see the shooter or the gun. My back was turned when it happened. I wish I knew more."

"Did Eddie ever say anything to you about fearing for his life or did he seem afraid at dinner?"

Melissa wiped her tears on the back of her hand and sniffled. "Eddie was always cautious, but no, I wouldn't say he seemed afraid that night. There were threats against him for sure. Eddie never told me who." Melissa broke eye contact with me and focused on Holden. "It was expected in his line of work."

Holden reached for her hand and took it in his. "Did Eddie tell you much about his work?"

"I knew enough," she said evenly. "I'm sure there were things Eddie didn't tell me though. We had known each other for more than twenty years and trusted each other. We were friends before there was ever anything romantic. Even at that, Eddie said there were things I was better off not knowing."

"You know that Eddie's business was criminal though, right?"

Melissa turned to face me; a hint of anger came over her face. "You can't judge him. You didn't know him. Eddie was one of the kindest, sweetest people you'd ever want to meet. Of course, I knew he was involved in illegal activity, but the heart wants what it wants. I was in love with him." Melissa broke down and put her face in her hands. "I still love him."

"I'm not judging him. Eddie didn't deserve what happened to him, but it's important to know who might have wanted to kill him. We must solve his murder."

Melissa raised her eyes to mine. "You're not going to be able to solve it." She turned to face Holden. "I'm glad you are home and care about what happened to Eddie, but no one is going to talk to you. People know more than what they will tell you. It will be better for you if you leave it alone."

Holden shifted in his seat and I could tell that something Melissa said impacted him. "Do you know more than what you're telling us, Melissa? It seems like you might," Holden said, looking uncomfortable now in a way he hadn't before.

Melissa stood and walked toward the front door. "I think it's time for you to go. As I said, I don't know who killed Eddie so I can't help you."

"But you do know more," Holden said, standing and walking toward her. "If you're afraid, I can protect you."

She shook her head hard enough her curls bounced. "There are things Eddie wanted to take to the grave, and I'm going to respect that."

Holden walked right up to her and stood toe to toe looking down at her. Melissa didn't budge. I got up from the seat and walked over to them. Nothing good would come of Holden pressing her too hard for information now. I reached out and tugged on his sleeve to go.

"Thanks for the information. If you want to tell us more, please call Holden. All we are trying to do is find who killed Eddie." I walked past them both and went to the door. It took Holden another minute but he followed me out.

As we stood on the porch, Melissa said one last thing before shutting the door. "Holden, you have to know at the end Eddie was a good man, but for him, there were worse things than being a criminal. I won't even share with you or with anyone what I knew. I'll tell you this though. It's what got him killed. Let it die with him."

Chapter 22

After throwing their luggage in the room, Sully informed them all he had a meeting with someone who might have information. He refused to tell them who his contact might be or what they might know.

Luke had started to argue, but Cooper stepped in. He slapped Sully on the back and said he'd be happy to go with him to the meeting. Even when Sully said he'd go alone, Cooper stuck to him like glue. Whether Sully wanted Cooper or not, he was going. On the way out of the hotel room, Cooper gave Luke a nod and wink letting him know he'd call with any updates.

That left Luke and Jack alone to scope out the neighborhood where Liv said she and Riley had been held. They weren't sure of the specific address but had a general idea given the cross-streets and description of the outside of the house. Neither had said much on the drive, but as Jack drove through the streets of the neighborhood, Luke stared out the window at the houses on the narrow streets. The area was rundown but not quite as bad as he had expected.

Jack turned down one street and then made a quick right on the next. He drove a few blocks and then pulled the SUV over to the curb. He cut the engine.

"This is the area," Jack said pointing to the street signs for East 3rd and P. Streets. "Doesn't look like much is happening around here."

Luke agreed. The street was desolate except for a few cars. He opened the door and got out to scan the houses on his side of the street. Jack did the same. It didn't take them long to zero in on the house Liv had described – two-story dirty blue siding with a front screen door off its hinge.

"It's right here, Jack." Luke walked over a small patch of grass to the sidewalk and then down two houses from where they had parked. He had his gun in the holster on his hip and he reached down to unclasp it.

Jack walked around the SUV and met Luke in front of the driveway. "No cars and no one around. Are you sure this is right?"

"It's the only house on the block with blue siding and you can see the street signs Riley saw from here." Luke walked in front of Jack up to the front door. He opened the screen as gently as possible to knock on the door. Before he could reach out, the screen door came off the other hinge and crashed to the ground with a clang and a rattle. "So much for that," Luke said with a sigh. He dragged it to the side of the porch and leaned it against the railing.

"If that wasn't enough to get the homeowner out here, we can assume no one is home," Luke said mostly in jest. He knocked on the door once and then harder. He called out, but no one answered. As they stepped off the porch and went to make their way to the driveway to walk to the back of the home, a woman called from across the street.

"You looking for those two girls?" she asked, leaning on her cane to cross the road. "Did you hear me? I asked if you were looking for those two girls?"

"We are," Luke said, walking over to her. "Have you seen them?"

"It was the craziest thing," she said, hitching her jaw toward the house. "Yesterday real early in the morning a white cargo van pulls up and the driver gets out. He walks around to the back and meets up with some other guy. They opened up the doors and pulled out two girls – both in handcuffs."

Luke couldn't believe what he was hearing. "Did you call the police?"

"I thought about it, but that Collins kid is not someone you rat out if you know what I mean. I have to live in this neighborhood." She held one arm out to the side while the other grasped the cane. "At almost seventy-eight, it's not like I'm moving soon unless it's to my final resting place."

"What did you see after that?" Jack asked, turning his head to Luke with a look that told him not to press his luck.

"Later that night, Collins came out and backed the van into the driveway and then was gone again. I couldn't see what they were doing back there though."

"Is that it?"

"No, it got weirder. About thirty minutes after Collins left, the other guy came walking down the driveway with the other girl – the redhead one. They came strolling down like they were pals. The handcuffs were gone and she wasn't trying to run from him or anything. They walked down the block together and then were out of sight." She pointed with her finger in the direction they had just come from. "He might have parked down the road because other than the van there were no cars in the driveway."

The woman's story seemed to match up with what Liv had said. Luke asked, "Do you know who owns this house?"

"Edna Collins, it's her grandson that was here. I can't remember his first name. He has always just gone by Collins."

Jack looked back at the house. "Is she home? No one answered and I'd like to speak with her."

The woman shook her head. "Edna is in a nursing home and has been for about a month. I don't know what the family is doing with the home. Collins, as far as I know, is the only one local and he's nothing but trouble."

Luke directed his attention toward the house. "We are going to try that side door. I want to see if they left any evidence behind. The redhead is my wife."

She closed her eyes and nodded once. "Do whatever you have to do. You won't get any trouble from me." She turned and shuffled back to her house.

"At least we know Riley is okay," Jack said. "Sounds like what Liv told us is accurate, at least."

Luke wasn't sure that made him feel any better. He walked up the length of the driveway and turned the knob on the side door, but it didn't budge. Luke followed Jack around to the back of the house. There wasn't anything out there though. The windows at the back of the home had the blinds shut. Even getting right up to the windows, nothing could be viewed inside the house. Luke stepped back and wiped his hands on his pants. He didn't even want to imagine how dirty the inside of the home might be if the outside gave any indication.

"Looks like a dead end," Jack said and walked back down the driveway with Luke to the SUV. "What do we want to do next?"

Luke toed the ground in front of him. He wasn't sure what to do next because they had few leads to go on. "Why don't we see if we can run down any leads on this Collins guy. It can't be too hard to find out his first name. Once we have that, we can run a search."

"You're looking for Collins?" a male voice said from behind Luke.

Luke turned around and came face to face with a guy about his age. He had a shaved head and a nasty scar ran down the right side of his face from temple to chin. "Yeah, do you know him?"

"Who are you?" he asked with a menacing tone that didn't escape Luke. The man postured himself for a fight.

Luke could have flashed his badge and said he was a cop but he knew that wouldn't win him any favors. He squared his shoulders and stood a little taller. "Collins might know something about two missing women who were last seen here. I'm looking to ask him a few questions. You know where I can find him?"

"Who are those women to you?"

Jack came around from the front of the SUV. "I'm a private investigator," he said reaching out his hand. The man didn't shake it, but Jack wasn't dissuaded. "We were hired to find the two women. Any information you might have will help." Jack reached for his wallet and pulled out a twenty-dollar bill. He offered it to the guy who just laughed at him.

"You think that's how much information goes for in this neighborhood?"

Jack put the money back in his pocket. "It's all I got on me. Do you know where Collins and the women are now?"

The guy smirked. "That seems to be the question everyone has."

"I don't understand," Jack said, glancing over at Luke.

"Don't worry about it. They aren't where they are supposed to be."

Luke stepped forward ever so slightly. "Where is that?"

The man just stared hard at Luke. "Don't play me for a fool. You're here, ain't ya? You know they are supposed to be here but nobody's home." He pulled a gun from the back of his pants and kept it at his side. "They are supposed to be here, but I said all along that we'd get screwed over. I told them, don't trust the brother. What do they do? Trust the brother and now he's going to pay, too."

Luke held his hands up in surrender. "I have no idea what you're talking about."

"Go back where you came from. Nobody is saving those girls." He turned and started to walk away, but Luke threw down his ace.

"What do you know about Noah Byrne and Holden Stone?"

The man advanced on Luke quickly, aiming the gun right at Luke's head. Luke sidestepped him, shoving the gun free from his hand, and then punched him hard in the ribs. Jack kicked the gun out of the way while Luke hit him again. The man was on the ground with his hands behind his back before he could even respond. Luke patted him down for other weapons while the man grunted and screamed, delivering threats no one took seriously.

It wasn't the most brutal or fanciest take-down Luke had ever delivered, but he was tired of playing games. He pulled handcuffs from his back pocket and slapped them on the man's wrists. Jack opened the SUV door and Luke jerked the man up from the ground and threw the man in the backseat.

Jack grabbed the man's gun from the ground and they piled into the SUV and took off. The man kicked at the back of Luke's seat and tried to free himself. When they were a few blocks away, Luke turned around and aimed his gun at the man. "Knock it off. Tell me your name right now."

The man seethed but stopped thrashing around. He didn't answer Luke's question and didn't look like he would. He breathed heavily in and out like an angry dog about to strike.

Luke wasn't having any of it. "Just tell me what I can call you or I might choose something for you that you're not going to like."

"Quin," the man said but nothing more.

"Fine, Quin, perfect," Luke said sarcastically. "What do you know about the kidnapping?" Quin said nothing, but Luke waved the gun in front of him. "If you think I'm above shooting you and dumping your body by the side of the road, think again. I came here to bring those women home and I'm not going to stop until I do."

It was obvious by how Quin had spoken that he had no idea that Liv had been released and Luke wasn't going to be the one to tell him. "Now, you reacted when I said Noah Byrne and Holden Stone so tell me what you know."

"Holden is Eddie's brother. I'm sure you know Eddie was murdered and we are going to avenge his death. The cops won't do anything about it, so we are going to take care of it as we should have at the start."

"What does that have to do with the women?"

Quin exhaled a breath in a sarcastic laugh. "It's not about the women. They are a means to an end."

"What would that be?"

"To kill their father, but I don't think that's going to happen." Quin locked eyes with Luke. "Holden double-crossed us. He's the one that needs to die now."

Chapter 23

Cooper vowed to stay on Sully no matter what happened, but the man didn't make it easy. He had tried twice already to shake Cooper. The first time was when they left the hotel. Sully entered a crowded elevator that had no room for Cooper. Sully told him he'd meet him at the lobby. That sent Cooper running to the stairs. He beat the elevator to the lobby and stood there gasping for breath when the elevator doors opened. Sully had said nothing but the look on his face upon seeing Cooper standing there said everything. They both played it off like the incident hadn't occurred and left in search of Riley.

Once they made it a few blocks from the hotel, Sully informed him that he had to meet someone at a local pub and that he needed to go alone. Cooper wasn't having any of it and followed right in step with Sully. Once they entered the bar, Sully pointed out a table and told Cooper to sit and wait while he went to get the guy he was meeting with.

It couldn't have been more than a few minutes later when Cooper, through the window, caught sight of Sully coming out of the alleyway that ran behind the pub. Cooper leaped from the table and ran out the front door of the pub and caught up with Sully on the sidewalk. The man had a scowl across his face and didn't even try to make an excuse.

"Why do you keep following me?" Sully barked.

"Why do you keep trying to dodge me? We are supposed to be working together."

Sully turned his head back toward the alley. "I work alone. Always have and always will."

Cooper stepped toward him but was forced to look up at Sully who was much taller. "Your daughter has been taken by someone connected to your work. Do you care about that at all?"

Sully reached his hands out and shoved Cooper back. "Of course I care, but Riley isn't in danger with Holden. He's the least of her worries."

"What's that supposed to mean? You didn't say anything like that before."

"You shouldn't have all come rushing to Boston to try to find her. You should have let me handle it. That's exactly what they want."

Sully tried to walk away from Cooper, but he grabbed the man's arm. "I get it, Sully. You're this tough lone wolf, traveling the world doing what you do. But this time, your daughter's life is at stake. She got all mixed up in something you started."

Sully turned on him fast, the anger and fire burning in his eyes. "You're right and it's up to me to stop it. Do you think you're skilled enough to take this on? Luke and Jack with their years in law enforcement? None of you even understand what's happening or what all this ties to. It's much bigger than you think. They took Eddie out and disappeared."

Sully turned and faced the road. "They are out there waiting though. They are out there and will take out anyone who gets in their way." He looked down at Cooper. "You're right. This is my responsibility and I'm the only one who can fix it. None of you should have come here. I told you that but you insisted. Now, you're getting in my way."

In one move, Sully put an arm around Cooper's neck and dragged him into the alleyway and out of sight. Cooper tried to kick and pull at the man's thick forearm but it was no use. Sully overpowered him. Cooper had never felt such strength or show of force. He couldn't even speak. He gasped for air and freedom but neither came. The next thing Cooper knew he felt a slight pinprick in his neck and the world became dark.

The stony concrete scratched at Cooper's back where his shirt had risen. Cooper laid his hands flat on the ground before he opened his eyes. His thoughts swirled like a tornado crashing through his brain and wreaking havoc.

Cooper opened one eye and then the other, blinking against the brightness. For a moment, he worried he had ended up in some CIA black site to be tortured or whatever those spooks did to people who got in their way.

As his eyes adjusted, relief washed over Cooper when realized he hadn't gone far at all. He pushed himself to a sitting position against a brick wall and took in his surroundings. He glanced right and then left at the alleyway Sully had dragged him into.

Cooper reached up and touched a tender spot on his neck. It was the last memory he had. Sully had injected him with something, a tranquilizer maybe, but Cooper knew they generally took a few minutes to take effect. This had been almost instantaneous and, even conscious now, the effects were still coursing through him. His limbs felt heavy and he had to fight off sleep.

Cooper took a few deep breaths and wiggled his arms around as best he could. He wanted to stand but assumed he might fall back over so he waited. His legs had a heaviness and the feeling of pins and needles that was annoying as much as it hurt. Cooper assumed whatever had been in that injection was CIA-made and not something available on the market.

As Cooper got his hands working again, he kneaded his fingers into his thigh muscles and began to bend his legs close to his body and stretch them out again. Normal feeling soon returned.

As Cooper planted one hand on the wall behind him and the other on the ground to stand, a metal door in the alleyway opened and a young kid carried out a bag of garbage. He got one look at Cooper and rushed towards him, dropping the bag near the door.

"Buddy, you okay?" he asked as he approached. "What happened? Someone mug you?"

"Something like that." Cooper pushed himself to a standing position. He swayed and the kid reached out to steady him. "I got it, thanks," Cooper said and leaned against the wall.

The kid stood there not moving. "You look like you're going to fall. What happened?"

"Took a hit to the head," Cooper lied and leaned his shoulder into the wall. He didn't realize standing would cause the entire world to spin. He took a few deep breaths and tried to shake off the effects of the drug. "You work in that pub out front?"

"Yeah, I came out the back door."

"Did you happen to see the guy I went into the bar with earlier?"

"I work in the back in the kitchen." The kid turned his head to look over his shoulder at the metal door and the bag of trash. "I have to get back to work. I can call someone for you if you need help."

Cooper waved him off. "I'm fine, just need a minute."

The kid left Cooper to it. He threw the trash in the dumpster and disappeared out of sight back into the building. The metal door slammed behind him. Alone again, Cooper used the wall as support as he made his way out of the alley. With each step, he grew a little stronger, which was good because he was almost out of wall to hold him up. He needed to call Luke but dreaded admitting Sully had gotten away from him.

Across the road in front of him was a public park and benches.

While it was a brisk day, Cooper needed to sit and regroup. He aimed himself toward that park, carefully crossing the busy street at the light. Each step felt like pushing himself through quicksand. The city streets were a bustle of people and cars even at mid-day. Cooper had never wanted to live in a big city and this trip to Boston only reinforced it.

Cooper gripped the back of the park bench and lowered himself to the seat. He had no idea where Sully could have gone and had no idea how to track him down. This wasn't going the way he had planned it. He checked his watch and saw only an hour had gone by. At least whatever Sully knocked him out with hadn't lasted that long. Just enough time for him to have made his escape. Sully hadn't even had a bag or anything in his hands. The syringe or whatever he used must have been in his pocket.

Cooper rubbed his forehead and braced himself for the headache he knew would come on soon. He punched in the number for Luke and waited as it rang.

"Not the best time, Cooper," Luke said as he answered. "We are at the Boston Police Department and I can't talk."

"Is everything okay?" Cooper asked, alarmed. The last he knew Luke and Jack were headed to the house where Liv said she and Riley had been held.

"Too much to go into right now. I'll update you when we meet up with you and Sully."

"Yeah, about that," Cooper started to say and his voice faltered.

"Is there a problem?"

Cooper cleared his throat. "There's no good way to say this, Luke. He tried to ditch me and when I caught up to him, he dragged me down an alleyway and injected me with something that knocked me out. He's gone."

Luke coughed once and then whistled. "I guess you're having a worse day than we are. Are you okay?"

"I'm still a bit shaky. I've sat down on a bench in a park not that far from our hotel." Cooper paused and then said more quietly, "Sully told me that we have no idea what we are dealing with and that he's not worried about the threat from Holden. He said Riley faces a bigger threat, but he didn't elaborate. He said he'd take care of it himself and that we shouldn't be here."

Luke cursed. "We need to meet up and share some info but not on the phone. I'm sitting here waiting to speak with the detective on the Eddie Stone homicide. I'm hoping he can provide some information. We also just brought in one of the thugs from Eddie's crew. He knows Holden turned on them. Riley, Holden...none of them are safe."

"Do you think that's what Sully was talking about?"

"I don't know, Cooper. I don't know." Luke made a plan to meet Cooper back at the hotel in ninety minutes. Until then, Cooper would sit on the bench and recuperate. He felt completely useless at the moment.

Chapter 24

Holden and I hadn't talked much on the walk back to the car after leaving Melissa's house. We drove in silence for most of the way until I asked, "Where are we headed now?"

"I'm not sure," he said not taking his eyes off the road. "We can't talk to any of Eddie's associates. They believe Sully killed Eddie. By now they should have figured out I'm on the run with you."

"How many guys did Eddie have here?"

"There was a core group of about twenty guys. Twelve of them are in prison. I only know a few. Noah, Collins, Quin, and two others I had minimal contact with. The rest I don't know where they are."

I suggested, "The only other two names thrown around were Danny Devaney and Frankie Coonan. I know Det. Nixon ruled them out but maybe they might know something. Let's talk to them now and get it out of the way. Let's start with Danny Devaney."

"You think it's that easy to walk up and talk to a mob boss?" Holden shook his head. "I don't even know if they'd speak to you."

I knew he was right. It wasn't going to be that easy if Holden was with me. I had an ace to play that couldn't be done in front of him. I had to go alone and told him as much. When he argued, I held my ground. "They know you're Eddie's brother. If you walk in there and start asking them for information, they are going to shut down. We probably won't even be granted a meeting."

"What makes you think you're going to walk in there and they will tell you?"

"I have ways of gathering information. Where can I find Danny?"

Holden pulled over to the side of the road and cut the engine. I wasn't sure where we were or what he was doing. He turned to me and put his hand on my shoulder. "I know this started with me kidnapping and threatening you, but by now, we both know I was never going to be able to do that. I can't have you get hurt trying to help me out of a mess."

I stared straight ahead and tried to keep calm. "Let me call home and get my husband and my friend Cooper here to help. There is no case the three of us haven't solved."

Holden rubbed his forehead. "If you do that, I'm going to prison and will probably be killed in my first week there. Eddie's guys will get to me inside."

I knew he'd go back on his promise to let me call home. "It seems you're out of options then. You can't talk to either Danny or Frank, and if you won't let me go alone, it seems we are going to be at a standstill."

I put my head back and closed my eyes. "You might as well finish me off now," I said dramatically. When he didn't say anything, I opened one eye and turned my head slightly toward him.

Holden was trying not to smile at me, but the corners of his lips turned up. "You're impossible, you know that, right?"

I shrugged. "You kidnapped me. No one said I was going to be easy. I always thought I probably wasn't a kidnap risk because I'm thoroughly annoying. Anyone who knows me could have told you that."

"I should have made inquiries first."

"There were a lot of things you should have done before attempting this idiotic plan."

"I know," Holden said with a weariness in his voice that hadn't been there before.

"Holden, listen, you brought me into this and refuse to let me go. At least, let me do what I'm good at so we can figure out who killed your brother and I can go home to my new husband. I just got married. This isn't exactly the honeymoon I had planned."

Holden's answer was to start the engine and pull back into traffic. We drove down narrow side streets, turning left and right until I grew dizzy and wasn't sure what area of Boston we were in anymore. I figured it out when road signs for Harvard started dotting the road. We were in Cambridge. "Where are you taking me?"

Holden kept his eyes on the road. "You said you wanted to speak to Danny Devaney so that's what we are going to do. Last I knew, he has a bar that he operates out of and there's a coffee shop down the road from it. I'll wait there and you can walk to the bar."

He pulled into a small parking lot adjacent to the coffee shop, which appeared to be full of students. Before I got out of the car, he leaned over and popped open the glovebox. The gun I had seen earlier in his waistband sat there.

He pulled it out and rested it in his lap. "I can't stop you from shooting me if I give you this. If you do, you do. I'm a walking dead man anyway. You can end it here if you want and run, tell them I took you." Holden handed me the gun. "There's no way I'm letting you walk into that bar unarmed."

I held the gun in my hand. I had assumed that when the moment came where there was a shift in power between us I'd run and get as far away from Holden as possible. I sat there staring down at the gun in my lap. I could shoot him right now or aim it at him and run for help. It would be easy enough to do. I knew Holden wouldn't even fight me on it.

I surprised myself because the only thing I wanted to do was go into the bar and talk to Danny and find out what he knew about Eddie Stone's murder. I smiled thinking of Luke who always told me I got too personally involved in cases. I glanced over at Holden and Det. Nixon's words rang in my head. He wasn't his brother. Holden got tied up in this as much as I did.

I made sure the safety was on and checked the magazine. "Whose gun is this?"

"It's mine and registered."

I shook my head at him. "You don't kill someone with a gun registered to you if you're planning to get away with it."

Holden looked out the driver's side window, his voice soft and distant. "I never planned to get away with it. I assumed someone in Eddie's crew would kill me, and if not, I'd turn myself in."

"For the love of it, Holden! You're a terrible criminal." I got out of the car and tucked the gun in my waistband. I walked down the street looking like one of the college students who were coming and going from the local shops. At the end of the row of businesses sat a dodgy-looking bar that I assumed no Harvard student would ever enter. I didn't even see a sign out front with a name.

I took a breath, put my hand on the brass doorknob, and turned it, pushing the door open as I went. I stepped into a dark room with red vinyl booths and a smattering of tables in the middle. A few feet in front of me there was a u-shaped bar with one guy tending it. There was no one else in the place. His eyes were fixed on a large flat-screen television overhead.

I cleared my throat and took a few steps toward him.

He glanced over at me. "We aren't open."

"I'm not here for a drink," I said, my voice almost a squeak and tinged with fear.

"Why are you here then?"

I mustered up some courage and walked right up to him. "I'm here to see Danny Devaney."

The guy had a shaved head and tattoos up both arms, some of them Celtic in design and others that didn't mean anything to me. He leaned over the bar on his forearms and laughed. "As cute as you are, he's not entertaining company today. Besides, what would a college student like you want with Danny?"

"I'm not a college student." I locked eyes with him. "Tell him Mickey Finnigan's daughter is here to speak to him."

The guy immediately pulled back and assessed me. "I didn't know Mickey had a daughter."

"There are lots of things I'm sure you don't know about Mickey, but I'm here on my father's behalf to speak to Danny."

The guy didn't say anything else. He turned, pulled open a section of the bar, and walked to a door in the back. Not even a minute later, he stuck his head out and waved me over.

Before I could enter, he frisked me, finding the gun shoved in my waistband. "College student you are not," he said, laughing. He waved the gun at me. "This will be at the bar and you can have it back when you leave." He held the door open and I walked into a scene that felt straight out of a mob movie.

Danny Devaney sat behind a large desk cluttered with paper and other items. He smoked a cigar that he held between his thick fingers. His brown eyes and ruddy complexion reminded me of my father, so did the man's size. Danny was probably a few inches shorter but no less thick and muscular even in his sixties. He had a tuft of white hair and an easy grin.

There was a large Celtic cross hanging behind his desk and a photo of St. Patrick on the wall. To my surprise, a photo of my father and Danny with golf clubs in hand hung next to it. It had to have been taken many years back. My father looked like he did in his youth. Much like I'd seen in my mother's photo albums, back when they were together.

Danny stood and pointed to the photo. "I'm friends with the man for nearly forty years and he never mentioned a kid. I'd say you're lying except you look exactly like him. Why didn't he tell me about you?"

"If you know Mickey, and I see you do, you know he's always got a trick or two up his sleeve."

"Where's your accent?"

"I grew up here in the states with my mother. I spent summers with my father and holidays." I shrugged like it was no big deal. "My mother found out what my father was into after I was born, and you know how it goes. This life isn't for some women."

Danny plopped down in his chair, the springs creaking under the weight, and proceeded to ask me what felt like fifty questions to confirm that I knew Mickey Finnigan. Things only someone close to him would know. Some of the answers were guesses on my part, but I seemed to pass muster. Danny waved me forward to his desk. "What can I do for your father?"

"You can tell me everything you know about Eddie Stone."

Danny's eyes lit up and he took a puff of his cigar. "That, kid, is going to take a while."

Chapter 25

Luke slammed his fist down on Det. Nixon's desk. "I don't care if you think Holden isn't capable of kidnapping my wife, it's what happened! You need to help us find her."

After getting as much information as possible from Quin, they had brought him to the Boston Police Department and dragged him through the front door. Quin had screamed that he had been kidnapped and Luke flashed his badge. That shut Quin up quickly and since then, the man hadn't said a word. He sat in lockup as the police tried to determine what was going on.

Luke had demanded to speak to the detective in charge of the Eddie Stone murder investigation. Det. Nixon brought him and Jack back to his office about an hour later. So far, they weren't doing a good enough job to convince the man anything criminal had occurred. All Quin said was that Luke and Jack had handcuffed him and threw him into the back of their SUV and brought him to the police station. He denied knowing anything about Eddie Stone's murder and any kidnapping plot involving Holden Stone and Riley and Liv. Quin acted like the innocent party who had been attacked on the street.

Det. Nixon had been familiar enough with Quin to know the man wasn't telling the truth, but he had no choice but to let him go.

"Nuisance criminal," Det. Nixon said when he sat down at his desk and looked up at Luke and Jack like they were wasting his time. Det.

Nixon had given Quin back his gun because it had been registered to him. Quin only had minor incidences with the law to date.

Det. Nixon focused on Luke. "I'm not saying this didn't happen, but it doesn't sound like the girls were in any danger." He folded his hands over his stomach and leaned back in his chair.

The situation was only made worse when Luke showed Det. Nixon Riley's photo.

He took Luke's phone in his hand and looked at the photo and then back up at Luke with a face that said he wasn't concerned. "She's a private investigator, right?"

"Yes," Luke said, glancing back at Jack and then to Det. Nixon in confusion. "How do you know that?"

Det. Nixon leaned forward and rested his arms on the desk. "I met with her this morning."

"You met Riley this morning?" Jack said, standing. It was the first time Luke saw him get as agitated as he felt meeting with the detective.

"I did. Holden asked for a meeting and I met them at a coffee shop near Boston Public Garden."

"I don't understand," Jack said, confusion written all over his face. "Holden asked to meet with you and he brought Riley with him? How did she seem?"

"She seemed perfectly in control of herself." Det. Nixon motioned with his hand for them both to sit down and they did reluctantly. "I'm not trying to be dismissive of you both. I can see that you're concerned for Riley's welfare and I do understand. The situation you described is quite concerning, but I'm not seeing evidence of a crime. I saw Riley with my own eyes. She flipped through the case file I provided on Eddie Stone and she asked pertinent questions. I didn't pick up any fear from her. She didn't try to signal for help in any way. I didn't pick up any tension between her and Holden. If anything, I'd say they were friendly."

"Friendly with her kidnapper?" Luke said with an exasperated laugh. "If Riley was acting friendly then that's what it was - an act. She is doing anything she can to keep herself safe from a killer."

Det. Nixon raised his eyebrows. "You think Holden is a killer?"

Luke couldn't get the words out because all he wanted to do was scream. He turned to Jack stone-faced.

Jack nodded and then turned back to Det. Nixon. "I appreciate your perspective on this, but you have to see where we are coming from. Riley and her sister disappeared the morning after the wedding without a word. The next day Liv comes back with a tale that they had been kidnapped and were being held here in Boston."

Jack went on to describe the circumstances of Riley and Liv's abduction and everything Liv had detailed for them about Holden and Collins and what was planned. When he was done, Jack said, "Surely, you can understand how we are concerned about Riley's wellbeing."

Det. Nixon agreed. "It's not that I don't understand, I do. You're here asking me to find Holden and arrest him and save Riley. You have two women that left a hotel on their own. One returned with a wild tale. The other I saw with my own eyes. I can bring Collins in for questioning. I wouldn't put anything past him, but Holden I assure you isn't holding Riley hostage now."

Luke knew there was no point arguing with the man so he changed the subject. "Let's say for the sake of argument that Riley is willingly helping Holden. Any idea where they are?"

"I suspect looking into Eddie Stone's murder," Det. Nixon said calmly.

"Why would you share information with them about an open investigation?" Jack asked.

Det. Nixon spun around in his chair and dug through some case files. When he turned back around, he slapped one down on his desk. "I didn't share everything with them. The Stones were well-respected members of the community here in Boston. They gave a lot to charity and supported the community and even the police. They didn't expect a lot in return. Even when Eddie got in trouble for petty crimes, his parents didn't expect us to turn a blind eye. They wanted Eddie to pay for his crimes. Eventually, they sent him away to school. You couldn't have had brothers less alike. Holden was an athlete and straight-A student. He excelled where Eddie failed." Det. Nixon tapped the file. "Eddie didn't fail because he wasn't smart. The kid was a genius, which is how he eventually grew his criminal empire. That was an embarrassment to the whole Stone family. After the deaths of their parents, Holden tried everything to help Eddie straighten out his life and when he couldn't, he washed his hands of him. When Eddie was murdered, Holden took it as a personal failure. He came back for the services and didn't want anything to do with the investigation or Eddie's life at all."

"Something changed," Jack said, interrupting.

Det. Nixon bobbed his head. "Something did change. I'm not sure what, to be honest with you. I'm as shocked as anyone that Holden reached out to me. To answer your question, I haven't been able to solve Eddie's murder. I haven't even come close. I hoped by giving Holden some information, he might be able to speak to some people that wouldn't talk to me, and if he makes headway in solving it, then it might help to appease some of his guilt."

It made sense to Luke. He might have even done the same. He wouldn't fault Det. Nixon for the decision. "Have you heard of Patrick Sullivan?"

Det. Nixon flipped through the case file and then glanced up. "Not a name I have or am familiar with in reference to this case. Should I know him?"

"He's who Holden and Eddie's guys believe killed him. He's Riley and Liv's father." Luke explained the connection without providing any information about Sully's CIA connections.

"Doesn't ring any bells for me," Det. Nixon admitted.

Luke had more questions for the detective but he was starting to feel like they were spinning their wheels. He needed the detective to bottom-line it for him. "Do you have any idea who killed Eddie Stone?" Before Det. Nixon could answer, Luke added, "I know you haven't made an arrest or come out publicly with anyone as a suspect or person of interest. I'm not asking for the formal line from the Boston Police Department. I'm asking detective to detective. Do you have anyone you think is good for this?"

Det. Nixon stayed silent for so long Luke figured he wasn't going to answer. Luke was about to stand and leave the man's office but Det. Nixon started talking.

"I believe it's a hit connected to Eddie's crimes. It's not personal. I can tell you that much. I've ruled out his local crew. He had no beef with them. If it wasn't for the money Eddie sent back, they'd have nothing. I've also ruled out anyone connected to his personal life."

Det. Nixon expelled a loud heavy breath. "The murder was meant to be public and send a message. Now, I don't know if it's a rival gang or someone connected to his life overseas, but I don't have anyone on any watch lists or anything like that known to be in the area at the time. I assumed that if it was someone international, they could have killed him over there. Why bother sneaking into the U.S. to handle it?"

The detective had missed something. Jack said it before Luke could. "Why would you assume that someone would have to come to the U.S. to kill Eddie? Most international criminal empires have factions in the U.S. already. Even Chinese and Russian gangs have people here. They might not be as well-known as the Italian and Irish mobs or the Mexican cartels but they are here. It might have been easier to get to Eddie here. Plus, on his home turf, his guard would be down."

"I admit I hadn't given that much thought. There was no evidence to suggest it though."

"You don't seem like you have much evidence pointing one way or the other," Luke challenged.

"True enough. What Jack said is certainly a possibility."

Jack sat back and folded his arms over his chest and closed his eyes. It was clear to Luke the man had something on his mind. They waited until Jack formulated his thought. His eyes opened and he postulated a theory. "If Eddie has an international criminal empire and making millions of dollars and funneling money back here, why would local rival gangs care? Eddie's guys aren't cutting into their turf. Given the specifics of the kidnapping and the fact that Holden and Riley seem to have broken away from them, Eddie's crew doesn't seem all that capable."

Det. Nixon pointed at Jack. "You've got me there. Eddie's crew is a bunch of bumbling idiots. It's why Eddie broke away from them at the start. Eddie may not have done well in school, but he was keen and intelligent. Street smarts got him further than most."

"Ruling out local rival gangs, that still leaves a lot of possibilities on the table," Jack said.

Det. Nixon pulled a pen from a cup of pens and pencils on his desk and jotted something down on a blue sticky note. He tore off the small square paper and handed it to Luke. "That's the number Holden called me from. It's the best I can do right now."

Chapter 26

Danny spent the next hour telling me everything I could have ever wanted to know about Eddie Stone. He went on and on and barely took a breath. There hadn't even been a break in conversation for me to ask any questions. It seemed Danny admired Eddie's drive and determination and the way he used his prep school contacts to build an international empire.

"Man," Danny said as he was wrapping up, "I was a kid from the streets. This life was all I knew. My father was a made man and so were his brothers. I tried early on to get Eddie to join us, but he had his ambitions higher. I couldn't blame the kid. He got out of the neighborhood. One of the few."

When Danny finally took a break, I asked what I was there to find out. "Do you have any information about Eddie's murder?"

Danny squinted. "What does Mickey want with that mess?"

"There's been some talk that people might be blaming him. That he put a hit out." I bit my lip. "You know Mickey, he doesn't like gossip. He figures if he can figure out who killed Eddie, the whole thing can be put to bed."

Danny pointed a finger to his chest. "Mickey doesn't think I had anything to do with it, does he?"

I smiled. "We both know if he did, I wouldn't be sitting here in front of you. You'd be dead already."

Danny laughed so hard his chest heaved up and down and his belly jiggled. "When you're right, you're right. Mickey is old school. That's why he's lasted so long in this game. Me and your pops have done things the right way." Danny shook his head. "I don't know who killed Eddie. I'm being straight with you about that. You can check but I even sent flowers to the wake."

"Danny, you'll find I am my father's daughter. We all know how it works with the Irish and the Italians. You'd bump Eddie off and send a check to the widow and flowers to the wake."

He chuckled again and winked. "Your father taught you well. That's not how these young guys operate. There's no honor anymore. They'd kill your father and take out your whole family."

His words made my stomach drop because he wasn't wrong. The Italian mafia and the Irish mob had changed over time as younger leadership came up. No longer was there the honor among men that Danny mentioned. It had become a free for all.

"You must know something," I stressed. "I'd take gossip at this point, anything that could point me in the next direction."

Danny furrowed his brow. "Why would your father send you on this task? He must have men that can handle this for him."

I understood why he asked. Mob bosses didn't involve their daughters in their affairs. "I guess I should have explained that. While I am my father's daughter and have his sensibilities, I've used my skills differently. I was an investigative journalist for years and then a private investigator. While my father has a lot of men who can do his dirty work for him, Mickey was looking for a more subtle touch this time."

"You should come work for me."

I laughed good-naturedly. "You know my father would shoot you dead before he'd allow that. As an honor to you, he sent me in to get as much information as I could. He could have used a heavier hand to handle this, but out of respect for you, here I am."

I gave him a sympathetic look. "Don't send me home empty-handed. That wouldn't bode well for either of us. You must know something." I could see on his face that he did. "Does it have something to do with Frank Coonan?"

"If it was that fool, I'd rat him out to you in a second and let Mickey take care of him." Danny remained quiet for a moment. His face constricted and his tone was serious when he spoke next. "No, it wasn't Frank. The whole Eddie thing has us all rattled. I put feelers out myself when it happened, figuring I was next. If it was a hit from one of us, the gossip mill would have been churning until we all knew the truth. Everyone was stumped. I have connections with some of the heads of the Italian families and no one took credit. That's the kind of thing they take credit for, you know?"

"Did people like Eddie?"

"He was ambitious. Once he got out of here, he didn't care about the local racket anymore. He went big time. If you're looking for someone, I'd search there. Russians, Chinese, or one of those cartels. It wasn't us. You give Mickey my word."

I exhaled. This wasn't getting me anywhere. "You told me all about Eddie's youth, but do you know much about Eddie's life in his last few years?"

Danny shrugged. "He wasn't around as much and when he was, he had changed."

"Changed, how?"

"He wasn't as affable. Eddie was this larger-than-life charismatic guy. The last time I saw him, maybe a year before he died, he had lost weight and seemed paranoid. One of my guys said maybe Eddie had turned rat and was all jumpy. You know what happens to rats in this business." Danny leaned back and by the look on his face, I knew our time had come to an end. There'd be no point pushing him harder.

I stood and brushed down the front of my pant legs, the clothes feeling foreign because they weren't my own. "I appreciate it, Danny. I'll let my father know you were very helpful."

Danny stood and came around his desk and wrapped me in a hug. He kissed each cheek. "You do that and tell him not to be a stranger around here. I have something special for him when I see him next."

I left Danny's office and walked back into the bar. The same guy was standing there in the same spot as when I had walked in. He glanced in my direction as I approached. "I didn't mean any disrespect earlier. You should have told me whose kid you were."

He thought he had disrespected the daughter of one of the most powerful international Irish mob bosses there was. An act of disrespect could have been a life sentence. I waved him off. "Don't worry about it. I'm sure you get lots of obnoxious college kids coming in here. Besides, I didn't tell you who I was. Don't sweat it."

"I appreciate it," he said and handed me my gun back.

"Where can I find Frank Coonan?"

The guy grimaced. "You don't want to talk to him."

"I have to and Mickey wasn't sure where Frank spends time these days." It was a risk because in all likelihood Frank was in the same place he always was. I just didn't know where that might be. The guy at the bar jotted down an address on a slip of paper and handed it to me. "You call me if Frank gives you an issue. I suspect knowing you're Mickey's daughter you'll be fine."

I smiled and nodded, leaving the bar without saying another word. It was only once the door closed behind me that I truly exhaled. Back in the 1970s after my father had joined the CIA and was a new fresh undercover officer, they had sent him to work on an organized crime taskforce with the FBI. Word on the street was a couple of the Irish and Italian families were getting into international drug smuggling and arms deals. The CIA had no authority and still doesn't to collect intelligence on U.S. citizens, but they needed the CIA cooperation to assess foreign connections overseas. Significant sums were also being funneled from America to Irish Republic Army operations in Northern Ireland. My father had been a natural choice. Not only did his size and stature command attention, but his thick Irish brogue and brooding Irish looks made him a natural. No one knew or suspected he had long since been an American citizen.

To pull it off though, my father had to create an entirely new identity, one he had perfected so well that the CIA kept him on the operation for his entire career. No one had ever suspected that Mickey Finnigan was CIA, and as a result, he was able to disrupt bombings planned by the IRA, take down international arms dealers across Europe, and prevent assassinations – all under the guise of running one of the largest criminal empires in Europe. I had no idea how he pulled it off, but it had garnered him the respect of the Irish mob across the United States. My father had become a boss's boss – head of a global crime family.

I did not know the ins and outs, and in truth, I shouldn't have even known my father's alias or any of the information I knew. My parents gave me the truth about his career when I graduated college. It started to make conversations I heard as a child make sense. I started putting two and two together.

I had heard my parents fighting about his work when I was young and had sneaked a look at the contents of boxes of documents my father kept in the attic before leaving us for good. Once I had even seen a passport in my parents' bedroom that had my father's photo and his alias. When I asked about it, I remember he had pulled me up on his lap and kissed me, and told me that sometimes parents played make-believe. I don't remember my response, but it was an exchange between us that never left my memory.

I didn't know then how powerful my father was in that other life, but as time went on, my mother told me more stories and it became clear. The names Danny Devaney and Frank Coonan had only been spoken a few times in my house when my father was around, and I knew never to mention them otherwise.

Chapter 27

I held my hands up to the glass and peered into the coffee shop window. Holden sat at a table drinking from an oversized mug and reading the newspaper like it was a leisurely Sunday morning. He appeared perfectly relaxed and comfortable amid the chattering college students. If he didn't have the car keys and it wasn't a ten-mile walk, I would have left him there and gone to Frank Coonan's place on my own.

With no phone, money, or ability to call a rideshare, I was at his mercy. There were three things I needed to do – find out how Eddie came by my father's real name, speak to Frank Coonan, and go through Eddie's financials.

I pushed open the door to the coffee shop and made my way over to Holden. I pulled out the chair and sat down. "You don't seem at all concerned I met with a mob boss," I said barely above a whisper.

Holden lowered the newspaper and raised his eyes to mine. "I thought we had already established you were fine on your own and better off without me."

"You could still worry."

He shook the newspaper and began folding it. "We have a strange relationship," he teased.

I hated that I was genuinely starting to like Holden. I hoped I wouldn't have to kill him later. "We need to go see Frank Coonan."

"I have no idea where to find him." Holden finished off the last of his coffee and offered to buy me something to eat or drink.

I declined the food and drink and slid the slip of paper to Holden that had Frank's address. "I found out while talking to Danny."

Holden picked up the paper and stood. "What else did you find out?"

"Not in here," I said standing with him.

He checked the address. "We'll need to drive to Frank's. It's too far to walk."

"Why do you think I didn't go without you?" I followed him out of the coffee shop to the sidewalk. I walked quickly to Holden's car because the last thing I needed was Danny or the guy behind the bar, whose name I never got, seeing me standing there with Eddie's brother.

Holden easily kept with my pace, never once questioning it. When we slid into the car, he turned to me and said, "Why would you ditch me? I figured I was growing on you." He turned the ignition and glanced in my direction. "Kidnapping aside, I'm not a bad guy."

"What's a little kidnapping between friends," I said lightly, making a joke of it even when I knew I shouldn't.

"We're friends?" he asked with a hopeful expression on his face.

"We're friends as long as you don't give me a reason to kill you." I turned and smiled at him as his eyes grew wide and he gulped. "Don't give me a reason and we'll be fine. Now, let's get to Frank Coonan's."

The tide certainly had shifted between us. I no longer felt like a kidnapped victim and assumed if I waited a few more hours, I could probably convince Holden to let me call Luke. By now, I assumed they were in Boston searching for me. Whether anyone had contacted Sully or not, I couldn't be sure. I didn't even know how to reach him directly to tell him that Eddie had blown his cover. It would have implications for him for sure. I had no idea about the inner workings of the CIA beyond what I saw in movies, but I knew enough to know a blown cover wasn't good.

A thought occurred to me at that moment that I tried unsuccessfully to shove aside. If Eddie had blown Sully's cover was that motive enough for my father or someone in the CIA to have killed him? Most CIA placements never last as long as my father's, but he had created an alternative life in such a way that the longevity of it was his ace. The man had staying power as the head of a global criminal empire. It put him in touch with all sorts of unsavory characters and international crime, and he funneled the information to any agency he wanted – CIA, NSA, FBI, MI-6, and beyond. Many government agencies relied on Sully's intel. The scope of suspects suddenly widened for me in a way that made me suck in a breath.

"Are you okay?" Holden asked, pulling over to the curb in front of the bar and grille where Frank was known to be.

I told him that I was fine even though I had rattled myself with thoughts of a government coverup. "Wait here," I said, opening the door. "I shouldn't be long."

A shot rang out as soon as my feet hit the cement. I ducked my head low not sure where it came from and pulled myself back in the car. I turned to Holden, who sat back frozen in his seat.

"Was that a gunshot?" he asked, looking forward out the windshield.

"Yes, but I…" I didn't get out the words because there was another one. This one hit the car in front of us. The shots were coming from across the street somewhere.

"We have to get out of here! Now!" I shoved the door open and kept low as I got out of the car. I moved to the side out of the doorway, keeping my head low. "Holden, now! Come out the passenger side door."

I inched down farther near the back tire and called Holden's name again as a third shot rang out. It hit closer than the others, but given my position, I had no idea where it hit. "Holden!" I yelled again and finally, his leg made an appearance coming out of the passenger door.

"What do we do?" Holden asked as he slumped low on the ground next to me.

Another shot ricocheted off the front of this car. We were pinned down as far as I could tell. There was a stretch of sidewalk in front of me from the car to the door to Frank's bar and I had no idea if it was open. The shots were coming from across the street and right now we were at least blocked by the car. My initial thought was that staying where we were and waiting it out would be the safest option, but a volley of shots blasted again. This time, a shot shattered one of the driver's side windows on Holden's car. The glass shattered and fell to the ground.

I reached out and grabbed Holden's hand. "Let's go! Now!" I pulled him as I bent forward and hustled toward the door of Frank's. Holden and I slammed through the door and threw ourselves on the floor, both of us out of breath more from fear than exertion.

"Are you okay?" I asked looking over at him. His face was ashen and his eyes were closed. "Holden," I said, nudging his side. "Are you hurt?"

"I'm fine," he said finally, his voice giving away how shaken he was. Gone was the tough exterior he had shown me the first time I saw him standing outside of the van and flashing a gun at me. It was clear now more than ever Holden was completely in over his head. That applied to both of us as soon as I put my hands flat on the dirty tile floor and went to push myself upright. As soon as I raised my head and focused my eyes forward, I realized we weren't alone.

Still on the floor, I counted five pairs of boots in front of me. Scanning up, five angry rough-looking men had guns pointed at us. The man standing farthest left in the row let out a string of curses.

"Who are you and what do you think you're doing in here?" he demanded. "Who is shooting out there?"

I got myself to a standing position as quickly as I could with my hands up in front of me and Holden did the same. I had no idea what Frank Coonan looked like so I wasn't sure if he was standing in front of me. "I'm looking for Frank Coonan." I turned and looked at the door behind me and back to them. "As per your other question, I have no idea who is shooting."

The man looked to be about my father's age. He had a head full of grayish-white hair and brown eyes. He wasn't much taller than I was and looked like he still lifted weights each day. He was the only one to lower his weapon as he advanced on me.

He got right in my face. "You barge in here in a hail of gunfire the least you could do is introduce yourself."

"Are you Frank?" I said, extending my hand. I put it back down when I realized he wasn't going to offer me his. "I'm Riley. I believe you know my father."

"I'm Frank. I don't know who your father is," he said. Then something in my eyes must have looked familiar because he took a step back and looked me up and down. He zeroed in on my face and recognition came over his. He told his men to let us be and the crowd dispersed.

"I didn't know he had a daughter. How is Mickey?" Frank said, walking over to a table. He motioned for us to follow.

At the mention of Mickey's name, I caught the look of confusion on Holden's face. I hoped he wouldn't say anything about Patrick Sullivan.

"Mickey is good. He's the reason I'm here, Frank," I said, sitting down. I gestured toward Holden who sat next to me. "This is Eddie Stone's brother Holden. We are looking into Eddie's murder."

Frank glanced over at Holden and then back to me "We'll get to that, but right now, we need to figure out why people are shooting at you before they start back up again. If they shoot up my bar, there's going to be blood in the street."

Chapter 28

L uke couldn't calm down. He paced back and forth in the hotel room, sat down, and then got back up again to pace. He couldn't sit still with the rage that ran through his veins. Det. Nixon had been useless. He provided no help and insisted it must all be a misunderstanding. Luke had asked to speak to another detective but had been told the same. Luke had no proof that Riley had been kidnapped. They wouldn't even bother to call Liv and listen to what she had to say.

Sully had attacked Cooper and left him in an alleyway. No one had eyes on him, which meant he could be working with them to find Riley or at cross-purposes. Luke didn't trust the man to keep Riley safe. They had been in Boston for several hours and had made absolutely no progress.

Cooper had met them back at the hotel and the three of them had been attempting to make a plan over the last hour. It wasn't much of a plan though. "At least you know Riley is safe, Luke," Cooper had said.

"Safe!" Luke stopped pacing long enough to turn and shout at Cooper. He pointed toward the window. "She is out there being forced to investigate a murder alone with a man who kidnapped her."

"I get it, Luke, but Det. Nixon said Riley seemed fine. Maybe we should have some faith that she knows what she's doing," Cooper said and then shared a look with Jack.

"Is that what you think, too, Jack? That Riley is fine?" Luke barked.

Jack, who had been sitting back on the chair with his arms folded across his chest, relaxed his posture. "Luke, I understand your frustration with the Boston Police Department. I was frustrated, too. Cooper is right though that we should be grateful that we know Det. Nixon had eyes on Riley and that she appeared fine. By all accounts, she hasn't been injured and was in good enough spirits. Good enough even to be asking questions about Eddie Stone's murder. They were sitting in a coffee shop. She could have screamed, yelled, or done anything to escape him at that point. I think all Cooper is trying to say is let's focus on the positive. Det. Nixon doesn't seem to think Holden is dangerous. He had eyes on her not too long ago so we know she's at least here in the city."

Luke blew out a breath. They were right. He knew for sure now that Riley was in Boston and they even had an area of the city where they had met with Det. Nixon, which wasn't that far from the hotel. It was more information than they had that morning.

"What do we do now?" Luke asked, running a hand over his bald head.

Jack shifted in the chair and looked across the table at Cooper. "Did Sully give you any indication where he was going or what he was doing?"

Cooper shook his head. "Sully left the hotel with me and said he had to meet a guy. He tried to ditch me once here at the hotel and then he did at that bar. I don't know if he was looking for someone or if he made that up. Whatever he was doing, he didn't want me with him."

"I don't think we will be able to track Sully so let's assume he's going to do his own thing to find Riley," Jack said. "Meanwhile, let's start taking the steps Riley might take while investigating. Maybe our paths will cross."

Luke pulled the slip of paper that had Holden's number out of his pocket. "Should we try to call him first?"

"I don't think so, Luke." Jack stood and grabbed his phone and wallet off the table. "Let's see if we can track them down by retracing their steps first. If we call now, we alert him that we are here and that might spook him. Det. Nixon said they are looking into Eddie's murder so let's do the same. Eventually, that should lead us to Riley."

"Where do we start?" Cooper asked.

"Let's start with some research. Find out where the murder happened and we'll start at the scene."

Luke walked over to the desk and pulled out the chair. He slumped down in the seat and straightened the laptop in front of him. He avoided looking at his reflection in the mirror because he wasn't ready to face everything that had transpired since the night of his wedding. Staring at himself would make him face a reality he wasn't ready for. He tipped his head down and focused on the laptop. He typed in Eddie Stone's name and pulled several news articles about the murder. Luke scanned them one by one until he was able to piece together a coherent story. He pulled the hotel pad of paper closer and grabbed the pen. He jotted down dates, times, and people's names.

It was the first time Luke felt productive. At first, Jack's idea didn't make much sense to Luke. Up until that point, their entire focus had been on trying to find Riley. That proved to be impossible. This was the next best thing.

With information to go on, Luke clicked off the internet and closed the laptop. "I have information," he said as he stood. "Let's start with the restaurant where the murder happened. It's walking distance from here." Luke checked his phone and pulled up specific walking directions. "It's not even a mile down the road." Together the three of them set out.

Mancuso Italian Restaurant was an upscale restaurant situated in the heart of Boston's financial district. Luke glanced at the menu that hung in a side window as Cooper and Jack assessed the area around. It was the kind of place that Luke would consider going for an anniversary dinner but not a place he'd frequent otherwise. He wasn't living that large. His detective salary was good for the lifestyle he and Riley wanted.

"It happened right here outside of the front door," Luke said, walking over to the door and looking around at the sidewalk.

"Were they coming or going from the place?" Jack asked.

"Leaving," Luke explained. "According to the news report I read, Eddie and his girlfriend had just had dinner and were on their way out. His girlfriend was a few steps ahead of him. Eddie was a few feet from the door when a black SUV pulled up and gunned him down. He died right here."

Cooper glanced around the area then back at the restaurant door. "Who tipped off the killer?"

"What do you mean?" Luke asked.

Cooper pointed to the road in front of the restaurant and then to the roads that ran parallel left and right. "There's nowhere to park and wait. I would assume a place like this has a valet at night so someone had to tip off the killer that Eddie was done with dinner and on the way out."

Luke hadn't thought of that. Seeing the scene now, Cooper was accurate. He also hadn't read that anyone else had been a witness. Det. Nixon also said as much. "I wonder where they keep the valet stand. I'm guessing that it's not in front of the door here. Otherwise, someone else might have been shot."

"Only one way to find out," Jack said, pulling open the door to the restaurant.

The place was quiet. There wasn't even a hostess waiting for them. A bar and waiting area sat off to the left and they made their way over. The bartender looked up as they entered.

"We only have about thirty minutes until we stop serving lunch and then we close down until five," the guy said, handing them menus.

"We appreciate that," Jack started, taking a seat on one of the round bar stools. "We aren't here for lunch though. I'm looking for some information about a murder that happened here near Christmas almost two years ago now."

"Eddie Stone," the bartender said.

"You working here then?"

"I was that very night. I don't know what happened though." The bartender leaned back and relaxed his posture. "I've been questioned by the police already. Who are you?"

Luke explained their connection to the case and pulled up Riley's photo on his phone. "Has she been in today to ask any questions about the murder?"

The bartender shook his head. "No one has been in here asking about Eddie Stone in a long time. What can I help you with?"

Cooper pointed toward the front door. "Where is the valet stand at night?"

"The side street to the north. We leave the front clear because so many people walk to the restaurant. We don't want them to have to dodge cars and valets as they enter."

"What time did Eddie Stone leave that night?" Luke asked, sitting next to Jack.

"I only know from news reports that he was shot close to ten that night. We are usually fairly cleared out by then, except for a few people finishing up a late dinner or lingering over drinks. From what I've read, Eddie was shot as soon as he left so I'd say just before ten that night."

"Any disturbances while he was here?" Jack asked.

"None. All was quiet as far as I can remember. This isn't the kind of restaurant that's rowdy or loud so something like that would stick in

163

my memory. There were only a few waitstaff left at that hour, too."

Everything the bartender said matched up to the news reports Luke had read. "Any talk amongst the staff about what people knew about Eddie's murder?"

The bartender seemed to think for a moment before answering. "It's going back some time so it's hard to remember what I knew before the murder and what I'm now remembering from reading about it. I don't think anyone here knew much about Eddie before that night. At least, I didn't and the people I spoke to who were working here didn't. What they wrote in the paper about him certainly wasn't common knowledge before the murder, at least as far as I knew."

Jack tapped on the bar. "How's the staff turnover here?"

"We are fairly steady. The owners are great, tips even better. People tend to stay. I've been here close to eight years and most of the waitstaff and kitchen staff as well. If you're thinking someone on the inside was involved, I'd say that's impossible. All the same staff are still here today. All good people."

Jack exhaled. "What about new people? Do you remember if anyone was recently hired before Eddie was killed and then left shortly after?"

He didn't respond for a few moments. Then he snapped his fingers. "You know, now that you mention it, yeah, there was." The bartender stood upright. "There was a guy working as a waiter who started work right before the murder and then I never saw him again after that night."

"No one thought it was odd?" Luke asked.

The bartender shook his head. "People didn't talk that much about it because they were so focused on what had happened with the murder. That's all anyone talked about for months." He shrugged. "Most people chalked up the guy leaving to the language barrier. They figured he was having a hard time not understanding English."

"I don't understand," Luke said. "What language did he speak?"

"German. The guy had just moved here from Germany or was on a work visa or something. I don't think I ever got the story. The guy fell under the radar because everyone was jacked up about the murder. He had only worked one shift before the murder and that night was his last. Now that I think about it, no one remembered hiring him either."

Chapter 29

Frank's men had left the bar armed to the teeth in search of the shooter. Holden sat at the table with his eyes pinned on me in a question that I couldn't answer. I didn't know what I was going to tell him. It was bad enough that Eddie had blown Sully's cover. I didn't want to be responsible for connecting those dots for anyone else. I'd have to think of something and keep my fingers crossed that Holden didn't say a word.

About thirty minutes after Frank's men left, they came back with a handful of shell casings. One of them handed the casings to Frank. "Whoever it was had a high-powered rifle. He shot from the top floor across the street. I don't think he was trying to kill anyone, just scare them."

"How do you know that?" I asked.

The guy turned to me. "Rifle like that – if he wanted to kill you, you'd be dead on the sidewalk out there or in the car as you pulled up. I don't know what you're doing, but someone doesn't want you doing it."

Frank left us alone at the table and walked to the back of the place with the other men. When he was gone, I focused on Holden. "Any chance that it's Eddie's guys?"

Holden shook his head. "They aren't that sophisticated. They will try to kill us eventually, but we should see them coming from a mile away."

I had figured as much if the rest of them were like Collins. "Then someone else is trying to scare us. Got any ideas?"

Holden smirked. "Mickey?"

"Not now," I mouthed. "Just follow along."

Before Holden confirmed that he would, Frank came over and sat down with us. "I got a few minutes to listen out of respect for your father."

"I'm looking for everything you know about Eddie Stone's murder."

Frank raised his eyes to Holden. "Why do you need me to tell you if his brother is right here?"

"I wasn't around my brother much," Holden said, his voice cracking. "We led different lives and our worlds rarely crossed. I don't know much more than I've read in the newspapers. This is the first time I'm back here in Boston looking into it. The cops haven't made much headway."

Frank smiled at him. "I know who you are, Holden. The next tech super genius, running a billion-dollar company. You are more like your brother than you know. You have the same drive and determination and head for business – you just chose to do something legit with your skills."

Holden didn't argue with Frank. He seemed quietly pleased to be compared to his brother in that way. It still didn't tell me what I needed though.

"Do you know anything, Frank? There have been some rumors swirling that Mickey is responsible for Eddie's death and that won't stand with my father." I gave him the same look I'd seen Sully make when he was dead serious about something.

Frank knew more. I could tell by his expression. He was debating whether or not to share it with me. I pressed him again about it and he stood and indicated for us to follow him. He guided us through a maze of tables and into an office space, much like the one in which I had met Danny Devaney. He closed and locked the door behind us.

Frank walked close and appraised us again. "I shouldn't be telling you this," he said looking me right in the eyes. When I didn't even blink, he made a flicking gesture with his hand like swatting away a bug. "I guess no harm can come from it now."

Frank sat down and gestured for us to do the same. "I'm going to give it to you straight. Eddie came to me probably six or seven years ago and told me that he'd been approached by someone high up in government who asked him to spy. He said the man would pay him for information. Given how close Eddie was to everything, he was given immunity for his crimes if he'd help to rat people out."

"My brother was an FBI informant?" Holden asked, disbelief evident in his voice.

"No, you're not understanding. Your brother was a spy. I don't know what agency contacted him or even if it was from here in the United States – CIA or NSA, who knows. It could have been an agency from the United Kingdom. Your brother was based in London after all."

A picture I didn't like was starting to come into focus. If it was Sully who had convinced Eddie to become an asset for him, it still didn't explain how Eddie had learned Sully's real name. Even in the spy game, Sully would have kept with his alias Mickey Finnigan. There's no way Sully would knowingly give anyone his real identity. "Did Eddie say who approached him?" I asked hesitantly not sure I wanted to know.

Frank shook his head. "Eddie never said and I never asked. When Eddie was killed though that was the first thing that came to mind."

There were so many things I didn't understand, I wasn't sure where to start with questions. Before I could say anything, Holden asked the obvious.

"Why would my brother come to you with information like this? I thought you were rivals. Why would he trust you?"

"It's not like it was in the old days," Frank said, leaning back in his chair and crossing his arms over his chest. "When your brother was working his way up in the neighborhood, I saw something special in him. A lot of us did. I tried talking him out of his life, but Eddie was dead set on it. He saw potential. He saw easy ways to make money that wouldn't require fancy boy education, as he called it. He was better than this life and I tried to tell him that."

"You couldn't talk him out of it though," Holden said sadly. "No one could. My father and I did everything we could to convince Eddie to turn away from the path he was on. Eddie would have been successful in any line of work he chose."

"That's right," Frank said. "Eddie was cunning and smart. After he got out of Boston and was growing his empire, he came to me and asked me to look in on his old crew from the neighborhood. He wanted them to join me. They refused, of course, but they were never competition for me so I did what Eddie asked."

I didn't understand why Frank would care. "Why were you willing to help Eddie?"

"He was a good kid but was after a kind of power I wasn't interested in. I'm happy here in the neighborhood. Eddie aimed for something bigger, and someone bigger than him thought they could use that drive for power for their benefit. I cautioned him about becoming a rat. I think at that point, Eddie saw other potential. He could run his criminal empire, be immune to prosecution and have the power of knowing a government owed him." Frank furrowed his brow. "He was naïve. We all know that's not the way it works. Once you turn spy, there's no going back to the life you had before."

Holden frowned. "Eddie threw his life away."

"Don't look at it like that, Holden. Your brother was brave to do what he did."

I was surprised to hear Frank say anything about someone becoming a government asset. "I thought ratting someone out was the deadliest sin of all in your world. You act like what Eddie did was noble. My father wouldn't take too kindly to rats."

"No, your father wouldn't." Frank remained silent for a moment and then leaned forward on the desk and looked at each of us. "That might be why Mickey is suspected in Eddie's murder, but I don't think it was him. I've never even heard that rumor about Mickey."

"Who do you think it was?"

"Take your pick," Frank said dramatically. "You've got the Chinese, Russians, French, or any host of multinational criminal networks." He looked directly at me. "You're right, we don't take too well to rats here. It's bigger than this though. This is about protecting countries and the fabric of governments. These guys Eddie was going up against are human traffickers, international drug smugglers, art thieves, arms dealers. They commit the kind of crimes that can take down entire countries. End of the day, we are all Americans. As far as I'm concerned, if it's what got Eddie killed, he died a hero."

Holden glanced over at me and I saw for the first time a hint of admiration for his brother. He turned back to Frank. "How do we find out more and confirm that's what Eddie was doing?"

"You don't. I don't know who Eddie was spying for. After we had that first conversation about it when Eddie asked me what I thought he should do, he told me later he agreed to do it. On his last trip home, he came here and told me it was harder than he ever thought it would be, but that it was more rewarding than anything he'd ever done."

Holden sat back, shifted his eyes between Frank and me. "Why wouldn't Eddie have told me?"

"He probably wasn't supposed to tell anyone," I said. "I'm sure a condition of doing this work was to keep it a secret."

"From me?" Holden asked. "I was Eddie's family. He told you,

Frank."

"Would you have believed him?" Frank asked. Holden didn't say anything. Frank pointed a finger at him. "Eddie loved you, but he knew you didn't approve of his life and his choices."

"It's true. I didn't. Eddie and I hadn't spoken much over the last few years."

"Eddie told me that if the time ever came, I should tell you what he was doing. Eddie wanted you to be proud of him. This was Eddie's redemption or at least a shot at it."

"Do you know anything, Frank, about what kind of information Eddie provided or who it might have incriminated?" Knowing this information now, it opened up our suspect pool to a list that was no longer manageable. I had no idea how to investigate something international on this scale – certainly not alone anyway.

"Eddie didn't tell me anything. I'm not even sure that's what got him killed. If I were looking into this though, that's where I'd start."

Holden's face registered the overwhelming feeling I had in my gut. I took a deep breath and tried to organize my thoughts. "I know from my father that the Irish are still active in Boston. What about the Italian mafia? Are there others?"

Over the next hour, Frank filled us in on all of the criminal gangs operating not only in Boston but in cities across the country, many of them connected to multinational criminal networks. I shouldn't have been surprised, but I was. It was like the United Nations of criminals – every nationality represented. I had no idea the underground current of criminal activity that pulsed through cities – all connected back to networks much larger.

Holden thanked Frank for the information and we got up to leave. I had forgotten about the person shooting at us as we had pulled up to Frank's place. Before we left, I asked, "Do you think the person shooting was trying to stop us from uncovering the truth about

Eddie?"

"I wouldn't put it past them." Frank went to the door of his office and opened it. "Is it just you two looking into Eddie's murder?"

"Just us," I said for the first time feeling out of my depth.

"You want some protection with you? I can send a few of my guys."

I thanked him but declined the offer, which seemed ridiculous to him. There was no way that I'd be able to speak freely about Sully in front of Frank's men. I was going to have a hard enough time explaining to Holden once we got out of there.

Chapter 30

Frank's men escorted us to the car and made sure we left without incident. I was a little surprised that the Boston Police Department hadn't shown up given the number of shots that had rung out earlier. I guess maybe they expected as much around Frank's place and no one called the cops. I knew he wouldn't.

Holden's driver's side window had been blown out and with the cold Boston air, it made for a chilly ride. As he pulled away from the curb, he turned to me. "What now?"

"Let's go back to your house and regroup. We can talk about all we know right now and piece together what makes sense and what doesn't. I feel a bit overwhelmed."

Holden made a right at the corner and we drove in silence for about ten minutes before he glanced across the console at me. "I want to ask why Frank called your father Mickey Finnigan. I just don't know if it's something you'll tell me or not."

I had been thinking of a way to lie. Instead, I dodged the question for now. "You told me earlier that you got the name Patrick Sullivan from Eddie's guy. Where did they get it from?"

"It was in one of Eddie's files. It looked like he was collecting information on him."

"Did it say anything about Patrick Sullivan being a criminal?"

"I don't know."

"What do you mean you don't know? Either you know or you don't. You were willing to kidnap me and kill my father and you're not even sure if he killed your brother."

Holden looked straight ahead and stopped at a light. "I meant that there was information about criminal activity on the page and financial information. Patrick's name also appeared there. Eddie had noted questions about wanting to find more about this person and there was an indication that he might be a threat. There was nothing directly tying Patrick to crimes. It was mostly biographical data – names, address in Troy, New York, and his daughters' names."

It didn't seem like they had connected Sully at all with Mickey Finnigan. "Did your files have the name Mickey Finnigan?"

"I don't know. I didn't go through all of them as I said. Who is he, Riley?"

I had no option but to give him a mix of half-truths. "Mickey Finnigan is my father, but it's an alias. After my parents were married and I was born, my father descended into his life of crime, much like your brother. My parents divorced and the only thing my mother asked of him was that he change his name so we were protected. I've been curious how Eddie uncovered his real identity."

"I don't know," Holden said, but there was more on his mind. "Why did you tell Frank that the rumors were about Mickey and not Patrick Sullivan? Why even bring up Mickey's name?" Before I could respond, Holden asked another question. "Aren't you afraid they might connect the two?"

"I thought of all of that. If they heard the name Patrick Sullivan, they weren't going to connect it to Mickey. You hadn't. I also couldn't go in there and ask about Patrick Sullivan because I look exactly like the man they know as Mickey. I had to gamble and I think I played it right."

Holden seemed to have bought it. He only asked one question.

"Were you ever going to tell me all that?"

"Probably not," I said and watched Holden's face fall. "I know you think we are in this together and that I should trust you by now. It's going to take longer, and I may never get there."

When we arrived at Holden's house, he parked and leaned his head back. "Do you think we are ever going to find who killed my brother or is this all pointless?"

"I can't promise you that we'll find the killer. Even Det. Nixon hasn't been able to make much progress. I think we are further along right now than we were this morning. Eddie's girlfriend said he was into something we didn't want to know about. Frank told us Eddie was acting as an informant. I'm guessing that was for the CIA. Either way, it sounds like Eddie was trying to do the right thing."

"This seems overwhelming." He turned to face me. "I'm out of my depth. I'm not an investigator. Put me in front of technology and I can handle it, no matter what it is. This is something different."

I knew what we needed. I broached the subject gently. "I know that you want to do this on your own, but there's a point in every investigation where outside resources are needed. I think we've reached that point. If we want this solved, we need to tap into expertise we have on hand."

Holden's face contorted in a question. "What resources are those?"

I held my breath and hoped he'd at least consider it. "My husband is a homicide detective. My mother's boyfriend is a retired homicide detective with more than thirty years of experience and my investigative partner used to be a homicide detective. I know they are here in Boston looking for me because Liv didn't just go back and tell Sully, she told all of them."

"Is Sully with them?"

"I have no idea where Sully is," I said honestly. "Holden, I wasn't lying when I told you that I don't have much contact with my father.

Your relationship with your brother parallels my relationship with my father. I don't know where he is or what he's doing."

Holden sat up straighter in his seat. "Do you think given the fact that Eddie might have been working for the CIA that he might have ratted out your father and he killed him for it?"

Holden was still operating under the misconception that my father was a criminal and I couldn't change that perspective. That said, when I heard that Eddie was working as an informant and given he had found out my father's real identity that certainly made me think that Sully could have killed him to protect his identity. CIA officers weren't supposed to do such things, but I was sure it happened more than we knew.

"I don't know, Holden. If I were looking at this objectively, I think we have to keep Sully on the suspect list. I don't think the way your brother was murdered though is Sully's style. I think he could just as easily have killed him in the United Kingdom or lured him someplace else. Sully wouldn't have risked coming back here to do it."

"Fair enough," Holden said and opened the car door. He hadn't said whether or not he wanted the help of Luke, Cooper, and Jack. I didn't push it and followed him out of the car and into his house.

Once we got inside, Holden went to the kitchen and started pulling things out of the fridge. He threw lettuce and a tomato and some turkey on the counter and then reached for the bread. He looked at me standing there at the threshold of the kitchen. "Let's eat first before we do anything. Tell me more about your husband. Will he kill me on sight?"

Luke would probably try to kill him on sight, but there was no way I was telling Holden that. "You have to expect that he's going to be angry. Jack and Cooper will be with him so they can calm him down."

Holden made two sandwiches and pulled a bag of chips from the cabinet. He poured us both some soda and handed me a plate and glass.

He motioned with his head toward the table. As he sat down, he said, "I think it might be better if I turned myself in and took responsibility for this. You can go back to your family and call it a day."

"Holden, I already thought about that. Eddie's guys know where to find me and my sister. I can't leave her and my mother in New York and go back home without this settled. If you go to prison, they will kill you." I took a sip of my drink. "We are in too far now. We have to see it through."

Holden took another bite of his sandwich and washed it down with his drink. He was about to say something when his phone chimed. Holden got up and went to the counter where he had left it. He looked at the screen and his face paled. "Go ahead and call your people. Noah Byrne is back in Boston and knows I took you. He said that when he gets his hands on us, he's going to kill us both."

"Is Noah the guy in Lake Placid who took my sister and hit me?"

"Yeah, he's the one who started all of this." Holden came over and sat back down at the table. "Noah was the one who found Patrick Sullivan's name and believes that's who killed Eddie. He's a bit of a hothead and drove the plan for the kidnapping."

"How did he get some of Eddie's things?"

"He went to Melissa's before I could get back to Boston. She said that he barged in one day and took some of Eddie's files."

"Holden, you seem like a rational guy. I still don't understand how you got so swept up in this."

"Noah pushed hard. They needed money to finance this and they knew I had it. Guilt can be a powerful tool."

Given Noah had lured me from my hotel room and whacked me in the back of the head, I knew he had no problem with violence. "To your knowledge, has Noah ever killed anyone?"

Holden stared down at his plate. "He said he has and Collins confirmed it. I don't know who or when though."

"Collins seemed easily pushed around even by you. I'm guessing Noah isn't like that at all." Holden confirmed that. The vibe I picked up from him told me more than his words. "Are you afraid of Noah?"

Holden raised his head and let his eyes meet mine. "I don't know anyone who is not afraid of Noah. Even Eddie used to say that Noah was unpredictable and could fly off in a rage. He holds a grudge and has been known to fight a man for looking at him the wrong way. I wanted to go to Lake Placid and handle this myself, but Noah wouldn't allow it. He said he'd take care of it and there was no arguing with him."

I put my hand on top of Holden's. "Let me call Luke. We will be a lot safer with him, Jack and Cooper around."

Holden nodded once and slid his phone to me.

Chapter 31

Luke, Jack, and Cooper waited until the restaurant manager was able to meet with them. They had explained the situation and wanted to see any information they might have on this German waiter who had only worked two days. The manager had been reluctant and explained a similar story as the bartender – that no one remembered formally hiring him.

Luke wanted the manager to check the employment files around that time to make sure. He had even offered to call Det. Nixon if that would make them more comfortable, but the manager balked at that. Instead, he allowed Luke back in the office with him to look for the information. He explained to Luke that the Boston police presence after the murder had slowed sales and he didn't want that again.

It turned out that the bartender had been right. There were no files on the waiter. He hadn't been officially hired and so no records of him existed. The manager had no explanation for how that happened. The guy showed up in a uniform to a shift and everyone assumed someone else had hired him. The waiter said enough right things that no one questioned it and he was on the schedule. He was gone from the restaurant as quickly as he had arrived.

Luke explained what he had found out to Jack and Cooper as they walked out of the restaurant. "This guy could be anywhere. He could be living here in Boston or long gone. We don't even have a name to go on."

"Eddie Stone had a girlfriend, right?" Cooper asked.

"Yeah," Luke said and checked his phone for a note he had written earlier while speaking to Det. Nixon. "Melissa Patton. I have an address but no phone number."

"Maybe she will know more." Cooper asked for the address and plugged it into his GPS. "We are going to need to drive. It's several miles away."

The three of them started to walk back to the hotel when Luke's phone rang. He checked the screen and the number was similar to Holden's work. "Let me get this. It might be Holden's office with more information."

"Det. Morgan," Luke said and was met with silence. When he heard the person on the other end, he reached out toward the wall of the building for support. Emotion overcame him and tears streamed down his face. He didn't even care that he was crying in public. He was so happy to hear Riley's voice.

"I'm okay, Luke," she reassured. "I need you to remain calm and level-headed. Can you promise me that?"

Luke wasn't going to make any promise he couldn't keep. "Where are you?" he demanded, motioning with his hand for Jack and Cooper. He told them it was Riley. Their excitement matched his own.

"I'm with Holden and we need your help."

"Help? Are you insane? Riley, when I get my hands on him, I'm going to rip him to shreds."

"Luke, that's not staying calm. I'll tell you everything. You have to promise not to call the police and not to hurt Holden when you get here."

"I can't promise that," Luke said angrily. He was sure now Riley had lost her mind. It was clear from her tone that she was okay and in control of herself.

"You have to promise or I'm not going to tell you where to find me."

Luke groaned and wanted to scream at her. Even kidnapped, Riley could be impossible. "I want you back safe. Are you safe? That's the only thing I care about right now."

"I'm safe from Holden, yes." Riley didn't say more.

"What aren't you telling me?" Luke knew there was something.

"I'll tell you when you get here."

Luke cursed. "Tell me now. If you want me calm, you're going to have to give me time to calm down before I get there. I can't even promise you that I will."

Riley let out an exasperated sigh, but Luke didn't care. She was expecting too much from him and he told her as much. "I've been out of my mind worried about you. Liv came back and told me that you were helping Holden investigate his brother's murder. I've been dying inside with worry, Riley."

"I know, Luke," Riley said, her tone softer. "I'm doing the best I can. I met with two Irish mob bosses today and when we pulled up to one, someone took a shot at us, several shots. We made it to safety though." Riley remained quiet for a moment and then she asked, "Is Sully with you?"

"No, your father attacked Cooper and took off," he snapped. "We have no idea where he is."

"He was with you?" Riley asked.

It hadn't occurred to Luke that Riley had no idea that her father was at the wedding or involved in any of this. He felt bad now for losing his temper with her. "This would be much easier if we could sit down and talk. Please, Riley, tell me where you are."

Riley gave him the address and how to get there. "Listen, Luke, I'm serious about no cops. This is delicate and both Holden and I are in danger. You, Jack, and Cooper have to come alone and make sure you haven't been followed. There is a lot we need to discuss."

Luke promised that much and hung up. He started to walk toward the hotel faster than before and Jack and Cooper followed. "Riley insists that we come alone. She said she is in danger and not from Holden." Luke explained about them being shot at. "I don't know what's going on or what she's gotten herself into, but we are getting her out of it."

"Be patient with her, Luke," Jack cautioned, picking up his pace to keep up with Luke. "You have no idea what Riley has been through since she was taken. Don't go off half-cocked thinking this is her fault. She's doing the best she can under difficult circumstances."

"That's exactly what she told me," Luke said and expelled a breath. He probably was too hard on her. He went from elated that Riley was safe to angry that she seemed to be doing fine without him. Luke had to remind himself that she hadn't taken off from the wedding by her own doing. The fact that Riley now seemed chummy with her captor and worried that Luke could hurt him galled him to no end.

Cooper slapped him on the back. "Who are you angry with?"

"I don't know," Luke said. "I felt like Riley was defending Holden. She was worried about me hurting him."

"You hurting this guy won't solve anything, Luke." Cooper opened the door to the hotel and Luke and Jack walked through. "Cut her some slack. She has a strange relationship with her father and she was kidnapped the morning after her wedding. No one would be in their right mind."

Luke didn't say anything as they navigated up to their room and he grabbed his laptop and phone charger. He looked around to see if they'd need anything else and when he was satisfied, they left again. The directions Riley had provided were close to the hotel – close enough to walk. Luke felt foolish that Riley had been so close in distance and he still hadn't found her.

On the walk over, Cooper and Jack tried to talk some sense into

182

him but he wasn't hearing any of it. Luke tried to clear his head and get in the right frame of mind. He had to fight his ego that he couldn't even protect his wife, anger that she hadn't told him about her father, and a general sense of unease that this was how they were starting married life.

Luke felt like a big ball of confused emotions and he was afraid of losing it. Cooper and Jack knew his temper could get the better of him and they were trying to talk him down. As much as Luke tried to do the same, as soon as he saw the black door and brick house at the address Riley had given him, his simmering boiled over.

"Hold this for me," Luke said, shoving his laptop bag to Cooper who grasped the strap in enough time before it hit the ground. Luke pounded his fist against the door.

As the door creaked open and a man who Luke assumed was Holden came into view, Luke launched himself through the doorway and punched him right in the face. Luke hit him again as Holden slumped in the foyer. He held his hands up in defense as blood spurted from his nose.

"I deserve it," Holden said, holding back the blood with his hands. "Hit me some more if you feel like it. I deserve whatever I get."

Luke reached down and grabbed Holden by the front of the shirt and jerked the man to his feet. He pulled his fist back to strike him again but stopped short when he saw Riley out of the corner of his eye.

"This is exactly what I told you not to do," she said, standing there with her hands on her hips in clothes that weren't her own.

The paleness of her face and subdued demeanor brought Luke back to reality. He let Holden go, dropping the man back to the floor, and grabbed Riley by the waist. He wrapped his arms around her and buried his face into her neck. He held back the tears as best he could. Luke wasn't prepared for her release of emotion as she sunk into him, crying harder than he had ever seen.

"It's okay, you're safe," he whispered to her. "You're okay. We're here now. Nothing is going to happen to you." Luke didn't know how long they stood there and held each other, but when he turned his head toward the doorway, Jack and Cooper were gone and so was Holden.

Luke released Riley and looked into her eyes. "We're alone," he said softly. "Tell me the truth. Are you okay?"

Riley swallowed hard and wiped the tears from her eyes. "I'm fine. I've been holding it all in trying not to seem afraid. I lost it when I saw your face."

Luke held her hands and stood back farther, assessing her. "Did he hurt you?"

"No, I'm okay," she reassured him. "Holden hasn't done anything to me. He was so good to me I forgot at times that he had kidnapped me. We have to talk about that though. I think Holden is in as much danger as I am. I don't think any of this was his idea."

"He had no plans of resuming his old life, Riley. I called his office and he sold his company, cleaned out his house, and took off."

"That's what I'm saying, Luke. He knew he wasn't going back to his old life. He told me at one point to call the police and he'd turn himself in. He's in danger and so is Sully. We have to see this through."

Luke didn't agree, but he also couldn't fight her. He leaned in, pulled Riley in his arms again, and let his lips meet hers.

Chapter 32

I was a little embarrassed that I had become so emotional when I saw Luke coming through the door. I knew there was no way he would remain calm. At least he hadn't hurt Holden too badly. I had been grateful that Cooper and Jack had taken Holden for a walk to give Luke and me some time to ourselves. They had been gone for about forty minutes and when they returned, the blood had been cleaned off Holden's face and bruises had started to form.

Luke and I were sitting in Holden's living room when the three of them arrived. Holden had gone upstairs to clean himself up. Jack had wrapped me in a hug and called my mother. I spoke with her briefly reassuring her that I was fine. Cooper seemed like he wasn't sure what to say, but I hugged him and thanked him for being there. Tears had formed in the corners of his eyes and he quickly wiped them away. He wasn't an emotional guy, but we had been through a lot together over the years.

With the four of us in the living room and Holden upstairs, Jack asked me what was going on. I wasn't sure where to start. I didn't know how much they knew about Sully, but this wasn't the time to hold back. "I'm sure you know by now Sully is a CIA officer. He's spent his whole career undercover."

"We know that much," Jack said. "What does this have to do with him? Did he kill Eddie Stone?"

"I don't know." I turned to Luke and reached for his hand. "There were so many times I wanted to tell you the truth. I knew I couldn't though. I hope you can forgive me."

"We can deal with that later," he said. "Tell me what you've found out so far."

I kept my voice low in case Holden returned. "Holden doesn't know my father is CIA. He believes Sully's cover - that he operates a global criminal network. That said, Eddie Stone somehow found out Sully's real name."

"What do you mean?" Cooper asked, sitting across from me in a leather armchair.

"Sully didn't go by his real name when he was undercover. He goes by Mickey Finnigan. That's how Eddie would have known him. Somehow, he got ahold of Sully's real identity. Eddie's guys have the name Patrick Sullivan, but I'm not sure if they have connected it to Mickey Finnigan. That's a dangerous unknown at this point. I don't know how much of Sully's cover has been blown."

Jack let out a soft curse, realizing the gravity of the situation. "I knew Sully would have used an alias, but it never occurred to me his cover might have been blown."

"That's not all. I learned from Frank Coonan, one of the crime bosses, that Eddie had told him he was approached to be an asset, an informant basically, for one of the government's spy agencies. CIA most likely. Frank wasn't sure because Eddie never gave him full details."

"Do you think it's true?" Jack asked.

That was a question I had failed to ask myself. I took Frank at his words. "I'm not sure. I had assumed Frank was telling the truth, but now that you ask, I don't have proof."

With eyebrows raised, Cooper asked, "Do you think Eddie was Sully's asset?"

"Possibly." I turned my head to the doorway to see if Holden was around yet. We were still alone. "I told Holden that when Sully took off and started his life of crime that my mother asked him to change his name. He has no idea that Sully is CIA and we need to keep it that way."

Cooper followed up his first question with another. "Do you think Sully has been compromised and that's why he killed Eddie?"

I had been weighing the likelihood of just that since Frank told me. I had no proof of anything and I told them that. "I have no idea how Eddie connected Sully's real identity and alias or why he knows the name Patrick Sullivan. All I know is he had my father's real name and research on him. That's what Eddie's guys are using. Both mob bosses I spoke to – Danny Devaney and Frank Coonan – know Sully as Mickey Finnigan and have no idea he is Patrick Sullivan. Holden never even heard the name Mickey Finnigan. I don't know what this means though at this point."

Luke said, "You don't know then for sure that Eddie connected the two. He might have just heard the name Patrick Sullivan but never connected it to Mickey. He might never have realized they were the same person."

This felt like it got more complex by the moment. "You're right," I conceded. "What I have is bits and pieces of a story that doesn't seem to make sense to me. We need facts and I have no idea how I'm going to get them."

Cooper rubbed a spot on his neck. "Sully injected me with something and left me in an alleyway. Whatever he's up to, he doesn't want us to know. Do you think Sully is the one who shot at you?"

My face contorted in concern. "One of Frank's guys said that given the caliber of weapon the shooter used if he had wanted to kill us, he would have. They speculated that the shooter was trying to scare us off. Do you think my father would shoot at me?"

Cooper had no response and he looked to Luke who turned in Jack's direction. "I think we have to be open to any possibility right now," Jack said. He hesitated and I encouraged him to speak freely. "Why aren't we going home, Riley? You're safe now. I don't understand why it matters now."

"Eddie's guys believe it was Patrick Sullivan who killed him. They are out for blood, Jack. If they came for us once, they will come again. This time though, Liv and my mom will be alone." I locked eyes with him. "Do you want to leave my mom and Liv at risk?"

"No," Jack said, shaking his head. "We can't do that, so what do we do now?"

"We have a mystery shooter after us and Noah Byrne, the man who kidnapped us in Lake Placid, is back in Boston. He already sent a text to Holden. He knows that Holden took off with me and has no intention of killing me or Sully. They are after us."

It was too much to ask the three of them, but I didn't feel like I had a choice. "We have to figure out if Eddie was really a CIA asset and then do the impossible – solve his murder."

"Do you have a way to reach Sully?" Cooper asked, standing. He shoved his hands in his pockets and rocked on the balls of his feet.

"No, only my mother does." I considered for a brief second calling my mom to contact him then thought better of it. "Sully has already shown us he's willing to attack you, Cooper. I have no idea if he was the one shooting at me. Let's leave him out of this right now."

Luke asked, "If Eddie was working as a CIA asset, there must be some kind of money trail, right? He's a criminal and running a global criminal network. He's going to insist on being paid."

"I didn't think most assets were paid," Jack said. "Most, like FBI informants, are compromised somehow or are doing it for ideological reasons."

Luke was right. I explained, "Eddie was a businessman though.

He wouldn't have done it unless he got paid. Holden said he has Eddie's financial records. I can look through them. I think Cooper should take a crack at speaking to Eddie's girlfriend, Melissa Patton. Holden and I spoke to her already and she said some strange things but wouldn't elaborate. It might have been she didn't want to talk in front of Holden."

Cooper agreed. I wasn't sure what Jack and Luke should be doing. For the first time in my career, I had no idea how to investigate a case. It was Jack who offered a suggestion. He told me about the German waiter working at the restaurant Eddie had been in the night he died.

"I think Luke and I should run down that lead. Maybe speak to Det. Nixon again and speak to Eddie's guys to see if we can get anywhere." Jack mentioned the guy they had run into while scoping out the house I had been held in.

"Don't you think it might be too dangerous to speak to them?" The last thing I wanted was to put Luke and Jack in danger.

That wasn't what was on Luke's mind though. He reached for my hand. "I don't want to leave you alone here with Holden. I don't think that's a good idea."

"I know it doesn't seem like it, but you can trust me," Holden said from the doorway to the living room. He entered the room, his face swollen and bruised, mostly around his nose and under his right eye. "I appreciate all of you helping with this. I don't know how I can ever repay you."

Luke stood and I worried he might hit Holden again. He got right up into Holden's face. "I'm not doing this for you. If it were up to me, you'd be in handcuffs right now. I'm doing this to keep Riley's family safe. I don't care about you or your brother."

Holden didn't respond at all. He held out his hand and there was a gold key in his palm. "I don't have much to offer you but take it. It's a key to this house. Come and go from here as you need to. No one even knows I own this. It's a safe house of sorts."

Luke didn't take the key. He stood there staring down at Holden. It was finally Jack who broke the tension. He plucked the key from Holden's palm and patted him on the back. "I appreciate it. Luke and I will be in touch when we know more."

With that, Luke hugged and kissed me goodbye. Holden went upstairs while I gave Cooper Melissa's address and directions to her place.

Before he left, Cooper reached out and hugged me. "We're going to figure this out."

Even though I had told Holden the very same thing, I had my doubts.

Chapter 33

"Your husband is intense," Holden said when I entered the bedroom where he had Eddie's files. He crouched low to the floor hunched over a box pulling out files and setting them in a pile. Then he stood and slapped the heavy haul on a desk in the corner of the room.

"What did you expect?" I asked. Holden didn't have an answer for me. I walked over to where he stood and glanced down at the files, flipping one of them open. He had been telling the truth. The papers were all financial. I closed it and leaned back against the wall. "You're lucky Luke went easy on you. What did Jack and Cooper say when you left the house?"

"At first, they threatened to beat the truth out of me and finish me off for Luke." Holden straightened up. "I told them everything. From how Noah first contacted me about my brother's death and his insistence that Sully was to blame to what my plan had been to now and now how things have changed. If they are going to help, they have a right to know everything. They are fiercely protective of you. How long have you known Cooper?"

"A few years. He is Luke's best friend from college and he and I met through Luke. We became investigative partners later. Jack is dating my mother. We are all fiercely protective of each other."

"I believed they'd kill me."

191

I locked eyes with him. "They would."

Holden looked away. "Is Luke always so intense? It doesn't seem to fit your personality."

"What do you mean?" I asked even though I had an idea of what he meant. Intense was not usually how people described Luke, except if they were suspects in an interrogation room. He could come off stern and serious. The more someone got to know him though, the more they realized he was a big softie. It was one of the most endearing qualities about him.

"You seem more relaxed than him, more flexible."

"Nature of the work, I guess. Luke is an amazing man. I wouldn't be so quick to judge him."

Holden held his hands up. "Not a judgment at all. If I were him, I'd have probably killed me. He's different than I expected is all."

"Were you not expecting a devastatingly handsome black man?" I said as the corners of my lips turned up.

Holden laughed and his face softened. "Something like that."

I let the subject drop because I saw no reason to defend Luke or talk about our relationship any further.

Holden motioned to the boxes on the floor and around a desk. "This is everything I have. As I said, unless it was to settle accounts, I didn't go through any of it. Where do you want to start?"

"These are the paper files. What about electronic files?"

Holden laughed again. "Eddie and I had very different views on technology. He was paranoid about it, and except for living expenses, rarely kept any electronic files. The entire internet could crash and Eddie would still be flush with cash and have a firm accounting of his assets."

"Not a bad way to live."

"I guess not if you're trying to hide things." Holden motioned with his hand. "Eddie was a good bookkeeper though. He may not have gone the easiest route, but his accounts were easy to settle. That's partly why I never went through any of this. Where do you want to start?"

"Any offshore accounts or ones that might have been hidden?"

Holden kicked a box towards me. "That's in here. Eddie had five offshore accounts. I closed them out but never read through the ledgers."

"I'll start with those. You take his main bank account."

"What am I looking for?" Holden asked as he pulled out the desk chair.

"Anomalies. Large payments from anyone. Payments of the same amount made consistently over time." I stood with my hands on my hips, dreading how tedious this would be. "Patterns that don't match up to anything legit."

Holden said he understood and offered me the desk if I wanted it. I declined and pulled the box over to a chair and ottoman in the corner of the room. I could at least be comfortable while I trudged my way through the task. I lifted the box to the ottoman and sat down on the chair. I flipped through the top file and noted that Eddie had dated them year to year. I'd start with the most recent and work my way back. I sat back on the chair, letting my body sink in and find a comfortable position. I kicked my feet up on the space left on the ottoman and started to read.

The files from all offshore bank accounts were in the file folder. I scanned one, which had nothing but continuous deposits of varying amounts from month to month. It didn't look like Eddie did much with this account other than deposit money.

I kept digging. Holden and I remained quiet as we each worked through the task. About an hour in, he got up and went downstairs. He came back with a tray of snacks and drinks for both of us. He set it down on the floor next to me, gave me a half-hearted smile, and went back to the desk. As I finished with one year of records, I put the papers neatly back in their folder and dropped it to the floor.

Nothing seemed strange to me in the first folder. It wasn't until I got another year back that I noticed something strange. There was a new account that had a series of deposits made quarterly spread over the previous five years. Each deposit was for two hundred and fifty thousand dollars – a million each year. This was exactly what I had been looking for. It was out of the Cayman Islands.

"Holden," I said and waited until he turned around in the chair and faced me. "Did you ever close out any account for Eddie out of the Cayman Islands?"

"The Cayman Islands?" he said more to himself than me. "I don't think so. I don't even remember seeing anything related to the Cayman Islands. Why?"

I pushed the ottoman away from me and walked over to the desk with the folder. I placed it on the desk in front of him and opened to the first page. "Right here, there is an account for Eddie Stone in the Cayman Islands. It wasn't in the most recent year of his records but the year before. It's exactly what I was looking for though. Consistent payments of the same amount quarterly over five years, including this last year here."

Holden picked up the folder and scanned through the information. "I don't understand," he said softly. He flipped through several more pages and read more. When he was done, he dropped it to the desk. "I only went through his last year of records to close accounts. This wasn't an account among them so I never closed it. I wonder if it's still open."

"The only way to know is to call." I pointed to the section from the deposits. "This money was transferred from another account. Try to find out that information. We can see if it was Eddie transferring the money in or if someone else was making the deposits. That's important to know."

Holden opened the desk drawer and grabbed a sheet of paper and pen. He jotted down the questions I wanted him to ask and then he called the number at the top of the statement. He got an automated system and worked his way through until he had a woman on the phone. Holden explained who he was and that Eddie had passed away. Of course, they wanted proof and told Holden they wouldn't be able to speak to him or answer any questions until the information was sent to them that verified his authorization on the account. Holden hung up to go get the necessary paperwork.

I didn't have the patience for this but knew it was the only way it was going to happen. Holden assured me that he had all the documents scanned on his laptop and could email them right now. He also had a list of Eddie's passcodes in case they needed those as well.

I couldn't sit there and wait for him to handle the matter, so I sat down and continued to scan through the records. Going back another year, I found the same account information. Nothing in any of the other accounts jumped out at me. Most of them had been large one-time deposits and money that sat there, collecting interest over time. Eddie hadn't withdrawn any of the money from the accounts and most had little activity. I went back another year and then another, working for close to an hour scanning through documents. As the account statement in the file had indicated, deposits went back five years. The first one started in March and the last payment was made five years later in December.

I could hear Holden talking downstairs. He was asking some of the questions I had told him to ask. I took that as a good sign that he had provided the paperwork the bank had requested and he was now approved to access Eddie's account.

I went to the doorway and listened in on Holden's side of the call. I didn't go all the way downstairs because it would annoy me if someone stood in front of me showing me their impatience while I was talking on the phone. I wouldn't do it to him either.

When I heard the stairs creak and realized Holden had ended the call, I scooted back to the chair and sat down, like I hadn't been eavesdropping.

"What did you find out?" I asked as he came through the door.

"With interest, there's close to six million in the account." Holden stood near the ottoman. "As far as they can tell, the money is coming from a business account in London."

"Did you get a name?"

"Farrell Investments. It doesn't mean much to me. Have you heard of them?"

I shook my head and motioned for Eddie to hand me his phone. He pulled it from his pocket and a quick internet search came back with a private equity firm in London. I told Holden and showed him their website. "Maybe you can call and see why they were sending money to your brother."

"Could they have been paying out from his investments?"

"I have no idea. It seems strange that it would be quarterly payments of the same amount for five years and there's no other record of this in Eddie's accounts. You said you thought you had found everything. Did you find other investments?"

"Yeah, Eddie had everything labeled and accounted for." Holden took his phone back and looked closer at the website. A few minutes later, he squinted and shook his head.

"Is something wrong?"

"These photos are faked," he said.

"What do you mean?"

Holden squatted down and pointed out photos from bios of people who worked at the company. "I don't think these photos are real people. I think they were digitally created."

Holden was a tech wiz so I didn't doubt what he was saying. I had no expertise in being able to tell a real photo from a fraud. "How do you confirm it?"

Holden stood upright and clicked the phone screen a few times. He didn't explain what he was doing and I couldn't see the screen. He kept at it until he found what he needed and turned the phone toward me. He had downloaded a photo and was running it through some program on his phone. "It's a digitally created image. This isn't a real person and my guess is Farrell Investments is a dummy corp."

Chapter 34

Cooper knocked on the door once and then again. "Melissa Patton!" he called out loud enough for the neighborhood to hear him. Cooper had been standing outside Melissa's door waiting for her to answer. He knew someone was home because he could hear movement inside. Finally, a woman peeked through the blinds on the living room window, pulling them apart slightly so she could look out.

"Who are you?" she asked, speaking loud enough for Cooper to hear her.

"My name is Cooper Deagnan. Holden Stone asked me to speak to you."

"Is Holden okay?" she asked in a panic, disappearing from the window. She reappeared as she pulled the door open.

"Holden's fine. Are you Melissa?" The woman standing in front of him barely came up to his chest. She had wide hips, a soft belly, and a pleasant face. In describing Melissa, Riley had said the woman looked like a sweet chubby toddler and she had been right. Cooper couldn't see this woman dating an international criminal.

"I am. Come in." Melissa moved out of the way and closed the door behind Cooper. "What's going on?" she asked as she guided him into the living room. She sat down on the couch and patted the cushion next to her.

Cooper sat but kept his guard up because he hadn't been anticipating it would be this easy. He turned his body to face her. "Holden said he came over and spoke to you earlier today about Eddie's murder. He told me that you indicated you might know more but refused to say. We need to know what else you know."

Melissa shook her head. "I can't tell you that. I'm not even supposed to know."

Cooper smiled at her loyalty. "I understand that you don't want to be disloyal to Eddie. I get it. I've been in similar situations, but nothing can hurt Eddie now. All Holden is trying to do is figure out who killed his brother. If you cared about Eddie, you should want to bring that person to justice."

"Of course, I cared about Eddie." Melissa chewed her lip and looked away. "I'm not supposed to say anything."

Cooper reached out and touched her gently on the arm. "Who asked you not to tell anyone?"

"Eddie. He said that he wasn't supposed to tell anyone and that bad things could happen if he did."

"Melissa," Cooper said softly and gently, drawing her attention back to him. "Something bad already happened. Eddie is dead and nothing you can do now will hurt him."

"I know," she said as fat tears rolled down her face.

Cooper could tell how much she was grieving, probably more so than any person he'd interviewed recently, but he needed the information. He decided to ease the pressure and change tactics. "How well do you know Holden?"

Melissa relaxed her shoulders and wiped her tears. "I don't know him that well. He's been helping me financially since Eddie died. That's what Eddie wanted. I knew Holden when we were young but hadn't seen him in years. Eddie told me that he didn't get along well with his brother, but he missed him. He said they fought a lot growing up and Holden was in California doing his own thing. The sad part is Eddie wanted to repair that relationship; he just didn't know how."

Melissa wiped her eyes again with the back of her hand. "I suspect they both had too much pride and neither wanted to be the first one to give in."

Cooper understood that. He didn't have a brother, but Luke was the closest he had and when there was tension between them, it was hard to take the first step. "You know Holden is a good guy, right?"

"He's been good to me so far. He's done everything Eddie wanted and he's nice and kind to me."

"You know that girl he came here with earlier today?"

"She said her name was Riley and that she was helping to investigate Eddie's murder."

"Right." Cooper lowered his head and locked eyes with Melissa. "Holden is so messed up over Eddie's death, he kidnapped Riley and her sister Liv. He and some of Eddie's guys here in Boston."

"No." Melissa's hand flew to her mouth. "Holden wouldn't do something like that."

"He did and it happened the morning after Riley got married this past weekend." Melissa didn't say anything so Cooper went on. "Some of Eddie's guys here in Boston think it was Riley's father who killed him. He had nothing to do with it, but they got some hairbrained idea to kidnap Riley and her sister and hold them hostage to draw out their father. Then they planned to kill all three of them."

"No, no," Melissa said adamantly. "I don't believe you. There's no way Holden would do something like that."

"Call him right now and ask him if you don't believe me." Cooper sat back and waited but Melissa didn't get up or reach for her phone, which sat on the coffee table. Cooper asked, "Do you know the guys Eddie hung around with here?"

"Eddie never brought them around me. He and I went to high school together so I've met some of them. When we were together, they didn't come around. Eddie made sure of that."

"Why was that?"

"He said they weren't good guys and he didn't trust them around me. That wasn't a world he wanted me in. That's why I wasn't with him in London. He told me I wouldn't like who he was there."

Cooper folded his hands in his lap pausing to see if she'd say anything else. It was clear to him Melissa had been through questioning before and she was skilled at it. She gave enough information to seem like she answered a question honestly but never more than asked. "What was that like for you being apart from him for so long?"

Melissa sighed and gave a half shrug. "It wasn't easy. We'd been together for a long time and still hadn't gotten married. Eddie said he could never marry me. He never wanted me to hold any blame or responsibility for the things he did. It was almost…" she trailed off.

"Like he was caught between two worlds?" Cooper asked, eyebrows arched as he finished her thought.

"Yeah, that's it." Melissa inched back on the couch until her side hit the arm and she relaxed back. "Friends often told me to move on from Eddie or I'd never get married and have children, which I'd still like to do. I was too in love with him to do that though. Eddie needed me. He used to tell me I was the only person he could trust. The only person that was real with him."

"That was probably true in his world. You meant a lot to him, but that's why it's so important that you tell me what you know." Cooper watched her face because he had already deduced Melissa was the kind of person whose face said everything. If she was happy, sad, angry, frustrated – the emotion was written all over her face. Right now, Melissa was conflicted. She wanted to tell Cooper, but she still felt a loyalty to Eddie.

Melissa wrung her hands and bit the inside of her cheek. Her eyes roamed all over the room finally landing on Cooper. "What are you going to do with the information?"

"I'll answer your question," Cooper said, "but first let's look at it another way. What are you most worried about if you share the information you have?"

"Eddie's reputation, primarily. But also, no one knows he told me. If the information starts to come out, I might be in danger."

Cooper couldn't argue with that. Melissa could very well be in danger and he told her as much. "Without knowing what you know, I have no idea how much danger you could be in. Think about it this way though. If you're worried that the person who killed Eddie could come after you if you disclosed information, he could come after you now to keep you quiet before you ever said anything. With people like that, even the hint that you have a secret about them could be dangerous for you."

Melissa shuddered. "I didn't think of it that way."

"I'm not trying to make any trouble for you," Cooper said sincerely. "All I want is to be able to help my friend and keep Eddie's guys from going after her and her family. Whether you realize it or not, Holden is in danger now, too. I know you've gotten closer to him and don't want to see anything bad happen to him. Finding Eddie's killer is the only way to protect them all."

"I understand," Melissa said. By her expression, Cooper knew she was ready to tell him. "Eddie was..."

Melissa never said more because the front living room window shattered and a bullet struck the wall across from where they sat. Cooper grabbed for Melissa's hand and pulled her to the ground as more shots rang out. "Stay down," Cooper said above the sounds of gunfire. He pulled her toward the hallway. "Is there another way out of here?"

All the color had drained from Melissa's face. Her eyes didn't seem to know where to land. She tried to speak but no words came out. She nodded once and pointed down the hall. As they began to crawl more gunshots rang out and Cooper put his hands on Melissa's backside and shoved her down the hall faster. He worried whoever was shooting at them would storm through the living room.

"Go, go, go!" he shouted to her. When they hit the kitchen, Cooper stood and opened the door. He grabbed the garbage can that sat near the door and launched it outside, waiting to hear footsteps or more gunshots. The can rattled on the cement but there was no other movement out back. The gunshots from the front still hadn't stopped. Windows from the second floor shattered next. They were bent on taking out everyone in the house.

"Anyone else here?" Cooper asked, realizing he should have found that out before he started the interview.

Melissa whispered in a shaky voice, "No, just me."

"Where does this door go?"

"There is an alleyway that goes left and right to the cross-streets or you can go left and then connect to another alley that goes to the road behind mine." That's the way Cooper would go then. Any possible avenue to get away from the front of the house and the person shooting at them. The gunfire had slowed and Cooper worried they might be coming around back.

"We have to go now!" Cooper grabbed Melissa's hand and dragged her through the kitchen door into the alley. They turned left and ran for it. Cooper had to slow his pace considerably so he wouldn't get too far in front of Melissa. She wasn't much of a runner and Cooper wondered if he could pick her up and carry her. He didn't think that would do much good.

Cooper turned to look behind him just as a man with a gun entered from the end of the block. He kept his eyes focused on the man long enough to memorize his face and then shoved Melissa down the alley that connected to the street behind hers.

"Run, Melissa!"

Melissa gasped for breath as she pumped her legs as fast as she could. Tears streamed down her face, which only made her breathing worse. "I can't run anymore," she said slowing to a walk.

Cooper turned behind him expecting to see the man with the gun at any moment. He had to think quickly. He grabbed Melissa's hand and pulled her into a driveway that connected to the alley. There was a truck that had lawn equipment and other items in the back. He quickly helped her into the bed of the truck and pulled the tarp over her.

He handed her his phone. "Don't move. Stay very still and be quiet. When you think the coast is clear, text Luke in my contacts and tell him what's happened."

"What are you going to do?"

"Lure the guy in another direction." Cooper went back into the alley and took off running.

Chapter 35

Luke and Jack waited as patiently as they could for Det. Nixon. The detective had been out of the office when they had arrived and they spent about an hour waiting for him to get back. As Det. Nixon rounded the corner in the detective's bureau, he saw them sitting on the bench outside of his office.

"You're back again," Det. Nixon said as he walked to his office and opened the door. "I don't think I can persuade you to leave so you might as well come on in."

Luke and Jack shared a look. They had already discussed that Jack would take the lead in speaking to the detective since Luke's temper was already high and hadn't cooled much since he had punched Holden in the face. Jack had cautioned him that taking a swing at Holden was one thing, going after a Boston detective was quite another.

Luke followed Jack into Det. Nixon's office. "We found Riley and Holden," Jack said as he took a seat across the desk. "Riley called us soon after we left your office. It seems you were right that she was holding her own. We can't fault you for letting us know what you saw."

Det. Nixon picked up a few papers on his desk and stacked them neatly in a pile. "I'm glad that you came around and saw things my way. Holden is a good guy."

Luke bit down on his tongue to stop himself from speaking. Jack glanced over at him because they had talked about this before. They had to give Det. Nixon a win if they were hoping to garner his support otherwise.

"Right, anyway," Jack started, "we are back here to see you because we think we found something significant regarding Eddie Stone's murder."

Det. Nixon stopped messing with the papers on his desk and raised his head to look at Jack. "What did you find?"

Jack looked to Luke to explain but he shook his head. He wasn't ready to speak quite yet. He didn't like Det. Nixon any more than he liked Holden. It was better that Jack took the lead.

Jack refocused his attention on Det. Nixon. "We spoke to a bartender at Mancuso's who said…"

Det. Nixon interrupted with a dismissive wave of his hand. "We already spoke to the staff there. They didn't have anything useful to offer."

Where Luke was ready to rip into him for interrupting, Jack just nodded. "Right, I understand that. I'm not faulting you for anything. I asked the bartender if they had any staff who had started around the time of the murder and then left. He told me about one guy, a German guy who no one remembers hiring."

"No one told us that at the time," Det. Nixon said, his voice stiff and cautious.

Jack shifted in his chair leaning a little forward. "It's happened to me more times than I can count in my career. I'm sure the staff was shaken after the murder. They can forget to disclose details, especially if they don't think it's significant. It occurred to us that given there is no parking outside of the restaurant that someone from the inside must have alerted the gunmen that Eddie was on his way out. That's the only way I could figure they were able to gun him down right as he was leaving."

"We considered the same but everyone we interviewed was clean."

"Of course," Jack said and then went on to detail what they found. "We don't think it was someone on their regular staff. From the sounds of it, the guy showed up one night and worked and was there the night Eddie was murdered. Then was gone never to be seen again. No one questioned it. One manager thought the other one hired him. Other staff didn't question it either. By the time anyone noticed and cared, the guy was gone and they were all freaked about the murder. Most of them thought the guy quit. The bartender said initially he thought it was because the guy was struggling to speak English."

Det. Nixon didn't say anything for a couple of seconds. Then he spun around in his chair and then rotated back to his desk with a file in his hand. He slapped it down on the desk and opened it. He scanned down the page his index finger lingering over the words. When he was done, Det. Nixon snapped it shut again. "No one we spoke to was German. I don't have a single name or notation here in the file regarding a witness like that."

"I'm just passing on information that might be helpful to you. What you do with it is up to you." Jack glanced over to Luke again and placed a hand on his shoulder to nudge him to speak.

"We found out something else," Luke said and then paused and corrected himself. "Riley found out something else. She met with Frank Coonan who indicated to her that Eddie might have been an informant for the CIA or another government agency." Luke could tell Det. Nixon was holding back a laugh, which didn't win him any favors.

"Riley doesn't seem like she'd be that gullible." Det. Nixon shook his head in disbelief. "I'd have trouble believing anything Frank Coonan had to say."

Luke sat stone-faced fighting his urge to yell. Through clenched jaw, he said, "If you think Riley is gullible, you don't know her. She didn't say she believed this. Riley said it's information she gathered and the murder has hallmarks of that. The bottom line is Riley is an excellent judge of credibility when interviewing and she believed Frank was credible. Now, like any good investigator, she is following that lead, which is all it is at this point."

"We checked every watch list and checked the airports for any known criminals coming in from overseas. There was no one around that time that jumped out at us. We ruled out fairly quickly that it was an international hit."

Luke smirked. "We never said this was someone from the outside. You'll have to excuse me I'm only a homicide detective out there in middle America, so you'll have to correct me if I'm wrong. Don't you have international criminal gangs operating here in Boston from China, Russia, Italy, Ireland, the United Kingdom, and beyond?"

Det. Nixon's lips were set in a firm line. "We do. What's the point? Eddie wasn't operating here in Boston."

"Right," Luke said, "but Eddie still had guys here who followed and took orders from him. He had a reach in Boston just like other international criminal gangs. I assume Eddie felt safe here. If he's out there ratting out his competition and someone finds out about it, there's going to be a price on his head. How easy would it be to have someone already here in Boston take him out?"

Det. Nixon still wasn't giving in. "We never found evidence of that."

Exasperated, Luke raised his voice. "It sounds like you never found evidence of anything, but the guy is still dead."

"Calm down, Luke," Jack cautioned. He turned his attention back to Det. Nixon. "You should be aware too that when Riley went to see Frank, she and Holden were shot at. They had to hide behind his car and it was Frank's guys who rescued them. Someone doesn't want them investigating Eddie's murder."

Det. Nixon didn't show any concern or shock that the shooting had occurred. "Why do you say someone was trying to stop them? There are many shootings in the neighborhood where Frank Coonan spends his time."

Jack clasped his hands together. "My understanding is that if the shooter had wanted to hit them, he could have. The shooter wasn't aiming at Frank's bar. They were aiming at Holden's car where Riley and Holden had been when the shooting started."

Det. Nixon didn't say anything as he picked up the phone on his desk and made a call. When the person on the other line answered, he asked some direct specific questions about a shooting in the vicinity of Frank's bar. The detective simply said, "I see," and hung up the phone. "It seems you're correct about the shooting."

Det. Nixon got up from his desk and went over to a five-drawer tan filing cabinet that was situated in the corner of the room behind where Luke and Jack sat. He unlocked it and slid out the second drawer from the top. He mumbled to himself as he pulled out file folders and flipped through information. Luke had no idea what he was doing or searching for so he remained quiet hoping the detective was finally taking him seriously.

The silence in the room was broken by Luke's ringing cellphone. He pulled it from his pocket and looked at the screen. He clicked a button to send the call to voicemail. He could call Cooper back after the meeting. A few seconds later the phone rang again. Luke did the same thing. He didn't have time to update Cooper yet and he didn't have any information to do so. Luke was about to put his phone back in his pocket when a text came through.

Luke read it twice in a matter of seconds. He stood so quickly his chair tipped backward. "We need to go. All of us, Det. Nixon. Now!"

Jack didn't stand right away. He raised his head to look up at Luke. "What's going on?"

Luke turned and headed for the door. "I'll explain on the way. We have to go now."

"Stop." Det. Nixon closed the file drawer and relocked it. "I need you to calm down and explain what's happening or I'm not going anywhere."

Luke released an exasperated sigh. "The text I just received was from Melissa Patton. She has Cooper's phone. When he was there speaking to her, someone shot up her house. They took off and now Melissa is hiding in the back of a truck and Cooper ran off to lure the shooter away. He's in danger!"

Hearing that, Jack jumped to his feet as well. "Where are they?"

Luke held up his phone and read the text again and rattled off an address.

"I know where that is." Det. Nixon took things seriously this time. He went to the phone and made a call for back-up. When he hung up, he grabbed his keys from the desk. "I'll drive. Units are already on the way. There were several 911 calls from the neighborhood. We'll find your friend and get this sorted out. I promise you that."

Luke didn't have a lot of faith in the man, but he had no choice right now other than to trust him. All Luke cared about was getting to Cooper.

Chapter 36

Cooper crouched low in the backyard of a house three blocks away from where he and Melissa had fled from her living room. After he left Melissa in the back of the truck, he had run as fast as he could down the alleyway. He turned around just as the gunman had reached the driveway where the truck had been parked. The gunman kept his pursuit of Cooper and had no idea he had passed Melissa, who was presumably his target. The ruse had worked so far.

The man stopped at one point and shot at Cooper. Given the distance, the man's aim was far off. Cooper kept running, turning down one alleyway and then another until he found a good hiding spot. While crouched low, he heard a volley of gunshots that made his heart stop cold. He remained where he was hidden. With no phone and no way to call for help, Cooper could only hope that Melissa had contacted Luke and that help would be arriving soon.

Cooper calmed himself and worked to catch his breath, allowing his breathing to become shallow and even. Melissa had been right on the precipice of telling him what he needed to know. The shooting couldn't have come at a worse time, or at the best time possible for someone who was looking to remain hidden. That's when it hit Cooper that there was a chance that someone had bugged Melissa's house. Until now, she hadn't been willing to disclose the information she knew. Right as she was about to, a hail of bullets came crashing down. If he ever got out of there, the first thing they needed to do was sweep her house for listening devices.

Cooper figured at any minute the homeowner would see him in their backyard and ask him what he was doing. He didn't know if the gunman was still out there looking or if Melissa had been found and shot. The uncertainty of it all caused a wave of nausea to course through him.

Relief finally came when sirens wailed around him. Cooper waited several minutes until he heard his name being called by familiar voices. Heavy foot stomps alerted Cooper that more than one person was coming to his rescue. He stood and walked the length of the backyard to the gates he entered from the alley. He stepped out and called Luke's name who he saw three houses over.

Luke turned, caught sight of Cooper, and jogged right over to him. "Are you okay? What happened?"

Cooper explained the events of the afternoon and how he split from Melissa intending to keep her safe. "I heard gunshots before I heard sirens. Is she okay?"

"She's down near the truck. When she heard the sirens, she flagged us down. You have to see this though." Luke turned in the opposite direction from where he had come and walked back the way Cooper had run from Melissa's house. "I don't know what we are dealing with here."

"What do you mean?" Cooper asked.

"You're going to have to see it to believe it." Luke didn't say any more.

Cooper followed until they reached a crowd of police officers standing in a circle in the alleyway. As they got closer, Cooper realized someone was lying on their back on the ground. Then he saw the blood pooled around the person and trailing from his body.

"Who got shot?" Cooper asked, worried it might have been a

bystander.

"I think it was the guy shooting at you. Would you be able to identify him?"

Cooper nodded. "When I was running, I turned and got a good look at him."

Luke touched one of the officers on the arm to get him to move out of the way. Cooper stepped through the parted crowd of cops and Jack until he stood on the side of the man's body. He glanced down and immediately knew it was the man who had been following and shooting at them. Blood stained the front of the man's shirt. It looked like he'd been hit in the side of the head. The blood that pooled under him was dense.

Cooper shifted his eyes away from the body and up to Luke. "That's him. I don't understand. Who shot him?"

"We don't know. He was here like this when we got here," an officer said off to Cooper's right. "You don't know anything about this? We thought maybe you took him out."

"No. I took off and he chased me and shot at me once but missed. I dodged him from one alley to the next and then hid. He never passed by where I was hiding. I heard gunshots before you arrived and worried that he had found Melissa." Cooper swiveled his head around looking for Melissa, but she was nowhere in sight. "Where is she?"

Luke pointed back in the direction of the truck. "She's back where you left her. The paramedics arrived and are giving her some oxygen and checking her vitals. She's pretty shaken up and running down this alley without shoes cut up her foot pretty badly."

"I didn't realize Melissa didn't have shoes on," Cooper said, feeling bad now that he had been annoyed at how slowly she had been running. "All I cared about was getting us out of her house."

"You did a good thing," Luke said, patting him on the back. He looked at one of the officers. "We have any identification on this guy yet?"

The officer looked to Luke and then to Det. Nixon, who assured him it was okay to speak honestly in front of them. He handed a wallet over in a sealed evidence bag. "His name is Leon Becker and he's got a New York driver's license. It says he lives in Queens. That's all we know so far."

Luke turned his head in the direction of Det. Nixon. "Name mean anything to you?"

Det. Nixon shook his head. "No idea. Never heard of him before. When I get back to the office, I can run him in the system." He pointed his finger between Cooper and Luke. "This isn't someone either of you knows?"

"Never seen him before in my life," Cooper said, not sure what the detective was getting at. "I don't normally have people chasing me down and shooting at me. I think he was watching Melissa's house. I'd bet money that if we go back there right now, we'll find surveillance equipment inside unless they already took it out while this guy chased us."

"What are you saying?" Det. Nixon asked, then held up a finger for Cooper to wait. He instructed the officers to wait until the medical examiner and the crime scene unit arrived and then walked around the body and pulled Luke and Cooper aside. Jack followed behind them.

When they were out of earshot of other officers, Det. Nixon asked his question again. "I don't understand what you're talking about. Why would anyone be after Melissa Patton?"

Cooper couldn't understand how Det. Nixon could be so dense, but he connected the dots for him. "Eddie told her that she was the only one he trusted. As a result, Melissa knows far more than she told you, Detective. I think she might even know who killed Eddie or at

214

least what led up to it. She was just about to tell me when shots rang out." Cooper brushed his hand through his hair and blew out a breath. "That's not a coincidence. I had been in that house for at least twenty minutes before the shooting started and the first shot happened just as Melissa was about to spill some secrets."

"What do you think she knows, Cooper?" Jack asked.

"I don't know but she was worried about ruining Eddie's reputation. She's extremely loyal to him and he seemed to care deeply about her. It wasn't a casual relationship."

"I'll bring her back into the station and talk to her," Det. Nixon said and started to walk back toward her.

"That's not a good idea," Luke called to his back. Det. Nixon turned with eyebrows raised and Luke continued. "She didn't tell you before. There's a good chance she won't tell you now. She was in the process of opening up to Cooper. Let him talk to her again and we can go back and search her house for surveillance equipment."

"I don't know about that." Det. Nixon hesitated, shifting his weight forward as if deciding the direction he'd choose.

Jack suggested, "I think it's worth a shot. If Cooper doesn't get anything, you can always bring her down to the station again and talk to her."

"Give it a shot," Det. Nixon said, his voice giving away that he wasn't fully convinced.

Cooper scanned the ground as he walked, looking for shell casings or any other clues. He hadn't realized just how far he had run away from where he had left Melissa. It was at least a good three-quarters of a mile down a maze of alleyways. Finally, he saw her in the back of an ambulance being tended to by an EMT.

"You okay?" Cooper asked as he approached. She had her right foot completely wrapped in a bandage from her ankle down to her toes.

She touched a scrape that ran down her right cheek. "I'll live thanks to you getting me out of there so fast. What was that about?"

Cooper leaned against the side of the ambulance and crossed his arms. "It's what I was trying to tell you. These people who killed Eddie have been watching you. You're not safe, Melissa. The only way out is to tell us the truth."

"What happened to the people shooting at us?" Melissa pointed down the road in the direction that Cooper had walked. "I heard a cop say someone was dead."

"I think the guy shooting at us is dead. His name was Leon Becker. Does that name mean anything to you?"

"I'm not sure," Melissa said. Cooper noted her face said otherwise.

"We don't have time for hesitation, Melissa. If they sent one guy to kill you, they will send another when they realize the job isn't done. The only way you're going to be safe is if you tell us what's going on."

She looked up at him. "It's hard betraying Eddie when I've spent practically my whole life being the person he trusted most." Melissa glanced down at her bandaged foot and thought long and hard.

Cooper understood her dilemma so he waited patiently while she considered it. In the end, he knew she'd do the right thing. He felt no need to push her. The events of the day had more than proven his point.

With tears in her eyes, Melissa raised her head to Cooper. "Eddie was an asset for the CIA. Right before he died, he had been involved in an international drug ring and realized it had ties back here to Boston. He never said who it was tied to here, but in the process, he got involved with Gregor Wolf, who is the head of an international criminal network in Germany. I don't know Eddie's involvement with Gregor Wolf. I don't know if Eddie was working with him or ratting him out. There was a connection that's all I know. Eddie was terrified of him though, and in the end, he was sure Gregor had found out what he was doing. He told me he went to the CIA for help. I don't know if he ever received it."

The pieces were beginning to fall into place. All Cooper thought about now was how to keep Melissa safe.

Chapter 37

Holden and I spent the rest of the afternoon into the evening going through Eddie's financial records. Nothing else jumped out at us other than the one account. We speculated that it might be money from the CIA or government agency he was spying for. I had no idea how that worked but the account was suspicious for sure.

I slapped the final folder on top of the pile and looked over at Holden who was still hunched over the desk. "I'm starving," I said, rubbing my growling stomach. I hadn't heard from Luke or Cooper and had no idea when they'd be back. "Any idea what you'd like to do for dinner?"

Holden turned in his seat. "Do you want to call your friends and see when they will be back? I can order from an Italian place down the road and pick it up."

"Sounds good to me." I reached for my phone to call Luke when the door below us banged open and Cooper called my name. I moved the ottoman out of my way and headed out of the room and down the stairs.

Cooper met me on his way up. "We need to talk. Luke, Jack, and Det. Nixon are on their way here. Melissa Patton is sitting in the living room."

"What happened?" I asked, realizing by the look on Cooper's face he had gotten more accomplished than I had.

"Come down and bring Holden. I'll explain more when everyone is here."

"Holden was going to order dinner. Should he wait?"

Cooper had already reached the bottom landing. He turned and looked at me debating for a moment. "We haven't eaten all day. Tell him to go ahead. We can get Jack to pick it up because we need Holden here."

I went back upstairs to tell Holden and found him staring down at his phone. He had a look of concern and fear on his face as he stared at the screen. "What's going on?"

Holden glanced up at me. "Noah keeps texting. He connected with Collins and now he knows for sure that I've backed out of the plan." Holden set the phone down. "He's gone on a rampage looking for us. He told me he killed Collins when he wouldn't tell him where to find us. I'm worried he's going to go after your mother and sister. Is there a way they can leave the house in Troy and stay somewhere safe?"

I thought for a moment about the best course of action and then raced downstairs to get Cooper's phone. I didn't want to call Det. Miles Ward from Holden's line. I found Cooper sitting with Melissa in the living room. I wanted to ask about her bandages but making sure my mother and sister were safe was the priority. I explained quickly what was happening to Cooper who handed his phone over immediately. I placed the call to a number I had memorized.

"Det. Ward," the Troy Police detective said as he answered.

"Miles, it's Riley…" I started to say but he spoke over me.

"I've been so worried! I'm glad Luke found you. Are you okay?"

I stepped back unsure of what he meant. I had no idea that Miles would have even known I was missing. I said as much and he explained that Luke had called him to check my mother's house when I first went missing. "I'm so happy you're safe," he said, the relief evident in his voice.

"I'm not yet, but right now I'm worried about Liv, Adele, and my mother who are all at the house in Troy." I explained as quickly as I could about what was happening in Boston without going into too much detail. "I can't handle things here if I'm worried about them. Is there any way you can help me?"

"Anything, Riley. I'll go over there and let them know what's going on. I'll stay and get a squad car out in front of the house, too. I'll handle it. Don't worry." Miles clicked off and I couldn't have been more grateful for an old friend's help.

Cooper asked, "Is Miles going to take care of it?"

"Yeah, he's going over and will stay there." I handed Cooper back his phone and looked down at Melissa. "What happened to you?"

She didn't get to answer because Luke, Jack, and Det. Nixon came through the door. Cooper explained about Noah Byrne's ongoing threat. Jack immediately reached for his phone to call my mother. I assured him I had spoken to Miles and he was on his way over.

"If you want to head home, Jack, we can handle this on our own," I said. The look on his face and that of Luke and Det. Nixon said otherwise. "Can someone please tell me what's going on? I've been sitting here in suspense since Cooper arrived."

"Where's Holden?" Luke asked, taking a seat.

"Upstairs. Should I get him?" When Luke said yes, I went to the bottom of the stairs and called Holden's name. He came down right away and we walked back into the living room together.

"This looks serious," Holden said when he saw the group of them. He sat in a chair across from the couch and waited. No one said a word. "Seriously, what's going on? Riley and I have been here all day going through financial records. We think we found something…" he trailed off when he finally saw Melissa through the crowd.

"Are you okay? What happened?" he said, standing and going over to her.

Cooper explained that when he'd been interviewing Melissa some-one had shot up the house and then chased them. "The guy who was shooting at us is dead. His name was Leon Becker. We don't know much about him or how he's wrapped up in this."

I didn't know what this meant for the case. "Does that mean he's the one who killed Eddie?"

"We don't know," Luke said. "Melissa gave us another lead to follow. She confirmed that Eddie was working as an asset for the CIA and was in the middle of an international drug deal in which he encountered a man by the name of Gregor Wolf, who is a crime boss out of Germany."

"I've never heard of him," Holden said, his face showing no emotion as he absorbed information about his brother. "Is Leon Becker connected to Gregor Wolf?"

"We don't know," Det. Nixon admitted. "Right now, I don't know anything about Leon Becker or Gregor Wolf, but someone bugged Melissa's house. That's how they knew when to strike."

I figured this was the best time to tell them about the payments I found. "Eddie was being paid quarterly from Farrell Investments. The money was directly deposited from this company to Eddie's offshore account in the Cayman Islands. It was a two-hundred-and-fifty thousand payment, quarterly, for a million each year. The payments go back five years."

"That's more than the CIA would have paid an asset," Det. Nixon said from across the room. "They will pay but it's peanuts, nothing like that sum. What did you find out about the company?"

"Nothing," Holden said and explained the research we did. "It's a dummy corporation. Someone is funneling money through them. The pictures on the bios are faked. None of those people exist."

Jack cleared his throat and all attention turned to him. "Riley, did you say Farrell Investments?"

"Yes, that's the name the bank gave us connected to the deposits.

Why?"

Jack almost had a smile on his face. "Terry Farrell was the architect of the SIS Building or MI6 Building as it's known. Could Eddie have been working for the CIA instead of just an asset? Those large payments could have been a mix of salary and operational expense."

"Is there a chance he worked for MI6?" Luke asked.

"No. He would have needed to have been a citizen of the United Kingdom. It's one of the basic requirements," Jack explained. "It would more likely be the CIA."

Everyone turned to Melissa for an answer. The poor woman seemed overwhelmed by the attention or maybe the pain of her injuries was setting in. "I have no idea," she said. "Eddie didn't share everything with me. I'd get bits and pieces and sometimes enough to put together something that made sense."

It reminded me of how my mother described her early relationship with my father before he told her what he did for work. There had been the early government employee lies. Then he said, as most spies do, that he worked for the State Department. My mother was like a bloodhound though and eventually sorted out that his work might involve something criminal. When she called him on it and even threatened to go to the police – the woman did not play around – Sully finally gave in and told her that he was a spy-in-training for a job at the CIA.

That's when they divorced and she demanded he use an alias for work. Sully had agreed, explained that most spies do anyway. I believed Melissa when she said that she didn't know for sure everything Eddie had been doing. I couldn't tell everyone this though because, at this point, I couldn't remember who knew what about my father. I was never good at lying because to lie well you need a good memory and that I didn't have.

"What's the plan?" I asked, looking down at my stomach as it growled.

Det. Nixon pointed at Holden. "I'm hoping Melissa can stay here with you until we sort out what's going on. Then we need to address your role in kidnapping Riley and her sister. I'd arrest you right now, but I don't think that's going to help matters."

All the color drained from Holden's face as he nodded in agreement.

"I don't think that's necessary, Det. Nixon," Luke said, surprising us all. "I don't believe Riley will press charges and neither will her sister. On the stand, Riley would be a hostile witness at best. Given Holden's lack of criminal background, I can't imagine he'd ever try something like this again."

He wasn't wrong. I wouldn't testify even if they arrested him. I was surprised that Luke wasn't going to push for it. Something had changed.

"Luke's not wrong," I echoed. "I don't want Holden arrested, but we still have Eddie's guys after us. Can we assume it was Leon Becker who shot at Holden and me?"

"We don't know and can't be certain there aren't others out there," Det. Nixon said. He left, assuring us he'd be in touch when he knew more. At the very least, it seemed we had given him some new avenues for the investigation into Eddie's murder.

When he was gone, Holden ordered dinner for all of us and Jack went to pick it up. I went to help Holden set the table for dinner. As I pulled a stack of plates from a cabinet I asked, "How do you feel knowing your brother might have been working for the CIA?"

Holden didn't answer me right away. He pulled silverware from a drawer and went over to the table and arranged them at each place setting. "I'm not sure. I want to see if we can confirm it first. If it's true, I'm going to live with a lot of guilt for not having more faith in him. At least, if it's true, Eddie died a hero."

"You may not ever know for sure. I don't know that the CIA will tell you the truth about Eddie and his work with them. Can you make peace with that?"

"I don't know that I'll ever make peace with this situation at all. I've done so many things wrong." Holden refocused his attention on the silverware, but his guilt and shame were palpable.

Chapter 38

I opened my eyes from the best night of sleep I could remember. Luke's arm was thrown across my stomach and his soft snores reminded me I was safe and loved. I had been in such a deep satisfying sleep that it took me a moment to remember where I was and that I wasn't home in Little Rock in the safety of my bedroom. I was still at Holden's house in Boston. At least Luke had spent the night with me, refusing to leave my side another night. Jack and Cooper had gone back to the hotel after dinner the night before. Holden had given Melissa a room in the house.

I stared at the ceiling, realizing I was waking up with my husband for the first time since we had been married, for real this time. I rolled over to my side and snuggled into Luke. I planted a soft kiss on his chest and rubbed my cheek against him. He stirred in his sleep and yawned as he roused himself from slumber. He stretched his arms around me.

"What time is it?" he asked as he glanced down at me and then kissed me on the lips.

"It's just before seven." If I could have burrowed myself anymore into him and under the warm blankets I would have. I now realized the toll this ordeal was taking on me. I had slept soundly for at least eight hours and I could have fallen asleep and slept another eight easily.

Luke rolled over to face me. "There's so much I want to talk to you about. I don't think this is the time or place to do it."

"We'll have plenty of time to do that later." It occurred to me we had already missed the flight for our honeymoon. "I was about to say we can do that on our honeymoon, but we missed the flight. What are we going to do?"

"Your mom called the airline and the hotel and put our reservations on hold. I haven't checked in with her to see if we lost money, but hopefully, the airline will let us reschedule even if we have to pay a fee."

"Do you still want to go?" I asked, my voice tinged with hope.

"Of course, I still want to go." He ran a hand over my hip. "Just because I said we need to talk doesn't mean that I'm not happy to be married. You have to admit, this was a lot to take on right after getting married. The information about Sully alone threw me for a loop."

I was glad that Luke didn't seem angry with me. Like Holden the night before, I was fighting guilt and shame for having gotten us into this predicament. I told Luke how happy I was that he was still excited about our life together. I promised, "I'll explain everything when the time is right. What do you think we should do today?"

"I think we need to regroup. I'll call Cooper and Jack and get them back over here and we can discuss everything we know to date." Luke rolled on his back and rubbed his eyes. "Information came so fast yesterday that I don't even know that I could name a suspect right now if I wanted to. We need to pin down some information and go from there."

I didn't disagree and wasn't even sure where things stood with the investigation. We rested there together for the next half-hour and then Luke took a shower while I called my mother on his cellphone.

"I can't believe your father got us into this mess," my mother said.

"This is what we've always worried about. He's on the run, Mom." I explained what Sully had done to Cooper and she gasped at the news. "I don't even know what's happening, but he got here and then took off. This doesn't leave the best impression."

"Jack didn't tell me about Cooper, but he told me that Luke and Cooper aren't too pleased with Sully. Frankly, Jack isn't either. I tried to tell Jack this is how Sully is and the reason we are no longer married." My mother paused and I waited because I knew she had more to say. "Jack asked me if I thought Sully was dangerous."

"Dangerous, how?"

"Jack wanted to know if I thought Sully could have killed that man Eddie. He also wanted to know if he was capable of harming him, Luke, or Cooper if they got in his way."

"What did you tell him?" I wasn't even sure how I'd answer that question. Just because Sully and I shared DNA didn't mean I knew the man.

"I told him it was probably best not to cross Sully because I didn't know." My mother dropped her voice lower. "I'm sure Sully has done things in the line of work that would horrify the both of us. Now whether that's eaten away at any conscience he might have had, I don't know. I don't trust him and don't suggest that anyone else does either."

My mother had left me with a message reverberating in my mind. When Luke opened the bathroom door with a towel around his waist and steam billowing behind him, he picked up my mood. "What happened?"

I told him about the call to my mother and what she said. I was waiting for Luke to be surprised or reassure me, but it didn't happen. Instead, he shrugged, "It's about what I'd expect of him."

I swiveled in bed until I sat on the edge with my feet on the floor. "Do you hate him that much?"

Luke didn't respond. He stood at the bathroom sink and brushed his teeth and finished his typical morning routine. I sat there dumbfounded by what my mother said and Luke's refusal to answer. When he came out of the bathroom, he fished around for clothes from his suitcase.

"Luke, answer me," I said when I couldn't take the silence anymore. "I know you and my father got off to a rough start, but do you hate him?"

"Riley," he groaned as he slipped on a pair of jeans, hopping from one foot to the other until they were on and buttoned. He pulled a green Henley shirt over his head and shoved up each sleeve. Finally, he stood with his hands on his hips and stared down at me. "I don't know what to say. Hate is a strong word. I barely know the man. What I do know, I don't like."

It was my turn to be quiet. Luke came over and sat on the edge of the bed next to me. He took my hand. "It doesn't mean that I don't love you or want anything to change. I like the rest of the people in your family. Jack is a great guy and someone I consider a real friend. I adore your mother. and your sister is growing on me." He laughed. "You have to admit, Sully hasn't made the best first impression."

"That's true," I conceded. I had a lifetime of dealing with Sully, and if I were being honest, there was a whole lot of time I spent not liking him. I needed to give Luke time and accept that if his feelings didn't change, that was okay, too. "How do you think Sully is wrapped up in this? I still have no idea how Eddie connected Sully's real name and his alias."

Luke pulled socks from his bag and tugged them on his feet. "I would suspect their CIA connections."

"If Eddie was just an asset, I can't imagine that anyone would tell him Sully's real name. I'm sure he wouldn't have shared it himself." I couldn't be sure of that though. I didn't know enough so I admitted, "Even though I've been dealing with Sully my whole life, I still don't know much about the spy game and the CIA."

"Me either, outside of movies," Luke said. "I'm going to head down and get breakfast and talk to Holden about the plan for the day." He kissed me on the cheek and stood. "I'll meet you down there."

Luke made it halfway out of the door when he turned and went back to his bag. He pulled out my cellphone and charger and handed them to me. "I haven't looked at this since the morning you were gone."

I was glad to have it back. I'd felt a little lost without it. Before Luke left the room, I said, "I appreciate what you said to Det. Nixon about Holden last night."

He leaned against the doorframe and looked at me. "If it were up to me, Holden would be in prison. I know you and I'm in no mood to fight you on that. I want to get this case solved and take a nice long honeymoon with you."

"Sounds good," I said even though I worried Luke thought he was compromising too much for me. "I'll be down soon."

I plugged the phone into the outlet near the bed and left it on the bedside table without turning it on. I went to take a shower and get ready for the day. After I was showered, I dried my hair and left it softly on my shoulders. I dug through the dresser for clothes.

Before I went downstairs, I checked my phone now that it had a charge. As I scrolled through, I noted calls from Luke, my mother, Cooper, and Emma from when I first went missing. I looked at my text messages next and it was more of the same, except for one recent text sent early this morning. I didn't recognize the number. The text was simple enough.

Meet me in front of your favorite childhood place in Boston. 4:00pm. Come alone.

I assumed it was Sully. Other than my mother and sister, he's the only one who knew that my favorite childhood place in Boston was the aquarium. More specifically the penguin exhibit. I wasn't sure if the message meant in front of the building or the exhibit. That was the least of my problems. I had no idea how I'd ever break away from everyone to meet him alone. I texted him back a simple message that I'd be there, but all the while, keeping my mother's message about not trusting him in the forefront of my mind.

Chapter 39

"We haven't had a chance to speak one on one," Luke said as he walked into the kitchen and found Holden sitting alone eating breakfast and reading something on his phone.

"No, we haven't, but I'd like to," Holden said, putting his phone on the table. He pointed to the cabinet where Luke could find a coffee cup and told him where other breakfast food could be found if he was hungry.

Luke was surprised that Holden wanted to speak to him at all and wasn't rushing out of the room to get away from him. Luke went to the cabinet and pulled out a cup and poured himself some coffee. He pulled a muffin from the tin near the coffeemaker and sat down with Holden.

As Luke sat, Holden said, "Before you say anything, let me explain myself." Luke motioned for him to go ahead. Holden looked past Luke and had a hard time looking him in the eye at first. "I don't know if you have any siblings, but I only had the one. I wasn't a very good brother for most of Eddie's life. I didn't agree with his decisions and how he led his life. For the most part, I shut him out of mine completely. He went his way and I went mine."

A tear formed in the corner of Holden's eye and he wiped it away before it fell down his cheek. "I never even sent Eddie a birthday card or called him to wish him a happy birthday for years. We didn't see each other on the holidays. I told him almost nothing about my life. The rare times he reached out, I would brush him off. My brother was a criminal as far as I was concerned. I was trying to build a legit business."

Holden looked down and rubbed his forehead. "Luke, I was the worst brother anyone could have had. The guilt after I learned Eddie had been murdered has been eating me alive. I was feeling so much guilt I couldn't even face Det. Nixon. I couldn't come back here and tell him I knew nothing about my brother or his life so how could I possibly know who killed him."

Holden raised his head. "It all changed when Noah told me he knew who killed Eddie. I'm not you. I'm not a detective, not a cop. I have no clue how to solve a murder, so it wasn't like I could investigate what Noah told me. I wasn't even thinking rationally. Suddenly, there was a way for me to erase my years of guilt and bring Eddie's killer to justice. I sold my business, my house, everything I had and came here. I didn't even think about it. I got that name Patrick Sullivan and sunk my teeth into it, no questions. It was my redemption."

Luke had been quiet until now. He was fighting the empathy he felt for the man because he knew just how Holden felt. "What changed then?"

"I saw how scared Riley and Liv were. Well, Liv really. Riley looked like she wanted to take my head off from the moment I saw her. I was a bit scared of her, to be honest. I saw the way Riley was willing to sacrifice herself for Liv and that just gutted me. I'm not a killer. I couldn't do to their family what someone did to mine." Holden toyed with the coffee cup in front of him. "When Riley offered me a way out, I took it. When she first approached me, I had real excitement that I tried not to show her. I was the kidnapper after all. I think Riley suspected right away I had no idea what I was doing. I just wanted to do right by my brother. I don't know if you can understand how guilt and grief can make you do things you'd never even think of doing."

Luke waited a moment to see if Holden would say anything else. "Did Riley tell you about my sister?"

Holden shook his head. "No. Riley hasn't told me anything about her life or yours. All we've talked about is solving my brother's murder."

Luke believed him. It wasn't like Riley to share personal information. For the first time though, Luke saw himself in Holden. He had killed himself for years trying to find his sister's killer after she had been murdered her freshman year of college. Although they had a good relationship, Luke felt responsible for not protecting her. He was a senior on the same campus and was getting drunk while someone was hurting his sister. For years after, he tried to find her killer, and each time he failed, the guilt swelled in him. By the time he figured out who had killed her, Luke could have killed the man easily. If he didn't have Riley and Cooper keeping him straight, Luke might very well be sitting where Holden was now. Luke understood Holden better than the man realized and told him as much without going into too many details.

Luke rested his cup down on the table. "I understand, Holden. My sister was murdered in college. I did everything I could to bring her killer to justice, so while I can't condone what you did, I do understand. I can't appease your guilt but killing the person who killed your brother won't solve anything. I'll help you find your brother's killer though. That I promise you." Luke meant it. Even if they couldn't solve it right now, Luke would continue to help Holden however he could.

Holden held up his phone. "I did a little research on Leon Becker this morning and I found one newspaper article from the New York Times that mentions his arrest several years ago in connection with the murder of a mob boss. They had a jury trial but weren't able to convict. Does that tell you anything?"

"Was there mention of his connection to any crime family?" Luke asked, not sure that one newspaper article would tell them what they needed to know but it was better than nothing.

"No. The article mentioned that Leon Becker has ties to New York City, Chicago, and Boston. It doesn't mention anything about mob connections."

Luke leaned back in his chair. "Does it say where he's from originally?"

Holden lowered his head and scanned through the article again. "It doesn't give me where he's from. It does mention that at the time of arrest he was in New York City for crimes committed there. Based on his age then, he'd be in his late forties now."

"I'll go upstairs and get my laptop in a minute and maybe we can track him down. I assume Leon's the one who shot at you and Riley before shooting at Melissa and Cooper. I think it would be too much of a coincidence otherwise." Luke finished off the rest of his coffee and muffin and Holden continued to read the article on his phone.

When Luke was done eating, he asked, "What's your end goal with this?"

Setting down his phone, Holden looked at Luke. "What do you mean – end goal?"

"What do you want to happen? If we find the guy who killed Eddie, what do you want to happen to him?"

Holden sat there and thought for a moment. It was longer than Luke would have liked because the answer should have been obvious. Holden stood and walked to the counter and poured himself more coffee. When he was done, he turned to face Luke.

"I know the right answer is we call Det. Nixon and let him handle it. Arrest and prosecution."

"You said that's the right answer. That's not what I asked you. What is it that you want?" When Holden still didn't respond, Luke stressed,

"You need to know this ahead of time, Holden. I don't want to track down this guy and have you make an irrational decision in the moment that you'll regret for the rest of your life."

Holden looked at Luke like he was still uncertain if he should say what was on his mind. Then all at once, he spoke with the anger Luke knew was just under the surface. "I want him dead. I want to put a bullet in his brain like he did to Eddie. I want him to suffer. I know I can't do that though so I'm struggling with what you want me to say. If I can't kill him, I'd like to spend five minutes alone with him and beat him until he's near death and take away everything in his life he holds dear."

Luke stood and walked toward Holden. They were finally getting somewhere. "You know you can't do that right?"

"I can't, you're right. I haven't been in a fight since grade school and even then the other guy won." Holden raised his head to face Luke. "I bet you think that's pretty pathetic."

Luke reached out and touched the man on his shoulder. "There's nothing pathetic about not going around beating up people. Grown mature men don't use their fists to solve their issues. I wanted to kill the man who murdered my sister. I dreamed about killing him. I nearly did. If Riley hadn't stopped me, I'd be living with that regret for the rest of my life. I asked the question because I don't want you to have to face that decision in the moment. I want you to think about it before you're in that situation."

Holden nodded in understanding. "I don't think we're going to find him anyway. If we don't, I don't know what that means for me. Noah will still be after me, and Riley and Liv will never be safe."

"We'll find the killer and stop Noah. Trust me, I wouldn't be here if I didn't think we could."

"Det. Nixon wasn't able to solve the case in more than a year."

Luke poured himself more coffee and then took a sip. "We have found out more in one day than it seems Det. Nixon found in over a year of investigating. We drew out Leon Becker and have a lead on the German guy from the restaurant. We have room to investigate."

Holden turned to him. "What do we start with first?"

"I'm going upstairs and getting my laptop. We are going to start with finding out who Leon Becker is and how he's tied up into this whole thing."

Chapter 40

"Jack," Cooper called as he walked out of the bathroom of the hotel after taking a shower and getting ready for the day ahead. "Luke called me and told me the news has released information on Leon Becker. He's tapping into his database now to try to get an address and more information about him."

Jack raised his head and glanced up at Cooper. "I just saw that on the news. The cops aren't releasing much information about this guy at all. I was thinking about the German guy at the restaurant. That can't be a dead lead. Someone over there has to know something. They can't just have a guy walk in off the street and start working there. Someone had to vouch for him – another waiter, a busboy, someone in the kitchen staff. There had to be someone."

Cooper sat down across from Jack at the table. "You don't think it's possible he just walked in there in uniform and started working?"

"At first when the bartender said it, I thought okay, maybe it's possible. The more I thought about it though, I don't think so." Jack sat back and stretched his arms over his head. "You saw the place. It's a high-end restaurant. It runs like clockwork. There must have been someone who added his name to the staffing roster that night and gave him a section in the restaurant to work. Anyone who has waited tables for five minutes knows it's an organized process."

"What about the bartender and the manager not knowing?" Cooper asked. He didn't think Jack was wrong. He couldn't wrap his head around how some random guy slipped into the restaurant and started working. Having an insider made sense.

"I imagine in a place like that there is a senior server who had the schedule for the floor. The manager might not readily know that and I don't think a bartender would either."

"What made you think of all of this?"

Jack laughed. "Adele. You've got one smart girlfriend."

"When were you talking to Adele?"

"I called the house trying to track down Karen because she didn't answer her cellphone. I wanted to see if Miles was there watching out for them. Adele answered and told me that Karen was taking a nap and Liv was in her room."

Cooper was glad Adele was settling in okay at Karen's house. He had been worried at first leaving her there alone, but Riley's family made it easy to feel comfortable. "Is Miles there keeping an eye on them?"

"He had just left but there is a patrol car outside of the house. Adele said Miles has been there off and on and spent last night there."

Cooper wanted to get back to the topic at hand because Jack was right. Adele was incredibly smart, which is what made her such a cunning defense attorney. "What did Adele say about the restaurant?"

"She said that she waited tables during college and there was no way the waitstaff was just going to let someone show up and take their tips without knowing who they were. Adele said if there is normally a night with five servers and six show up, people are asking questions, especially in a place like that with long-term staff."

"I didn't even think in those terms," Cooper admitted, brushing his hair back with his hand.

"I didn't either, but I've never waited tables. I guess I never thought much about the inner workings of a restaurant."

Cooper tapped at the table with his index finger wondering how it could be sorted out. "What do you suggest we do?" he asked after a moment.

Jack pulled up the restaurant website on his phone and turned the screen around to Cooper. "I think we should go to lunch and chat with some of the staff."

That sounded like a plan. Cooper told Jack he'd be happy to go with him and would let Luke know. Before he called Luke though, his cellphone rang.

"I was just about to call over there," Cooper said to Riley instead of hello. "I think Jack and I are going back to the restaurant to check out a few things we might have missed yesterday."

"That's good," Riley said and hesitated.

"Is there something wrong?"

"You alone?"

Cooper eyed Jack across the table. "Jack is here. What's going on?" He could tell by her hushed tone that something was up.

"Listen, don't tell Jack. Sully sent me a text to meet him later today at a location only I would know. He said to come alone though and I don't think that's a good idea."

The news didn't surprise Cooper, but he didn't like it one bit. He was surprised that Riley had enough sense not to go alone. Maybe being kidnapped had finally knocked some sense into her about the dangers she faced. He couldn't tell her not to go because Riley was going to do whatever she wanted anyway. He had to be diplomatic. "What's your plan?"

"Well, I..." Riley trailed off.

"I'm not going with you if that's what you're thinking."

"Why not? I want you there."

Cooper debated getting up and taking the call outside. When he saw the concerned look on Jack's face, he decided that this would be better in the open. "Riley. Your father injected me with something and left me in an alleyway. You'll have to forgive me that I don't want to be anywhere around him. I can't see how connecting with him right now will help anything."

Jack sat there shaking his head at Cooper and mouthing, *No, no, no.*

Riley groaned loud enough for Jack to hear her across the table. "I know what my father did to you, but I need you. You don't have to be around us. He said to come alone so I figured we could go over there together earlier than planned and you could watch from a distance."

"Your father will know. Don't put anything past him." Cooper wasn't sure what else to say so he finally just said what he should have at the start. "I don't think you should go at all."

"I have to and I'm not telling Luke. He will freak out and won't let me out of his sight."

Cooper's anger rose. "You're putting me in a terrible position here. I'm not going to hide this from Luke and lie to him to protect you when you want to do something ridiculous." Cooper knew if he didn't go with her that she'd go alone. "What will you do if I don't go with you?"

"I don't know."

"Yes, you do."

"I'm going, Cooper, with or without you. I know what my father did to you wasn't right. I have to assume though he did that for good reason."

Cooper knew he didn't have much of a choice. He didn't want Riley to go alone, but she was stubborn enough to go without him. The one thing he wasn't going to do was keep it a secret from anyone. He just wasn't going to tell Riley that.

"I haven't known Sully long, but I know him well enough to know that he is going to know if you bring someone with you. How are you getting around that?"

"We can go separately. I don't need you to meet Sully with me. I need you to watch my back."

"You don't trust him either," Cooper said.

"Not fully." Riley paused and then explained herself. "I trust him not to harm me. He's a trained liar. It's what he does for work, so yes, naturally there is some mistrust there. Even my mother said I shouldn't fully trust him. Right now, though, I have to trust enough that he must have a good reason for wanting to see me. Are you in or not?"

Cooper could tell Riley was losing patience with him. "I'm in. Give me the details of what you need from me." Riley spent the next fifteen minutes hashing out an acceptable plan with Cooper. He still didn't like the idea, but her reasoning and strategy were sound.

When he hung up, Jack looked across the table and shook his head at him in disapproval. "This is a dumb idea."

Cooper explained his reasons and then picked up his cellphone from the table. "I'm not going alone. Luke is coming with me. Riley just isn't going to know that."

"Do you want me there, too?"

"If you want to be."

Jack leaned back. "I might as well be. Nothing good can come from this meeting."

Cooper smiled. "We are all going to feel pretty stupid if we get there and he wants to give her a wedding gift or congratulate her or even just say goodbye."

"We can only hope it goes that well." Jack motioned with his chin toward Cooper's phone. "You better call Luke before he makes other plans for the day. I'll meet you downstairs when you're done and we can hit the restaurant."

Cooper made the call to Luke, who answered so quickly it was like he was sitting on top of the phone. "Luke, we need to talk. Don't tell

Riley I'm calling though."

Luke told him to hold on while he found a more private place to talk. When he got back on the line, he cursed. "What has she done now?"

Cooper explained about Sully's text and that Riley had reached out to him for help. "I think Riley didn't want to stress you out or was worried you might talk her out of it."

"What I said this morning about Sully probably didn't help any. I think she might have been hinting around. I'm happy she reached out to you. What's the plan?"

"We are all going. Jack, too." Cooper filled Luke in on the plan and worked out a way for Luke and Jack to be there, too. "I don't care at this point if Sully sees us there or not. She can't go alone."

Luke agreed. "We might as well see what he has to say. It may be useful information. We have a few avenues to investigate but not many."

Cooper updated Luke about what Adele said about the restaurant and Jack's plan to dig a little deeper.

"I didn't even consider that," Luke admitted. "Then again, I've never worked in a restaurant. What time are you going?"

"Jack is waiting downstairs for me. What's your plan?"

"I'm going to run down some leads on Leon Becker."

"Call me if you need anything," Cooper said before he hung up. He exhaled a breath and sat at the table for a moment longer. Then he pushed himself up from the chair and got himself ready to go meet Jack. He figured if he sat too long, he would go down a rabbit hole of worrying about Luke and Riley. This was no way for anyone to start a marriage.

Chapter 41

I found Luke and Holden sitting at the kitchen table together, pleased they seemed to be getting along. "Where's Melissa?" I asked as I poured myself some coffee.

Holden glanced over at me. "She left early this morning for her sister's house. I dropped her off at the train station before seven. Her house is destroyed so she can't go back home and she didn't feel comfortable staying here. It's probably for the best she gets out of here anyway. I can't blame her for that."

I carried my coffee cup over to the table and sat down. "Do you think she told us everything she knows?"

"I'd assume so," Luke said. "If yesterday didn't scare her into telling the truth I don't know what would. Cooper said Melissa was ready to tell him the truth before the shooting started. I can only imagine that after, she had no reason to hold back."

Holden nodded. "I would agree with Luke about that. I talked with her this morning on the way to the train station and she apologized for not telling me sooner. She had felt like she was protecting me from whatever got Eddie killed. She realizes now it only put both of us in more danger."

"What will happen with her now?" I asked as I took a sip of coffee.

"I'll help her find a new place to live and see that she's taken care of as Eddie wanted. She'll have plenty of money so that won't be an issue."

Holden stood from the table and set his coffee cup in the sink. "I'm heading upstairs to go through more of Eddie's financial documents I didn't get to yesterday. Let me know if you need anything."

When Holden was gone, Luke opened his laptop. "I want to do a search on Leon Becker and see what I get back." Before he did, he told me about Cooper and Jack's plan to go back to the restaurant.

"That seems like a good idea." I fiddled with a pen sitting on the table. "Do you have any suspects yet?"

Luke raised his head from his laptop. "I was going to ask you the same thing."

I knew if Luke was asking me instead of jumping in with his opinion that he wasn't far along. "I have no handle on this at all and it's beyond frustrating," I admitted.

"Let's talk about what we know then," Luke suggested, moving aside the laptop and turning in his chair to face me.

I started first with the details of Eddie's death. The most important being that someone probably tipped off the killer because the hit outside the restaurant went too smoothly for it to be random. "We have Jack and Cooper hunting down that possible suspect right now."

"Det. Nixon never disclosed any vehicle information and there were no witnesses who got a plate number. Is that correct?"

"Correct. There were no witnesses and I don't believe any cameras picked it up either. There is no way to identify the large black SUV or its driver." I scanned through my memory to see if there was anything else that stuck out to me about the night Eddie died and came up short. Luke didn't have anything else to offer on the night in question.

"Do we know what Eddie was doing home?" Luke asked. "My understanding is he didn't come home here to Boston all that often. I know it was Christmas but was there any other reason?"

"I never asked that question. I heard Christmas and assumed he wanted to be with his family, but he and Holden weren't speaking and his parents were deceased. Maybe it was just to see Melissa. I was so focused on other things that it didn't even occur to me to ask why."

"Maybe Holden knows," Luke suggested. "It might be relevant."

I didn't think Holden would know, but it wouldn't hurt to ask. As I left the table, I gave Luke a quick kiss before I went upstairs. I jogged up the staircase and found Holden sitting at the desk going over a financial document like he said he would be doing. He jumped in his seat when I said his name.

"Sorry, didn't mean to startle you," I said, coming into the room and standing near the desk. "Luke and I were just going over some information and we realized neither of us asked why Eddie was home in Boston when he was killed."

"I asked Melissa that back when it happened. It was around the holidays so I assumed that's why he was back, but she said Eddie had a meeting here with someone in Boston. He never told her who though."

"Did he have the meeting or was he killed before it happened?"

Holden looked at me wide-eyed. "I never asked. Do you think it's significant?"

"I'm not sure. It might be nothing, but I think we need to find out." When I was looking yesterday, I thought there had been a box with date books in it. I wasn't sure if that was only financial information or if it contained anything related to Eddie's schedule. "Where is that box with date books in it?"

Holden pointed to a pile of boxes stacked neatly against the wall. "It's the second box in from the left. What are you looking for?"

I went over to the boxes and sat on the floor. I pulled the box Holden mentioned closer to me and tugged off the lid. "I saw some calendars in here the other day. It might have Eddie's schedule."

"I flipped through one of those after Eddie died and some do have names and dates. I never looked further though." Holden glanced down at me. "With his aversion to technology, Eddie never kept an online calendar so if there was something of importance, it would be written down."

Holden went back to looking at the financial file opened in front of him while I dug through the box. I opened one datebook and found Eddie had scribbled names, notes, phone numbers, and other information on specific dates. He never noted times of meetings and it seemed to be hit or miss where he filled in information. It was clear though that he used the datebook as more than just a calendar for his schedule. He kept notes in it. The problem was Eddie used shorthand and it didn't make a lot of sense to me.

I put one date book aside and dug back in the box to find the datebook for the year of Eddie's murder. I opened the first page and saw the same scribbled handwriting. As I flipped through, some writing caught my eye. Eddie's handwriting had become messier and a little more frantic. By October of that year, there were pages filled with notes from conversations with people and Eddie's impressions. No one's name was spelled out though. Most had initials instead of names and some just had one letter.

I flipped through November so fast that I nearly missed one note on the fifteenth. As I read the simple sentence, a chill ran down my spine. Eddie had written: *Who is Patrick Sullivan?*

It seemed six weeks before Eddie died, he hadn't connected Patrick Sullivan to Mickey Finnigan. Nothing indicated where Eddie had come across the name. I flipped pages slowly, scanning over the contents for anything relevant. There was nothing else until I reached December. There on the twentieth was a note to meet Bruce Campbell. Eddie didn't have any details for the meeting – a time or address or even who the man was. The name didn't mean anything to me and when I asked Holden, he didn't know either.

I set that date book aside and pulled out more, going back a few years. Slowly, I made my way through each one. The name Bruce

Campbell appeared three times – one meeting a year for the past three years. Not all the meetings were held in December but all of them were in Boston. No addresses were provided just the city name. According to Melissa, Eddie had come back the night of the nineteenth. He had arrived right before the meeting.

"You have no idea who this person is?" I asked Holden again, standing up and brushing my pant legs down.

He turned slightly in the chair to look at me. "I've never heard of him."

"He's not a lawyer or anyone you dealt with while handling Eddie's estate?"

"Definitely not. I would remember the name."

It would take some digging. I knew Luke was downstairs checking out Leon Becker so he could probably throw Bruce Campbell's name into the database. As I left the room, Holden lowered his head to continue reading through the financial documents. I didn't know what he was looking for and wondered if Holden was avoiding being around Luke by making himself appear busy. That was fine by me. There wasn't much investigating that Holden could do.

I walked back to the kitchen and Luke seemed hard at work. He was taking notes from something he was reading on his laptop. "Did you find something?" I asked as I sat down next to him.

Luke jotted down a few more lines and then raised his head to look at me. "Leon Becker has a fairly long rap sheet. Holden found one newspaper article but searching for prior criminal offenses, I came back with a treasure trove of information. He's been in and out of state prison in Massachusetts, Rhode Island, and New York. The man gets around. He's been arrested three times on murder charges, two of which led to jury trials where he was acquitted. The third one the only witness went missing before the trial started so they couldn't proceed. Leon's defense attorney got the case thrown out for lack of evidence."

"Did you figure out if Leon is connected to any crime family?"

Luke leaned back and stretched. "Not that I can see. It doesn't mean he isn't though. Some of the charges certainly indicate he might be. One of his known associates is connected to a crime family in New York City. There's nothing to indicate why he'd be after you or Melissa."

"Unless he was hired by someone." I remembered what Frank Coonan had said about the person shooting us knowing what they were doing and had intended to scare rather than harm us. With Melissa, clearly, the intent was to kill her and stop her from speaking.

"That could very well be the case, but he's dead so there's no way to know for sure." Luke pointed to the datebook I had set on the table. "What do you have there?"

"Eddie used date books to track his schedule." I slid the book across the table towards Luke. "He didn't detail specific times, but there are names and dates and some notes. He met with a man named Bruce Campbell a few days before he was killed. I want to see if you can search for any information on him. Holden has no idea who he is."

Luke didn't open the book and see for himself. He asked me how to spell the name and I opened the datebook and spelled it as Eddie had written it. Luke typed it in and we waited for a result to come back.

Luke whistled. "The plot thickens. FBI Special Agent Bruce Campbell runs the organized crime division here in Boston." Luke rattled off more information and an address. "Maybe we should pay him a visit."

I checked the time on my phone. I had a few hours before I'd have to meet Sully. "Let's go to his office now. He might not see us but it'll be better than calling and him turning us down."

Chapter 42

J ack and Cooper waved to the bartender they had spoken to
yesterday as the hostess guided them to the table. A young woman
named Molly was their server and had promptly come over to
get their drink order and tell them about lunch specials.

Jack had chatted with her amicably, making her laugh a few times
in what he told Cooper was "priming the pump" before hitting her
with hard questions. Cooper laughed because for him it was just good
old-fashioned flirting and the first time he realized that Jack was a
charmer.

When Molly came back with their drinks, Jack asked. "How long
have you been working here, Molly?"

She smiled as she set down Cooper's water. "I've been here for the
past five years. I'm working while going to Boston College."

"Good hockey team," Jack said and leaned in a little towards her.
"Did you happen to work around the time Eddie Stone was murdered
outside of the restaurant?"

Molly frowned. "I worked that night. It was terrible. Nothing like
that had ever happened here before and we were all quite upset, as
you can imagine."

Jack explained that he was a private investigator working with
Eddie's brother to find out what happened since the police hadn't
solved the case yet. Molly nodded in understanding, praising him for

helping out. "We understand that there was a server on that night that quit shortly after. Do you know who I'm talking about?"

"The German guy?" Molly asked, her face registering surprise.

"That's him. Do you remember his name?"

"I think it was Toby or at least that was the name he gave us."

Jack thanked her for the information. "It struck me as odd that he could show up and start working that night without ever really being hired. Didn't all of you servers mind that there was an extra person on shift that night?"

"Oh, he wasn't extra. Toby was on the schedule. One of the regular servers had been told not to come in because we had a new person," Molly said, lowering her voice so the tables around them couldn't hear. She glanced over her shoulder like she was worried she might be in trouble for sharing the information and then added, "Ethan, who made the schedule that night, was fired about a month later. We all heard it was because he had stolen some money, but I always thought it was related to Toby."

"Why did you think that?" Jack asked, taking a sip of his water.

"Ethan was the head server who made the schedule. He let some random guy walk in off the street and put him on the schedule. No one had questioned it at first. It was during the holidays and we were busy and most thought Toby was some holiday help. When Toby was gone a few days later, that's when people started to question it, but I don't think it ever really got figured out."

Jack sat back in his seat. "What's Ethan's last name?"

"McBride." Molly looked back over her shoulder again. "I need to take your order and get back to work."

Jack thanked her for the information and then they placed their order. When Molly left, Jack turned to Cooper. "What do you think?"

"I think that was the easiest interview I've ever witnessed."

Jack smiled. "I had nothing to do with it. You can tell Molly is still a little annoyed that the whole thing happened. She was motivated to tell someone."

Cooper pulled out his phone and typed in the name Ethan McBride. A Facebook profile came up first and then several links came back to pay sites to get information about a person. Cooper didn't need that. He texted Luke the name and told him he needed an address. "I asked Luke to run his name in the database."

"Hopefully, he'll find us some information. If we can narrow down who Toby is then we are one step closer to the killer."

"Do you think Ethan would know?" Cooper asked, taking a sip of his drink. His stomach growled even though he hadn't thought he was that hungry when they arrived.

"He might," Jack said. "There's no telling if Ethan knew he was setting someone up for murder or not."

Jack and Cooper watched as the restaurant filled up around them. A few minutes later, Molly came back with their food. As she set down Jack's plate, she said, "I hope you won't tell anyone what I told you. I don't want to get in trouble. The owners are pretty sensitive about the murder and don't like us gossiping."

"My lips are sealed," Jack assured her. "Let me ask you one more thing and then we can pretend we never had this conversation."

"Just one more and that's all you get." Molly winked at him.

"Do you happen to have an address for Ethan?" Jack asked with a smile.

"I knew where he lived a few years ago. No idea if he's still there." Molly gave Jack the address and then walked away from the table.

Cooper typed the address in a note file on his phone. A moment later, Luke responded to his text with the same address that Molly had provided. "Looks like the address Molly gave you is going to be our best bet. Luke came back with the same."

Jack looked down at his food. "We'll go after we eat. This looks delicious and I haven't eaten anything that looked this good since the night of Luke and Riley's wedding."

Cooper laughed. "That was only a few nights ago."

"I'm old, Cooper," Jack said, taking a bite. "Who knows how many delicious meals I have left. Each one counts."

Cooper laughed and dug into his lunch. He knew that Jack wasn't married to Karen and wasn't Riley's father, but he couldn't help but think of him that way. Without any living parents of his own, it was easy for Cooper to see Jack as a reliable, stable father figure. He enjoyed the man's company.

When lunch was over, Jack insisted on paying and left a more than generous tip for Molly. She blushed as they said goodbye and wished her well. Once on the street, Cooper plugged Ethan's address into his phone's GPS and they walked the seven blocks to his apartment on the third floor of a brick brownstone that looked like it was out of the price range of a fired waiter.

"Wonder what else this guy does for work?" Jack asked, turning the handle on the main door. He pushed it open and stuck his head inside. "Stairway straight ahead," he said, turning back to look at Cooper. "Let's just go up instead of ringing the bell. Harder to say no to us if we are standing outside his apartment door."

Jack and Cooper stepped into the foyer and took the winding staircase to the top floor. There were two doors and they weren't sure which one belonged to Ethan.

"Let's try the front one first." Jack hit his knuckles against the door and waited. "He might have a new job and not be home in the middle of the day."

Cooper pointed to the other door. "I heard someone moving around in there so someone is home."

Jack waited a moment longer and then they moved down the hall to the other apartment door. Before Jack could knock a man with messy light brown hair that fell over his forehead answered. He had on shorts and a tee-shirt from a band Cooper didn't recognize.

"Can I help you?"

"Are you Ethan McBride?" Jack asked.

The man raked his hand through his messy hair. "Yeah? What's going on? Are you with building inspection or something?" He looked behind him before Jack could answer. "It's kind of messy in here, but if you give me a minute, I'll clean up."

"That's not necessary," Cooper said. "We have a few questions for you about when you worked at Mancuso's."

Ethan groaned. "Man, I got fired from there ages ago. What do they want now?"

"They don't want anything. We want to know about Toby." Jack looked toward the stairs. "We can do this inside if you'd rather."

"Yeah," Ethan said with a frustrated sigh. "Come on in."

Jack and Cooper followed him into the messy space. Clothes were strewn on the floor and tossed over chairs. There was an old pizza box sitting on the coffee table with mold growing on an uneaten slice. It had been there so long it had stopped smelling. There was nowhere for them to sit among the mess so they stood. Ethan did the same.

"What do you want to know?"

"I'm going to get right to the point, Ethan. How do you know Toby?" Jack asked.

"I don't, really."

"You must. You added him to the schedule at Mancuso's without him being actually hired," Cooper said.

"Who are you guys?" Ethan said and then chuckled. "I probably should have asked you that before I let you in here."

Jack introduced Cooper and himself. "We're private investigators looking into the murder of Eddie Stone."

"Murder?" Ethan said, pulling back in disgust. "What do you think

I know about any murder?"

"We don't know that you do," Jack said evenly. "We believe that Toby does and you're our link to him."

Ethan stepped back and turned, shoving clothes off a chair, which landed in a heap on the floor. He sat down and put his head in his hands. "Man, that was a messed-up situation. I didn't know he had anything to do with a murder. He was inside the restaurant when that guy got shot. I don't get it."

It was clear from this guy's demeanor and body language that he didn't know he'd been set up. Cooper believed he wasn't involved in the murder. He looked over at Jack, and by his expression, it seemed he felt the same. "We think Toby alerted someone outside when Eddie Stone was ready to leave. The timing of the shooting was too perfect. We believe there was someone on the inside alerting the shooter when it was time to pull up in front."

Ethan didn't say anything one way or the other. He chewed on his lip and looked up at Cooper like he wanted to say something but didn't.

Cooper pressed. "We are trying to keep you out of trouble so it's in your best interest to tell us how you came to know Toby and add him to the schedule. It's even more suspicious because Toby barely spoke English. How did you expect to pull this off?"

Ethan laughed. "Toby spoke English. The accent was something he liked to do from time to time."

"He wasn't German?" Jack asked.

"He's as American as you and me. He lives in the North End as far as I remember."

Chapter 43

Luke and Riley walked into the main entrance of the FBI building in Chelsea, Massachusetts. There was a lobby desk with a receptionist sitting behind it and two security guards standing by. The receptionist was currently on the phone so they took a seat on one of the couches and waited. She eyed them suspiciously while she continued her call. FBI agents and other staff were coming and going while they sat there, but no one asked why they were there. Luke had his badge on a chain around his neck.

When the receptionist was done, she set the phone down and waved them over. "Can I help you?"

Luke handed her his credentials and introduced them both. "I need to speak with Agent Bruce Campbell. I might have some information on a case he's been working."

"Is he expecting you?" the woman said, staring up at him.

"No. He's not. I only became aware of his involvement in the case about an hour ago so I came right over."

"I see." She picked up the phone and punched in a number. "I don't know if Agent Campbell is available or willing to see you but we can check."

That was all Luke had been hoping for. Before they left, Riley had wondered if they should call Det. Nixon before coming to see Agent Campbell. Although Luke would have appreciated the heads-up if he had been the detective on the case, he wasn't impressed with Det. Nixon and wanted to get right to the source of the information without any red tape getting in the way.

The receptionist spoke to someone and then hung up. "He'll be right down. You can have a seat and wait."

"At least he's willing to talk to us," Riley said, sitting back down on the couch.

"You're being quiet. Not like yourself at all."

Riley smiled. "I figured the FBI would rather hear from a homicide detective than a private investigator. I'm not even licensed to be working in Massachusetts."

"You're not getting paid so you're probably off the hook."

"Right," Riley said absently.

They waited a few more minutes until a tall man with an athletic build wearing a gray suit, blue shirt, and striped tie walked toward them. They stood as he approached, and he reached his hand out to Riley and then to Luke. "Det. Morgan, I'm Agent Bruce Campbell. You said that you might have some information on a case."

"I do," Luke said. "I'm not sure of your involvement but it relates to the Eddie Stone murder case."

Agent Campbell pulled back. "Let's go upstairs to my office to discuss this."

Luke and Riley walked in step with Agent Campbell through the lobby and to the elevator. The agent didn't say anything and neither did Luke or Riley as they rode to the fifth floor. Luke assumed that he'd want to have some privacy before discussing anything. As the elevator doors opened, Agent Campbell pointed to the left and they followed. He escorted them to a small office with the agent's name on the door. He motioned for them to go in and then he closed the door behind them.

Rounding his desk, he sat down and clasped his hands together on the desk. "How do you know Eddie Stone?" he asked.

"We don't," Riley said. "I recently came in contact with Eddie's brother, Holden, who is looking into his brother's death. We have been assisting him."

Luke sat back in the chair and assessed the agent. He gave nothing away on his face like most law enforcement, which in this case, bothered Luke because he couldn't get a good read on him. Luke decided to level with the agent. "We've been in contact with Det. Nixon, the Boston police homicide detective on the case. It's been quite complex since we started a couple of days ago and I don't have full confidence in Det. Nixon. He seems good, but we've come across information in this short time he should have known from the start."

Agent Campbell zeroed in on Luke. "What is it you do for the Little Rock Police Department?"

Luke had told him already when he first introduced himself but he explained again. "I'm the head of the homicide bureau and have been for a few years. I've been on the police force my whole career."

"The Eddie Stone case brought you here?"

"No," Luke said and hesitated. There wasn't a great way to explain his involvement without throwing Holden under the bus or bringing up Riley's father. Luke decided to go with an abridged version of the truth. "Riley and I got married recently in New York and Riley recently met Holden and he asked for her assistance."

Agent Campbell sat back. "You said yourself Det. Nixon is handling the homicide case so I'm not sure why you'd come to me with information."

Riley looked to Luke and back to Agent Campbell. "We know that Eddie was scheduled to meet with you during the time he came to Boston when he was killed. I had hoped you could shed some light into that meeting."

"Why would you think that I'd have a meeting with Eddie?"

Riley smiled the way she did when she was trying to disarm someone. "Agent Campbell, we could sit here all day and volley these questions back and forth. We are all trained in interrogation and interview techniques. Luke and I know how to play the game. I think we'd be better off and save a good deal of time if we were all truthful with each other."

Luke could tell that Agent Campbell wanted to smile at Riley's candor, the corners of his lips turned up ever so slightly.

"Proceed then," the agent said.

"We know that Eddie Stone is in some way connected to the CIA, whether he was employed by them full time or as a paid asset," Riley explained. "We know that he was gathering intel on arms deals, drug deals, and the like. We know based on notes in his datebook that he had an appointment with you right before he was murdered. There were also appointments with you once a year for the last couple of years. Finally, we know that whatever Eddie was working on at the time of his death was connected to Gregor Wolf in Germany and had a connection back here to Boston. What we don't know is who killed him."

The agent appeared impressed. "You found all that out in just a few days?"

"That's not all," Luke responded. "We also know that someone was after Melissa Patton, Eddie's girlfriend. One of our other investigators went to her house to speak to her and right before she could disclose the information Riley just shared, they shot up her house. When they ran, he chased, attempting to kill them. That man's name is Leon Becker. I have had a look at his rap sheet."

Riley added, "The day before that, someone shot at Holden and me when we went to interview Frank Coonan."

"You went to interview Frank Coonan?" Agent Campbell asked, looking skeptical. "I can't imagine he would have told you much.

You're lucky you got out of there alive."

"Quite the contrary," Riley said. "Frank is the one who told us Eddie had been recruited by a government agency. He wasn't sure if it was the CIA or another group."

"Frank told you that?"

"Yes, he was rather forthcoming with information."

"Why would he trust you?"

Riley looked to Luke, but it wasn't his secret to share so he didn't say anything. She turned her attention back to Agent Campbell. "My father is respected in certain circles and I had an in with Frank."

Agent Campbell raised his eyebrows. "Care to share more about that?"

"No. I can't even if I wanted to." Riley leveled a look at him and it seemed that Agent Campbell understood. At least, he didn't press the issue. Riley went on. "It was Frank's men who got us out of harm's way that day. They never found who was shooting, but I assume it might have been Leon Becker."

"I don't understand how you think I can help." Agent Campbell peered over the desk at them.

Riley looked at Luke and he explained. "We were hoping you could share why you were meeting with Eddie, and if you think it might have played any part in his death. We have a ton of conflicting information and not a lot makes sense. I'll be honest with you, Agent Campbell, I can't even get a good read on a suspect."

"You mentioned Leon Becker. Wouldn't he be a suspect?"

Luke nodded. "Sure, we have but it's bigger than one person. That much is obvious."

"Why do you say that?"

Agent Campbell's questions were starting to annoy Luke. He understood why the man was asking him. He'd be doing the same if he were on the other side of the desk. He was losing patience to play along though.

"How is it not obvious?" Luke asked, hating the sarcastic tone in his voice. "There were at least three people involved in Eddie's death." When Agent Campbell didn't bite, Luke counted it down on his fingers. "The person driving the SUV, the shooter, and the person in the restaurant who tipped them off that Eddie was on his way out the door."

Agent Campbell looked at him with a curious expression on his face so Luke explained how the timing of the hit was a little too perfect to be random. Agent Campbell smiled. "You certainly know what you're doing, Detective."

"Little Rock may be in the middle of nowhere to you, but last I checked, it's still at the top of the list for one of the most violent mid-sized cities. Not a reputation we are proud of but it's brought a level of experience generally only gained in bigger metropolitan police departments."

Agent Campbell sat there for a few beats not saying anything. Luke wasn't sure if the agent was willing to share any information at all. It could be a wasted trip, but Luke still felt like it was worth it to try. He felt no closer to solving the case now than when he started. That's what made what Agent Campbell said next so shocking.

"I wouldn't share this information if the operation were still ongoing, but with Eddie's death, all investigation has stopped," Agent Campbell noted. "Eddie had come across information about individuals here in Boston heavily involved in a major international drug smuggling operation. He did the right thing and shared that with the FBI. I had been meeting with him and working to find out more details as his investigation evolved. It wasn't a primary focus of his, but when he came across information, he shared it with me. We met when he was back here in Boston and were in fairly close contact."

"You said his investigation. Was Eddie working with the CIA as an asset or was he employed by them? We've never had a straight answer on that."

"You're probably hearing conflicting information because the relationship evolved." It was obvious to Luke that Agent Campbell was trying to weigh his words carefully much the way Riley had when speaking about her father. Finally, he exhaled and got it straight.

"Eddie had been approached by the CIA. My understanding is he started as an asset for another CIA officer and then the relationship evolved. That's all I'm at liberty to share."

"Are you able to tell us who he was referencing here in Boston?" Luke asked, figuring that would be a solid lead and potential suspect for Eddie's murder.

"I'm afraid I can't. He was dealing with lower-level criminals, and as far as I knew, had yet to discover who the boss was here." Agent Campbell sat back and frowned. "I've always suspected that his murder was directly connected to the last investigation Eddie was involved with. Someone here in Boston figured out what Eddie was doing and silenced him before he could talk."

That's exactly what Luke had been worried about.

Chapter 44

"American?" Cooper asked, confused more now than before. He folded his arms across his chest and stared down at Ethan. Jack was doing the same.

"Yeah, Toby was from here. He only faked the German accent." Ethan shook his head and laughed. "It wasn't only German. Toby could fake just about any accent you asked him to do."

"How long have you known him?" Jack asked.

"It was a friend of a friend kind of thing," Ethan explained. "Before you ask, no I can't put you in touch with the guy who initially asked me to allow Toby to work those two nights."

Jack scowled down at him. "What reason did they give you that Toby needed to work at the restaurant those two nights?"

"It was only supposed to be one night and then Toby told me he needed to come back the next night, too."

"You didn't answer my question," Jack said, clearly losing patience. "What reason did they give you to add Toby to the schedule?"

Ethan looked away and mumbled, "I didn't ask. They said he needed to be at the restaurant that first night and I made it happen. Then when Toby said he needed to come back one more night, I made that happen, too."

"How can you sit there—" Jack started but Cooper cut him off.

"Let me guess, Ethan, you did it for the money?"

Ethan nodded. "My friend offered me five grand to allow Toby on the schedule. It was simple enough. I knew neither of our managers paid that much attention to what the servers were doing. I called off one server and added Toby in her place. He had experience so it was seamless. I had no idea why he wanted to be there, but Toby didn't cause a scene or mess anything up, so when he said he needed to come back, I didn't question it."

"You didn't question that someone was willing to pay you that much money?" Jack asked and whistled. He turned to Cooper. "I think if someone was asking me something like that and offering me that kind of cash, I'd be worried what they were getting me involved with."

"Me, too," Cooper said. "Let me guess, Ethan, the guy who offered you the money knew you were desperate for some cash?"

"I had some gambling debts to pay off."

Now they were getting somewhere. Ethan had been the perfect patsy. Cooper relaxed his arms at his sides. "Who did you owe the gambling debts to?"

"A bookie on the south side. His name was Collins. I don't know that I ever knew his first name."

Cooper's ears perked up and so did Jack's who turned and looked at him in a question. That was the name of the guy involved with Riley and Liv's kidnapping. He had been a part of Eddie's old crew. "Do you know who this bookie worked for?" Cooper asked.

"What do you mean?" Ethan looked up at Cooper squinting.

"Organized crime, you know, the mob." Cooper was starting to wonder if this guy had any smarts at all. "Most bookies, at least the ones in this city, are connected to the mob – Italian, Irish, don't matter they all work the same." Cooper had no idea if that were true, but Ethan didn't seem to know much of anything.

Ethan shook his head. "I don't know anything about all that. My friend knew I was in deep and needed the cash. He came to me a couple of days later and told me he had a way for me to make some quick money, more than enough to pay off Collins. I took it, man. It was as simple as that."

Except it wasn't that simple at all. Cooper was trying to connect the dots and it was nearly coming into focus but not quite. "What's the name of your friend that came to you with this offer?" Cooper pressed.

"I'm not telling you that." Ethan stood. "I've said enough."

As Ethan tried to pass, Cooper stood blocking his way. "Eddie Stone was murdered that night and we believe Toby was involved. You played a role in that whether you think you did or not. I'd think you'd want to redeem yourself here and help us find his killer."

"I have no idea who killed him!" Ethan suddenly screamed at the top of his lungs.

Cooper and Jack remained calm in the face of his tantrum. "I don't think you know who killed him," Cooper said, "but I think you can help us put the pieces together so we can figure out who did."

Ethan shook his head. "No, you guys need to go. I should never have let you in here."

"Who are you afraid of?" Jack asked, stepping out of the way so Ethan could go by him.

"I'm not afraid. I'm just done with that chapter of my life and don't want to revisit it."

Jack took a few steps toward him, speaking to Ethan's back. "What does that mean?"

Ethan turned to him and raked a hand through his messy hair. "It means I don't run with those kinds of people anymore. I don't gamble. I don't do drugs. I haven't even had a drink in over a year. I may be a complete slob, but I've got it together. I'm done with my past and not revisiting that chapter of my life for anything – even if it means solving a murder."

Cooper hated playing this card, but desperate times. "We'll go and thanks for speaking to us." He pulled his wallet out of his pants pocket and retrieved a business card and handed it to Ethan. "If you want to be on the straight and narrow, your conscience is going to eat you up. Think about if it were someone in your family. Wouldn't you want justice?"

"That's a low blow, man." Ethan took the card though and looked at it. "You're a long way from home."

"That's how important solving Eddie Stone's murder is to us."

"Toby Wahl. You can probably still find him in Boston," Ethan said before closing the door.

Cooper went down the stairs and Jack followed behind him. They didn't say anything to each other until they were on the street and about a block away.

Jack stopped on the sidewalk and turned to Cooper. "This feels like it has come full circle."

"Collins, right? I thought the same." Cooper stared up the road. "Do you get the feeling all of these people are interconnected?"

"Boston isn't that big." Jack blew out a breath. "I wonder how Collins would feel knowing he was paid off with blood money that helped to get his friend killed."

Cooper turned back to Jack. "I don't think I'd ever want to be the one to tell him that. What do you think we should do next?"

"Hunt down Toby Wahl."

"We'll have to go back to Holden's to get Luke to search in the database for us."

Jack pointed down the road to the corner where there was a coffee shop. "We won't need to do that. Let me make a call and I'm sure I can get an address."

Cooper followed Jack down the road and into the shop. Jack grabbed a table near the window while Cooper went up to the counter and ordered coffee for both of them. He paid and then went to stand by the counter where the orders were placed when they were ready. Cooper glanced over and watched as Jack spoke to someone on the phone. He should have known being a cop for so long that Jack would still have connections. Cooper pulled his phone from his pocket and checked the time. They had a couple of hours before he'd have to meet Riley.

The young woman called Cooper's name and he stepped forward to grab the coffee cups. He carried them over to the table and set one cup down in front of Jack and then pulled out the chair across from him. Cooper sat down and got comfortable as Jack wrapped up his call.

"I have an address for Toby in the North End," Jack said as he placed his phone on the table.

"How did you get it so quickly?"

"I called Miles. I wanted to check to see how things were going back in Troy anyway, and I figured he'd be able to pull me the information I needed."

Cooper took a sip and savored the taste. This wasn't a chain shop they were in but a place that seemed eclectic and local to the neighborhood. "How are things back there?"

"Good. Miles has been at the house on and off between things he had to handle. He slept there last night and he has another officer rotating with him. He said he got some flak from his supervisor but then he mentioned my name and they cleared it."

"You still have pull there, don't you?"

Jack sipped his coffee and stared out the window. "You work someplace more than thirty years it starts to feel like home. You see them more than your own family." Turning back to Cooper, he said, "I was the longest-serving detective they had. I call in favors when needed but don't abuse the privilege."

Cooper understood that. He had only been a detective for a few years with the Little Rock Police Department before he went out on his own. Captain Meadows had asked him a few times to come back, even throwing more money at him, but it wasn't what Cooper wanted. He knew though that if he needed anything that they'd be there for him.

Jack was the direct opposite of his father, who had bounced around from job to job never providing Cooper much stability growing up. With his mother passing when he was still a baby, his father was all he had. It was what had made Cooper so commitment-shy but determined to stay in one place and build something for himself. If there was any man he wanted to emulate, it was Jack, and Cooper told him exactly that.

Jack smiled. "I'm here for you, Cooper, anything you need. I'm glad you can turn to me. Riley and Luke, too."

There was something Cooper wanted to know but didn't want to pry. Curiosity got the better of him. "Are you planning to marry Karen?"

Jack laughed. "Wondering my intentions? I could ask the same about you and Adele."

Cooper held his hands up in defeat. "I didn't want to do anything to take the focus away from Riley and Luke, but as soon as I get back to Little Rock, that's the plan."

Jack chuckled. "Same. I have the ring already. Karen and I already discussed it. Most of my stuff is already at her house. We wanted to tell Riley when she got back from her honeymoon."

"You should still. I'm sure she could use some good news."

Jack nodded and tipped back the rest of his coffee. He got up and tossed away the empty cup. "Let's go catch a killer so Riley and Luke get to have a honeymoon."

Chapter 45

L uke and I walked out of the FBI office not sure if we knew more than when we walked in. He held the door for me and I stepped out into the sunlight. "Do you think Agent Campbell was telling us the truth that he doesn't know who Eddie was investigating in Boston?"

"I think so," Luke said, stopping for a moment.

"How could Eddie not have known who it was?"

"Eddie wasn't investigating someone here in Boston. He was working undercover and came upon information about someone in Boston. It's two different things." Luke shifted his body to turn toward me. "If I'm investigating an international drug ring and Americans keep popping up as part of that investigation then I'm going to realize there are ties back here, which would fall under the FBI's jurisdiction. Eddie might have come across some lower-level people in a crime syndicate that he was dealing with but never had access to the boss. I'm sure they have systems to protect the people at the top."

"Have you worked many organized crime cases?" It occurred to me that I didn't know more about Luke's experiences before we met.

"Almost none. It's not that the south doesn't have organized crime, we do, but I'm dealing more with street gangs. Those street gangs might be connected or have an allegiance to a broader criminal syndicate, but I rarely see that at the local level. If there are ties, it generally falls out of my jurisdiction. We've never, to my knowledge, been able to make a big connection like that."

We walked to Luke's car and got inside. He started the engine, turned the heat on for us, and let it warm up. "The mob or mafia, whatever you want to call it, has organization hence the name organized crime which street gangs don't usually have or at least not as far-reaching."

"That makes sense. When Agent Campbell said Eddie's role with the CIA evolved. It almost sounds like he was working for them directly. Would it surprise you if he was?"

"Not necessarily," Luke said, reaching forward and turning the car vents more toward us now that the air had warmed. "Good criminals understand the criminal mind and become an asset to law enforcement under the right circumstances. Eddie had first-hand knowledge of how those operations work. He might have needed training on how to collect the intel and pass it to his superiors and some access to spy equipment and even a bigger budget to do the work, but I suspect at the heart of it, he had a good handle on the inner workings of it. He probably knew much more than a CIA officer who had never committed a criminal act."

"What do you think happened to the men working with Eddie over in London? How did he make that transition?" I was fascinated by this and how it all worked. I didn't expect Luke to have all the answers.

"How does it work with your father?" Luke asked, narrowing his eyes at me. "I assume he's not a one-man operation? If he's supposed to be coming off like the head of a crime syndicate, how does he work it?"

"I've never really asked, but I assume he has a team of other CIA officers working with him from time to time. He never was a criminal though and went legit. It's the transition I'm most interested in."

Luke put the car in drive and left the parking lot. "That's an answer I don't have. I'm sure that the CIA helped him with that. I'm sure keeping the appearance of the head of a large crime syndicate was part of his cover so the criminal activity of his people might have continued. There might have even been arrests of some of his lower-level people, but I'm sure none of them knew Eddie's real mission. That's how it works with confidential informants for the FBI. They have a fine line to walk."

I stared straight ahead wondering what the next steps might be. If I were being honest with myself, I was exhausted. I wanted to be on my honeymoon with Luke instead of in Boston working on a homicide case. My mother and sister flashed in my mind and I remembered why I was doing this – to keep my family safe. I turned to Luke. "Now that we have real confirmation that Eddie was working with the CIA, I think we should have Holden call and try to get some information from them."

Luke gave me a sideways glance. "I don't think they will provide much information."

"I think it's worth a shot at this point. It's not like we have anything to lose." I tried to stifle a yawn, but Luke saw it.

"You tired?"

"Exhausted. I wanted to wake up with you the morning after our wedding and have a nice relaxing couple of weeks. Instead, I've been running around Boston." I tugged on the shirt I was wearing. "I haven't even worn my own clothes since the day I was taken."

Luke changed lanes and I watched as his fingers tightened around the steering wheel. "We can quit this anytime. Just say the word and we can be on a flight out of here. I hate that you've gone through this."

"I hate that you woke up and I was gone. I hate that you were scared and panicked and that the cops probably initially looked at you like you did something to me." I reached over and touched his arm and his muscles relaxed. "It's a few days in our life together. I hate all of it, but we can make it work."

Luke continued driving toward Holden's house. I was going to ask Holden once we arrived to place a call to the CIA headquarters in Langley, Virginia, and see what he could learn. I glanced down at the clock in the car. I would need to leave for the aquarium to meet Sully soon after I arrived. I still wasn't sure what I was going to tell Luke. A few more miles passed while I rolled around excuses that I could make for why I had to leave the house. I glanced over at my husband and my heart swelled. Lying wasn't any way to start a marriage. He was on my side even if I didn't always agree with what he wanted me to do.

"Luke," I said softly. "I have to tell you something, but I don't want you to get angry with me."

Luke's eyes shifted toward me and his lips curled up in a smile. "Sully texted you and you're going to meet him?"

"Cooper told you?"

He laughed. "Of course, Cooper told me. There was no way he was letting you go meet Sully without telling me. I'm coming with you, and I think Jack is as well. We've got your back."

"Sully told me to come alone, Luke. The last thing I want to do is antagonize him. I told Cooper he could watch from afar but he needed to stay out of sight."

"Then that's what I'll do as well." He pulled over in an open spot a couple of blocks away from Holden's house. I was surprised he had even found a spot this close. Luke cut the engine and turned to me. "We will figure it out. You don't have to do this or anything else alone."

I didn't know what to say. When it came to Sully, I always felt alone. There were so many secrets surrounding his work that it was never anything I could share with people. I reached for Luke's hand and linked my fingers through his. "I appreciate that."

"I mean it. I'm always here for you." Luke rubbed a hand over his bald head and blew out a breath. "This probably isn't the time or place to say this. You hide things from me because you think it's better for me or that I'll stop you from making what I would consider crazy decisions. You're a great investigator and I need to step back and let you be you. I can't tell you the number of cases I've had where I was stuck or backed into a corner because of my own rigid thinking and you offered up something I never thought of. You're willing to take risks I'd never take. You're willing to throw out a wild theory and see where it lands. I could never do that. I need to get better at respecting your choices."

For the second time in a matter of minutes, I didn't know what to say. This had been a sticking point in our relationship since we started dating. Now, it seemed Luke was changing his tune.

"I have never felt disrespected. I know that you care about my safety. It's nice that you said that and I'll be more inclined now to keep you in the loop. No one likes feeling scolded." I leaned back and looked over at him. "It's okay that we are different. You have rules to follow that I don't have. I think our differences are what make us work so well together."

Luke smiled. "You're probably right about that."

With that settled, we got out of the car and walked to Holden's house. Luke used the key to unlock the door and we stepped inside. I stopped short as Holden rushed toward us. He had a bloody nose and another bruise forming on his face.

"What happened to you?" I asked.

Holden pointed to the door. "I went out to get some food and when I was walking back, Noah saw me. He dragged me into an alley and he roughed me up. He demanded to know where you were and what I was doing. He had a gun and threatened to kill me right there, but he's desperate to get to you."

"What did you tell him?" Luke demanded, raising his voice.

"I didn't tell him anything, I swear. I told him that we were close to finding Eddie's killer and that it wasn't Patrick Sullivan." Holden lowered his eyes to mine. "I told him, Riley, how you've been doing everything you can to help find who killed Eddie and that you brought in other people to help. He didn't care. Noah said no matter what we find, he knows it was Patrick Sullivan who killed Eddie. He wanted me to bring you to him right then. I struggled with him and thankfully some people passed by the alley and saw us. It gave me a chance to get away."

"You said Noah doesn't know about this house, right?" Luke asked.

"No one knows. Eddie didn't even know about it. It's not in my name but rather a corporate name. There would be a lot of hoops to jump through to find it."

"Okay," Luke said, his shoulders relaxing. "You stay here, Holden. Don't leave the house again. If you're not out there, he can't find you. He can't trace you back here."

Holden said, "He knows I'm staying somewhere though and he found me in this neighborhood. I was only a few blocks away. It's only a matter of time before he finds us here."

"We aren't going to let that happen," Luke said. He glanced down at me. "We need to find the killer now."

I wanted that, too, but it was easier said than done.

Chapter 46

Cooper and Jack made it to Boston's North End quicker than they expected. Cooper was surprised to see the tightly packed row houses and cobblestone streets. Some of the small houses looked like they might have been there since the early days of the Revolutionary War. They had even passed Paul Revere's house on the way there.

"It's too bad we can't sightsee while we are here," Cooper said as they turned down Tileston Street.

"You've never been?" Jack asked, as he glanced down at his phone and then up at the numbers on the houses.

"Never. This trip is only the second time I've been in the Northeast."

"You'll have to come back when you have more time. I can show you around." Jack stopped in the middle of the sidewalk and pointed to a small house two up from where they stood. There was a sign that simply said *Bakery* above the door.

As they approached, the smell of freshly baked bread wafted through the air and Cooper caught the scent. "I wouldn't mind living above a bakery if it always smelled like this."

Jack patted his belly. "If I did, I'd eat it constantly and that wouldn't be good for my growing midsection."

Cooper reached for the handle to open the door but had to step out of the way as it swung open for a customer exiting the building. It was then Cooper noticed two doors inside the small foyer. One to the left going to the bakery and another door straight ahead that probably went to the apartment above it.

Cooper stepped into the foyer and tried the handle of the door leading upstairs. It turned and he pulled the door open. "Unlocked," he said over his shoulder to Jack. "I think we should go right up instead of ringing the bell. We can have the element of surprise as we did with Ethan."

Jack agreed and they climbed the steep narrow staircase to the top. Once on the second-floor landing, there was another door straight ahead. Cooper knocked once and waited. He raised his hand to knock again but didn't need to. A young man pulled open the door and looked up at Cooper. "Can I help you?" he asked.

"I'm looking for Toby Wahl."

"That's me," he said, stepping into the hall.

Caught off guard, Cooper hesitated. The man standing in front of him was probably no more than five-foot-six and had short sandy brown hair and a trim build. His pants barely stayed up on his narrow hips and his arms looked like they had never lifted anything heavier than a can of soup. Toby didn't look the part of someone involved in a mob-style hit.

"Is there something you need?" Toby asked.

It was Jack who finally spoke up. He introduced Cooper and himself and explained briefly why they were there. "Is there someplace we can talk?"

Toby looked back at the apartment. "My girlfriend and daughter are inside. Can we go downstairs to the bakery? There are a few tables down there where we can sit and talk."

"You might not want an audience for this conversation," Jack said.

Toby sighed. "It's my brother's shop. My family has owned the bakery since the 1940s."

"Lead the way," Jack said and motioned with his hand toward the stairs.

Toby led them down the stairs and through the door. Once inside, he walked to the back of the bakery to a side table. As they sat, Toby waved to the man and woman behind the counter and asked Jack and Cooper if they wanted anything. When they declined, Toby sat across from them and took a breath. He glanced down at his hands folded on the table and then back up at them. "I assume you're here to ask me about my involvement in the Eddie Stone murder?"

"Why would you guess that?" Cooper asked, still assessing the man not sure what to make of him. He had no reason to be so forthcoming with them.

"I assumed it would catch up to me because my life is finally on track. Karma, right?" Toby frowned.

Jack sat back on his chair and looked over at Toby. "Tell us what happened."

"First thing you should know is I had a gambling problem. I'd bet on anything and I did for years. I'd win enough to feed my habit and make it worth it. I never thought I had a problem." Toby looked over at the counter. "Everyone around me knew I had a problem, but no one could convince me of that. That is until I lost big and didn't have the money to pay up. The guy threatened to kill me. He threatened my family and the bakery. It wasn't in my name so they couldn't take it from me even if they wanted to and they tried. When that didn't work, they threatened to burn it down if I didn't pay up."

Cooper glanced around. "It's still standing."

Toby nodded. "Barely. I begged and pleaded for more time to pay. I owed close to twenty thousand. My brother didn't have it and my parents weren't going to bail me out again. I was too ashamed to go to friends. I did the next best thing or so I thought. I asked if I could work off my debt to him."

"How'd that go?" Cooper asked, not sure whether to feel sorry for the guy or not.

"At first, it was just stupid stuff – odd jobs and errands. Nothing that bad. It was more embarrassing than anything. Then he came to me with a request that I thought was equally as stupid – go be a waiter at Mancuso's for a night and let him know when Eddie Stone was leaving. I didn't even know who Eddie Stone was at the time. The guy showed me a photo. Eddie never showed up the first night so I had to go back there. All I had to do was call a number when Eddie paid the check and he was headed out."

Toby locked eyes with Cooper. "I swear I had no idea they were going to kill him. I thought maybe they'd rough him up or something. I had no idea I set someone up to be murdered."

"Why didn't you go to the cops when you knew?"

Toby raised his palms. "Why do you think? I mean they were going to burn down my family's bakery for being late with a debt. What do you think they'd do to me and my family if I ratted them out?"

Toby had a point. Cooper still wasn't sure what to make of the guy who was sitting there so forthcoming with information. "Did the cops or anyone come and speak to you?"

"Never. I kept waiting. I figured they'd connect the dots eventually." Toby had a wide-eyed look of surprise on his face. "No one ever did."

Jack shifted his eyes back to Cooper and then landed squarely on Toby. "Why tell us now if you've gotten away with this for so long?"

Toby sat back in his chair and pointed upstairs. "I have a wonderful girlfriend and we just had a baby six months ago. I'm a father now and I have a perspective I didn't have before. I paid off my gambling debt and got the help I needed. I'm tired of looking over my shoulder." He stayed quiet for a moment. "I had no idea when I agreed to do it that someone would die. If I had, I wouldn't have done it. I've lived with the guilt for every hour of the day. It's time I man up and do what's right, if not for me then for my family."

This was the moment of trust and would tell Cooper how committed Toby was to doing what was right. "Who was the person you called to notify that Eddie Stone was leaving the restaurant that night?"

"I don't know that and that's the truth. They gave me a number and I called. I didn't know the person on the other end of the phone. It surprised me because I thought I knew who I was calling, but that's not who answered." Toby leaned forward on the table and dropped his voice an octave. "I'll tell you who I owed the debt to and who set me up to work at the restaurant."

"Good enough," Jack said and Cooper agreed.

"Noah Byrne."

Cooper wasn't sure he had heard correctly so he asked the question again and Toby provided the same answer. Jack and Cooper sat there not speaking. Cooper was sure Jack felt as shocked as he did. Noah Byrne worked for Eddie and was the one driving the theory that Patrick Sullivan had killed Eddie. Now, Toby was sitting there telling him it was Noah who helped set Eddie up to be killed. It didn't make any sense at all.

"I'm not lying," Toby said defensively when he saw the looks on their faces. "I told you I was going to tell you the truth and that's what I did. You look like you don't believe me."

Jack recovered faster. "It's not that we don't believe you, Toby. Did you know that Noah is connected to Eddie Stone? They were friends. Noah is one of the reasons we are here investigating. Noah told Eddie's brother he knows who the killer is so he's incriminating someone else."

Toby shook his head adamantly. "That's not right. I owed a debt to Noah and that's who made all the threats. That's who I ended up doing work for to pay off the debt and then told me I needed to be at Mancuso's Italian Restaurant and when. He told me that there was some deal made with some guy Ethan at the restaurant and I'd have no problem working the shift. He gave me the uniform and told me to show up."

"Have you had any contact with him since?" Cooper asked, still confused about Noah's involvement.

"Not in months." Toby expelled a breath. "After I found out what had happened, I went to Noah and told him that I couldn't believe what they had set me up to do. He acted as if nothing had happened. He said he had no idea what I was talking about. I figured he thought that I was wearing a wire and helping the cops. He didn't admit to anything. Noah made subtle threats about keeping my mouth shut, and that if I kept saying the things I was saying, bad things would happen to me and my family. Noah never admitted he even knew Eddie. It was a surreal conversation."

Cooper looked to Jack to see if he had any more questions. When he didn't say anything, Cooper asked one more. "Would you be willing to speak to the Boston police detective assigned to the case?"

Toby nodded. "You know how to reach me if you or the cops need to know anything else." When there was nothing else and Cooper said he could go, Toby stood from the table. He looked down at Cooper and Jack one last time. "I really am sorry. I had no idea that I was setting someone up for murder."

When he was gone, Jack turned to Cooper. "What did you make of that?"

"That was a curveball I wasn't expecting. Why would Noah tell Holden he needed to track down Patrick Sullivan because he was responsible when he was involved all along?"

"You believe Toby?" Jack asked, standing from the table.

"I do," Cooper said honestly. "He seemed like he was telling the truth and didn't have much reason to lie. He didn't have to speak to us at all." Cooper looked at his watch. "I'm going to need to get back to meet with Riley."

Jack glanced at the door. "I think I'm going to go back and put a little pressure on Ethan to see if Noah is the person he knew. I want some confirmation that Noah is involved before we are off on another wild goose chase. You think Riley will be okay without me?"

"We're fine. I think that's a great idea that you go back to Ethan's. We need confirmation about Noah before we can do anything with it."

Jack jotted down directions so Cooper could find the New England Aquarium. It turned out he was a lot closer than he realized. It was only a little more than a mile from the bakery. He could easily walk it and get there on time.

Chapter 47

I paid the entrance fee to the New England Aquarium and made my way inside. I stopped for a moment and looked up at the sign overhead which gave directions to the different exhibits. It had been a long time since I had visited the aquarium, but the penguin exhibit was always my favorite. I recalled that there was a winding ramp that connected the floors and the exhibit was right there in the middle so visitors could look down at them.

The aquarium had African penguins, which were also called jackass penguins because they made the same sound as a donkey braying. It was funny that's where my father wanted to meet. My mother had called him that more than once.

My eyes shifted back and forth as I walked through the exhibits. I didn't see anyone that looked familiar. I knew Cooper and Luke were there someplace keeping an eye on me. I approached the penguin exhibit and watched a little boy about five years old point to the penguins and talk to his mom who stood beside him. He smiled as he watched them play and giggled when they made their braying sound. It was soothing standing there watching them. I hated that the penguins weren't in the wild but appreciated being able to watch them. It was a weird mix of emotions.

"You could stand there for hours as a kid. Your mother would have to drag you away," the familiar voice said behind me.

I hesitated to turn around as anger I didn't know I had bubbled up inside me. "I don't appreciate you drugging my friend and leaving him in an alley." I turned to face him.

Sully had a ball cap pulled low to shield a good portion of his face. He had lost some weight since the last time I saw him, which at the moment, I couldn't recall how many years it had been. There were deeper wrinkles around his eyes, but his cheeks were still ruddy and his smile still wide.

"I did it for his own good," Sully said. He reached for me but thought better of it and pulled his hand back. "I know you probably don't believe that. There are things you don't understand."

"Then tell me so I do understand." I leaned back on the edge of the penguin exhibit railing.

"I can't do that."

"You can. You won't. There's a difference." I glanced past him and wouldn't make eye contact. "Why did you want to meet me?"

This time Sully reached out and put a hand on my shoulder. I felt like shrugging it off but figured being defensive wouldn't get us anywhere. "I wanted to see you. I didn't mean to disrupt your wedding. I was here in the States handling a few things and thought I'd see my daughter on her wedding day."

"You could have told me and joined the rest of us like a normal person instead of sneaking around the venue."

Sully pursed his lips together and shook his head. I made the same face. "That wouldn't have worked. I didn't want to upset your mother. Believe it or not, I was trying to keep you safe. I had no idea this was going to happen."

I wasn't going to debate with him about how much angrier my mother was now that Liv and I had been kidnapped. Sully often used my mother and work as an excuse for being less than a decent parent.

I looked him right in the eyes that were the same shape and color brown as mine. "Did you kill Eddie Stone?"

"Not directly. No."

"What does that mean?"

Sully glanced to his left and his right. "I shouldn't tell you this."

I pushed myself off the wall and tried to shove past him. Sully was like a wall though. I stepped right and he blocked my path. I slammed right into him, my head hitting his chest. He placed both hands on my shoulders and moved me back. "You don't get to stalk off and be angry right now. There is too much at stake."

I tipped my head back to look at him. "I'm well aware of that. You're not telling me anything useful though." I grunted. "You're not telling me anything at all and I'm better off on my own."

Sully stepped toward me. "Eddie Stone was my asset," he said quietly. "I'm the one that decided to bring him in initially. We worked well together at first. We had even set it up so we looked like rivals. Eddie got cocky though especially after the CIA offered him officer status and trained him. He stopped taking my advice."

"He went rogue. Is that what you're trying to say?"

"Not exactly."

"What are you saying then?"

"Eddie took risks he shouldn't have been taking. Melissa, for instance, knew too much. He was being paid by the Germans, too. I was working to get to the bottom of what he was being paid for, but I never did figure that out."

"Gregor Wolf?"

Sully narrowed his eyes. "How do you know that name?"

"It came up in our investigation," I admitted. I was hesitant to say more. Not that I knew much more. "Is he involved in Eddie's death?"

"Not that I know of."

"Then how is he connected?" I asked and Sully stared down at me. For the first time, I felt what Luke probably felt when he was trying to get information out of me. It was a mixture of annoyance like Sully didn't trust me and outright disrespect. I tucked it away as a good life lesson in the marriage. "You need to answer me, Sully."

"Sully?" he asked with a sarcastic tone. "What about Dad?"

"When you start acting like a father, then I'll call you Dad but not a moment sooner." I pointed past him and raised my voice. "You have us running around like chickens with our heads cut off and you're lurking in the shadows with critical information. Do you know that I was shot at?"

No words came out of Sully's mouth but his look said everything. Not only did he know, but I was sure he had been the one shooting at us. I jabbed a finger into my chest. "You shot at your daughter? Are you trying to kill me? Is that why you brought me here?" The tears had started to form and heat drifted up my chest into my neck and cheeks. I was sure I was flaming red at the moment.

"Riley, you have to calm down. It's not what you think." Sully looked around us and noticed people starting to stare. "I'm going to have to walk away if you don't calm down. You are drawing attention to us."

I wanted to throw an all-out five-year-old tantrum. I had no desire to compose myself. I felt like throwing myself on the ground and kicking and screaming, just letting out every frustration and emotion bubbling up inside of me. I couldn't do that or I'd get no information.

I roughly brushed my hand across each cheek and slapped the tears away and took a deep breath. "Explain now or I'm calling the police."

"I got intel that Leon Becker was in one of those buildings ready to take out Holden. I couldn't get a position on him so I did the next best thing. I shot at you and Holden so you'd get down and get out of the way." He stared deep into my eyes. "I saved your life and then I saved Cooper and Melissa."

Sully caught me so off guard that I stepped back and bumped into the railing behind me. "That was you? How was Leon Becker connected to all of this?"

Sully moved past me and stood at the railing staring out at the penguins. "I can see why the penguins were your favorite when you were little. It's hard not to smile watching them." He reached back for my hand. "Watch them with me and I'll tell you what I know."

I turned around to face the exhibit and shook my hand free of his. "I'm listening."

"As I started to say, Eddie was an asset for me. He brought us great intel, so much so the CIA offered him a job. We were set up as rivals. Eddie did okay for a while, but the CIA doesn't pay as well as criminal activity. He was around all that money, but it wasn't his. He was making deals with CIA money and carrying out criminal acts during work for the government. He wasn't banking the kind of money he made before when he was doing the same job. It had become all risk and no reward. He got greedy."

"I would think that happens often."

Sully shook his head. "It doesn't. I make a great living better than most. The difference between Eddie and me is that the CIA is a lifelong commitment for me. I'm doing it because I care about the service I provide to my country. No one does this because it's just a job. Eddie, I think, was getting off on playacting for a while, but a leopard doesn't change its spots."

"You think Eddie went back to a life of crime."

"I know he did. I got intel that he was. I tried talking to him about it. It was risky – not only was he risking his freedom, but he was putting other CIA officers at risk."

"I found payments in an offshore account that belonged to Eddie. They were regular quarterly payments over the last several years. The deposits came from Farrell Investments. Jack said Terry Farrell is the name of the architect of the MI6 building. We wondered if they were paying him or if it was money the CIA had given him for operations."

Sully raked a hand down his face and chuckled. "I can't believe my kid found the evidence I couldn't."

I looked up at him. "What do you mean?"

"Gregor Wolf. Farrell Investments is a dummy corporation of his. He likes the irony of using something connected to MI6. It's a blatant slap in the face to MI6. They have been trying to bring him down for years."

"Eddie was working for Gregor Wolf?"

"We weren't sure of the relationship. We had trouble pinning down evidence, especially after Eddie died. We believed that Eddie was tipping off Wolf about operations because he seemed to slip through the cracks at every turn. It frustrated the CIA and MI6. How much was in that account?"

"It was about a million a year."

"Sounds about right. Are you able to share that account information with me?"

"Sure. It's back at Holden's house." I thought of Holden who spent his life believing his brother was a criminal and only now recently started to believe his brother was a good guy serving his country. I worried what this would do to him to learn that his brother hadn't changed so much after all.

"Do you think Leon Becker was hired by Gregor Wolf to kill Eddie?"

"No. That isn't Wolf's style. If Wolf was going to kill Eddie, it would be far more brutal than a shot to the head. Trust me on that."

"Then who?"

"I don't know. That's why I've been back in the U.S. I've been compromised, Riley. Eddie got ahold of my real name as you know. I don't know how he did, but he did. It's not safe for me in Europe right now. I don't know who he told. We also don't know what other CIA officers might be compromised." Sully looked back out at the penguins. "I've been here trying to figure out who killed Eddie, but I haven't made much progress."

After more than thirty years with the same alias, if I were Sully and Eddie had compromised me, I might have killed him myself. That isn't what Sully was saying though. I breathed a sigh of relief. I didn't realize until that moment how much I believed down deep that Sully might have killed Eddie.

I told Sully about seeing the note in Eddie's datebook. "I don't know if Eddie ever connected your real name to your alias."

"He did and it's a risk I can't take."

I understood that. "You don't have any ideas who killed Eddie?"

"It's someone tied to Eddie's past. That's all I know for sure."

Chapter 48

"The Boston connection has come up a few times during our investigation," I said while taking a step closer to Sully in a sign of goodwill. I still wasn't ready to hug him or behave in any way like a daughter would with her father, but it was the best gesture I had. "I spoke to FBI Special Agent Bruce Campbell who told me Eddie had uncovered a Boston connection during an international drug smuggling case and he was feeding intel to the FBI."

"I had the same intel. I haven't spoken to Agent Campbell myself but the agency has. I'm surprised he shared any information with you at all."

"Luke and I can be persuasive. He said Eddie never provided the name of the head of the crime syndicate here in Boston. Do you know who that might be?"

"We never did find that out," Sully said, glancing around the area again. "It's not the Chinese or Russians. That much I know for sure. I believe Eddie was giving up this information to knock out the competition for Gregor Wolf."

The area had cleared out for the most part. There was no one near us as we spoke. I wasn't sure if he was looking for someone specific or just scoping out the area. "Are you waiting for someone?"

"No." He refocused his attention on me and his face softened. "If anyone other than Eddie has connected Patrick Sullivan with Mickey

Finnigan, I'm as good as dead. I've been in this business a long time and my cover is deep. Impenetrable, I thought. Since I found out Eddie knew my real identity, I've been laying low and constantly on alert."

"When did you find out Eddie knew your real name?"

"My boss at the CIA alerted me about a year ago."

Eddie had been dead for more than a year. "You didn't know Eddie knew your real name until after he died?" I asked, surprise in my voice.

"When the CIA cleaned out his home in London, they came across a document connecting my alias with my real identity. He had the real identities of two other CIA officers as well. We don't know how much research he had done. There were no dates of birth or family connections, but the names alone rang alarm bells. The two other officers were immediately reassigned. They hadn't been using their aliases for long so it was an easy reassignment. I'm far more entrenched. I have an entire life and business built around Mickey Finnigan. They thought about staging Mickey's death and reassigning me, but too many people knew me as Mickey at that point."

I thought about my earlier meetings that week and the connection to Sully. "I don't know if Eddie told anyone. I met with Danny Devaney and then went to see Frank Coonan. I introduced myself to both of them as Mickey Finnigan's daughter and they didn't even flinch other than to say you never talked about me."

Sully stood dumbfounded. He went to speak but could only shake his head. A moment passed and I wasn't sure what he was thinking. Finally, he spoke. "I don't know what to say. That was brazen and bold and dangerous. How could you put your life at risk like that? I knew you were outside of Frank Coonan's place. I had no idea you said you were my daughter – well Mickey's daughter. Did you tell them your last name?"

"No, of course not. I just said my name was Riley. It was obvious though, Sully, especially to Danny. We look so much alike." Thinking back on Danny, I laughed. "He quizzed me about you. He asked me questions to see if I knew you as he does. I had no idea your relationship was that close."

"How did you connect Mickey Finnigan to them?" he asked, his voice tinged with worry.

I told Sully about overhearing conversations between him and my mom and the things I found in the attic when I was young. "It's kind of hard to forget that kind of information. I didn't want to meet with them, but I figured a rival of Eddie's might be the most likely suspect."

"I assume you don't believe they did it?" Sully leaned his hip on the railing and peered down at me.

"I wouldn't think so. Frank Coonan was the one who told me that Eddie went to work for a spy agency. Frank had no idea which one. He said that Eddie had come to speak with him about it. I guess they were close."

Sully nodded and expelled a breath. "Frank was Eddie's mentor in a way. He looked after him when he was running around the streets when he was young. I'm not surprised by what he told you."

I brushed my hair out of my face. "Do you think it could be Frank or Danny?"

"I wouldn't think so. Eddie's guys weren't doing much. They are both fairly local. I can't see either of them having the capacity to be involved in an international drug-smuggling operation unless something has drastically changed."

That was exactly the assessment I had and told him as much. "Where do we go from here?"

"You should go back home and let me finish this."

"I can't, Sully. Noah Byrne is still after me because he's convinced Patrick Sullivan killed Eddie. He just beat Holden to a pulp and threatened us again. There is a detective I know from the Troy Police Department at Mom's house watching over her and Liv. I can't let this go and pretend we aren't all still at risk."

He reached out and touched my cheek. "I can't watch over you and find Eddie's killer at the same time. As long as you're here, I'm focused on keeping you safe and watching my back."

I wasn't going to back down and leave this to him. I didn't trust him that much at the moment. "I think we are going to have to find a way to work together then." I folded my arms over my chest and stared up at him. "That means no more knocking out my friends."

The corners of his lips turned up. "I only did that to protect him. I like Cooper and the last place he needed to be was with me. It was safer for him to be with Luke and Jack. I couldn't shake him though. I can see that he's good at what he does."

"There were other options."

"Trust me, there weren't." Sully smiled down at me and changed the subject. "I like Jack, too. He's a good choice for your mom."

That surprised me. It hadn't occurred to me to even ask how he felt about her dating because they had been divorced for so long. "Jack's a good guy. I like him, too."

Sully grew quiet and I wasn't sure what to say. He had a far off look on his face. "The CIA wants me to retire. They demanded I retire and choose some other alias to live out the rest of my days."

That wasn't necessarily a surprise. He was close to sixty-two years old. I wasn't sure how much longer he anticipated working. I didn't see the problem. "Is that a bad thing? You might be able to spend some time with Liv and me now. It would be nice to get to know you."

"That's an upside. The pension more than covers my needs, but I can't even imagine a life like a normal person."

"You'll figure it out," I said and reached out and squeezed his hand. "None of us are going to be able to move on to anything though if we don't figure out who killed Eddie Stone. Cooper texted me before I came here and told me he had interesting news to share. He didn't specify what it was. He said it was too much to go into in text, but it sounds like he and Jack made some progress." I told Sully about them going back to the restaurant because they thought they might have a lead there. "I'll know more when I see them again."

Sully raised his eyebrows. "I assume they're here someplace? I can't imagine they'd let you meet me here alone."

"They are out there."

Sully reached out and pulled me into a hug. He kissed the top of my head. "Good. I can't be the only one watching out for you." He released me and kept his hands on my shoulders. "Go find them and I'll be in touch. Use the number I texted you from and let me know what Jack and Cooper find."

"You don't want to come back to the house with me?"

Sully shook his head. "It's not safe for me to be around all of you. Trust me, I'll make contact when the time is right." He stared down into my eyes for a few more seconds and then brushed past me without saying another word.

I watched him until he rounded a corner and was out of sight. I turned back to watch the penguins for a few more minutes and thought about what I should do next. I half expected Cooper and Luke to rush to me right after Sully left, but they were still keeping their distance.

I pulled my phone from my pocket and sent Luke a quick text, telling him I'd meet him and Cooper outside of the main entrance in ten minutes. He texted me back almost immediately confirming. I slid my phone back into my pocket and stood there for a moment longer. The heaviness of my meeting with my father and uncertainty of when I'd see him again or what the future would hold hung over me.

I turned to go and slammed right into a man a few inches taller than me. "I'm sorry. I didn't see you there." When I tried to move past him, he gripped my arm hard enough to leave a bruise and shoved a gun into my side. I lurched forward from the pain as it made contact.

He leaned in. "Make one false move and I'll kill you on the spot. Then I'll take out a few of these kiddies running around."

I knew the voice even if I didn't recognize the face. It was Noah. "What do you want? My father didn't kill Eddie."

Noah pulled me past the penguin exhibit moving us in the opposite direction from the main entrance where Luke and Cooper would be waiting for me. He spoke low into my ear as we moved. "This is bigger than Eddie."

I tried to pull my arm free but that only made his grip tighter. I scanned around for someone who might be able to help me. I worried if I tried to make a break for it that he'd kill me on the spot or kill one of the children. I was doing everything my training had taught me not to do. Never go with the man with a gun. Let him kill you on the spot was the advice always given. Rarely will they do it. If you go, you're only in for worse. I knew I was making the wrong decision, but as my brain worked on overdrive, I didn't see much of an option.

As an employee passed us, I mouthed the words *help me*. The woman stopped immediately and turned to us. Noah pointed the gun at her and told her to get out of there. When she didn't move fast enough, he pulled the trigger missing her by mere centimeters. I let out a scream and she threw herself on the floor. Chaos erupted around us with parents reaching for their children, shielding their small bodies with their own. Others screamed and ducked for cover. It all happened so fast I couldn't process it.

I used it as an opportunity to make a break for it. I didn't make it more than a few feet when Noah ripped me back by my hair and knocked me across the head with the butt of the gun. A grunt of pain escaped my lips and a wave of dizziness took hold.

It wasn't the smartest decision he could make because I was a heavy girl to try to carry or drag out of the place. He anticipated that though and leaned low into my ear and pointed across the room at a woman with two small children. "Come with me now or I'll kill all three of them."

I knew he wasn't kidding so I allowed myself to be jerked upright. He moved me toward the back of the aquarium. There was a flurry of people running so no one noticed us. Noah had the gun deep into my side and out of sight of people passing. We reached the back door and Noah shoved it open and dragged me into the cold air before anyone had a chance to find us. We were in a narrow alleyway and there was a car a few feet ahead of us.

He kept the gun jammed into my side and pulled open the backseat driver's side door and shoved me inside. I tried to brace myself with my hands but the force was too much. My left wrist snapped and I face-planted into the seat. Noah slammed the door closed, nearly closing it on me. I pulled my foot inside just in time.

As I sucked in a breath and tried to temper the pain shooting across my forehead and wrist, I righted myself in the seat. That's when I realized we weren't alone. Sitting in the passenger seat turned around looking at me was a familiar face – the bartender from Danny Devaney's bar.

"I knew there was something off about you from the start."

"What's going on?" I asked, looking down at my wrist which was already swelling.

"You'll see," Noah said and started the car. He gunned the engine and took off down the road. I turned back to the door to see if anyone had come out the way we did but there was nothing but an empty alleyway.

Chapter 49

Luke and Cooper shoved through the throngs of people fleeing the aquarium. They could only move a few feet at a time as the crowd shoved them back with nearly every step. It was like wading upstream with a heavy current going the other way.

"Do you see her?" Luke shouted above the crowd.

"No. She's got to be in there."

Luke grabbed an older man as he shoved past him. "What happened inside?"

"There's a guy with a gun. He shot at an employee and took off with a woman." The man didn't stick around to answer any more questions. He pulled away from Luke and moved with the crowd.

"Sully?" Luke asked, turning to Cooper over the heads of shorter people.

"Anybody's guess."

Luke squared his shoulders low, almost like a linebacker, and used his body weight to shove through the crowd until both he and Cooper reached a clearing at the same time. He found a man with a New England Aquarium shirt on. Luke flashed his badge. "What's going on here?"

"Are you with the Boston Police?"

"No, Little Rock. I was supposed to meet my wife outside, but we heard a gunshot and then saw all the people rushing out. We heard from a man that the gunman may have a woman hostage."

The man pointed behind him. "Back there, but you can't be in here. The cops are on their way." He tried to physically move Luke in the direction of the crowd going out the door. Luke didn't budge. He lifted his head in the direction he wanted Cooper to go and the two of them kept pushing until they reached a spot against a wall free of the crowd.

Luke motioned with his hand to the vast space of the building ahead of them. "Let's go canvass the place. I don't want to unholster my gun because if the cops come running in here, they are going to shoot first and ask questions later."

Cooper agreed and they set off in opposite directions. Luke watched as Cooper made his way to a winding ramp that led up to the second floor. Luke meanwhile made his way to the first exhibit area on the first and started his search there. The place had emptied considerably, which made the search easier. Luke moved from one exhibit area to the next. There was no sign of Riley or Sully.

Only moments before, Luke had been inside the aquarium standing on the second floor while Riley and Sully talked at the penguin exhibit below. He had watched them. While he couldn't hear what they were saying to each other, their interactions had gone from cold to serious. They seemed to leave things a bit more positively. Cooper had been waiting outside in case there was trouble.

Luke saw Sully leave and walk away from Riley so he wasn't sure what had happened. Had he turned around and taken her once Luke's guard was down or was it someone else? Luke couldn't be sure. After Riley had texted that she'd meet him outside, that's where he went. He figured she probably needed a moment to herself. Assuming at that point Riley was safe, he took his eyes off her. Luke hoped he didn't live to regret that decision.

The deeper Luke got into the building the quieter it became. There was a haunting stillness about the place that unnerved him. He searched each exhibit on the first floor and found nothing. Luke looped around and started to head back towards the front but on the opposite side of the building than he had searched previously. He made it through three exhibits and then came to an exit door that was slightly ajar. He patted the gun on his hip but didn't pull it from the holster.

Luke nudged the metal door open wide enough to stick his head out but stopped when two uniformed cops screamed for him to put his hands in the air. He backed away from the door slowly with his hands up. His badge hung around his neck on a chain. "I'm Det. Luke Morgan with the Little Rock Police Department," he said slowly facing the cops.

"Get down on the ground!" one of the cops yelled.

Luke did as they asked and dropped to his knees, his hands still in the air as adrenaline and fear coursed through him. "Call Det. Nixon. He knows who I am. The woman who was taken is my wife. I was searching before you arrived."

With guns still pointed at him, one officer used his radio while the other asked him what had happened. "I don't know," Luke said. "Please, take my identification. I swear to you I was outside when it happened. I have to find my wife."

The officer didn't say a word. He kept his gun trained on Luke until the other cop finished his conversation over his radio. Finally, he motioned for Luke to stand. He still didn't make any fast moves because the cop still had his gun pointed at him.

Luke pointed. "You mind lowering your weapon, please?"

The officer lowered it but didn't relax his posture. He stared Luke down like he might make a sudden move toward him. Luke tried reassuring him again but nothing seemed to work. He wasn't sure if the cop was young or just on edge. "Is there a supervisor or detective on the scene yet?" Luke asked.

"Det. Nixon is coming into the building now," the officer who had radioed in said.

They waited like that in a silent stalemate for a couple of minutes until Luke heard Det. Nixon barking orders. His voice gradually grew closer and closer. When he appeared, Cooper was at his side. Det. Nixon walked right over to him. "What's going on?"

Luke explained about Riley meeting with her father without going into too much detail. He told the detective where he had been in the building and how he left. "I wasn't outside more than a few minutes when there was a gunshot and everyone came rushing out. I didn't see Riley among them. I heard from a witness that the gunman has a woman hostage. That's all I know right now. The first floor is clear. I searched it."

"Upstairs, too," Cooper said.

"What's out there?" Det. Nixon asked as he shoved open the metal door Luke never had a chance to explore. He stuck his head out and then back in quickly. "It goes to an alleyway, but there is no one out there now." Det. Nixon turned to Luke. "It's a way out if you didn't see her come out the front door."

"Any chance we can see the surveillance video?" Luke asked, sharing a look with Cooper. They didn't have a lot of time to waste standing around.

"I've got security queuing it up for me." Det. Nixon started to walk back the way he had come but stopped and motioned for Luke and Cooper to join him. "We can watch it together."

Luke and Cooper moved quickly to catch up with Det. Nixon who seemed to take one step for their two. The man could move fast when he desired. Det. Nixon led them to a door marked for staff, shoved it open like he owned the place, and then proceeded down a long narrow corridor. When he reached the door marked security, he hit his knuckles against the door once and then pushed it open.

"You got that video feed ready for me?" he asked, moving into the small office space to give Luke and Cooper room to enter.

Luke didn't catch the name of the guy sitting behind the desk because he was so focused on the still image of Riley and Noah Byrne. The security guy swiveled his laptop so all of them could see it and then hit play. At once, the screen came alive with Noah shoving Riley forward through the aquarium. Her face registered the fear Luke felt at that moment. Luke watched as Noah jammed a gun into her side and shoved her toward the section of the aquarium where he had just been standing.

Just as Luke thought he'd seen the worst of it, Noah aimed his gun at an employee and pulled the trigger. As Riley said something and tried to pull away, he bashed her across the head with the butt of his gun. She dropped to her knees and raised her hand to her head. He didn't even give her time to react before he yanked her up, pointed the gun at a mother and her children, and then shoved Riley through the metal door.

Luke grunted. "Do you believe me now that they kidnapped Riley?"

Det. Nixon didn't say a word. He cursed in anger and then reached for his phone. He called into the station and put out an all-points bulletin for Noah Byrne and then asked for units to head to an address that he gave them. When he was done, Det. Nixon turned to Luke. "If he's at his house, they will get him."

"If he's not there?" Cooper asked.

"We can check a couple of addresses near there, but otherwise, I have no idea."

"Luke, I have information about Noah I was going to wait to share," Cooper said and all eyes turned to him. He explained what they had learned earlier about Ethan McBride and Toby Wahl. "When Jack and I interviewed Toby, he said it was Noah who told him to work at the restaurant the night Eddie was killed and to phone in when he was leaving. I think Noah was directly involved in Eddie's murder."

Det. Nixon shook his head. "That can't be right. Noah had an alibi for that night. He wasn't even in Boston. He was at the Mohegan Sun Casino in Connecticut. We have him on surveillance video. He never left. I don't even think he took a call. He sat playing blackjack for most of the night and flirting with a hooker until he took her back to his room."

"That measures up," Cooper explained. "Toby said that when he called the number Noah provided, he was surprised when someone else answered. We've thought all along more than one person was involved."

Det. Nixon still didn't seem to understand. "I thought this all started because Noah went to Holden and named Eddie's killer. Why would he risk making Holden look for his brother's killer if he was guilty all along? That doesn't make a lot of sense."

Luke blew out a frustrated breath. "Nothing about this case has made sense from the start. I'm going to make some calls and see if I can track down where else Noah might spend his time."

Chapter 50

We pulled up in front of a familiar bar and Noah put the car into park and cut the engine. I had no idea why we were back at Danny Devaney's bar or what these two had in store for me. I didn't have much time to give it any consideration because as soon as Noah got out and slammed his door shut, he opened my door and dragged me out of the car by my wrist – the one still throbbing in pain. I yelped and he leaned over and smacked me across the face. The sting ran up my cheekbone and across to the bridge of my nose. It was probably the worst thing he could have done because fire raged in my belly. I didn't know how today would end, but I knew if I had anything to do with it, Noah wouldn't be alive to see the sunrise.

I didn't say a word but exhaled short hot breaths out of my nose like a bull ready to charge. The bartender, whose name I still didn't know, pulled open the door and Noah shoved me hard. I landed in a heap on the floor of the empty bar.

"Back there." The bartender pointed to Danny Devaney's office where I had met with the man earlier.

Noah yelled, "Go and don't give us any trouble. As I told you before, it's going to be my pleasure to put a bullet in your head. I'm just mad your sister got away."

I started to walk toward the door because I couldn't stand looking at him anymore. What he said next stopped me in my tracks.

Noah let out a sinister vile laugh. "Don't worry. As soon as you and your father are dead, I'm going to kill your sister and maybe even your mother."

I wanted to turn and charge him and beat his face to a bloody pulp with my fists. I was sure I wouldn't make it even a few feet to him before he or the bartender shot me. I had to get out of there alive and protect my mother and sister. I remembered then that my phone was in my pocket. Noah hadn't searched me or taken it away from me. There was no way for me to reach for it and call for help without them seeing. It was like a security blanket at the moment, knowing it was there had to be good enough.

I marched forward to Danny's office and stepped through the doorway. Behind the desk sat Danny Devaney with his eyes trained in my direction.

"You've got a lot of explaining to do," he said through a puff of cigar smoke.

I took a confident step into his office. "How do you think Mickey is going to react knowing one of your goons kidnapped me?"

Danny laughed a loud obnoxious belly laugh and then took another puff of his cigar.

I had no idea how to play this. "What do you want?"

Danny pointed to the chair in front of his desk. "Sit down."

I took a deep breath and approached the chair. The last thing I wanted was my back toward the door and to be any closer to Danny than I already stood. I didn't see many options though.

"Why are you in Boston?" he asked, even though I had already told him the first time we met.

I took a seat and explained the events of the last week including being kidnapped by Noah the morning after my wedding. I splayed my arms wide. "It seems I'm stuck here so I'm trying to make the best of a bad situation. I figured if I find Eddie's killer then maybe Noah will let me go."

Danny leaned back in his chair and continued to smoke his cigar. He took long puffs and blew the smoke in the air, the smell of which was turning my stomach.

When I couldn't take any more silence, I blurted, "Why am I here? I have better things to do."

Danny pointed at me with the cigar between two of his fat stubby fingers. "You're going to tell me all about Patrick Sullivan. You are his daughter after all."

I swallowed hard. I wondered if I could tell Danny what I told Holden about my father's alias in the criminal work. I chose avoidance for now. "I think we should just cut through all the clutter here and be straight with each other."

Danny interrupted. "That's what I've been waiting for, sweetheart."

I opened my mouth to speak, but at that moment, my father's loud voice boomed from the bar and Danny shot to his feet. The sounds of a commotion – tables turned over, the sound of punches landing, grown men grunting and yelling, and then my father giving up in defeat. I stood from my chair and ran to the door before Danny could stop me. There was my father with the bartender standing over him with a gun to his head.

Danny came up behind me and shoved me out of the way. "Evan, let him go," he said waving his hands at the bartender. Danny pulled Sully to his feet. "I knew if we grabbed your daughter, you'd show your face eventually." He turned to the bartender. "Did you take his guns?"

Evan walked over to Sully and began to pat him down. He pulled a gun from an ankle holster and another from the back of his pants. Noah stood there looking on with a smug smile plastered across his face. When Evan decided Sully was free of any weapons, he tried to shove him forward to Danny. My father didn't budge. It was like shoving a wall.

Sully locked eyes with me for the first time and gave me a nod like it was all going to be okay, but I had no idea how that was even possible. It was three against one and we had no weapons. Danny turned back toward me and motioned for me to go back into his office. Sully followed behind me.

"Now," Danny said as he made his way back around his desk, "we are going to have a little chat." Looking to Sully, he said, "I'm sorry about my sons. They don't have the old school refinement that we once had."

"Sons?" I asked, confusion evident in my voice.

"Evan and Noah are both my sons from different mothers," Danny said matter-of-factly. "Noah doesn't have my last name. It worked out perfectly."

I sat in the chair that I had been in and Sully pulled up the chair next to me. "Noah was Eddie's friend though. I don't understand."

Danny laughed at me. "You're quite naïve on how this works, aren't you? I sent Noah to work with Eddie to keep an eye on him. You don't come to this neighborhood and start pulling rank and building a crew of guys without the locals taking notice. Then he left and I thought we had rid ourselves of him for good." He chuckled. "Little did I know what he was really up to. It seems I have rats all around me."

Danny narrowed his eyes at my father. "What should I call you – Patrick Sullivan or Mickey Finnigan. You are the same man, are you not?"

My father, his voice calm and steady, asked, "How'd you make the connection?"

"Eddie, of course. He told Melissa he found out Mickey Finnigan's real identity was Patrick Sullivan and then we found out Eddie was going to the FBI."

I knew they had found listening devices in Melissa's house. My father had been right – Eddie talked too much. I looked across the desk and frowned. "You killed Eddie."

"I didn't pull the trigger, no. I'm too old for that kind of a mess. I happily ordered the hit though."

"Leon Becker?" Sully asked.

Danny shook his head. "We wanted it a bit more personal. Evan handled it for me. I needed to make sure the job was done right. I hired Becker to take care of other matters, but it seems you bested him after all."

I was trying to connect the dots as best I could in my head. It wasn't making sense to me and Danny saw the confusion on my face.

"I thought you were the smart daughter." When I didn't say anything, he shrugged and explained. "I've grown my operation more than anyone knows. I have men across Europe. Eddie started making connections back to Boston and we killed him before he figured out it was me. He had already mentioned the connection between Mickey and Patrick so I figured you were working with Eddie.

"Killing you," he said, pointing to Sully, "wasn't such an easy task. I had to get a bit creative to draw you out. As you know, I called and asked you to meet me and you refused. I hired three hitmen to take you out and you killed each of them. After a little research, I came to learn about Riley and Liv. I figured using them would draw you right to me. We roped in Eddie's brother because we planned to kill him, too. I didn't know what Eddie might have told him or left behind for him to find. Convincing him that Patrick Sullivan killed his brother proved helpful with the whole operation."

"Why didn't you kill me the first time I came here?" I asked.

"There was no point yet. We didn't have confirmation that Sully had followed you here. We figured if we took out Holden, you'd have to ask Sully for help." Danny waved his hand dismissively. "Turns out

Sully was already here and stopped that from happening."

Sully said evenly, "I wasn't working with Eddie so I didn't have all this information about you. The drug operation wasn't my focus. It was Eddie's. You're telling me now and there's only one way this is going to end. You're going to jail or you're leaving here in a body bag."

"Big talk for a man without a gun." Danny picked up his cigar from the ashtray on his desk and took a puff. "You can decide who wants to watch the other one die first. I'll give you that much." Danny set the cigar down and opened his desk drawer. He pulled a gun out and pointed it at my father.

Sully didn't flinch. He looked calmly at me. "Is there anything else you want to know about Eddie's murder?"

My heart raced and my palms were a sea of perspiration. I couldn't believe Sully sat there so calmly asking me that. I couldn't do anything except shake my head.

"Good," he said, smiling at me and patting my knee. He rose from his seat. "Well, then. It's about time we get out of here." Sully looked down at Danny. "Last chance. Jail or body bag?"

"You're too arrogant for your own..." Danny never got the final words out of his mouth.

Out of the corner of my eye, there was a flash of movement as Sully reached up under his shirt and threw what looked like a silver-handled knife right at Danny. I turned in time to see the final moments of his life. The man's eyes bulged in his head and he tried to speak, but it was blood that rushed from his mouth. The knife had lodged right in his throat. His hand shook like he might fire his gun but it dropped from his hand and he slumped forward on the desk.

I sat in stunned silence at the swiftness of my father's calm actions. He reached his hand down to my shoulder and I looked up to him.

He smiled reassuringly at me. "I never liked guns. They make too much noise. Ready to get out of here?"

CHAPTER 50

All I could do was look at my father too stunned to speak.

Chapter 51

Luke pounded his fist on the door and screamed Riley's name. Cooper and Luke had gone back to the neighborhood where Riley and Liv had been held. In an online search, Luke had found an address for Noah, but so far, even the cops had failed to find him.

Back at the aquarium, Det. Nixon had assured Luke they would do everything possible to locate Noah and Riley. Luke couldn't sit still and wait for them to be found. He had played this wait and see game in Lake Placid and he wasn't going to do it again. He did not doubt that Det. Nixon would be doing everything he could. He didn't doubt the skill or commitment of the Boston Police Department.

Right now, though, it wasn't good enough for Luke. He needed to be pounding the pavement himself and so Cooper and Luke left the aquarium and headed to the address they pulled up online. It was a rundown house that looked abandoned. There was no car in the driveway and no lights on in the house. Since they had been standing there no one had come to the door and there hadn't been a peep from inside.

Cooper reached for Luke's arm and pulled him away from the door. "Luke, I don't think anyone is here. Beating that door isn't going to help."

"I know," Luke said, shrugging off Cooper's hand. He turned around to face Cooper. "I've tried calling Riley and the phone rings but goes to voicemail. I have no idea how to reach Sully and don't even know if he'd help or make the situation worse. I'm so stupid for letting her out of my sight."

"Luke, you couldn't have done anything. She was out of sight for less than ten minutes. Long enough for you to walk outside." Cooper stepped off the porch and Luke followed. They stood on the sidewalk at the edge of the grass facing one another. "What do you want to try next?"

Luke blew out a frustrated breath and rubbed a hand over his bald head. "I have no idea. We'd need to go back to Holden's house for me to get my laptop and check my database, which would at least give me the address on Noah's driver's license and any past addresses in the system. Have you called Jack? Maybe he's closer and can run by Holden's and do that."

Cooper held up his phone. "I texted him about Riley and he texted back that he was at Ethan McBride's house. Jack is like a dog with a bone. He thinks Ethan knows more than he told us."

"Do you think that, too?"

"He wouldn't tell us the name of his contact, but once Toby told us who he was involved with I assumed Ethan was holding back Noah's name."

"That makes sense," Luke said. He wasn't sure what to do next. He felt like he did when he first arrived in Boston, like they were shooting in the dark hoping for a lead. "Ask Jack to go back to Holden's and search in the database. He is closer and Ethan sounds like a dead end."

Luke walked back to the car while Cooper sent off the text. He pulled open the driver's side door, slid in, and tried to call Riley again. Her phone rang and rang and then went to voicemail. Riley had a bad habit of leaving her phone on silent so there was a chance she wasn't even hearing it ring or Noah had taken it from her. Luke glanced out the passenger side. Cooper's head was lowered reading something on his phone.

While he waited Luke called their cellphone company hoping that without a warrant, they might be able to trace Riley's phone. Riley had been adamantly opposed to having her "find her phone" turned on because she didn't want to spend her life tracked. Not that Luke would abuse the privilege. She just hated the idea of it. He didn't much like it either, but it certainly would make times like this that much easier.

"I think we got something," Cooper said, breaking Luke out of his train of thought.

"What is it?" Luke asked, turning his head to look at Cooper.

Cooper slid in and angled his phone so Luke could read the message from Jack. "Ethan finally broke down and told Jack the truth. Noah was the connection but so was Evan Devaney. They are both Danny Devaney's sons."

Luke tried to process the information as quickly as possible. It meant that Noah was working for Eddie but related to another crime boss. "He was a plant for his father. He was never Eddie's friend."

"Right. I don't know why or the ins and outs of it all, but Jack thinks Riley is probably wherever you can find Danny Devaney. Ethan didn't have that information. He only dealt with Noah and Evan. Jack's on his way to Holden's right now."

Luke knew finding Danny's main place of business should be easy enough. He grabbed for his cellphone and placed a call to Det. Nixon. He cursed when the detective didn't answer the call. Luke left a quick message providing the details that Cooper had just told him and then hung up. Luke sat for a moment thinking through all the information Riley had told him about her investigation before they found one another. It hit him all at once.

He scrolled through his phone until he found the contact that Riley had added for him. It rang only once before Holden answered. "When you were with Riley earlier this week and she went to speak to Danny Devaney, where did you go?"

"That was one of the first places we went," Holden said and then paused. "I stayed in a coffee shop but there's a bar a few doors down. I don't remember the name of it."

"Give me directions then," Luke said. It would have been easier to have the name of the bar to pull it up on GPS, but Luke would take what he could get. He gave Holden his current location as a starting point.

Holden gave Luke detailed directions on how to find the place. "Is everything okay?"

"Not anything I have time to explain right now. Jack is on his way to your place." With that, Luke hung up. He felt no loyalty to warn Holden about what was happening and didn't have time to explain the danger that Riley could be in.

Luke started the car and took off in the direction that Holden had explained. He only hoped that he'd find Riley in time.

As they drove, Cooper asked, "Do you think we should have Jack meet us there?"

Luke stared straight ahead looking for the next road sign. "No, let's leave Jack out of harm's way. He's done enough to help us this time." They rode the rest of the way in silence.

Luke thought he might be lost but then the coffee shop Holden mentioned came into view. The area was close to Harvard and the bar at the end of the block looked distinctly out of place.

Luke pulled over to the curb down the road from the bar and cut the engine. He pointed out the place for Cooper. "That's the place. I don't want to pull up in front. Det. Nixon didn't get my message yet or this place would be crawling with cops. You want to go this alone?"

"Do we have another choice?"

Luke was about to respond when a gunshot rang out followed by another two in quick succession. "That's your answer."

Luke and Cooper got out of the car as people in other businesses flowed into the streets, looking around for the source of the sound. Luke and Cooper both drew their weapons and headed for the bar. "People around here act like this is commonplace," Luke said, noticing the looks on people's faces. They looked more annoyed than alarmed.

As they passed the coffee shop, Luke flashed his badge to onlookers. "Call 911," he said to a man and woman who stood just outside the coffee shop door.

They proceeded slowly down to the bar. The shooting had stopped but they got low as they approached. Luke took one side of the door as Cooper flanked the other. Luke crouched and faced the building while attempting to look through a small slit in the window covering. What he saw made his blood run cold.

Sully lay motionless on the ground with a man with a gun in his hand standing over him. The gun was pressed into Sully's forehead. Luke turned slightly and saw Riley on the ground tears streaked down her face and begging for her father's life. Another man had her by the hair and his gun aimed at her.

Luke had to think quickly. He and Cooper had almost no cover. They could storm the building but were sure to be shot at in the process. He didn't feel like he had much of a choice though. Luke turned back to face the street and looked over at Cooper. He used hand signals to explain what he saw and mouthed an explanation he hoped Cooper would understand. Luke moved over an inch toward the door and tried the doorknob. To his surprise, it turned and the door inched open.

It was enough that Luke could inch open the door a little and then a little more. He could hear the men yelling and Riley crying. They were so caught up in what they were doing they hadn't noticed the door opening. Luke stood against the wall near the opening and Cooper did the same. Luke worried that he might hit Riley, but they had to act now before these men did anything else. At least there were only two of them.

Luke moved into the bar first and Cooper followed. They each had their gun aimed at one of the men. "Put the guns down now," Luke said, his voice not sounding like his own. It was filled with anger and rage that bubbled up unexpectedly. The events of the week had finally caught up to him. He didn't care if the men killed Sully, but he wasn't going to let anyone harm Riley, even if he had to die trying.

Riley's head snapped in his direction. There was a faint smile on her lips before her face filled with fear. "You shouldn't be here," she said quietly, barely loud enough for him to hear her.

"Get out of here!" the one holding Riley shouted.

The other moved away from Sully and took a step toward Luke. "You have no business here."

The men had no idea who he and Cooper were. Luke held up his badge. "I'm a cop and I'm not going anywhere. Put your guns down now!"

Cooper inched toward the side of the room and slowly made his way toward Riley. Luke remained dead center of the room. It split their attention which had been the plan. Cooper had more cover where he stood with tables between them than Luke did. His only goal was to keep his eyes on him.

The one near Sully laughed. "Then looks like we are going to have to kill you, too."

"You're not killing anyone," Luke said, wondering why they hadn't fired at him yet. They had a clear shot. "Let them go and we all walk out of here."

The man kicked Sully hard in the ribs. "He killed my father. No one is walking out of here alive."

"Fine," Luke said. "You can have him. I don't much care, but she is coming with me."

Riley glanced up at Luke and then in one swift movement pulled a knife from behind her back and stabbed the man in the leg. He yelped in pain and aimed his gun at her head, but before he could pull the trigger his brain exploded right before Luke's eyes. Cooper had fired a shot that hit the man in the side of the head.

The other man squeezed off one round toward Cooper but that was all he got. Luke fired two shots and he dropped to the ground. Luke rushed over to him and kicked the gun away from his open hand. He leaned down and checked for a pulse but there was none. He had hit the man in the center of his chest. He was probably dead before he hit the ground.

Riley pushed herself up from the floor and ran to Luke who stood and wrapped his arms around her. The feel of a vest under her shirt surprised him but it wasn't the time for questions.

"I'm so glad to see you," she cried into his chest.

As Luke held Riley, he looked over at Cooper, who had slumped against the wall. "You hit?" he asked.

Cooper shook his head. "Stunned but no damage."

Luke kissed the top of Riley's head and told her how much he loved her. He closed his eyes and said a silent prayer for having kept them safe. He had no idea what Riley was doing with a knife or what happened before they got there, but it didn't matter now. She was safe. Much to Luke's amazement, when he opened his eyes, Sully had sat up against the wall and was watching them.

"Great job, son. I had it under control but you did well." Sully pushed himself to a standing position.

"It didn't look like you had it under control," Luke said, confusion in his voice.

Sully didn't respond. Instead, he pulled out his phone and walked to the front of the bar. "All clear," he said. "You've got three to clean up." He slid the phone back into his pocket and then looked once at Luke and Riley and then over at Cooper. "What do you say we get out of here? I'm famished."

"We need to wait for the Boston Police Department," Luke said, not sure what was happening.

Sully waved him off. "It will be taken care of." He stepped out of the bar. "Let's go."

Riley turned her head to look at Luke who was at a total loss for words. "I'll explain everything later," she said planting a kiss on his lips.

Luke laughed. "I'm not sure I'll believe you."

Epilogue

I had been back at my mother's house for more than twelve hours and she was still doting on me. The four of us – Jack, Cooper, Luke, and I – had arrived at close to eleven last night. My mother and sister rushed me at the door, hugging me and asking if I was okay. Adele did the same to Cooper.

I assured them I was fine but that all I wanted was to take a shower, put on my pajamas, and sleep in my bed. My mother had shared a look with Jack and he nodded, giving his confirmation that I was doing well. It made me laugh the way they could already communicate without words the way many long-time couples could. I had gone upstairs and gotten ready for bed while Jack and Luke gave an abridged version of what had happened.

After Sully, Luke, Cooper, and I had left the bar the night before, we headed back to Holden's house. We got a call later from Det. Nixon. He asked Luke and Cooper a few questions and then cleared us all from any wrongdoing. He considered it case closed. Det. Nixon didn't seem to care about the particulars or that both of Danny's sons had been killed as well. All Det. Nixon needed were enough details to write his report. He was more than happy that we had solved Eddie Stone's murder. All in all, it took a lot off his plate.

When I told him what I could about Eddie's involvement with the CIA, Det. Nixon understood why the case had been so hard to solve.

He expressed regret though that he hadn't been able to connect the dots and had cleared Noah when he shouldn't have. I couldn't blame him. Noah being Danny Devaney's son had been a shock to us all. Det. Nixon had been briefed when the CIA had stepped in so I wasn't on the hook for explaining much. In the end, my family was safe and that was all that mattered.

I was grateful that Sully had come back to Holden's with us. He spent a good deal of time telling Holden about Eddie and his involvement with the CIA – both the good and the bad of what his brother had done. Holden seemed relieved that it was over and told us he'd learn to make peace with his brother's life and death. He still felt like he needed to be punished in some way for what he had done to Liv and me, but we all assured him that it was water under the bridge at that point. He was going to stay in Boston for a while until he made some life decisions.

We left Sully in Boston. He said that he had some cleanup to do but that he'd be in touch soon. I wasn't sure how long that would be or what exactly his "cleanup" meant, but after what we had been through, I hugged him goodbye and told him how much I appreciated what he had done for me. I wouldn't have made it out of Danny Devaney's alive without him.

Now, I stood in the kitchen with my mother, sister, and Adele while Luke, Cooper, and Jack said they had errands to run. My mother had made me thick French toast, bacon, and eggs and didn't complain once about the calories I was consuming.

She leaned against the counter sipping her coffee and locked eyes with me. "Jack and Luke filled us in last night about what happened after they got to the bar but what happened before? Luke said it was your story to tell." She glanced at Adele and I knew she was wondering if it was okay for me to talk in front of her.

"No more secrets, Mom," I said, raising my eyes to her. "I told Jack,

Luke, and Cooper everything last night. I might as well tell you all now."

"Go on then," she said, sitting with us at the table.

"Sully saved me. That's the bottom line."

"He's the one that got us into this," Liv countered. Mom had told me that Liv was still angry with Sully and I understood it, but I also knew that she didn't know everything.

"He didn't intentionally get us into this. It was a chain of events that was set off when he got Eddie Stone to be an asset for him. If you want to blame Sully for his work, then I guess that's your right, Liv." I glanced over at her and reached for her hand. "Whatever you decide is what I'll support. I'm just trying to cut him some slack."

"Go on with what happened," my mom urged.

I told them all about how Sully recruited Eddie and that he was so good the CIA had offered him a job. "Sully still isn't sure how Eddie found out his real identity. Eddie had only known him by Sully's alias. An internal CIA leak maybe. Sully isn't sure." I filled them in about the course of events that led to Eddie ratting out Danny Devaney to the FBI to limit the competition for Gregor Wolf. These were names I was sure I wasn't supposed to be throwing around, but I was done with secrets as I had said.

"I figured out a little too late Danny's connection to Noah and Evan. They had set this whole thing up to flush out Sully because they thought he had been working with Eddie to bring down Danny."

I took a sip of the coffee in front of me and leaned back. "Sully showed up at Danny's knowing he'd be caught. He figured he'd either sacrifice himself for me or get us both out of there. After Sully killed Danny, we were able to use what Danny had in his office – guns, bulletproof vests, and Sully gave me his knife. He showed me how to use it. When he gave the signal, I was supposed to stab one of the men. Sully would shoot the other one and then the one I stabbed. We had a solid plan until Luke and Cooper walked in."

Adele laughed but the worry line on her forehead creased. "Those two don't always have the best timing."

"Sully used it to his advantage. He gave me the hand signal we had worked out and I went for it." They all grimaced at the thought of me stabbing someone. I only wished it had been Noah instead of Evan. He was dead though so I couldn't complain.

I turned to my mother. "The CIA wants Sully to retire."

"That will never happen."

"He might not have a choice."

My mother rolled her eyes as the front door opened. In walked Luke, Cooper, and Jack. They all had ridiculous smiles on their faces and I knew immediately they had been up to something. I looked to Luke for some kind of hint but he gave nothing away.

I got up and hugged him and was about to tell him that I had just told my mother all about what had happened but he shushed me. He pointed to Jack who had walked over to my mother and wrapped his arms around her as she sat at the table. Before I knew what was happening, he dropped to one knee beside her and proposed.

He held the ring in his hand. "I know this isn't the most romantic proposal, but I couldn't think of any more perfect spot than this kitchen where we have spent so many nights. You know how much I love you, and your daughters are like my own. Will you marry me?"

My mother who rarely showed emotion started to cry and said yes over and over again. She got up from her chair and hugged and kissed Jack. I was so overcome with emotion it took me a moment to realize that Adele and Cooper were no longer with us in the kitchen. As my mother came over and hugged me, I asked Luke where they were. He smirked and shrugged.

Jack leaned down and kissed me on the cheek and Liv rushed to hug him. A moment later, amidst the noise of congratulations, Cooper and

Adele walked back into the kitchen from the living room. Cooper's face was bright red and he had a smile from ear to ear. Adele held up her left hand and flashed her own diamond engagement ring. The kitchen erupted in cheers and well wishes. I couldn't think of anything that would have made me happier. Dusty danced around our feet wagging his tail and each of us had a broad smile on our faces. It was the perfect way to wrap up the trip before Luke and I left on our honeymoon two days later.

Luke hugged me and kissed me. "They thought you might be angry if they proposed now since our wedding didn't end so well."

I shook my head. "I'm so happy and glad we are all here for it. I think it's perfect." There was a knock on the front door and I let go of Luke long enough to answer it. I made my way through the hall with Dusty in tow and pulled open the door and stepped back in surprise. It was Sully.

He wrapped me in an awkward hug. "I came to talk to all of you," he said and then brushed past me and made his way into the house before I could stop him.

The noise in the kitchen ceased as he walked in. I walked in behind Sully and saw how surprised they all looked. My mother's face had gone from joy-filled to annoyance in seconds flat.

"I didn't mean to interrupt the joyous occasion, but I thought I'd tell you all that I'm retiring. I have to go down to Langley and wrap up a few things, but I'm done in a month." Sully looked around at each of us. "I thought I'd just let you girls know in case you'd like to spend some time with me. I'm not sure what I'm doing next, but I'm going to be stateside from here on out."

My mother fell back into Jack, who caught her against his chest. Liv looked at me in shock. If aliens had landed in my mother's kitchen, I don't think anyone would have been more surprised. I turned in time to catch the look between Jack and Luke. Neither of them looked happy.

Sully, who was undeterred by everyone's surprise, reached down and snatched a piece of bacon off my plate and popped it into his mouth. "I think this is going to be fun. What are we celebrating?"

Luke reached for my hand and pulled me into him. I leaned up and kissed his lips. "At least, life is never boring," I said, trying to hide my smile. I couldn't worry about this now. We finally had our honeymoon in front of us.

Also by Stacy M. Jones

Watch for Riley Sullivan Mystery Series Book #6
 THE NIGHT GAME - Fall 2021

Access the Free Mystery Readers' Club Starter Library
 Riley Sullivan Mystery Series novella "The 1922 Club Murder"
 FBI Agent Kate Walsh Thriller Series novella "The Curators"
 Harper & Hattie Mystery Series novella "Harper's Folly"

Sign up for the starter library along with launch-day pricing, special behind-the-scenes access, and extra content not available anywhere else. Hit subscribe at
 http://www.stacymjones.com/

Please leave a review for Boston Underground. Reviews help more readers find my books. Thank you!

Have you read them all?

FBI Agent Kate Walsh Thriller Series
 The Curators
 The Founders

Riley Sullivan Mystery Series
 The 1922 Club Murder
 Deadly Sins
 The Bone Harvest
 Missing Time Murders
 We Last Saw Jane

Harper & Hattie Magical Mystery Series
Harper's Folly
Saints & Sinners Ball
Secrets to Tell
Rule of Three
The Forever Curse

Made in the USA
Coppell, TX
21 December 2021

69222654R00194